REDWALL

A Tale of Redwall

Tales of
Redwall
- Lord Brocktree
- Martin the Warrior
- Mossflower
- The Legend of Luke
- Outcast of Redwall
- Mariel of Redwall
- The Bellmaker
- Salamandastron
- Redwall
- Mattimeo
- The Pearls of Lutra
- The Long Patrol
- Marlfox
- The Taggerung

Click onto the Redwall website and
discover more about the legendary world of
Redwall and its creator, Brian Jacques!
http://www.redwall.org

BRIAN JACQUES

❖

REDWALL
A Tale of Redwall

Illustrated by Gary Chalk

RED
FOX

REDWALL
A RED FOX BOOK : 1 86 230330 4

First published in Great Britain by Hutchinson,
an imprint of Random House Children's Books

Hutchinson edition published 1986
Beaver edition published 1987
Red Fox edition published 1990

Papers used by Random House Children's Books are natural,
recyclable products made from wood grown in sustainable forests.
The manufacturing processes conform to the
environmental regulations of the country of origin.

Red Fox Books are published by Random House Children's Books,
61–63 Uxbridge Road, London W5 5SA,
a division of The Random House Group Ltd,
in Australia by Random House Australia (Pty) Ltd,
20 Alfred Street, Milsons Point, Sydney, NSW 2061, Australia,
in New Zealand by Random House New Zealand Ltd,
18 Poland Road, Glenfield, Auckland 10, New Zealand,
and in South Africa by Random House (Pty) Ltd,
Endulini, 5A Jubilee Road, Parktown 2193, South Africa

THE RANDOM HOUSE GROUP Limited Reg. No. 954009
www.kidsatrandomhouse.co.uk/redwall

A CIP catalogue record for this book is available from the British Library.

Printed and bound in Great Britain by
Bookmarque Ltd, Croydon, Surrey

REDWALL ABBEY
AND
SURROUNDING
COUNTRYSIDE

MEADOW

N

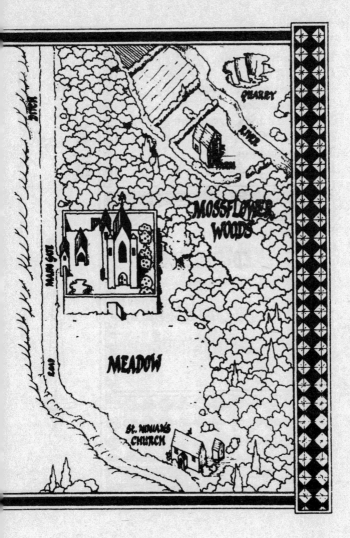

QUARRY

RIVER

MOSSFLOWER WOODS

MAIN GATE

ROAD

MEADOW

St. NINIAN'S CHURCH

Who says that I am dead
Knows nought at all.
I – am that is,
Two mice within Redwall.
The Warrior sleeps
'Twixt Hall and Cavern Hole.
I – am that is,
Take on my mighty role.
Look for the sword
In moonlight streaming forth,
At night, when day's first hour
Reflects the North.
From o'er the threshold
Seek and you will see;
I – am that is,
My sword will wield for me.

*(Rhyme from beneath
the Great Hall tapestry)*

It was the start of the Summer of the Late Rose. Moss-flower country shimmered gently in a peaceful haze, bathing delicately at each dew-laden dawn, blossoming through high sunny noontides, languishing in each crimson-tinted twilight that heralded the soft darkness of June nights.

Redwall stood foursquare along the marches of the old south border, flanked on two sides by Mossflower Woods' shaded depths. The other half of the Abbey over-looked undulating sweeps of meadowland, its ancient gate facing the long dusty road on the western perimeter.

From above, it resembled some fabulous dusky jewel, fallen between a green mantle of light silk and dark velvet. The first mice had built the Abbey of red sandstone quarried from pits many miles away in the north-east. The Abbey building was covered across its south face by that type of ivy known as Virginia creeper. The onset of autumn would turn the leaves into a cape of fiery hue, thus adding further glory to the name and legend of Redwall Abbey.

BOOK ONE

The Wall

1

Matthias cut a comical little figure as he wobbled his way along the cloisters, with his large sandals flip-flopping and his tail peeping from beneath the baggy folds of an over-sized novice's habit. He paused to gaze upwards at the cloudless blue sky and tripped over the enormous sandals. Hazelnuts scattered out upon the grass from the rush basket he was carrying. Unable to stop, he went tumbling cowl over tail.

Bump!

The young mouse squeaked in dismay. He rubbed tenderly at his damp snub nose whilst slowly taking stock of where he had landed: directly at the feet of Abbot Mortimer!

Immediately Matthias scrambled about on all fours, hastily trying to stuff nuts back into the basket as he muttered clumsy apologies, avoiding the stern gaze of his elder.

'Er, sorry, Father Abbot. I tripped, y'see. Trod on my Abbot, Father Habit. Oh dear, I mean. . . .'

The Father Abbot blinked solemnly over the top of his glasses. Matthias again. What a young buffoon of a mouse. Only the other day he had singed old Brother Methuselah's whiskers while lighting candles.

The elder's stern expression softened. He watched the little novice rolling about on the grass, grappling with large armfuls of the smooth hazelnuts which constantly seemed to escape his grasp. Shaking his old grey head, yet trying to hide a smile, Abbot Mortimer bent and helped to gather up the fallen nuts.

'Oh Matthias, Matthias, my son,' he said wearily. 'When will you learn to take life a little slower, to walk with dignity and humility? How can you ever hope to be accepted as a mouse of Redwall, when you are always dashing about grinning from whisker to tail like a mad rabbit?'

Matthias tossed the last of the hazelnuts into the basket and stood awkwardly shuffling his large sandals in the grass. How could he say aloud what was in his heart?

The Abbot put his paw around the young mouse's shoulders, sensing his secret yearnings, for he had ruled Redwall wisely over a great number of years and gained much experience of mouselife. He smiled down at his young charge and spoke kindly to him. 'Come with me, Matthias. It is time we talked together.'

A curious thrush perching in a gnarled pear tree watched the two figures make their way at a sedate pace in the direction of Great Hall, one clad in the dark greeny-brown of the order, the other garbed in the lighter green of a novice. They conversed earnestly in low tones. Thinking what a clever bird he was, the thrush swooped down on the basket that had been left behind. Twisters! The basket contained only hard nuts, locked tight within their shells. Feigning lack of interest, lest any other birds had been witness to his silly mistake, he began jauntily whistling a few bars of his melodious summer song,

14

strolling nonchalantly over to the cloister walls in search of snails.

It was cool inside Great Hall. Sunlight flooded down in slanting rainbow-hued shafts from the high, narrow stained-glass windows. A million coloured dust-motes danced and swirled as the two mice trod the ancient stone floor. The Father Abbot halted in front of the wall on which hung a long tapestry. This was the pride and joy of Redwall. The oldest part had been woven by the founders of the abbey, but each successive generation had added to it; thus the tapestry was not only a priceless treasure, it was also a magnificent chronicle of early Redwall history.

The Abbot studied the wonderment in Matthias's eyes as he asked him a question, the answer to which the wise mouse already knew. 'What are you looking at, my son?'

Matthias pointed to the figure woven into the tapestry. It was a heroic-looking mouse with a fearless smile on his handsome face. Clad in armour, he leaned casually on an impressive sword, while behind him foxes, wildcats, and vermin fled in terror. The young mouse gazed in admiration.

'Oh, Father Abbot,' he sighed. 'If only I could be like Martin the Warrior. He was the bravest, most courageous mouse that ever lived!'

The Abbot sat down slowly on the cool stone floor, resting his back against the wall.

'Listen to what I say, Matthias. You have been like a son to me, ever since you first came to our gates as an orphaned woodland mouse, begging to be taken in. Come, sit by me and I will try to explain to you what our Order is all about.

'We are mice of peace. Oh, I know that Martin was a warrior mouse, but those were wild days when strength was needed. The strength of a champion such as Martin.

15

He arrived here in the deep winter when the Founders were under attack from many foxes, vermin, and a great wildcat. So fierce a fighter was Martin that he faced the enemy single-pawed, driving them mercilessly, far from Mossflower. During the rout Martin fought a great battle against overwhelming odds. He emerged victorious after slaying the wildcat with his ancient sword, which became famous throughout the land. But in the last bloody combat Martin was seriously wounded. He lay injured in the snow until the mice found him. They brought him back to the Abbey and cared for his hurts until he regained his strength.

'Then something seemed to come over him. He was transformed by what could only be called a mouse miracle. Martin forsook the way of the warrior and hung up his sword.

'That was when our Order found its true vocation. All the mice took a solemn vow never to harm another living creature, unless it was an enemy that sought to harm our Order by violence. They vowed to heal the sick, care for the injured, and give aid to the wretched and impoverished. So was it written, and so has it been through all the ages of mousekind since.

'Today, we are a deeply honoured and highly respected Society. Anywhere we go, even far beyond Mossflower, we are treated with courtesy by all creatures. Even predators will not harm a mouse who wears the habit of our Order. They know he or she is one who will heal and give aid. It is an unwritten law that Redwall mice can go anywhere, through any territory, and pass unharmed. At all times we must live up to this. It is our way, our very life.'

As the Abbot spoke, so his voice increased in volume and solemnity. Matthias sat under his stern gaze, completely humbled. Abbot Mortimer stood and put a wrinkled old paw lightly on the small head, right between the velvety ears, now drooping with shame.

Once more the Abbot's heart softened towards the little mouse. 'Poor Matthias, alas for your ambitions. The day of the warrior is gone, my son. We live in peaceful times, thank heaven and you need only think of obeying me, your Abbot, and doing as you are bidden. In time to come, when I am long gone to my rest, you will think back to this day and bless my memory, for then you will be a true member of Redwall. Come now, my young friend, cheer up; it is the Summer of the Late Rose. There are many, many days of warm sun ahead of us. Go back and get your basket of hazelnuts. Tonight we have a great feast to celebrate – my Golden Jubilee as Abbot. When you've taken the nuts to the kitchen, I have a special task for you. Yes indeed, I'll need some fine fish for the table. Get your rod and line. Tell Brother Alf that he is to take you fishing in the small boat. That's what young mice like doing, isn't it? Who knows, you may land a fine trout or some sticklebacks! Run along now, young one.'

Happiness filled Matthias from tail to whiskers as he bobbed a quick bow to his superior and shuffled off. Smiling benignly, the Abbot watched him go. Little rascal, he must have a word with the Almoner, to see if some sandals could be found that were the right fit for Matthias. Small wonder the poor mouse kept tripping up!

2

The high, warm sun shone down on Cluny the Scourge.

Cluny was coming!

He was big, and tough; an evil rat with ragged fur and curved, jagged teeth. He wore a black eyepatch; his eye had been torn out in battle with a pike.

Cluny had lost an eye.

The pike had lost its life!

Some said that Cluny was a Portuguese rat. Others said he came from the jungles far across the wide oceans. Nobody knew for sure.

Cluny was a bilge rat; the biggest, most savage rodent that ever jumped from ship to shore. He was black, with grey and pink scars all over his huge sleek body, from the tip of his wet nose, up past his green and yellow slitted eye, across both his mean tattered ears, down the length of his heavy vermin-ridden back to the enormous whip-like tail which had earned him his title: Cluny the Scourge!

Now he rode on the back of the hay wagon with his five hundred followers, a mighty army of rats: sewer rats, tavern rats, water rats, dockside rats. Cluny's army –

18

fearing, yet following him. Redtooth, his second-in-command, carried a long pole. This was Cluny's personal standard, and the skull of a ferret was fixed at its top. Cluny had killed the ferret. He feared no living thing.

Wild eyed, with the terror of rat smell in its nostrils, the horse plunged ahead without any driver. Where the hay cart was taking him was of little concern to Cluny. Straight on the panicked horse galloped, past the milestone lodged in the earth at the roadside, heedless of the letters graven in the stone: 'Redwall Abbey, fifteen miles'.

Cluny spat over the edge of the cart at two young rabbits playing in a field. Tasty little things; a pity the cart hadn't stopped yet, he thought. The high warm sun shone down on Cluny the Scourge.

Cluny was a God of War!

Cluny was coming nearer!

3

Beneath the Great Hall of Redwall, candles burned bright in their sconces. This was the Cavern Hole of the mice.

What a night it was going to be!

Between them, Matthias and Brother Alf had caught and landed a fully-grown grayling. They had fought and played the big fish for nearly two hours, finally wading into the shallows and dragging it to the bank. It was nearly two pounds in weight, a tribute to Brother Alf's angling skills combined with the youthful muscles of Matthias, and their joint enthusiasm.

Constance the badger had to be called. Gripping the fish in her strong jaws, she followed the two mice to the Abbey kitchen and delivered the catch for them. Then she made her farewells; they would see her at the Jubilee feast that evening, along with lots of other Mossflower residents who had been invited to share the festivities.

Brother Alf and Matthias stood proudly beside their catch amidst the culinary hustle and bustle until they were noticed by Friar Hugo. Busy as he was, the enormously fat Hugo (who would have no other title but that of Friar) stopped what he was doing. Wiping the perspiration from his brow with a dandelion which he held with his tail, he waddled about inspecting the fish.

'Hmm, nice shiny scales, bright eyes, beautifully fresh.' Friar Hugo smiled so joyfully that his face disappeared amid deep dimples. He shook Alf by the paw and clapped Matthias heartily on the back as he called out between chuckles, 'Bring the white gooseberry wine! Fetch me some rosemary, thyme, beechnuts and honey, quickly. And now, friends, now,' he squeaked, waving the dandelion wildly with his tail, 'I, Hugo, will create a *Grayling à la Redwall* that will melt in the mouth of mice. Fresh cream! I need lots of fresh cream! Bring some mint leaves too.'

They had left Friar Hugo ranting on, delirious in his joy, as they both went off to bathe and clean up; combing whiskers, curling tails, shining noses, and the hundred and one other grooming tasks that Redwall mice always performed in preparation for an epic feast.

The rafters of Cavern Hole rang to the excited buzz and laughter of the assembled creatures: hedgehogs, moles, squirrels, woodland creatures and mice of all kinds – fieldmice, hedgemice, dormice, even a family of poor little churchmice. Kindly helpers scurried about making everybody welcome.

'Hello there, Mrs Churchmouse! Sit the children down! I'll get them some raspberry cordial.'

'Why, Mr Bankvole! So nice to see you! How's the back? Better now? Good. Here, try a drop of this peach and elderberry brandy.'

Matthias's young head was in a whirl. He could not remember being so happy in all his life. Winifred the otter nudged him.

'I say, Matthias. Where's this giant grayling that you

21

and old Alf hooked, by the claw! I wish that I could land a beauty like that. Nearly a two-pounder, wasn't it?'

Matthias swelled with pride. Such praise, and from the champion fisher herself, an otter!

Tim and Tess, the twin Churchmouse babes, felt Matthias's strong arm muscles and giggled aloud in admiration. He helped to serve them two portions of apple and mint ice cream. Such nice little twins. Was it only three months ago that he had helped Sister Stephanie to get them over tail rickets? My, how they had grown!

Abbot Mortimer sat in his carved willow chair, beaming thanks as one by one the new arrivals laid their simple home-made gifts at his feet: an acorn cup from a squirrel, fishbone combs from the otters, mossy bark sandals made by the moles, and many more fine presents too numerous to mention. The Abbot shook his head in amazement. Even more guests were arriving!

He beckoned Friar Hugo to his side. A whispered conference was held. Matthias could only hear snatches of the conversation.

'Don't worry, Father Abbot, there will be enough for all.'

'How are the cellar stocks, Hugo?'

'Enough to flood the Abbey pond, Father.'

'And nuts? We must not run short of nuts.'

'You name them, we've got them. Even candied chestnuts and acorn crunch. We could feed the district for a year.'

'Dairy produce?'

'Oh that, I've got a cheddar cheese that four badgers couldn't roll, plus ten other varieties.'

'Good, good, thank you, Hugo. Oh, we must thank Alf and young Matthias for that magnificent fish. What fine anglers they are! There's enough to keep the entire Abbey going for a week! Excellent mice, well done.'

Matthias blushed to his tail's end.

'The otters! The otters!'

A loud, jolly cry went up as three otters in clown costumes came bounding in. Such acrobatics! They tumbled, balanced and gyrated, cavorting comically across the laden tabletops without upsetting as much as a single sultana. They ended up hanging from the rafters by a strand of ivy, to wild applause.

Ambrose Spike the hedgehog did his party piece. He amazed everyone with his feats of legerdemain. Eggs were taken from a squirrel's ear; a young mouse's tail stood up and danced like a snake; the incredible vanishing–conker trick was performed in front of a group of little harvest mice who kept squeaking, 'He's got it hidden in his prickles.'

But had he? Ambrose made a few mysterious passes and produced the conker, straight out of the mouth of an awestruck infant mouse. Was it magic?

Of course it was.

All activity ceased as the great Joseph Bell tolled out eight o'clock from the Abbey belfry. Silently, all the creatures filed to their allotted places. They stood reverently behind the seats with heads lowered. Abbot Mortimer rose and solemnly spread his paws wide, encompassing the festive board. He said the grace.

> 'Fur and whisker, tooth and claw,
> All who enter by our door.
> Nuts and herbs, leaves and fruits,
> Berries, tubers, plants and roots,
> Silver fish whose life we take
> Only for a meal to make.'

This was followed by a loud and grateful 'Amen'.

There was a mass clattering of chairs and scraping of forms as everyone was seated. Matthias found himself next to Tim and Tess on one paw, and Cornflower Fieldmouse on the other. Cornflower was a quiet young mouse, but undoubtedly very pretty. She had the longest eyelashes Matthias had ever seen, the brightest eyes, the softest fur, the whitest teeth. . . .

Matthias fumbled with a piece of celery, he turned to see if the twins were coping adequately. You never could tell with these baby churchmice.

Brother Alf remarked that Friar Hugo had excelled himself, as course after course was brought to the table. Tender freshwater shrimp garnished with cream and rose leaves; devilled barley pearls in acorn purée; apple and carrot chews; marinated cabbage stalks steeped in creamed white turnip with nutmeg.

A chorus of ooh's and ah's greeted the arrival of six mice pushing a big trolley. It was the grayling. Wreaths of aromatic steam drifted around Cavern Hole; it had been baked to perfection. Friar Hugo entered, with a slight swagger added to his ungainly waddle. He swept off his chef's cap with his tail, and announced in a somewhat pompous squeak, 'Milord Abbot, honoured guests from Mossflower area and members of the Abbey. Ahem, I wish to present my *pièce de résistance*—'

'Oh get on with it, Hugo!'

After some icy staring about to detect the culprit, and several smothered sniggers from around the room, the little fat friar puffed himself up once more and declaimed firmly: '*Grayling à la Redwall*'.

Polite but eager applause rippled round as Hugo sliced the fish, and placed the first steaming portion on to a platter. With suitable dignity he presented it to the Abbot, who thanked him graciously.

All eyes were on the Father Abbot. He took a dainty fork loaded precariously with steaming fish. Carefully he transferred it from plate to mouth. Chewing delicately, he turned his eyes upwards then closed them, whiskers atwitch, jaws working steadily, munching away, his curled up tail holding a napkin which neatly wiped his mouth. The Abbot's eyes reopened. He beamed like the sun on midsummer morn.

'Quite wonderful, perfectly exquisite! Friar Hugo, you are truly my Champion Chef. Please serve our guests your masterwork.'

Any further speech was drowned by hearty cheers.

4

Cluny was in a foul temper. He snarled viciously.

The horse had stopped from sheer exhaustion. He hadn't wanted that: some inner devil persuaded him that he had not yet reached his destination. Cluny's one eye slitted evilly.

From the depths of the hay cart the rodents of the Warlord's army watched their Master. They knew him well enough to stay clear of him in his present mood. He was violent, unpredictable.

'Skullface,' Cluny snapped.

There was a rustle in the hay, a villainous head popped up.

'Aye, Chief, d'you want me?'

Cluny's powerful tail shot out and dragged the unfortunate forward. Skullface cringed as sharp dirty claws dug into his fur. Cluny nodded at the horse.

'Jump on that thing's back sharpish. Give it a good bite. That'll get the lazy brute moving again.'

Skullface swallowed nervously and licked his dry lips.

'But Chief, it might bite me back.'

Swish! Crack! Cluny wielded his mighty tail as if it

were a bullwhip. His victim screamed aloud with pain as the scourge lashed his thin bony back.

'Mutiny, insubordination!' Cluny roared. 'By the teeth of hell, I'll flay you into mangy dollrags.'

Skullface scurried over on to the driver's seat, yelling with pain. 'No more! Don't whip me, Chief. Look, I'm going to do it.'

'Hold tight to the rigging back there,' Cluny shouted to his horde.

Skullface performed a frantic leap. He landed on the horse's back. The terrified animal did not wait for the rat to bite, as soon as it felt the loathsome scratching weight descend on its exposed haunches it gave a loud panicked whinny and bucked. Spurred on by the energy of fright it careered off like a runaway juggernaut.

Skullface had time for just one agonized scream before he fell. The iron-shod cartwheels rolled over him. He lay in a red mist of death, the life ebbing from his broken body. The last thing he saw before darkness claimed him was the sneering visage of Cluny the Scourge roaring from the jolting back-board, 'Tell the devil Cluny sent you, Skullface!'

They were on the move again. Cluny was getting nearer.

5

Down in Cavern Hole the great feast had slackened off.

So had a lot of belts!

Redwall mice and their guests sat back replete. There were still great quantities of food uneaten.

Abbot Mortimer whispered in Friar Hugo's ear, 'Friar, I want you to pack up a large sack with food, hazelnuts, cheese, bread, cakes, anything you see fit. Give it to Mrs Churchmouse, as secretly as you can without attracting attention. Poverty is an ugly spectre when a mousewife has as many mouths to feed as she does. Oh, and be sure that her husband doesn't suspect what you are doing. John Churchmouse may be poor but he is also proud. I fear he might not accept charitable gifts.'

Hugo nodded knowingly and waddled off to do his Abbot's bidding.

Cornflower and Matthias had become quite friendly. They were young mice of the same age. Though their temperaments were different they found something in common, an interest in Tim and Tess the twin church-mice. They had passed a pleasant evening, joking and playing games with the little creatures. Tess had clambered on to Matthias's lap and fallen asleep, whereupon baby Tim did likewise in the velvety fur of Cornflower. She smiled at Matthias as she stroked Tim's small head. 'Ah, bless their little paws! Don't they look peaceful?'

Matthias nodded in agreement.

Colin Vole tittered aloud and remarked rather foolishly, 'Ooh, would you look at Matthias an' Cornflower there, a-nursin' those two babbies like they was an old wedded couple. Well, crumble my bank!'

Brother Alf reprimanded him sharply. 'Here now, you keep a latch on that silly tongue of yours, Colin Vole! Don't you know that some day Matthias will be a Redwall mouse? And don't let me hear you slandering young Cornflower. She's a decent mouse from a good family. Mark my words, Master Vole, I could say a thing or two to your mum and dad. Only last evening I saw you playing "catch the bulrush" with that young harvest mouse. What was her name now?'

Colin Vole blushed until his nose went dry. He flounced off, swishing his tail, muttering about going outside to take the air.

Matthias caught a nod and a glance from the Abbot. Excusing himself to Cornflower, he deposited the sleeping Tess gently upon his chair and went across to him.

'Ah, Matthias, my son, here you are. Did you enjoy my Jubilee Feast?'

'Yes, thank you, Father,' Matthias replied.

'Good, good,' chuckled the Abbot. 'Now, I was going to ask Brother Alf or Edmund to go on a special errand, but they are no longer young mice and both look quite weary at this late hour. So, I thought I might ask my chief grayling-catcher to carry out this special task for me.'

Matthias could not help standing a bit taller.

'Say the word and I'm your mouse, sir.'

The Abbot leaned forward and spoke confidentially. 'Do you see the Churchmouse family? Well, it's such a long way back home for them on foot. Good Heavens, and there are so many of them! I thought it would be a splendid idea if you were to drive them home in the Abbey cart, along with any others going that way. Constance Badger would pull the cart, of course, while you could act as guide and bodyguard. Take a good stout staff with you, Matthias.'

The young mouse needed no second bidding. Drawing himself up to his full height he saluted in a smart military fashion. 'Leave it to me, Father Abbot. Old Constance is a bit slow-thinking. I'll take complete responsibility.'

The Abbot shook with silent laughter as he watched Matthias march off with a soldier-like swagger. Flip flop, flip flop; he tripped and fell flat on his tail.

'Oh dear, I'll have to get that young mouse some sandals that aren't so big,' the Abbot said to himself for the second time that day.

Well, what a stroke of luck. Fancy Cornflower's family living so close to the Churchmouse brood! Matthias was only too glad to offer them a lift home.

Would Miss Cornflower like to sit next to him?

She most certainly would!

Cornflower's parents sat inside the cart, her mum helping Mrs Churchmouse with the little ones, while her dad chatted away with John Churchmouse as they shared a pipe of old bracken twist.

Friar Hugo came out and dumped a bulky sack next to Mrs Churchmouse. 'Abbot says to thank you for the loan of bowls and tablecloths, ma'am.' The fat friar gave her a huge wink.

'All comfy back there?' called Matthias. 'Right, off we go, Constance.'

The big badger trundled the cart away as they called their goodnights. She nodded at Methuselah, the ancient gate-keeper mouse. As the cart rolled out into the road a sliver of golden moon looked down from a star-pierced summer night. Matthias gazed upwards, feeling as if he were slowly turning with the silent earth. Peace was all about him; the baby mice inside the car whimpered fitfully in their small secret dreams; Constance ambled slowly along, as though she were out on a night-time stroll pulling no weight at all; the stout ash staff lay forgotten on the footboard.

Cornflower dozed against Matthias's shoulder. She could hear the gentle lull of her father's voice and that of John Churchmouse, blending with the hum of nocturnal insects from the meadow and hedges on this balmy summer night.

The Summer of the Late Rose . . . Cornflower turned the words over in her mind, dreamily thinking of the old rambler which bloomed in the Abbey gardens. Normally it was in full red flower by now, but this year, for some unknown reason, it had chosen to flower late. It was covered in dormant young rosebuds, even now, well into June – a thing that happened only infrequently, and usually heralded an extra-long hot summer. Old Methuselah could only remember three other such summers in his long lifetime. Accordingly he had advised that it be marked on the calendar and in the Abbey chronicles as 'The Summer of the Late Rose'. Cornflower's head sank lower, in sleep.

The old cart rolled on gently, down the long dusty road. They were now over halfway to the ruined church of Saint Ninian where John Churchmouse lived, as had his father, grandfather, and great grandfather before him. Matthias had fallen into a deep slumber. Even Constance was unable to stop her eyelids drooping. She went slower and slower. It was as if the little cart and its occupants were caught in the magic spell of an enchanted summer night.

Suddenly, and without warning, they were roused by the thunder of hooves.

Nobody could determine which direction the sound was coming from. It seemed to fill the very air about them as it gathered momentum; the ground began trembling with the rumbling noise.

Some sixth sense warned Constance to get off the road to a hiding place. The powerful badger gave a mighty heave. Her blunt claws churned the roadside soil as she propelled the cart through a gap in the hawthorn hedge, down to the slope of the ditch where she dug her paws in, holding the cart still and secure whilst John Churchmouse and Cornflower's father jumped out and wedged the wheels firmly with stones.

Matthias gasped with shock as a giant horse galloped past, its mane streaming out, eyes rolling in panic. It was towing a hay cart which bounced wildly from side to side. Matthias could see rats among the hay, but these were no ordinary rats. They were huge ragged rodents, bigger than any he had ever seen. Their heavy tattooed arms waved a variety of weapons – pikes, knives, spears, and long rusty cutlasses. Standing boldly on the backboard of the hay cart was the biggest, fiercest, most evil-looking rat that ever slunk out of a nightmare! In one claw he grasped a long pole with a ferret's head spiked to it, while in the other was his thick, enormous tail which he cracked like a whip. Laughing madly and yelling strange curses, he swayed to and fro skilfully as horse and wagon clattered off down the road into the night. As suddenly as they had come, they were gone!

*

Matthias walked out into the road, staff in hand. Stray wisps of hay drifted down behind him. His legs trembled uncontrollably. Constance hauled the Abbey cart back on to the road. Cornflower was helping her mum and Mrs Churchmouse to calm the little ones' tears of fright. Together they stood in the cart tracks amid the settling dust.

'Did you see that?'

'I saw it, but I don't believe it!'

'What in heaven was it?'

'What in hell, more like.'

'All those rats! Such big ones, too.'

'Aye, and that one on the back! He looked like the Devil himself.'

Seeing Matthias still stunned by what had happened, Constance took over the leadership. She wheeled the cart around.

'I think we'd best head back for the Abbey,' she said firmly. 'Father Abbot'll want to know about this straight away.'

Knowing that the badger was far more experienced than himself, Matthias assumed the role of second-in-command. 'Right, Cornflower, get in the cart and take charge of the mothers and babies,' he said. 'Mr Field-mouse, Mr Churchmouse, up front with Constance, please.'

Silently the mice did as ordered. The cart moved off with Matthias positioned on the back providing a rear-guard. The young mouse gripped his staff tightly, his back to his charges, facing down the road in the direction the hay cart had taken.

6

The horse had got away safely.

It was the hay cart that suffered most damage. Bolting recklessly from side to side down the road, the blinkered animal failed to see the twin stone gateposts on its right – skidding crazily, the cart smashed into the uprights. There was a loud splintering of shafts as the horse careered onwards, trailing in its wake reins, tracers and shattered timber.

His lightning reflexes serving him well, Cluny leaped clear. He landed catlike on all fours as the hay cart upended in the roadside ditch, its buckled wheels spinning awkwardly.

Feeling braced after his mad ride and the subsequent narrow escape, Cluny strode to the ditch's edge. The distressed cries of those trapped beneath the cart reached his ears. He spat contemptuously, narrowing his one good eye.

'Come on, get up out of there, you cringing load of catsmeat,' he bellowed. 'Redtooth! Darkclaw! Report to me or I'll have your skulls for skittles.'

Cluny's two henchrats pulled themselves from the

ditch, shaking their heads dazedly.

Crack! Slash! The whiplike tail brought them swiftly to his side.

'Three-Leg and Scratch are dead, Chief.'

'Dead as dirt. The cart crushed 'em, Chief.'

'Stupid fools,' snarled Cluny. 'Serves them right! What about the rest?'

'Old Wormtail has lost a paw. Some of the others are really hurt.'

Cluny sneered. 'Aah, they'll get over it and suffer worse by the time I'm done with them. They're getting too fat and sluggish, by the tripes! They'd not last five minutes in a storm at sea. Come on, you dead-and-alive ragbags! Get up here and gather round.'

Rats struggled from the ditch and the cart – frantic to obey the harsh command as quickly as possible. They crowded about the undamaged gatepost which their leader had chosen as a perch. None dared to cry or complain about their hurts. Who could predict what mood the Warlord was in?

'Right, cock your lugs up and listen to me,' Cluny snarled. 'First, we've got to find out where we have docked. Let's take a bearing on this place.'

Redtooth held up his claw. 'The Church of Saint Ninian, Chief. It says so on the notice board over yonder.'

'Well, no matter,' Cluny snapped. 'It'll do as a berth until we find something better. Fangburn! Cheesethief!'

'Here, Chief.'

'Scout the area. See if you can find a better lodging for us than this heap of rubble. Trail back to the west. I think we passed a big place on the way.'

'Aye, aye, Chief.'

'Frogblood! Scumnose!'

'Chief?'

'Take fifty soldiers and see if you can round up any rats

35

that know the lie of the land. Get big strong rats, but bring along weasels, stoats and ferrets too. They'll do at a pinch. Mind now, don't stand for arguments. Smash their dens up so they won't have homes to worry about. If any refuse to join up, then kill them there and then. Understood?'

'All clear, Chief.'

'Ragear! Mangefur! Take twenty rats and forage for supplies. The rest of you get inside the church. Redtooth, Darkclaw, check the armour. See if there are things about that we can use as weapons: iron spike railings – there's usually enough of them around a churchyard. Jump to it.'

Cluny had arrived!

7

Matthias had never stayed up all night in his life. He was just a bit tired, but strangely excited. Great events seemed to have been set in motion by his news.

Immediately upon being informed of the hay cart incident, the Abbot had insisted upon calling a special council meeting of all Redwall creatures. Once again Cavern Hole was packed to the doors, but this time it was for a purpose very different from the feast. Constance and Matthias stood in front of the Council of Elders. All about them was a hum of whispers and muttering.

Abbot Mortimer called order by ringing a small bell.

'Pay attention, everyone. Constance and Matthias, would you please tell the Council what you saw tonight on the road to Saint Ninian's.'

As clearly as they could, the badger and the young mouse related the incident of the rat-infested hay cart.

The Council began questioning them.

'Rats, you say, Matthias. What type of rat?' inquired Sister Clemence.

'Big ones,' Matthias replied, 'though I'm afraid I

couldn't say what kind they were or where they had come from.'

'What about you, Constance?'

'Well, I remember that my old Grandad once knew a sea rat,' she answered. 'Going by his description, I'd say that's what they looked like to me.'

'And how many would you say there were of these rats?' Father Abbot asked.

'Couldn't say for sure, Father Abbot. There must have been hundreds.'

'Matthias?'

'Oh yes, Father. I'd agree with Constance. At least four hundred.'

'Did you notice anything else about them, Constance?'

'Indeed I did, Father Abbot. My badger senses told me right off that these were very bad and evil rats.'

The badger's statement caused uproar and shouts of 'Nonsense. Pure speculation,' and 'That's right! Give a rat a bad name!'

Matthias silenced the hubbub. Raising a paw, he shouted aloud, 'Constance is right. I could feel it myself. There was one huge rat with a ferret's skull on a pole. I got a good look at him – it was like seeing some horrible monster.'

In the silence that followed, the Abbot rose and confronted Matthias. Stooping slightly, he stared into the young mouse's bright eyes. 'Think carefully, my son. Was there anything special you noticed about this rat?'

Matthias thought for a moment.

'He was much bigger than the others, Father.'

'What else? Think, Matthias.'

'I remember! He only had one eye.'

'Right or left?'

'Left, I think. Yes, it was the left, Father.'

'Now, can you recall anything about his tail?'

'I certainly can,' Matthias squeaked. 'It must have been the longest tail of any rat alive. He held it in his claw as if it were a whip.'

The Abbot paced up and down before turning to the assembly.

'Twice in my lifetime I have heard travellers speak of this rat. He bears a name that a fox would be afraid to whisper in the darkness of midnight. Cluny the Scourge!'

A deathly hush fell upon the creatures in Cavern Hole. Cluny the Scourge!

Surely not? He was only some kind of folk legend, a warning used by mothers when youngsters were fractious or disobedient.

'Go to sleep or Cluny will get you!'

'Eat up your dinner or Cluny will come!'

'Come in this instant, or I'll tell Cluny!'

Most creatures didn't even know what Cluny was. He was just some sort of bogey that lived in bad dreams and the dark corners of imagination.

The silence was broken by scornful snorts and derisive laughter. Furry elbows nudged downy ribs. Mice were beginning to smile from sheer relief. Cluny the Scourge, indeed!

Feeling slightly abashed, Matthias and Constance looked pleadingly towards the Abbot for support. Abbot Mortimer's old face was stern as he shook the bell vigorously for silence.

'Mice of Redwall, I see there are those amongst you who doubt the word of your Abbot.'

The quiet but authoritative words caused an embarrassed shuffling from the Council Elders. Brother Joseph stood up and cleared his throat. 'Ahem, er, good Father Abbot, we all respect your word and look to you for guidance, but really . . . I mean. . . .'

Sister Clemence stood up smiling. She spread her paws wide. 'Perhaps Cluny is coming to get us for staying up late.'

A roar of laughter greeted the ironic words.

Constance's back hairs bristled. She gave an angry growl followed by a fierce bark. The mice huddled together with fright. Nobody had ever seen a snarling, angry badger at a Council meeting.

Before they could recover, Constance was up on her hind legs having her say. 'I've never seen such a pack of empty-headed ninnies. You should all be ashamed of yourselves, giggling like silly little otter cubs that have caught a beetle. I never thought I'd live to see the Elders of Redwall acting in this way.' Constance hunched her heavy shoulders and glared about with a ferocity that set them trembling. 'Now you listen to me. Take heed of what your Father Abbot has to say. The next creature who utters one squeak will answer to me. Understood?'

The badger bowed low in a dignified manner, gesturing with her massive blunt paw. 'The floor is yours, Father Abbot.'

'Thank you, Constance, my good and faithful friend,' the Abbot murmured. He looked about him, shaking his head gravely.

'I have little more to say on the subject, but as I see that you still need convincing, here is my proposal. We will send two mice out to relieve the gatehouse. Let me see, yes . . . Brothers Rufus and George, would you kindly go and take over from Brother Methuselah? Please send him in here to me. Tell him to bring the travellers' record volumes. Not the present issue, but the old editions which were used in past years.'

Rufus and George, both solid-looking sensible mice, took their leave with a formal bow to the Abbot.

Through a high slitted window, Matthias could see the

rosy-pink and gold fingers of dawn stealing down to Cavern Hole as the candles began to flicker and smoke into stubs. All in the space of a night events had moved from festivity to a crisis, and he, Matthias, had taken a major role in both. First the big grayling, then the sighting of the cart; large happenings for a small mouse.

Old Brother Methuselah had kept the Abbey records for as long as any creature could remember. It was his life's work and consuming passion. Besides the official chronicle of Redwall he also kept his own personal volume, full of valuable information. Travelling creatures, migratory birds, wandering foxes, rambling squirrels and garrulous hares – they all stopped and chatted with the old mouse, partaking of his hospitality, never dreaming of hurting him in any way. Methuselah had the gift of tongues. He could understand any creature, even a bird. He was an extraordinary old mouse, who lived with the company of his volumes in the solitude of the gatehouse.

Seated in the Father Abbot's own chair, Methuselah took his spectacles from a moss-bark case, carefully perching them on the bridge of his nose. All gathered around to hear as he opened a record book and spoke in a squeak barely above a whisper.

'Hmm, hmm, me Lord Abbot Cedric. It is Cedric, isn't it? Oh botheration, you'll be the new Abbot, Mortimer – the one who came after Cedric. Oh dear me, I see so many of them come and go, you know. Hmm, hmm, me Lord Abbot Mortimer and members of Redwall. I refer to a record of winter, six years back.' Here the ancient mouse took a while to leaf through the pages. 'Hmm, ah yes, here it is. "Late in November, Year of the Small Sweet Chestnut, from a frozen sparrowhawk come down from the far north . . ." – Peculiar chap, spoke with a strange accent. I repaired his right wing pinfeather – ". . . news of a mine disaster, caused by a large savage sea rat named Cluny. It seems that this rat wanted to settle his army in the mine. The badgers and other creatures who owned the mine drove them out. Cluny returned by night, and with his band of rats gnawed away and undermined much of the wooden shoring. This caused the mine to collapse the next day, killing the owners." '

Brother Methuselah closed the volume and looked over his glasses at the assembly. 'I have no need to read further, I can recite other misdeeds from memory. As the hordes of Cluny the Scourge have moved southwards over the past six years, I have gathered intelligence of other incidents: a farmhouse set alight, later that same year . . . piglets, an entire litter of them eaten alive by rats . . . sickness and disease spread through livestock herds by Cluny's army. There was even a report brought to me two years ago by a town dog: an army of rats stampeded a herd of cows through a village, causing chaos and much destruction.'

Methuselah halted and blinked over his spectacles. 'And you dare doubt the word of our Abbot that Cluny the Scourge exists? What idiotic mice you are, to be sure.'

Methuselah's words caused widespread consternation. There was much agitated nibbling of paws. Nobody could doubt he spoke the truth; he was already old and wise when the most elderly among them was a blind hairless mite, puling and whimpering for a feed from its mother.

'Oh my whiskers, what a mess.'
'Hadn't we better pack up and move?'
'Maybe Cluny will spare us.'
'Oh dear, oh dear, what shall we do?'
Matthias sprang to the middle of the floor brandishing

his staff.

'Do?' he cried. 'I'll tell you what we'll do. We'll be ready.'

The Abbot could not help shaking his head in admiration. It seemed that young Matthias had hidden depths.

'Why, thank you, Matthias,' he said. 'I could not have put it better myself. That's exactly what we will do. We'll be ready!'

8

Cluny the Scourge was having nightmares.

He had lain down in the Churchmouses' bed for a well-earned rest while his army were going about their allotted tasks. He should never have tried to sleep on an empty stomach, but weariness overcame his hunger.

In Cluny's dream everything was shrouded in a red mist. The cries of his victims rang out as barns blazed, and ships foundered on a stormy red sea. Cattle bellowed in pain as he battled with the pike that had taken his eye. The Warlord thrashed about, killing, conquering and laying waste to all in his dream.

Then the phantom figure appeared.

At first it seemed a small thing, a mouse in fact, dressed in a long hooded robe. Cluny did not relish meeting with it – he could not tell why – but the mouse kept getting closer to him. For the first time in his life, he turned and ran!

Cluny went like a bat out of hell. Glancing back, he saw all the carnage, death and misery he had caused in his career. The big rat laughed insanely and ran faster: on and on, past scenes of desolation and destruction wreaked by him, Cluny the Scourge. Floating through the red mists he could still see the strange mouse hard on his heels. Cluny felt himself filled with hatred for his pursuer. It seemed to have grown larger; its eyes were cold and grim. Deep inside, Cluny knew that even he could not frighten this oddly-garbed mouse. Now it was wielding a large bright sword, an ancient weapon of terrible beauty. The battle-scarred blade had a word written upon it that he could not make out.

Sweat dripped from Cluny's claws like stinging acid. He stumbled. The strange figure was closer; it had grown into a giant!

Cluny's lungs felt as if they were bursting. He realized that he had slowed up and the mouse was getting closer. He tried to put on an extra burst of speed, but his legs would not obey. They ran more and more slowly; more and more heavily. Cluny cursed aloud at his leaden limbs. He saw he was trapped in deep icy mud. For the first time he knew the meaning of mindless fear and panic.

He turned slowly. Too late. The enemy was upon him; he was rooted helpless to the spot. The avenging mouse swung the sword up high; a million lights flashed from its deadly blade as it struck.

Bong!

The loud toll of the distant Joseph Bell brought Cluny whirling back from the realms of nightmare to cold reality. He shivered, wiping the sweat from his fur with a shaky claw. Saved by the bell.

He was puzzled. What did the fearful dream mean? Cluny had never been one to put his faith in omens, but this dream . . . it had been so lifelike and vivid that he shuddered.

A timid paw tapping on the door snapped Cluny from his reverie with a start. It was Ragear and Mangefur, his scavengers. They slunk into the room, each trying to hide behind the other, knowing that the poor results of their search were likely to incur the Chief's wrath. Their assumption was correct.

Cluny's baleful eye watched them as his long, flexible tail sorted through the paltry offerings which had dropped from their claws. A few dead beetles, two large earthworms, some unidentifiable vegetation, and the pitiful carcass of a long-dead sparrow.

Cluny smiled at Ragear and Mangefur.

With a sigh of relief they grinned back at him. The Chief was in a good mood.

At lightning speed the big rat's claws shot out, and grabbed them both cruelly by the ears. The stupid henchrats yowled piteously as they were lifted bodily from the floor and swung to and fro. In a fit of rage, Cluny bashed their heads together. Half senseless, they were hurled towards the doorway, with his angry words ringing in their skulls. 'Beetles, worms, rotten sparrows! Get me meat. Tender, young, red meat! Next time you bring me rubbish like this, I'll spit the pair of you and have you roasted in your own juice. Is that clear?'

Mangefur pointed an accusing claw at his companion. 'Please, Chief, it was Ragear's fault. If we'd gone across the fields instead of up the road—'

'Don't believe that big fat liar, Chief. It was him who suggested going up the road, not me—'

'Get out!'

The scavengers dashed off, bumping clumsily into each other in panic as they tried to get through the door together. Cluny slumped back on the bed and snorted impatiently.

Frogblood and Scumnose were next to report.

They bore news that cheered Cluny up somewhat. They'd obtained over a hundred new recruits, mainly rats

46

but with a good scattering of ferrets and weasels, and the odd stoat. There had been some who needed convincing. These had been press-ganged by a savage beating from Frogblood coupled with the threat of a horrible death. They were soon convinced that the wisest course was to enlist in Cluny's horde. Others were hungry nomads, only too willing to join up with the infamous Cluny. They were greedy for plunder and booty and pleased to be on what they were sure would be the winning side. Lined up in the churchyard, the recruits were supplied with weaponry by Redtooth and Darkclaw. Impassively they stood in ranks awaiting the Warlord's inspection.

Cluny nodded his approval. Scurvy rats, hungry ferrets, sly weasels, bad stoats: exactly what he needed.

'Read 'em the articles, Redtooth,' he snapped.

Redtooth swaggered back and forth on the churchyard paving as he recited the formula from memory. 'Right, eyes front. You're in the service of Cluny the Scourge now, me buckoes! Desert and you'll be killed. Retreat and you're under sentence of death. Disobey and you'll die. I'm Redtooth, Cluny's number one rat. You will obey the word of your Captains. They take orders from me. I take orders from Cluny, remember that. Now, if any one, two, or a group, or even all of you together want to try and beat Cluny and lead the horde, this is your chance.'

Without warning Cluny charged headlong into the new recruits, lashing out wildly with his scourging tail. He bowled them left, right and centre with his massive strength. Baring his teeth and slitting his eye, he whipped fiercely away until they fell back and scattered in disorder, hiding behind gravestones. Cluny threw back his head and roared with laughter.

'No guts, eh? Ha, it's just as well! I don't want dead 'uns on my claws before I find a proper battle for you to fight.

And make no mistake, when the right time comes I'll see you fight, aye, and die too. Now, raise your weapons and let's see if you know who your master is.'

A motley collection of evil-looking implements was framed by the cloudless sky as wild cries rang out from the newly-inducted recruits.

'Cluny, Cluny, Cluny the Scourge!'

9

Abbot Mortimer and Constance the badger meandered through the grounds together. Both creatures were deep in thought. Had they spoken and voiced their thoughts, they would have mentioned the same subject, the safety of Redwall.

Down long ages the beautiful old Abbey had stood for happiness, peace, and refuge to all. Diligent mice tended the neat little vegetable patches which every season gave forth an abundance of fresh produce: cabbages, sprouts, marrows, turnips, peas, carrots, tomatoes, lettuces and onions, all in their turn. Flowerbeds, heady and fragrant with countless varieties of summer blooms from rose to humble daisy, were planted by the mice and husbanded by the hard-working bee folk, who in their turn rewarded Redwall with plentiful supplies of honey and beeswax.

The two friends wandered onwards, past the pond. Early morning sunlight glinted off the water, throwing out ripples from the fish caught by the overnight lines which were baited and left to drift each evening by Brother Alf. Ahead of them lay the berry-hedges – raspberry, blackberry, bilberry; and the strawberry patch where every August sleepy baby creatures could be seen, their stomachs full after eating the pick of the crop. Gradually they made their way around the big old chestnut trees into the orchard. This was the Abbot's favourite spot. Many a leisurely nap had he taken on sunny afternoons with the aroma of ripening fruit hovering in his whiskers: apples, pears, quince, plums, damsons, even a vine of wild grape on the warm red stone of a south-facing wall. Old Mother Nature's blessing lay upon a haven of warm friendliness.

Now with the threat of Cluny upon Redwall, the two old friends assessed the beauteous bounty of their lifelong abode. Sweet birdsong on the still air tinged Constance's heart with sorrow and regret that this peaceful existence would soon pass. Gruffly she snuffled deep in her throat, blinking off a threatening teardrop. The Abbot sensed his companion's distress. He patted the badger's rough coat with a gentle paw.

'There, there, old girl. Don't fret. Many times in our history has tragedy been forestalled by miraculous happenings.'

Constance grunted in agreement, not wishing to disillusion her trusting old friend. Deep within her she knew a dark shadow was casting itself over the Abbey. Furthermore, it was happening in the present, not in bygone days of fabled deeds.

Matthias seated himself to an early breakfast in Cavern Hole: nutbread, apples and a bowl of fresh goatsmilk. Cornflower, along with other woodland creatures granted sanctuary, was sleeping in makeshift quarters provided by the good mice of Redwall. Matthias felt that he had grown up overnight. Duty was a mantle that he had taken willingly upon his shoulders. If there were a threat to Redwall from outside it must be dealt with. The mice of Redwall were peaceful creatures, but that must not be taken as a sign of weakness. Stolidly he munched away as he confronted the problem.

'Eat heartily, Matthias. No point in facing trouble on an empty stomach. Feed the body, nourish the mind.'

The young mouse was surprised to see that old Brother Methuselah had been watching him, his eyes twinkling behind the curious spectacles he invariably wore. The ancient mouse sat down at the breakfast table with a small groan.

'Don't look so surprised, young one. Your face is an open book to one of my years.'

Matthias drained the last of the milk from his bowl, wiping cream from his whiskers with the back of a paw. 'Give me your advice, Brother Methuselah,' he said. 'What would you do?'

The old mouse wrinkled his nose. 'Exactly the same thing as you would – that is, if I were younger and not so old and stiff.'

Matthias felt he had found an ally. 'You mean you would fight?'

Methuselah rapped the table with a bony paw. 'Of course I would. It's the only sensible course to take.'

He paused and stared at Matthias in an odd manner. 'Hmm, y'know there's something about you, young feller. Did you ever hear the story of how Martin the Warrior first came to Redwall?'

Matthias leaned forward eagerly. 'Martin! Tell me, Brother, I love hearing about the warrior monk.'

Methuselah's voice dropped to a secretive whisper. 'It is written in the great chronicle of Redwall that Martin was very young to be such a warrior. He could have been the same age as yourself, Matthias. Like you, he was impulsive and had a great quality of youthful innocence about him when he first came to our Abbey. But it is also written that in times of trouble Martin had the gift of a natural leader, a command over others far superior to him in age and experience. The chronicle says that they looked to Martin as some look to a strong father.'

Matthias was full of wonderment, but he could not help feeling puzzled. 'Why do you tell all this to me, Brother Methuselah?'

The old mouse stood up. He stared hard at Matthias for a moment, then, turning, he shuffled slowly off. As he went, he called back over his shoulder, 'Because, Matthias . . . he was very like you!'

Before the young mouse could question the old one further, the Joseph Bell tolled out a warning. Sandals flapping, Matthias dashed out into the grounds, nearly colliding with the Abbot and Constance, who, like everyone else, were heading for the gatehouse.

Brothers Rufus and George had an incident to report. A large evil-looking rat, covered in tattoos and carrying a rusty cutlass, had turned up at the gate. He had tried to gain entry by pretending he was injured. Limping about, the rat explained that he had been in a hay cart which overturned into the ditch. Would they come with him and render assistance to his friends, many of whom were lying trapped beneath the cart, crying out for help?

Brother Rufus was no fool. 'How many rats were travelling in the cart altogether?' he asked.

'Oh, a couple of hundred,' came the glib reply.

Then why, reasoned Brother Rufus, did the rats not give aid to their own companions? Surely all two hundred were not trapped? The rat evaded the question and made a great show of rubbing his injured leg. Could they not take him in and dress his wound and perhaps give him a bite to eat at least?

Brother George agreed, on condition that the rat surrendered his weapon.

The rat made as if to do so, then suddenly lunged at Brother George, only to be sent sprawling by a blow from Brother Rufus's staff. Realizing that he was up against two big competent mice who would stand no nonsense, he became abusive and foul-mouthed.

'Ha! Just you wait, mice,' he raged. 'There's a whole army of us camped down in the church. When I tell Cluny how you treated me, ho ho, just wait, that's all. We'll be back, by the fang we will.' With that he slunk off, cursing all mice.

The grim news was digested in silence by the assembled creatures. Mrs Churchmouse began sobbing. 'Oh dearie me. Did you hear that, m'dear? They must be living in our home at Saint Ninian's church. Oh, whatever shall we do? Our dear little home, full of dreadful rats.'

Mr John Churchmouse tried to comfort his wife as best he could. 'There, there, hush now, Missus. Better to lose a house than lose our lives. A good job we've been given sanctuary here at Redwall.'

'But what about the other creatures in the area?' cried Matthias.

'Sensible mouse,' said Constance. 'Is Ambrose Spike anywhere about? He'd better do the rounds and tell them to take sanctuary here at the Abbey as quickly as possible. Spike'll come to no harm. Once he curls up, there's nothing can touch him.'

This idea was greeted with enthusiasm. Brother Alf went off to find the hedgehog.

The Abbot suggested they all go inside the Abbey and await further developments. Matthias piped up again, 'I think we'd best mount a guard on the walls.'

53

One of the older mice, Sister Clemence, chided Matthias as an upstart. Her voice was stern and condescending. 'Novice Matthias, you will be silent and do as your Abbot commands.'

Much to everyone's surprise, the Abbot came to Matthias's defence. 'One moment, Clemence, Matthias speaks sense. Let us hear what he has to say. We are none of us too old to learn.'

All eyes were turned on the young mouse. Boldly he outlined his plans for the defence of Redwall.

It was eleven o'clock on that glorious June morning. Mossflower Woods and the meadowlands stirred to the brazen voice of the great Joseph Bell. John Churchmouse heaved on the bellrope as he had been told to by Constance and Matthias.

Bong! Boom! Bong! Boom! Even the small creatures in wood and field who could understand no language save their own, knew what it meant. 'Time of danger, place of sanctuary.'

Carrying what simple belongings they needed, woodlanders and their families hurried from far and near to gain the safety of the Abbey before the storm of Cluny broke upon them – squirrels, mice, voles, moles, otters, all save the birds of the air, who were safe anyway. Up the long dusty road they came, mothers protectively herding young ones whilst fathers provided a rearguard.

Brother Methuselah stood at the gate with the Abbot. He translated fully to each group of creatures the Abbot's message, in turn construing back to the Father Abbot their grateful thanks with pledges of help and loyalty to Redwall Abbey. For what creature had not been freely given the aid and special knowledge of the kindly mice? All knew that they owed their very existence to the Abbot and his community.

Healing, aid, food, shelter, and good advice were

granted to all. Now was the time to unite and repay, to give any help that was possible. Before much longer Redwall would require the skills and knowledge of all its woodland allies. It would be gratefully given!

Matthias and Constance stood on top of the high perimeter walls, watching the road. It was noon, and the sun shone directly overhead. Despite the heat, Matthias had ordered all the mice to put on their hoods. It served a double purpose, to shield their eyes from the sun and create a camouflage effect. Silently each one stood, armed with a stout staff. The high red sandstone walls were far too lofty to be scaled by any normal creature. Instinctively Matthias knew this was a good defence and a formidable deterrent.

Constance could feel her hackles beginning to prickle. She sniffed the air and shivered despite the heat that shimmered in waves across the meadowlands. The big badger nudged Matthias.

'Listen to that.'

Matthias pricked up his ears and looked at her, questioning.

'Even the birds have stopped singing,' Constance said quietly.

The young mouse gripped his staff tighter. 'Yes, it's the silence we can hear. The grasshoppers, too, have gone quiet.'

Constance peered down the road as she spoke. 'Strange for a summer day, little friend.'

Bong!

Every creature standing on the ramparts twitched with fright as the loud voice of the Joseph Bell rang out, and John Churchmouse shouted from his position high in the belfry, 'They're coming, down the road! I can see them. I can see them!'

10

Cluny's army halted at the sound of the Joseph Bell. As the dust settled, Fangburn looked to his leader for approval.

'They're ringing that big bell again, Chief. Ha! ha! Maybe they think it'll frighten us off.'

The Warlord's eye rested balefully on his scout. 'Shut your mouth, fool. If you'd done as I ordered and come right back to report, the way Cheesethief did, we might have been inside that Abbey by now!'

Fangburn slunk back into the ranks. He hoped Cluny had forgotten, but Cluny rarely forgot anything on a campaign. The element of surprise had been lost: now he must try another ploy, the show of force. The mere sight of a fully armed horde had worked before, and he had little doubt it would prove effective now. Ordinary peaceful creatures were usually panic-stricken at the sight of Cluny the Scourge at the head of his army. The rat was a cunning general, except during the times when his mad rage took control of him, but what need of berserk fits for a bunch of silly mice?

Cluny knew the value of fear as a weapon.

And Cluny was a fearsome figure.

His long ragged black cloak was made of batwings, fastened at the throat with a mole skull. The immense war helmet he wore had the plumes of a blackbird and the horns of a stag beetle adorning it. From beneath the slanted visor his one eye glared viciously out at the Abbey before him.

Matthias's voice rang out sharp and clear from the high parapet, 'Halt! Who goes there?'

Redtooth swaggered forward and took up the challenge in his Chief's name, as he called back up at the walls, 'Look well, all creatures. This is the mighty horde of Cluny the Scourge. My name is Redtooth. I speak for Cluny our leader.'

Constance's reply was harsh and unafraid, 'Then speak your piece and begone, rats.'

Silence hung upon the air while Redtooth and Cluny held a whispered conference. Redtooth returned to the walls.

'Cluny the Scourge says he will not deal with badgers, he will only speak with the leaders of the mice. Let us in, so that my Chief may sit and talk to your Chief.'

Redtooth dodged back as his request was greeted by howls of derision and some loose pieces of masonry from the ramparts. These plump little mice were not as peaceful as they first looked.

The rats looked to Cluny, but he was eyeing the Abbot who had joined Constance and Matthias. They appeared to be consulting quietly. Cluny watched tensely; there seemed to be some disagreement between the old mouse and his two advisers. They conferred awhile; then Matthias came forward to the parapet. He pointed at Cluny and Redtooth with his staff.

'You there, and you also. My Abbot will talk with you both. The rest must remain outside.'

A rumble of protest from the horde was silenced by a crack from Cluny's tail. He lifted his visor.

'We agree, mouse, let us in.'

'But what about hostages for safe conduct?' hissed Redtooth.

Cluny spat contemptuously. 'Don't talk wet. D'you imagine a load of mice in funny robes could take me captive?'

Redtooth gnawed anxiously on a split claw. 'Maybe not, Chief, but have you cast a weather eye over that badger?'

Cluny answered quietly out of the side of his mouth, 'Don't worry, I've been watching her. A real big country bumpkin. No, these are mice of honour, they'd sooner die than break their word to anyone. You leave this to me.'

As Cluny and Redtooth made for the gatehouse door, Constance shouted, 'Put down your weapons, rats. Throw off your armour to show us that you come in peace.'

Redtooth spluttered angrily. 'Hell's teeth! Who does that one think she's ordering around?'

Cluny shot him a warning glance. 'Quiet. Do as she says.'

Both rats took off their armour and placed it in a pile on the road. Matthias cried down to Cluny, 'If you really are Cluny the Scourge, then we know of your tail. It is a weapon. Therefore you will knot it tightly around your waist so that it cannot be used.'

Cluny laughed mirthlessly. He squinted at Matthias and cracked his tail dramatically.

'Young mouse,' he called. 'You do right to ask this thing, for truly you are looking at Cluny the Scourge.'

Having said this he took his tail in his claws, and pulled the poison war spike from its tip. Tossing it on the armour pile, Cluny hitched his tail in a knot around his middle.

'Now will you let us in, mice? You can see we are unarmed.'

Ponderously the heavy gate inched open. The two rats passed through a bristling forest of staves. The gate slammed shut behind them.

Cluny mentally estimated the walls to be of immense thickness as he and Redtooth, ducking their heads, emerged from the tunnel-like arch into the Abbey grounds, where Constance and Matthias were waiting in the sunlight. The defenders followed the two rats closely, menacing them with staves.

Matthias rapped out a curt command, 'Leave us, mice. Go back to your duties on the wall.'

Unhappy at leaving the Abbot unguarded, the mice hesitated to obey the order to withdraw. Cluny addressed Matthias scornfully, 'Here, mouse, watch me shift 'em.'

Suddenly he whirled upon the apprehensive creatures. The single eye rolled madly in its socket as Cluny bared claws and fangs, snarling, 'Ha harr! I've got a powerful hunger for mice! You'd best get aloft on those walls. Ha harr!'

Cluny leaped into the air. The mice scattered in panic.

Constance stopped the proceedings with a loud angry bark. 'Here now. Enough of that, rat. You are here to talk with the Abbot. Get along with you.'

Matthias was glad he was walking behind the rats; he blushed with shame. Cluny had sent the defenders scattering like butterflies in a whirlwind. Matthias was furious; the enemy now knew he was dealing with un-trained and untested soldiers.

As the party walked towards Cavern Hole, Cluny could sense hostility emanating from the young mouse who flip–flopped behind him in over-large sandals. Strange for one so young to be counted as a Captain, he thought. Moreover, the little fellow didn't seem to fear him. Ah, but enough of that. Cluny would deal with him when the time came. Meanwhile, the big rat gazed about his surroundings in secret admiration. What an astounding place!

He allowed himself a peek at the future. One day this would be called Cluny's Castle. He liked the sound of that. Secure from attack, living off the fat of the land, in his mind's eye he saw it all: those mice and the woodland creatures enslaved, living just to serve him. He would hold sway as far as the eye could see; power; an end to his rovings; a dream come true; King Cluny!

Entering the Abbey, the party stopped to make way for a pretty little fieldmouse bearing a tray.

'Oh, Matthias,' she said. 'I've brought some refreshments for you and—'

'Thank you, Cornflower. Put them down on the table,' said Matthias abruptly.

Redtooth nudged Cluny. 'Cornflower, eh. Satan's nose, she's a pretty little one for you!'

Cluny remained silent. He stood insolently watching Cornflower set the table in Cavern Hole. A pretty one indeed!

The Abbot indicated chairs. They all sat except Cluny, who lounged against the table using the chair as a footstool. He glared at Redtooth until he stood and waited alongside his Chief. Idly Cluny picked up a bowl of honeyed milk and sampled it.

Slop! He spat it out on the floor.

The Abbot folded his paws into the wide sleeves of his habit and stared impassively at the Warlord. 'What do you want at Redwall Abbey, my son?'

Cluny kicked the chair over and laughed madly. As the

60

echoes died around the room his face went grim.

'Your son, ha. That's a good one! I'll tell you what I want, mouse. I want it all. The lot. Everything. Do you hear me?'

Matthias's chair clattered on its side as he sprang forward, breaking free from the restraining paws of the Abbot.

'Listen, rat, you don't scare me! I'll give you our answer. You get nothing! Now do you understand that?'

Shaking with fury, Matthias allowed himself to be pulled back on to the chair. The Abbot turned to Cluny.

'You must forgive Matthias. He is young and head-strong. Now, as to your proposal, I am afraid it is out of the question. Should you or your army require medical attention, food, clothing or help upon your way, you will find us only too willing to assist—'

Cluny interrupted rudely by pounding upon the table until the Abbot was silenced. He pointed a claw at Red-tooth.

'Read them the articles.'

Redtooth held up a tattered parchment. He cleared his throat. 'These are the articles of surrender to be obeyed by all creatures who come under the claw of Cluny the Scourge or any of his commanders. *One*: surrender will be total and unconditional. *Two*: Cluny will execute the leaders of all who choose to oppose him. *Three*: all property conquered will belong solely to Cluny the Scourge. This includes homes, food, crops, land, and additionally all creatures dwelling on said property: they shall be owned by Cluny—'

Thwack!

Redtooth got no further. Unable to contain himself, Matthias sent his staff ripping through the middle of the articles. As the torn document fluttered to the floor, Redtooth launched himself at Matthias with a snarl.

The rat was actually in mid-air when a huge blunt paw knocked him flat. He lay stunned with Constance standing over him.

'Why pick on a small mouse? Surely a big strong rat like you can deal with an old badger? Come on, try me for size.'

It was only the timely intervention of Abbot Mortimer that saved Redtooth's life.

'Constance, would you please let the rat up? Much as I would like to see him get his just desserts, you must remember we cannot break the law of hospitality in our Abbey.'

Redtooth staggered shakily to his feet, backing warily away from the badger. Cluny spoke as if nothing had occurred, 'You, Abbot mouse, you have until tomorrow evening to give me your answer.'

Not normally given to anger, the Abbot stared Cluny in the eye, his face a mask of cold fury.

'I will not need until tomorrow, rat. You can have my answer now. How dare you come here with your robber band to read articles of death and slavery to me? I tell you that neither you nor your army will ever set paw or claw inside Redwall, not while I or any of my creatures have breath in our bodies to fight and resist you. That is my solemn word.'

Cluny sneered and turned on his heel. Followed by Redtooth, he stamped out. On the stairs between Cavern Hole and the Great Hall he stopped and turned, his cold voice echoing between both chambers, 'Then die, all of you: every male, female, and young one. You have refused my terms. Now you will suffer the punishment of Cluny. You will beg on your knees for death to come swiftly, but I shall make your torment loud and long before you die!'

It was then that Constance did something that creatures would speak of in years to come.

Exerting the full strength of a female badger, she lifted the massive Cavern Hole dining table. It was a huge solid oaken thing that no dozen mice could even move. Dishes clattered and food spilled as Constance heaved the table above her head. Her voice was a roar. 'Get out, rats! Leave this Abbey! I'm weary of your voices. Hurry before I break the laws of hospitality and ask the Abbot's pardon later. Go, while you still have skulls.'

With the best grace he could muster, Cluny walked rather quickly up the stairs, followed by Redtooth, who laughed nervously. 'Big country bumpkin, eh, Chief? One more word from you back there and she'd have thrown that table and crushed us.'

Remembering who it was that he had spoken to in this insolent fashion, Redtooth cringed, expecting Cluny to deal him a blow for impudence. But nothing happened.

Cluny was standing transfixed.

Oblivious to all about him, even Matthias and the Abbot who had followed him out, Cluny stood staring at the tapestry.

'Who is that mouse?' he gasped.

Matthias followed the direction of the rat's gaze. He walked to the tapestry with his paw outstretched.

'Do you mean this mouse?'

Cluny nodded dumbly.

Matthias, still with his paw outstretched, declared proudly, 'This is Martin the Warrior. He founded our Order, and I'll tell you something else, rat. Martin was the bravest mouse that ever lived. If he were here today he'd just take up his big sword and send you and all your bullies packing. Those of you he didn't chop up into crow meat.'

Much to everyone's surprise, Cluny allowed himself to

be shown out. He was like one in a daze all the way back to the gatehouse.

A hush fell over the mice on guard as Cluny and Redtooth were let out on to the road. Swiftly, the horde gathered around the Warlord and his lieutenant. They awaited orders. Deputizing for Cluny, Redtooth called out, 'Form up. Back to the church, everyone.'

Cluny marched automatically, shaking his head in disbelief.

Martin the Warrior. The mouse who pursued him through his nightmares. What did it mean?

As Redtooth marched away, a voice hailed him from the wall. He turned and looked upward. The torn articles – the parchment wrapped around a fistful of rotting vegetables – splattered in his face. Livid with rage he clawed the foul mess from his eyes and saw Constance leaning over the parapet with a wicked grin of delight on her striped muzzle.

The badger shouted mockingly, 'Don't forget to call again, rat. I'd be delighted to see you. We've got some unfinished business that I'm looking forward to settling. Just you and me, Redtooth! Bye now.'

Before the rat could reply, she had vanished from sight.

11

Later that evening Brother Alf was patrolling his stretch of wall when he noticed a movement in the ferns at the edge of Mossflower Wood. Constance and Matthias were summoned hastily. They peered over the parapet as Brother Alf pointed to where he had seen the ferns moving.

'Over there, to the right of that aspen. Look, they're moving again.'

Matthias had better nocturnal vision than either of his friends. He was the first to recognize the forlorn figure that rolled on to the grass.

'It's Ambrose Spike. He's hurt. Quick, let's get down there.'

'Hold fast,' Constance warned. 'It may be a trap.'

Matthias was loth to hang about whilst a creature was lying injured within his sight, but he had to heed his friend's advice. There just might be some of Cluny's rats lying in ambush for any creature that ventured into the shadowy fringes of Mossflower. However, Matthias was growing impatient.

'We can't leave poor Ambrose lying out there, Constance. He'll die. We've got to do something.'

The badger sat down with her snout between her paws. 'Yes, we've got to think. Anyone got an idea?'

The two mice joined her. Hardly had Matthias sat down when he leaped up again.

'I've got it. Stay here. I'll be back in a tick!'

Brother Alf watched the little figure flip-flopping off. He gave a sigh and shook his head. 'What do you suppose our Matthias is up to?'

The badger smiled affectionately. More and more she was coming to trust Matthias's natural skill as a leader and tactician. 'Don't fret, Brother Alf. Whatever it is, you can bet your habit it'll be an original Matthias gem. That youngster has got more in his head than a pile of acorns.'

Brother Alf looked out at the still form in the grass. 'It may be too late. Ambrose isn't even twitching. Look, he's not rolled up in a ball any more.'

Further speculation was curtailed by the appearance of Matthias. With him were half a dozen moles.

Their leader glanced out at the hedgehog. He scratched some hasty calculations on the wall with his claw, then turned to Matthias. 'Oi I think we can get yon 'edgepig back, sur. You'm get us outen the gate and stan' watch.'

Turning to his team, the Foremole (for that was his official title) began discussing tunnel width, coupled with reverse prickle drag, forward traction, and all the other specialist details that are routine to the average qualified tunnel-mole.

Matthias whispered to Constance and Brother Alf, 'The Foremole and his crew are first class at rescue work. They've often rescued burrowers from cave-ins. All we have to do is stand guard by the south-east wicket gate until they're safely back.'

'Right. What are we waiting for? Let's go,' said the badger.

Silently they slid through the small green-painted iron door, Matthias straining his eyes anxiously to see if there were any signs of life in the hedgehog. He still lay about a hundred and fifty mouse paces from where they stood.

The moles unravelled a rope sling. Foremole stood watching as two of his team started the dig.

Matthias looked on in wonderment. One minute they were above ground, a moment later there was a veritable shower of loam and topsoil as they vanished beneath the earth: nature's own technicians.

In a trice they were back, moist snouts poking from the excavation. They made their ground report to the Foremole.

'Harr, he'm be noice an' soft, sur. Baint no rock nor root to stop us'ns, straight furrer we'em a-thinking.'

Satisfied, the Foremole moved towards the test hole with the rest of his team. 'Oi'll dig ahead, you'm woiden workin's. Gaffer and Marge, foller up a-shorin.' He tugged his snout respectfully to Matthias and Constance. 'You'm gennelbeast bide by 'ere 'til us back.'

Another quick shower of soft dark earth and the moles were lost to view beneath the ground surface.

Constance sniffed the breeze as Matthias turned his ears to the night-time woodland sounds. They watched the ground humping into a continuous hillock that progressed further as the moles tunnelled towards Ambrose Spike. The night remained calm and still, but Matthias and Constance stayed alert, both knowing if they failed to observe this rudimentary law of nature, the penalty could be fatal.

Matthias did a little shuffle of excitement. 'Look, they've come up right under poor old Ambrose! My word, what splendid moles. Good heavens, he's vanished completely! They must have him inside the tunnel.'

In a surprisingly short time the tunnellers were back. Emerging from the hole, they carried the hedgehog in the rope sling across their backs, refusing any help from the badger or the mouse. The Foremole merely tugged his snout.

'Nay, may, you uns on'y getcher paws durted.'

As swiftly as possible Ambrose was hurried to the Abbey infirmary and sick bay. He was attended by the Abbot himself. A hasty diagnosis revealed that the hedgehog was suffering from a long jagged wound that ran from the back of his ear to the tip of his paw. Brother Alf nodded sympathetically.

'That's probably what caused old Ambrose to pass out. Pain and loss of blood. He must have travelled a fair way in that condition. D'you think he'll live, Father Abbot?'

The Abbot chuckled quietly. He cleaned the long ugly wound and applied a poultice of herbs. 'No cause for alarm, Brother Alf. Ambrose Spike is made of leather and needles. Tough as a boulder, this old ruffian is. Look, he's beginning to come around already.'

Sure enough, after some peculiar grunts and much curling and uncurling, the hedgehog opened his eyes and looked about. 'Oh my aching ear. Father Abbot, you wouldn't see a poor son of the Spike suffering like this without a drop of last October's nutbrown ale to wet his parched gullet,' he pleaded.

All the creatures laughed aloud with delight and relief at seeing their old friend alive and well once again.

Matthias was astonished at the amount of nutbrown ale which Ambrose supped before he deemed himself fit enough to make a report. The hedgehog smacked his lips noisily.

'Aaaahhh, that's better. Now, let me see. I did as you asked me, gave as many creatures fair warning as I could.

The Joseph Bell helped a great deal to warn everyone. Well, to cut a long story short, it must have been near noon when I stopped at Vole Bank. I told the Voles the bad news, and blow me if that little ninny Colin Vole didn't go to shrieking and screaming all over the place as to how they'd all be murdered in their beds. Believe me, there was no way of silencing the daft young thing. Anyhow, his noise must have alerted a pack of those rats who were out foraging. Before you could say "knife" they were upon us. There was such a gang of them that I couldn't do anything. I had to curl up. They carried off young Colin and his mum and dad, but try as they would there was no laying claws on Ambrose Spike, no sir. Then one of them had a go at me with a point of an iron churchyard railing. Stabbed away at me, the devil did. They reckoned I was dead. Said I was too spiky to eat, so they dragged the Vole family off and I lay still until the coast was clear. I made it as far as Mossflower and that's all I can remember. Er, is there any more left in that jug? This wound's giving me jip. I need ale for medicinal purposes, Father Abbot.'

Matthias groaned and hung his head in despair. The Vole family taken captive; death or slavery was all the wretched creatures could look forward to. Emboldened by the rescue of the hedgehog, Matthias was about to suggest that he and Constance, together with some hand-picked helpers, venture to undertake a rescue mission to Saint Ninian's church. It was as if the Abbot and Constance both read his thoughts at the same time. Abbot Mortimer sighed and shook his head at Matthias. The badger was more voluble.

'Matthias, forget it. Abandon any hopes you have of snatching the Vole family from under Cluny's nose. Imagine it, a few of us going up against several hundred armed rats in their own camp. Ridiculous. A fat lot of good we'd be as defenders of Redwall with our heads fixed to Cluny's standard. Matthias, you're a very brave young mouse, so please try to set an example to the rest by not becoming a foolish or dead one.'

On reflection, Matthias could see the wisdom of the badger's counsel. Long after they had all retired for the night he sat up thinking. A hundred mad ideas pounded through his brain, each one wilder than the last. Feeling at a loss, he wandered up into the Great Hall and stood in front of the tapestry. Without consciously realizing it, he found himself talking to Martin the Warrior.

'Oh Martin, what would you have done in my place? I know that I'm only a young mouse, a novice, not even a proper Redwall member yet, but once you were young too. I know what you would have done. You'd have buckled on your armour, picked up your mighty sword, gone down to that church and battled with the rats until they released the Voles or perished beneath your blade. But alas, those days are gone. I have no magic sword to aid me, only the advice of my elders and betters, to which I must listen.'

Matthias sat down upon the cool stone floor. He gazed longingly up at Martin the Warrior, so proud, so brave. What a dashing figure he cut. Looking back down to himself in his baggy green robes and oversized sandals, Matthias felt hot tears of shame and frustration spilling from his eyes and dripping on his young whiskers. Unable to stop himself, he wept freely; then the soft touch of a gentle paw on his back caused him to look around. It was Cornflower.

Matthias wished he were dead!

He quickly turned his face away, knowing she could see his tears.

'Cornflower, please go away,' Matthias sobbed. 'I

don't want you to see me like this.'

The little fieldmouse, however, would not go. She sat down on the floor next to Matthias. Taking the edge of her pinafore she softly wiped away his tears. For such a shy little mouse she had quite a bit to say.

'Matthias, don't be ashamed, I know why you cry and grieve. It is because you are kind and good, not a hard-hearted pitiless rat like Cluny. Please listen to me. Even the strongest and bravest must sometimes weep. It shows they have a great heart, one that can feel compassion for others. You are brave, Matthias. Already you have done great things for one so young. I am only a simple country-bred fieldmouse, but even I can see the courage and leadership in you. A burning brand shows the way, and each day your flame grows brighter. There is none like you, Matthias. You have the sign of greatness upon you. One day Redwall and all the land will be indebted to you. Matthias, you are a true Warrior.'

Matthias, with his eyes dry and his head held high, stood up; he felt himself stand taller than ever before. He helped Cornflower to her feet and bowed to her.

'Cornflower, how can I ever thank you for what you have said. You too are a very special mouse. It is late now. Go and get some rest. I think I will stay here a while longer.'

The fieldmouse untied her headband. It was her favourite one, pale yellow bordered with the cornflowers after which she was named. She tied it to Matthias's arm, the right one, just above the elbow. A maiden's colours for her champion warrior.

Silently she crept off. Matthias could feel his heart beating against his chest. He spoke to the image of Martin.

'Thank you, Warrior. You spoke to me through Cornflower. You gave me the sign that I asked of you.'

12

At the Church of Saint Ninian, Cluny sat in the wreckage of what had once been a pulpit. Redtooth, Darkclaw, Cheesethief, and Fangburn lounged about at his feet on old burst hassocks. Cluny was in one of his strange moods again. He showed little interest in the captive Vole family, merely ordering that they be kept under guard until he found time to deal with them. Most of his army slept in the choir loft or the lady chapel. The rest were posted on sentry-duty outside.

Cautiously, his Captains watched the Warlord. Cluny's long tail swished, restlessly, the single eye stared at a carved eagle holding the rotting lectern on its outspread wings. What thoughts occupied the dark devious mind of Cluny the Scourge? Finally he looked up and spoke.

'Go and get the Shadow. Bring him here to me.'

Darkclaw and Fangburn scurried off to obey the command. Silently the others waited, their eyes glinting in evil anticipation.

The Chief had a plan. Like all of his schemes it would be cunningly simple and wickedly brilliant. There was no better General than Cluny when it came to strategy.

The Shadow had been with Cluny for many years. Nobody was sure if he was rat or weasel, or even a bit of both. He was very lithe and wiry, and his long sinewy body was covered in sleek, black fur. There was no hint of another colour in his coat; it was blacker than moonless midnight. His eyes were strangely slanted, black without any brightness in them. The eyes of the Shadow were like those of a dead thing.

He stood before Cluny, who had to strain his one eye against the darkness of the church to make sure he was really there.

'Shadow, is that you?'

The reply sounded like a whisper of wet silk across a smooth slate. 'Cluny, I am here. Why do you want the Shadow?'

The Captains shivered at the sound of the voice, Cluny leaned forward. 'Did you see the walls of that Abbey today?'

'I was there. The Shadow sees all.'

'Tell me true. Could you climb them?'

'No beast I know of could climb those walls.'

'Except you?'

'Except me.'

Cluny gestured with his tail. 'Come closer then. I will tell you what must be done.'

Shadow sat on the top pulpit step. Cluny issued his orders. 'You will climb the Abbey wall. Many sentries patrol the top, so take the utmost care. If you get captured, you are of no use to me. There is no point in one creature trying to attack the gatehouse and open the door alone, it is too well guarded. So forget the gate.'

The Shadow gave no hint that Cluny had inadvertently read his mind. He remained motionless as Cluny continued, 'Once you have scaled the wall, make for the main Abbey door. Should it be locked for the night you will use all your skill to open it without any noise. It is vital that you get inside. The first room you will find yourself in is the main one. The mice call it Great Hall. Walk in, turn around, and on the left wall facing you is a long tapestry covered in pictures and designs. Now listen carefully. In the bottom right-hand corner of that tapestry is a picture of a mouse dressed in armour, leaning on a big sword. I want it! Cut it, rip it, or tear it out, but get it for me. I must have it! Don't come back without it, Shadow.'

Puzzlement was written on the faces of the four Captains who had overheard the others.

A picture of a mouse?

Cluny had never been known as a collector of pictures.

Fangburn whispered to Cheesethief, 'What use is a picture of a mouse to the Chief?'

Cluny heard. He came to the edge of the pulpit. Grasping the sides of the lectern he surveyed his small congregation like some satanic minister.

'Ah, Brother Fangburn, let me explain. I will tell you why it is that you and all your kind will forever remain servants, while I shall always be the master. Did you not see the faces of those mice today? The mere mention of Martin the Warrior sends them into ecstasies. Don't you see, he is their symbol. His name means the same to those mice as mine does to the horde: in a different way maybe. Martin is some sort of angel; I'm the opposite. Think for a moment. If anything were to happen to me, you'd all be a leaderless rabble, a headless mob. So, if the mice were to lose their most precious omen, the picture of Martin, where would that leave them?'

Redtooth slapped his haunches. He rocked to and fro, sniggering with uncontrolled glee.

'Brilliant, Chief, diabolical! They'd just be a crowd of

74

terrified little mice without their wonderful Martin.'

Cluny's tail banged down on the rotting lectern, smashing it into several fragments.

'And that's when we'll strike!'

The powerful tail lashed backwards, wrapping itself around Shadow's body. He was dragged forward, face to face with his master. Cluny's rancid breath blasted into Shadow's face as he ground out each syllable.

'Bring that picture back here to me. Do this, and your reward will be great when I sit on the Abbot's chair in Redwall Abbey. But fail me, and your screams will be heard far beyond the woodland and meadows!'

Cluny the Scourge had spoken.

13

The sun's first rays flung wide the gates of dawn. The inhabitants of Redwall were already up and about. After breakfast the Abbot issued daily orders. All those not employed defending the Abbey would husband the crops and gather in supplies for the larders in the event of a prolonged seige. Young otters collected watercress and fished; Cornflower headed a party of mice to reap the early cereal crops; more youngsters tended the salad gardens. The bright summer morning hummed to the bustle of industrious woodlanders.

Ambrose Spike, now sufficiently recovered, sat in the storeroom taking stock: lots of nuts and preserved berries from last autumn; apples and pears a-plenty. Unfortunately, the hedgehog could not check the cellars; Brother Edmund and Friar Hugo had the only two keys. He licked his lips at the thought of barrels of nutbrown ale, strong cider, creamy stout, and the little kegs – ah, the dear little kegs! – full of elderberry wine, mulberry brandy, black-currant port, and wild grape sherry.

'Yurr, 'edgepig. Where'm us a-puttin' these roots an' dannylines. 'Asten up, they'm roight 'eavy.'

Ambrose sighed wistfully as he attended the two moles staggering under a bundle of dandelions and tubers.

'Arr, 'old 'em liddle taters steady, Bill. Yurr, tip 'em up, leggo.'

More baby moles. Ambrose pawed the bandage on his wound. A hedgehog's work was never done.

Matthias and Constance stood in the cloisters. They had taken charge of weapon training. The woodlanders were each showing off their special skills. In more peaceful days, these skills had only been used at fairs and sporting contests, but now, when the need arose, they would be used to more deadly effect.

The otters carried bags of smooth pebbles which they hurled from vine slings with great force and accuracy. Groups of fieldmouse archers nocked thistledown shafts to the strings of their longbows. Many a marauding bird had been driven off by these same tiny archers. Bands of Redwall mice practised at thrust and parry with staves.

Below the wall on the Abbey grass the Foremole directed his crew as they dug a trench. This was lined with sharpened stakes by a solitary beaver. A system of ropes and pulleys carried the baskets of stone and trench-debris up to the ramparts. Defenders piled it in heaps at the edge of the parapet.

Matthias took a group of Redwall mice to instruct in the use of the quarter staff – he had discovered in himself a natural skill with the long ash pole. None of the mice had ever competed in any type of violent sport; they were awkward and timid. But as it was a personal choice between learning cudgel and wrestling from Constance or quarter staff from Matthias, to a mouse they had opted for the latter.

Matthias found he had to be quite severe with them. Accordingly, he dealt out some hefty blows and hard falls to make the more timid souls angry enough to retaliate.

'Keep that head guarded, Brother Anthony!'

Thwack!

'I warned you, Brother! Now look out, I'm coming after you again.'

Thwack!

'No, no! Don't just stand there, Brother! Defend yourself! Hit out at me.'

Thwack, crack!

This time, Matthias sat down hard, rubbing dazedly at his sore head. Constance chuckled.

'Well, Matthias, you've only yourself to blame. You asked Brother Anthony to hit out at you and, my word, he certainly obliged. I'll have to recruit him for my cudgel class! He shows promise.'

Matthias stood up, smiling ruefully. He rested on his staff. 'Yes, he's very strong, but I do wish that we had some real weapons of war – swords and daggers and such like. We won't kill many rats with wooden staves.'

'Maybe not,' the badger replied. 'But you must remember that we are here to defend, not to attack or kill.'

Matthias threw down his staff. He took a dipper of water from an oaken pail, drinking deeply, then splashing the remains over his aching head.

'A wise observation, Constance, but you try telling that to Cluny and his horde. See how far you get.'

Lunch that day was served out in the orchard. Matthias lined up with the other woodland creatures to collect his food: a bowl of fresh milk, a hunk of wheaten loaf and some goats-milk cheese. Cornflower was serving. She gave Matthias an extra large wedge of the cheese. He rolled up the sleeve of his habit and pulled out the corner of her scarf.

'Look, Cornflower, a very close friend gave me this last night.'

She laughed at him. 'Get along, and eat your lunch, warrior mouse, or I'll show you my deadly aim with a piece of this cheese.'

Strolling through the dappled shade of the orchard, Matthias sought out old Methuselah. Slumping down beneath a damson tree the young mouse munched away at his lunch. Methuselah was sitting with his back against the tree, his eyes closed in an apparent doze. Without opening them he addressed Matthias. 'How goes the practice war, young stavemaster?'

Matthias watched some of the tiny ants carrying off his fallen breadcrumbs as he answered, 'As well as possible, Brother Methuselah. And how are your studies coming along?'

Methuselah squinted over the top of his spectacles. 'Knowledge is a thing that one cannot have enough of. It is the fruit of wisdom, to be eaten carefully and digested fully, unlike that lunch you are bolting down, little friend.'

Matthias set his food to one side. 'Tell me, what knowledge have you digested lately, old one?'

Methuselah took a sip from Matthias's milk bowl. 'Sometimes I think you have a very old head for such a young mouse. What more do you wish to know about Martin the Warrior?'

Matthias looked surprised. 'How did you know I was going to ask about Martin?'

Methuselah wrinkled his nose. 'How do the bee folk know there is pollen in a flower? Ask away, young one, before I doze off again.'

Matthias hesitated a moment, then blurted out,

'Brother Methuselah, tell me where Martin lies buried.'

The old mouse chuckled drily. 'Next you are going to ask me where to find the great sword of the Warrior mouse.'

'B–but how did you know that?' stammered Matthias.

The ancient gatehouse-keeper shrugged his thin shoulders. 'The sword must lie buried with Martin. You would have little use for the dusty bones of a bygone hero. A simple deduction, even for one as old as I am.'

'Then you know where the Warrior lies?'

Methuselah shook his head. 'That is a thing no creature knows. For many long years now I have puzzled and pored over ancient manuscripts, translating, following hidden trails, always with the same result: nothing. I have even used my gift of tongues, speaking to the bees and others who can go into places too small for us, but always it is the same – rumours, legends, and old mouse tales.'

Matthias crumbled more bread for the ants. 'Then the Warrior's sword is only a fable?'

Methuselah leaned forward indignantly. 'Who said that? Did I?'

'No, but you—'

'Bah! Nothing of the sort, young mouse. Listen carefully to me. I have an uncanny feeling that you may be the one I have been saving this vital piece of information for.'

Matthias forgot his lunch. He listened attentively.

'About four summers ago I treated a sparrowhawk who had pulled a sinew in her foot. She could not use her talons properly. Hmm, as I remember, I made her promise never to take a mouse as prey. She was a fierce, frightening bird. Have you ever been close up to a sparrowhawk? No, of course you haven't. Well, let me tell you, they can hypnotize small creatures with those savage golden eyes. Born killers, they are. But this hawk said something that made me think. She talked of the sparrows, called them winged mice, said that many years ago they had stolen something from our Abbey: a treasure that belonged to the mice. Wouldn't say what it was. Just flew off. Huh, who expects gratitude from a sparrow-hawk, anyway?'

Matthias interrupted. 'Have you ever spoken to the sparrows about this "something"?'

Methuselah shook his head. 'I'm too old. I can't climb up to the roof where they nest. Besides, the sparrows are odd birds, forever quarrelling and chattering on in their strange voices. They are warlike creatures, extremely forgetful and completely savage. They'd throw you from the roof and kill you before you had a chance to get near their tribal nests. Yes, I'm far too old for that sort of thing, Matthias, and anyhow, I'm not too sure that the sparrow-hawk's story was true. Some birds can be dreadful liars when they have a mind to be.'

Matthias tried questioning Brother Methuselah further, but the warm sun had worked its magic upon the old gatekeeper as he sat in the orchard savouring the peace and tranquility of a June afternoon. This time there was no deception. He was genuinely fast asleep.

14

Clouds drifted across the sky, obscuring the thin sliver of moon. The Joseph Bell tolled out its midnight message to the slumbering countryside. A warm soft drizzle was falling over the parched meadows and dry woodland, bringing relief after the hot dry day, damping down the dust from the road.

In the ditch a frog opened its eyes, disturbed by some slight noise from the hedgerow. It blinked. Was that three figures creeping along, or two?

The frog remained perfectly still. There seemed to be two figures, and some sort of shadow. The moon came out from behind a cloud.

It was two huge rats . . . and a dark shadowy *something*!

They crept along under cover of the hedge towards the big dwelling of the mouse-folk. Rats were hunters; thankfully they had not noticed him. The frog stayed motionless and let them pass. It was none of his business.

Cluny, Ragear and Shadow padded noiselessly towards Redwall. This was such an important mission that Cluny had decided to come along and supervise it personally. Around Shadow's waist was strapped a skin pouch. It contained a thin strong rope, a padded grappling hook, a vial of oil, some lockpicks and a dagger: Shadow's usual burgling kit.

Ragear ambled proudly along, thrilled that he had been specially picked to accompany his Chief on such a vital task. Little did he know that Cluny had only included him as an insurance. If they should get into a tight corner, Ragear would serve as an expendable fool. That way Cluny could make good his own escape.

The trio halted beneath the lofty Abbey walls. Cluny silenced them with a wave of his tail, then vanished into the night. Ragear felt distinctly nervous at being left alone with the Shadow. He attempted a whispered conversation.

'Nice drops of rain, eh, Shadow? Good for the grass. Blow me, these walls are pretty high. I'm glad it's you climbing them and not me. I'd never make it. Too fat, hahaha.'

Ragear's voice trailed off. He fumbled with his whiskers, wilting beneath the basilisk stare of Shadow's dead black eyes. He shuddered and fell silent.

Within ten minutes Cluny was back. He nodded up at the parapet. 'I've been up and down the length of the wall for a fair distance. The sentry mice are all asleep, the fools! They've never had to do guard duty before – as soon as night falls so do their eyelids. That's what soft living does for you.'

Ragear's head bobbed in agreement. 'You're right, Chief. If they were in our army and old Redtooth caught them snoozing he'd—'

'Shut your trap, stupid,' Cluny hissed. 'Are you ready, Shadow? Now don't forget your instructions.'

The Shadow bared his yellowed fangs and started

climbing. Slowly he made his way upwards, like a long black reptile, his claws seeking hidden niches and crevices in the sandstone. Ever upwards, sometimes stopping spreadeagled against the surface as he figured out his next movement, taking full advantage of every crack and joint in the wall. No other animal in Cluny's army could have attempted such an ascent, but the Shadow was a climbing expert. He concentrated his whole being on the job in hand, sometimes clinging to the stones by no more than a single claw. Below on the ground Cluny and Ragear strained their eyes upwards. They could hardly make out his shape but could just see him, not far from the top of the wall.

The Shadow shifted position and levered with his back legs and tail. Now he wedged his claws into a fissure and stretched upwards, gaining inch by inch.

On top of the wall Brother Edmund was snoring gently. He was nestled in a pile of rubble, wrapped in a warm blanket with his hood up against the light rain. Edmund was oblivious of the long sharp claws that latched themselves over the parapet edge. A moment later the sleek black head appeared; two dense obsidian eyes stared at the sleeping mouse. The Shadow had succeeded in climbing the Abbey wall.

Like a sinuous black lizard he slithered past slumbering creatures and around rubble heaps, never once making a sound. Friar Hugo mumbled gently in his sleep, and moved his head so that his cowl slid off. Drizzle fell upon the fat friar's face, threatening to wake him. Gently as a night breeze, Shadow replaced the hood. Pausing for an instant, Shadow looked about before descending the stone steps from the ramparts to the cloisters. Using shrubs and bushes as cover he moved furtively forwards, never taking any needless chances or making sudden movements. Sometimes he stopped and waited, letting the minutes tick away as he planned his next progression, gliding like a cloud's shadow cast upon the ground by the moon.

The door to the Great Hall was not locked. Shadow judged that the latch was probably old and creaky. He took out the vial of oil and lubricated the latch and hinges. Carefully he inched the door ajar – apart from a tiny squeak it swung effortlessly open. Sliding inside, he released the door by mistake. A swift night breeze slammed it shut with a dull thud.

Shadow cursed inwardly and flung himself behind a nearby pillar. He lay inert, not daring to breathe; one, two, three minutes, good! Nobody had been disturbed by the noise. He ventured out to inspect the tapestry that hung upon the wall.

A black moth on a moonless night would not have escaped Shadow's notice. He needed no lamp to scrutinize the thing before him. So this was the picture of the warrior mouse that Cluny lusted after. Using his razor-sharp fangs he began gnawing into the ancient tapestry, working from the tasselled hem upwards.

Matthias tossed and turned in his bed, exhausted, but unable to sleep. His mind revolved around a host of problems and schemes: the sword, Martin's grave, defence of the Abbey, Cornflower. Finally, after much kicking and rumpling of sheets, sleep started to take over. He was somewhere in a long deserted room, not unlike Great Hall. A voice called to him, 'Matthias.'

'Oh, go away,' the young mouse muttered drowsily. 'Get someone else. I'm tired.'

But the voice persisted, boring into his mind. 'Matthias, Matthias, I need you.'

He peered down the length of the darkened hall. 'What is it, why do you need me?'

Matthias began to walk towards the voice. He could hear a wicked snigger followed by a cry of despair. 'Matthias, help, don't let them take me.'

He ran forwards. The hall seemed to grow longer.

'Who are you, where are you?'

Far ahead in the murky darkness Matthias could vaguely distinguish a figure leaning out from the wall. It was a mouse in armour.

'Please, Matthias, you must help me quickly!'

Bump.

Matthias landed on the floor of his bedroom. Sheets were tangled about his body. Slowly he sat up and rubbed his eyes. What a strange dream: the long hall, the plea for help, the armoured mouse. . . .

Matthias felt the fur on the back of his neck rising.

Of course, it had to be!

The Great Hall; Martin the Warrior; something terrible was going on downstairs. He was needed urgently.

Matthias kicked the sheet from him as he leaped up and dashed headlong from the bedroom, along the dormitory corridor and helter skelter down the spiral staircase. Through Cavern Hole he clattered in the darkness, stumbling and tripping over furniture, his heart hammering loudly and legs pumping like twin pistons. Matthias fell over the top stair and went sprawling into the Great Hall. He lay on the floor, gazing through the gloom to the tapestry. Martin was still there, but . . . *he was moving.*

Was it the breeze? No, it couldn't be. The likeness of the Warrior mouse was jiggling about as though it were being tugged in some way. Matthias could see a shadow, but there was nothing to cast it. He jumped to his feet and ran forwards as the picture of Martin was ripped away from the tapestry.

A rat held it!

There was no doubt in Matthias's mind. It was a rat, entirely black from tip to tail, barely distinguishable from the night itself.

Shadow heard the footsteps on the floor behind him. With cold, calculated detachment he wheeled about as his opponent charged. He was certain to defeat such a small creature in combat, but his orders were to get the picture, not to fight little mice. Besides, there was always the additional hazard that the mouse might hang on to him and shout for help until it came. Like a wraith of oily smoke Shadow completed a clever double manoeuvre. Bowling his body into a forward roll he knocked Matthias down like a skittle. Bounding up he slipped around the door, slammed it and fled off through the cloisters.

Matthias sprang up, roaring at the top of his voice, 'Stop that rat! Stop that rat!'

Immediately the mice on sentry duty were alerted. As the Shadow ran he saw Constance dash across the grounds at an angle which cut him off from the stairs up to the ramparts. Switching direction, he made for the next set of stairs, silently cursing the badger. Now he would have to use his climbing rope to descend quickly to the road.

Matthias emerged from the Abbey. He saw Shadow change direction. Thinking fast, he ran diagonally, catching up with the thief at the foot of the stairs. Throwing himself in a flying tackle, Matthias grabbed the Shadow by the legs, sending him crashing on to the lower steps.

Still clinging to the tapestry, the Shadow wriggled like an eel. Turning over on to his back, he kicked savagely at the young mouse's head with a free foot. Matthias tried valiantly to hang on, but his larger and heavier opponent kicked him viciously in the face, again and again. The big bony foot with its sharp claws pounding and gouging away soon took its toll. Matthias went limp and blacked out.

Constance had mounted the far steps. Gaining the ramparts, she ran along, dodging the heaps of rubble. She saw Matthias go down under the onslaught of kicks and ran even faster, impeded by mice all around who scattered in panic, thinking they were under mass invasion. The only one besides Constance who had the sense to see what was happening was Cornflower's father. Being nearer the top of the stairs than the badger he ran straight into the intruder. Shadow was struggling to get out his climbing rope.

'Surrender, rat, I've got you,' cried Mr Fieldmouse as he grabbed hold of the thief. But, rummaging in his pouch to free the rope, Shadow's claw had closed on the handle of his dagger. He drew it out swiftly and drove it twice into the fieldmouse's unprotected body.

Constance arrived just as the victim fell wounded. Shadow turned on her with the dagger upraised. Constance swung her paw round in a mighty arc, and it caught Shadow square on the chin. The force of the blow lifted the thief clean off his feet, and, before Constance could grab hold of him, he overbalanced and hurtled over the edge of the parapet with a horrible scream. Downwards he plunged, his body thudding off the unyielding masonry. He landed in the wet roadway with a sickening crunch.

Cluny came dashing towards the stricken Shadow, with Ragear scuttling in his wake. Despite his appalling injuries, Shadow managed to lever himself up on one paw.

'Cluny, I'm hurt, help me,' he gasped.

The piece of tapestry lay upon the road. Cluny snatched

it up eagerly. Behind him he could hear the gatehouse bolts being withdrawn amid the shouts of angry mice. Ruthlessly he kicked at Shadow's broken body.

'Get up and run for it or stay here, fool. I don't carry cripples or bunglers.'

Leaving the injured Shadow to the mice, Cluny sped off across the road. He covered the width of the ditch with a mighty leap and ran off across the meadows. In open country he could outdistance any mice that dared follow him. Waving the tapestry, Cluny laughed in exhilaration as he put on an extra burst of speed.

Ragear had panicked completely. He could not jump the ditch, so he scuttled off down the road in the opposite direction from the way they had come.

A group of mice led by Brother Alf tried fording the ditch and climbing up into the meadow. Unfortunately, the rain had made the going hard and slippery. Cluny was long gone, and the tapestry with him.

Turning back to Redwall, the pursuers came upon Matthias. He was leaning on Friar Hugo's arm in a dazed condition. Painfully he staggered up the road to where the Shadow lay. Wincing, he cast about, searching the muddy roadway for the fragment of tapestry.

'It's got to be here somewhere,' cried Matthias. He fell upon the injured Shadow, searching his waist pouch.

His flat black eyes clouding over, the Shadow watched Matthias. Laconically he spoke. His voice was strangely calm. 'Too late, mouse. Martin is with Cluny now.'

It was the last thing the Shadow ever said. He gave one final shudder and lay dead.

15

Dawn arrived as if it were aware of the previous night's events. Heavy, grey skies and steady rain prevailed over Redwall and the Mossflower area.

Abbot Mortimer looked old and stern as he addressed the assembly in Cavern Hole. The atmosphere was decidedly subdued.

'Sleeping at your posts, allowing the enemy into our Abbey to steal that which we hold most dear! Is this the way you defend us?' The Abbot's shoulders slumped wearily. There was an awkward hush – anger and guilt lay thick upon the air. The kindly old mouse shook his head and held up a conciliatory paw.

'Forgive me, friends, I criticize you unjustly. We are all creatures of peace, unskilled in the art of war. Yet when I saw the late rose this morning, I could not help but notice that its leaves are all shrivelled; the tiny rosebuds have died. Martin the Warrior is gone from our Abbey. He has left Redwall. We are forsaken. There will be hard and sorrowful days to come without him amongst us.'

The mice and woodland creatures shuffled their feet

and gazed at the floor. They knew the truth in their Father Abbot's words. But hope springs eternal. There was one voice raised, that of Matthias:

'A bit of good news,' he said. 'I have just come from the infirmary. Mr Fieldmouse is out of danger. He will live.'

The relief was audible throughout Cavern Hole. Tensions were eased; even the Abbot temporarily forgot his gloomy predictions.

'Thank you, Matthias,' he cried. 'What heartening news. I must say that the terrible injuries received by Mr Fieldmouse almost had me believing the worst. But look at yourself, my son. You should be resting. You face is still swollen after the fight with the black rat.'

Matthias gave a lopsided grin. He shrugged cheerfully. 'Don't worry about me, Father Abbot. I'll be all right.'

The mice smiled with pride. A brave little warrior, Matthias; he put new heart into them. Their resolve strengthened as he continued, 'Huh, black rat indeed! He didn't even scratch me. Well, only a bit. But where is he now, this sly one? Deep under the soil, if the insects are doing their job properly. Listen to me, friends. We of Redwall are a tough old lot to kill off. They couldn't finish Ambrose Spike, could they? Why, even the black one armed with a dagger couldn't slay Mr Fieldmouse, so what's a scratch or two to a mouse like me?'

Cheers for Matthias's speech rang to the rafters. Constance sprang up beside him, shouting heartily, 'That's the spirit, friends! Now let's see you all back out there at your posts. We'll be wide awake this time, and heaven help any dirty rats that come marching up to Redwall this day!'

With wild yells very uncharacteristic of peaceful mice, the friends seized their staves and charged out, fired with new zeal. After a while Constance accompanied the

Abbot to see Mr Fieldmouse, while Matthias went with Methuselah to the Great Hall. Together they surveyed the torn tapestry.

The young mouse stood with his paws folded, an expression of disgust upon his features. The old gatekeeper patted his shoulder. 'I know how you feel, Matthias. I could see you were only putting on a brave face for the benefit of the others. That is good. It shows you are learning to be a wise leader. You hide your true feelings and encourage them not to give up hope.'

Matthias gingerly touched the swellings on his face. 'Aye, that's as may be, old one. But you can see as well as I that Martin is gone. Without him I do not think we can win.'

Methuselah nodded in agreement. 'You are right, my young friend, but what's to be done?'

Matthias staggered slightly. He leaned against the wall, rubbing a paw across his brow. 'I don't know. In fact, the only think I know right now is that the Abbot was right. I think I'd better go and lie down for a bit.'

Refusing Methuselah's help, the young mouse left the old one gazing at the torn tapestry. He tottered off unsteadily in the direction of the dormitory.

On the spiral staircase he met Cornflower.

'Hello there,' he said, as cheering as he could. 'How is your father?'

Cornflower looked at Matthias solicitously. 'He's doing fine, thank you, Matthias. I'm just going to get some herbs for the Abbot. Shouldn't you be lying down? Your face looks terribly puffy.'

Matthias winced and leaned against the banister. 'Yes. As a matter of fact, I'm just going to my room for a good long rest. But don't you worry, before long I'll make those rats pay dearly for hurting your father.'

Matthias staggered weakly into his room – but the

moment he closed the door he became a different mouse. With bright eager eyes he groped under his bed and brought forth the waist pouch that had belonged to the Shadow. Tucking the long dagger into his belt, he wrapped the climbing rope around his shoulder and said aloud to himself, 'Right, Cluny, you and I have a score to settle.'

Keeping a mound of earth between himself and Brother Rufus, Matthias silently looped the rope around a projection at the edge of the parapet. Fortunately for him, Rufus was looking in the opposite direction. Matthias started to slide down the rope on the Mossflower side of the wall, where the woods came close up to the Abbey.

He had imagined the descent would be very difficult, and surprised himself by handling it with ease, his confidence growing as he slid swiftly and noiselessly to the fern-covered ground. Crouched in the undergrowth, he mentally rehearsed his plan of action. He would go through the woods to Saint Ninian's church, avoiding the road which was being watched by sentries. Once at the church he would discover where the piece of tapestry was kept; then he would create a diversion of some kind. While Cluny's horde was occupied he would snatch the tapestry and get back to Redwall with all speed.

Matthias ducked deeper into the ferns and was soon just a silent ripple making through the lush summer green of Mossflower towards the Church of Saint Ninian.

16

At the camp of Cluny the Scourge the rat army was girding itself up for war.

Weapons were being sharpened upon churchyard headstones. Under the critical eye of Redtooth a band of rodents was gnawing off a length of planking from a rickety lych-gate fence at the rear of the church. Others collected stones to provide ammunition for slings, while some coiled ropes about their bodies.

Inside the church Cluny sat up in the choir loft, the image of barbaric authority. He held the scourging tail in one claw, while gripped in the other was his war standard, topped by the ferret skull with the addition of the tattered tapestry square depicting Martin the Warrior. He gazed proudly at it as his armourer dressed him for war.

At Cluny's feet were the Vole family. They were bound. He flicked his tail at them and sneered. 'Ha, look at me, you spineless little creatures! Did you ever see such a leader of fighting animals as Cluny the Scourge? Soon I will have every creature that moves down on its bended knees to me.'

Mr Abram Vole glared defiantly at his captor. 'You

filthy great bilge rat, why I'll—'

'Silence!' roared Cluny. 'Hold your tongue, vole, or I will deal with you and your family here and now before I set out to conquer your precious Abbey. Do you see my new battle flag? That is Martin the Warrior. Yes, the same one who is supposed to protect that doddering old Abbot and his witless mob of mice. Now Martin is mine, it is more fitting that he travels at the head of real warriors. He will lead us to victory!'

Cluny ranted and raved on, the light of madness in his eye. 'Death and desolation shall be the reward of those who dare stand against Cluny. The only ones I will spare are those I might choose to serve me.'

Mrs Vole struggled upright but was forced back down by Scumnose and Fangburn. Chattering with rage she shouted at Cluny, 'You'll never bend Redwall to your evil will. Good will prevail! You'll see, Cluny. We are tied up, but our minds are free.'

Crack!

Cluny lashed out with his long tail, sending the Vole family flat upon the floor. Mr Abram Vole struggled to shield his wife and son with his body as the tail flailed out a second time.

'A touching little speech, vole, but you wrong me. I don't want to capture the spirit of Redwall. I mean to kill it! Take these whining creatures out of my sight. Lock them in the hut out at the back. Leave them to imagine what their fate will be when I return.'

Colin Vole shrieked in terror. His mother and father struggled bravely as they were dragged off.

Redtooth marched in and saluted Cluny.

'The horde is ready to march, Chief.'

The rat armourer set the war helmet firmly upon Cluny's head. He snapped the visor down and kicked aside the rat who had fixed the poison barb on his tail.

Striding out into the churchyard, Cluny climbed up on the wrecked gatepost. His fierce eye gazed out across the mighty army: black rats, brown rats, grey rats, piebald rats, skulking weasels, furtive stoats and sinuous ferrets, all gathered round, their weapons glistening and dripping with the rain. As Cluny exhorted them they roared back their frenzied replies:

'Where does Cluny's army go?'

'Redwall. Redwall.'

'What is the law of Cluny?'

'Kill, kill, kill.'

'Who will lead you to victory?'

'Cluny, Cluny, Cluny the Scourge!'

Springing down among his army, the Warlord waved the banner high overhead. With a mighty shout the horde of Cluny the Scourge marched out upon the road to Redwall Abbey.

STEALTHILY

17

Ragear was hopelessly lost!

Separated from Cluny, he could not think for himself. Scuttling off down the road in the wrong direction, he had kept on going in a state of funk. Frightened by the sound of a bird chirping suddenly, he rushed blindly into Mossflower Wood, and pressed on, deeper and deeper into this strange new territory. It was only with the arrival of pale dawn that he stopped, slumping down under some bushes. Exhausted, soaking wet and dispirited, he curled up into a wretched damp ball and slept.

Some time about mid-morning, Ragear was awakened by the sound of footsteps. As Matthias tramped past he lay low, silently congratulating himself. What a find, a little mouse! He would take him prisoner and bring him back alive to Cluny. That way he could gain some prestige. Cluny might even forget that he panicked and deserted at the Abbey.

Matthias risked a swift glance over his shoulder. There was a rat clumsily trying to stalk him, a fat awkward-looking rodent, but nevertheless an enemy. The young mouse strode onwards, his mind working coolly and without fear, confident that he could handle the situation.

Breaking twigs underfoot, stumbling ineptly from tree to tree, Ragear watched the mouse and fantasized.

'There was six of 'em, Chief, they tried surrounding me, but I fought like a devil! Then I says to meself, Ragear, says I, you'd better capture this last one and fetch him back for the Chief to question.' Then Cluny'll say to me, 'Ragear, good old Ragear, I knew I could depend on you. Why d'you suppose I took you along in the first place? Mangefur, bring food and wine for my old pal, Ragear the Brave.' Ha, yes, then I'll pat the Chief on the back and say, 'By Satan's whiskers, you old rodent! Have you never thought of retiring and letting me lead the horde? Why, with a gallant warrior like me in comm—'

Thwack!

A long whippy larch branch sprang forward suddenly. It crashed into Ragear's head, poleaxing him.

Matthias stepped out of hiding, rubbing his hands – it had been a strain holding the branch back for so long. Uncoiling Shadow's climbing rope, he bound Ragear paw and claw to a sturdy oak. The young mouse could not afford to wait around for the rat to regain his senses, there was still a deal of travelling to be done. He pressed onwards, leaving his senseless enemy bound to the tree.

The rain stopped. Within minutes the hot June sun burst down on Mossflower, as if in apology for its absence. Clouds of steaming mist arose from the woodland floor, mingling with the golden shafts slanting down through the trees. The birds began singing. Each flower and blade of grass was decked out in jewelled pendantry with necklaces of sparkling raindrops.

The sudden warmth flooded over Matthias, cheering him onwards. Humming a tune beneath his breath, he strode out with a will, almost breaking from the cover of the trees straight out into the flat meadowland. He checked himself just in time. Directly ahead lay a vast overgrown area which was neither pasture nor meadow. It was the common land that had once belonged within the curtilage of Saint Ninian's.

Matthias crouched at the edge of the woods. He could see the back of the church. There were ten or twelve rats patrolling it, some distance away. Before he dealt with that problem there was still the common land to be crossed. Clumps of thistle and slight ground hummocks would be his only cover. The young mouse spoke his thoughts aloud. 'Hmm, this could present a little problem.'

A strange voice answered him. 'Problem, a little problem? Well at least it's not a fully grown adult problem.'

Matthias squeaked aloud with fright. Whirling about, he looked for the source of the mystery voice. There was no one about. Taking a grip on himself, he squared his shoulders and called out boldly: 'Come out here this instant and show yourself!'

The voice answered. It seemed to come from directly in front of him. 'Show m'self indeed! How many pairs of eyes d'you want, young feller, eh, eh? Fine state of affairs, bless m'soul! What, what!'

Matthias narrowed his eyes and looked hard . . . still nothing.

'I warn you, come out and show yourself,' he shouted irritably. 'I'm in no mood for playing games.'

As if by magic a lanky hare popped up right beside Matthias. An odd patchworked creature, his fur was an ashen hue with blots of grey and light-brown flecked white on the underbelly. He was very tall, with formidable hefty hind legs and a comical pouched face topped off by two immense ears which flopped about of their own accord. With a courtly old-fashioned manner the hare made a leg, bowing gracefully. His voice carried a slightly affected quaver.

'Basil Stag Hare at your service, sir! Expert scout, hindleg fighter, wilderness guide, and camouflage specialist, ahem, liberator of tender young crops, carrots, lettuce, and other such strange beasts. Pray tell me whom I have the pleasure of addressing, and please state the nature of your little problem.'

Matthias decided the peculiar hare was either slightly mad or tipsy, but his outmoded manner was certainly friendly. The young mouse humoured him accordingly, bowing low with a paw at his waist.

'Good day to you, Mr Basil Stag Hare. My name is Matthias. I am a novice in the order of Redwall mice. My immediate problem is to cross this land to the church over yonder without being discovered by the rats who are guarding it.'

Basil Stag Hare tapped one of his huge feet gently on the ground. 'Matthias,' he laughed. 'What an odd name, to be sure!'

The young mouse laughed back as he replied, 'Not half as odd as your own name. Whoever heard of a hare being called Basil Stag?'

The hare disappeared momentarily. He reappeared next to Matthias. 'Ah well, Hare's the family name, don't y'know. My parents named me Basil, though the old mater wanted me to be called Columbine Agnes. Always longed for a young gel, she did.'

'But why Stag?' Matthias inquired.

'Noble creatures, stags,' the hare sighed. 'Did I ever tell you I wanted to be one; a magnificent royal stag with great coathanger antlers? So, I went down to the jolly old river one night and christened m'self Stag! Had two toads and a newt as witnesses, y'know. Oh yes.'

Matthias was unable to hide his merriment. He sat down and chuckled. Basil started chuckling too. He sat down beside Matthias.

'I think I'm going to like you, m'boy,' he cried. 'Now, what about getting you to that church? Why, there's nothing simpler. But enough time for that later, young rip. How about telling me what brings you here? I love listening to a good yarn, y'know. Oh, by the way, I hope you like fennel and oatcakes. Of course you do! You'll share lunch with me – of course you will – young 'un like yourself.'

In a flash Basil had lugged a haversack from the undergrowth and was spreading a repast on the grass between them. For the next half hour Matthias related his story between mouthfuls of the hare's tasty luncheon. Basil listened intently, interrupting only when he required clarification on some point.

Matthias finished his tale and sat back awaiting comment. Basil's long ears flopped up and down like railway signals as he digested his food and his friend's information.

'Hmm, rats. I knew they'd come eventually, through intelligence on me grapevine, y'know. Could feel it in the old ears, too. As for Redwall, I know it well. Excellent type, Abbot Mortimer. Splendid chap. I heard the Joseph Bell tolling out the sanctuary message. Huh, even had some cheeky old hedgehog-wallah telling me to run for it. Couldn't go of course. Dear me no. That'd never do. Chap deserting his post; bit of a bad show, what, what? I prefer me own company, y'know. Present company excepted, of course.'

'Oh, of course,' Matthias agreed. He had taken enormously to the hare. Basil sprang up in a smart military fashion and saluted.

'Right, first things first! Must get you across to the church, young feller me mouse. I say, that green thing-ummyjig you're wearin' – habit, isn't it? Capital camouflage. You just try lying down anywhere in the shadows. Believe you me, you'd have trouble finding yourself. Top hole cover, absolutely!'

Basil stopped and ruminated for a moment. His ears lay flat, stood up, then pointed in opposite directions. He continued, 'Now, when you've liberated your bit of tapestry or whatever, make straight back across the common. I'll be waiting, never fear. Good! Well, come on, young bucko. We can't sit about here all day like two fat rabbits at a celery chew. Up and at 'em! Quick's the word and sharp's the action! Nip about a bit, young un.'

Again Basil vanished only to reappear some three metres out on the common. 'Come on, Matthias. Tack to the left and wheel to the right. Bob and weave, duck and wriggle. Look, it's easy.'

Matthias hurried to follow, keeping in mind Basil's instructions. Surprisingly, they seemed to work perfectly and before long the two friends had covered nearly three-quarters of the common land. Matthias could even count the whiskers on some of the rats. He covered his mouth with a paw to stifle a giggle.

'It's really very simple, isn't it, Basil? How am I doing?'

The hare bobbed up beside him. 'Capital! Bung ho! Like a duck to water, young feller. Flop me ears if you aren't the best pupil I've ever had. By the way, is there anything I can do to help?'

Matthias stopped and looked serious. 'Yes, there is, Basil. But I feel reluctant to ask you to involve yourself in my fight.'

Basil Stag Hare snorted. 'Rubbish. My fight indeed! D'you fondly imagine that I'd sit there munching at the old nosebag while some ugly great rodent and his band of yahoos run about conquering my countryside? Huh, never let it be said in the mess that Basil Stag Hare was backward in coming forward! Ask away, Matthias, you young curmudgeon.'

The hare puffed out his narrow chest and stood with paw on heart, his eyes closed and ears standing straight up. He awaited orders. The young mouse, hiding a smile at Basil's noble pose, said admiringly, 'Oh, Mr Hare, you do look heroic standing like that! Thank you!'

Basil opened one eye to look at himself. Yes, he did look rather gallant; a bit like the Monarch of the Glen, or the Stag at Eve. Not that a young mouse'd understand anything of that nature.

Matthias expressed his wishes to the 'Stag'. 'Would it be possible for you to create some kind of diversion while I'm getting the tapestry? Could you keep the rats occupied, Basil?'

The hare twitched his ears confidently. 'Say no more, laddie. You've come to the right stag. Listen carefully. You cut across the flank to their left. They took a piece of planking out of the fence by the lych gate. That's where you'll slide through. When you've got what you came for, then make your exit the same way. I'll be somewhere about keeping an eye on you. Right, off you go.'

Matthias went swiftly, still remembering to bob and weave as Basil had taught him. He made it with ease to the fence, glancing back to check on his companion.

Basil went into a speedy run. He cleared the fencetop at a bound and tapped the nearest rat on the back.

'I say, old thing, where's this leader feller. Cluny, or Loony, whatever you call him?'

Completely staggered, the rat stood slack-jawed. Basil left him and popped up beside another rat.

'Phew! Dear, dear, don't you chaps ever take a bath? Listen here, you dreadful creature. D'you realize that you

103

niff to high heaven? Er, by the way, did your parents ever call you Pongo, or did they smell as bad as you?'

It took the rat-sentries a moment or two to recover from their surprise. Then they let out yells of rage and tried to seize the impudent hare.

It was like trying to catch smoke with their claws. Basil ran rings round them, keeping up a steady stream of insults and adding to the rats' bad temper. They shouted angrily:

'Grab that big skinny rabbit, lads.'

'Big skinny rabbit yourself! Catsmeat!'

'I'll stick his damned guts on my pike.'

'Temper, temper! Tut tut! Such language! If your mother could hear you!'

'Blast, he's as slippery as a greased pig.'

'Some of my best friends are greased pigs, bottle-nose. Oops! Missed me again, you old butterfingers you.'

Matthias chuckled quietly and shook his head in admiration. He watched twelve rats falling over each other and bumping heads as they chased his friend around the common land. Every now and then Basil would pause and strike his 'Noble Stag' attitude, letting the rats get to within a whisker of him. Nimbly he would kick out with his long powerful legs and send them all sprawling in a heap. Adding insult to injury he danced around the fallen sentries, sprinkling them with daisies until they arose, cursing him, to continue the chase.

Wary that there might be other rats about, Matthias climbed into the church through a broken stained-glass window. He dropped down into the lady chapel. The young mouse wrinkled his nose in disgust. The beautiful old church was rank with the heavy odour of rats. Furniture was overturned, statuary broken, walls stained; the pages of torn hymn books lay about everywhere.

Where was the fragment of tapestry?

And where was Cluny with the rest of his army?

Instant realization sent a leaden weight thudding into the pit of Matthias's stomach!

They had gone to attack Redwall. Cluny must have the tapestry with him. Matthias felt sick at the thought.

Hastily he climbed back out of the window. Halfway across to the fence he noticed a small shed. Somebody was pounding upon its locked door and calling his name aloud.

'Matthias, quickly, over here in the hut.'

Through a small gap in the door he could see the Vole family. Their paws were tightly bound. Colin Vole huddled piteously on some dirty sacking in a corner, whilst Mr Abram Vole and his wife battered away at the door with their paws tied together. Matthias called through the crack to them, 'Stop banging! Stay quiet! I'll have you out of there as soon as I can break the lock.'

Matthias cast about for something that would force the padlock and hasp. Doubtless some rat had the key, but there was no time for that.

By a stroke of luck he found an iron spike that had been thrown at Basil by one of the rats. Forcing the spike in the hoop of the lock Matthias levered away.

'It's not budging,' he muttered.

From the corner, Colin Vole started to weep aloud. 'Oh we'll be locked in here until Cluny gets back. I don't want to face him again! Do something, Matthias! Save me!'

Despite the Voles' wretched predicament, Matthias could not help showing his contempt for Colin. 'Do stop whining, Colin! It doesn't help matters. Keep your voice down. There may still be rats about. Stop thinking of yourself all the time. Try to be brave like your mum and dad.'

In his frustration Matthias swung the spike at the lock. It bounced off, lodging deep between the hasp and the woodwork. He grunted in exasperation, pulling it savagely towards himself to loosen it. Taken off balance, he went head over tail. The hasp had broken; it came away bringing with it some twisted rusty screws. The door swung open.

Drawing his dagger, Matthias hastily cut the bindings from the paws of the Voles, issuing orders as he worked. 'Follow me and do as I say. Move as quickly and quietly as you can.'

Cautiously, they slid through the broken fence and began making their way across the common. There was no sight of the rat sentries. Matthias guessed that they were off somewhere, still trying to catch the elusive hare.

It was mid-afternoon. The common was peaceful and sunny; butterflies perched on thistle flowers and grasshoppers serenaded each other with their ceaseless cadences. Abram Vole insisted on shaking Matthias by the paw and congratulating him. 'Matthias, thank you with all my heart for saving my family. We thought we were doomed.'

The young rescuer looked grim.

'We're not back home yet by any means, Mr Vole, and even if we do make it back to the Abbey, I dread to think what we may find.'

Mrs Vole nodded vigorously. 'Aye, we saw them leave the church to march on Redwall. Cluny was leading the villains with Martin's picture tied to his banner. My oh my, you never did see so many wild rascals in all your born days.'

Matthias's brow creased in a worried frown. 'I wish I hadn't sneaked off from the Abbey this morning. I do hope Constance has all the defenders on the alert.'

It was only seconds later that Matthias wished he had also been on the alert.

The sentry rats had become tired of chasing Basil. Wearily they made their way out of the woods and back to the common land. They sat on the grass behind a low hummock taking a break together.

Matthias and the Vole family walked straight into the middle of them.

18

Cluny massed his forces in the roadside ditch opposite
Redwall Abbey. He stood well back in the meadow
behind the ditch, surrounded by his captains. Here, where
he was out of range, he could direct the entire operation.

But at the moment he was not having things all his own
way. For a start, he did not have many archers. Rats are
notoriously bad at bowmaking and the fletching of
arrows.

From the ramparts of Redwall the field and harvest
mice sent down volley after volley of tiny arrows which,
while they had no great killing power, were causing much
wounding and discomfort in the ranks of Cluny's horde.

Standing beneath his banner which was rammed into
the earth, Cluny cracked his tail. 'Redtooth, Darkclaw,
tell the sling-throwers to stand ready. When I give the
signal I want to see a good heavy barrage of stones hitting
the top of that parapet. That'll make them keep their
heads down. Frogblood, Scumnose, you two will
organize the gangs with the scaling ladders and grappling
hooks. See they all get up on top of that wall, and no
blunders.'

The rat captains marched off to the ditch to make ready. Cluny held his tail up to give the signal.

On top of the wall the mouse-archers kept up their relentless hail of arrows into the ditch. Constance strode up and down, holding a heavy cudgel in her paws as she urged them on. 'That's the stuff to give 'em, mice! Keep those bows twanging!'

Knowing the supply of arrows was not endless, the badger looked to the heaps of rubble and stone along the parapet edges. 'Brother Rufus! Foremole! Be ready to shift that lot overboard at a moment's notice.'

Smack, clank, bang, thud!

A hail of sharp stones and pebbles whizzed upwards, rattling against the masonry as Cluny waved his tail in the meadow below. Taken unawares, several mice were felled and a mole lay stunned.

'Get your heads down, everyone! Lie flat!' Constance shouted.

The defenders instantly obeyed as the showers of missiles increased. Running along the ramparts, bent double, the Abbot cried out, 'Stretcher-bearers! Over here! Help me to get the casualties down into the cloisters.'

Winifred the otter lay alongside Constance and whispered to her, 'Hear that scraping? Cluny's lot are putting something against the walls. It's my guess they'll be trying to climb up while we've got to lie low.'

Even as Winifred spoke two grappling hooks with climbing ropes attached came clanging over the parapet and lodged in the joints.

'Stay low, my friends,' whispered Constance. 'Give them a bit of time to get off the ground. I want plenty of rats to be high up before we make a move. Pass the word along.'

Below in the meadow, Redtooth waved his cutlass and

laughed wildly. 'Your plan is working out, Chief! Look, there's old Fangburn and his gang nearly at the top of the wall.'

Cluny lifted his visor to get a better view. It was too late to call out against what he saw happen next.

A veritable avalanche of earth and rocks cascaded over the parapet. It smashed straight on to the main ladder. Rats screamed aloud and grasped at mid-air as they were swept from the ladder to the road below. The ladder fell sideways, cannoning into another one that had been set up beside it. As both ladders fell there were scenes of mass chaos. Badly wounded and shocked, the survivors on the roadway tried to crawl back to the safety of the ditch, only to be buried beneath rubble which thundered down on them. Many lay trapped beneath the heavy ladders that had fallen. The air resounded with screams and moans.

Cluny ranted and swore. Leaving his standard, he rushed across the meadow. Taking the ditch in a single leap, he darted across the road. Grasping a hanging rope he began hauling himself up claw over claw. As the solitary beaver gnawed through the last strands, the rope parted. Cluny fell from a fair height and sprawled on the dusty road in an undignified heap.

Cluny flung himself into the ditch. Regrouping the sling-throwers and a few archers he ordered them to await his command.

At the top of the walls the last climbing rope had been severed. A hearty cheer rent the air as the Redwall defenders broke cover to survey their handiwork.

'Fire!' Cluny roared.

Stones and arrows sped upward with devastating effect. Several mice and woodlanders cried out and fell. The results heartened Cluny. All was not lost. He began devising a new plan.

In Mossflower Woods, Ragear was struggling with the rope that bound him to the oak tree. He could hear far-off sounds which meant only one thing. His Chief was attacking the Abbey.

Straining his neck downwards at an uncomfortable angle, Ragear was able to get his teeth into the tough climbing rope. If he could manage to free himself he might be able to sneak back and join the horde. He could mingle with them and deny that he had ever been missing. Cluny might also take a lenient view of his desertion if he could distinguish himself during the battle.

The rope tasted foul. Ragear could tell by its scent that it had once belonged to the Shadow. He'd never liked that surly poker-faced rodent! Ragear congratulated himself as his teeth bit through another strand.

'Ha, take that, rope, and that! No rope can keep Ragear prisoner for long, heh, heh, heh! Poor old Shadow, if only you could see your lovely rope now!' Ragear straightened up for a moment to ease his neck.

The laughter died on his lips. A horrified gurgle bubbled from his throat. Icy claws of terror gripped his chest.

Swaying hypnotically a foot from his face was the biggest, strongest, most-evil-looking adder that had ever been born.

The rat was completely petrified. The breath seemed to freeze in his lungs. The sinister blunt head moved in a lazy rhythm, its forked tongue flickering endlessly in and out, the round, beadlike jet eyes never leaving his for an instant. Its voice was like dry leaves rustling in an autumn breeze.

'Asmodeus, Asmodeussssssss,' it hissed. 'So kind of you to untie yourself, rat! Come with me, I will show you eternity! Asmodeus, Asmodeussssssss.'

It struck with lightning speed! All that Ragear felt was a

sudden sharp sting to the side of his neck. His limbs became flaccid, his eyesight shrouded by a dark mist. The last words Ragear ever heard on this earth were uttered in the adder's sibilant hiss.

'Asmodeus, Asmodeussssssssssss!'

Cluny scratched the floor of the ditch with his claw. It was all there, the design for his next move. He would attack the Abbey secretly from the Mossflower side.

It would be a surprise manoeuvre. A handpicked squad led by him would carry out the mission. Dressed in Cluny's war helmet and armour, Redtooth would stay back in the meadow. His disguise would be sufficient to fool the defenders from the distance of the high walls. The rats in the ditch were ordered to continue pressing home the attack until Cluny and his party scaled the walls from behind and fought their way across the grounds to open the Abbey gates.

After issuing orders to his remaining Captains, Cluny, accompanied by a score of assorted rats, weasels, stoats and ferrets, crept off along the course of the ditch. They carried with them the long plank from Saint Ninian's lych-gate fence. Silently they travelled in a northerly direction, until they were out of sight of the walls. Climbing out of the ditch they crossed the road into Mossflower woods.

Cluny sat on a fallen tree trunk and told his squad what was required of them. 'I'll wait here with the plank carriers. The rest of you split up and search the area for any big high trees growing near the Abbey walls. Make sure that the tree you pick is higher than the wall itself and not too difficult to climb. Got that? Right, get going.'

Cluny watched them strike off into the undergrowth. His previous good mood had deserted him. He was working himself into a foul temper over the day's performance from his mighty conquering horde. Shown up by the simple tactics of woodland creatures and mice! He snorted and dug his powerful claws into the rotten tree trunk, sending beetles and woodlice scurrying as he tore out a chunk of the spongy timber. Oh, he had had them frightened at first. As a commander he knew the power of fright, but once they had gained the upper hand in the initial skirmish the mice lost their fear and became bolder. That was when the battle had started to go against him. Granted, he had scored one or two small victories, but they were nothing to brag about. He couldn't use them as an example to put fresh heart in his troops.

Cluny's only hope was that the mice would become over-confident and eventually make a mistake. It was the old waiting game. Just let them make one slip; that was all he needed. Meanwhile, he had a greater obstacle to overcome than mice: the walls. It was those same accursed walls that were ruining all his plans. Cluny tore viciously at the rotting log until great chunks of it flew through the air. If this scheme worked he wouldn't have to worry about walls any more. He would be inside those walls like a fox among day-old chickens.

Cluny sniffed the air. His senses told him the searchers were returning. Cheesethief and a ferret named Killconey came crashing out of the underbush. They were trembling and twitching. Both looked as if they had been badly scared.

It was some time before Cluny could get any sense out of them. Cheesethief spoke haltingly, glancing back fearfully over his shoulder. 'Er, er, we, like . . . we got a bit lost, Chief.'

'Lost? Where?' Cluny snarled.

Killconey pointed a shaky claw. 'Over that way, yer honour, and didn't we find a great strappin' oak?'

113

'Was it close to the wall?'

Cheesethief shook his head. 'No, Chief, it was further out into the woods. Look what I found wrapped around the trunk.'

He held out the chewed and broken climbing rope. Cluny snatched it. 'This looks like the Shadow's climbing rope. He's dead. What are you fools trying to tell me?'

Killconey whimpered pitifully. 'It's Ragear, yer honour.'

Cluny seized the unlucky pair and shook them soundly. 'Have you both gone raving mad? D'you mean to tell me you're frightened of that fool Ragear?'

Cheesethief fell to his knees, sobbing. 'But you didn't see him, Chief. He was just lying there. His face was all swollen and his tongue was sticking out. It had gone purple. Ugh! He was all sort of bloated like . . . it was horrible!'

Killconey bobbed his head vigorously in agreement. 'Aye, so 'twas. Didn't we see him with our very own eyes, sir? Pore ould Ragear, and him going backwards all the time.'

'Going backwards?' echoed Cluny.

'Indeed he was,' said the ferret, 'and your man here says to me, says he, "there's something pulling Ragear along." Sure, we couldn't see what it was for all the bushes, so we pulled them to one side between us, and what did we see?'

'Well, what did you see?' barked Cluny irritably.

Killconey stopped and shuddered. He spoke incredulously, as if he were unable to believe himself. 'We saw the biggest snake you ever clapped eyes on. The father of all serpents! He had poor Ragear's body by the feet and was dragging it along backwards.'

Cluny's one eye widened. 'What did this serpent do when it saw you?'

'It let go of Ragear and looked at us,' squeaked Cheesethief. 'The serpent stared at us. It kept on saying, "Asmodeus, Asmodeus".'

Cluny scratched his head with a sharp, dirty claw. 'Asmodeus? What's that supposed to mean?'

'Do ye not know? 'Tis the dreaded name of the divvil himself, sir,' wailed the ferret. 'I know because me ould mother told me so, and she always said never to look a serpent in the eye. So I sez to me mate here, "Cheese-thief," sez I, "don't look. Run for your life!" And that's exactly what we did, sir. Oh, you'll never know how horrible it was. I'd rather be tied in a blazin' barn than go back there, so I would! The great scaly body of the—'

'Quiet, fool,' said Cluny. 'I think I hear the others coming back. Now straighten yourselves up, and not a word to anyone about this serpent thing, or you'll feel my serpent across your backs.' Cluny's long tail waved menacingly under their noses. They took his point.

A weasel called Scragg came running up. He reported smartly with great efficiency. 'High tree near the Abbey wall, Chief, elm I think, much higher than the wall, lots of branches jutting out, just the job for climbing.'

'How far to this tree?' Cluny asked.

'About ten minutes' march to the east,' Scragg replied.

When the rest of the party arrived back, Cluny had them form up in single file. They marched eastwards at a smart pace.

The high tree did prove to be an elm, an ancient giant covered in gnarled bumps and handy branches. Cluny sized it up: exactly what he wanted, the perfect distance from the wall. He turned to his commando squad.

'Listen, we're going to climb this tree. When we get up high enough I'll find a strong branch that we can bridge to the wall with the plank. If we go carefully, the mice won't suspect a thing. Before they can gather their wits about them we'll be inside Redwall.'

19

It was difficult to tell who was the more surprised, Matthias and his party or the rat sentries.

There was a second's pause, then they scattered. One or two of the rats were a bit slow off the mark, but not as slow as Colin Vole and his mother, who were roughly grabbed by the faster sentries.

Matthias dodged, wriggled, and ran free, tripping a rat who was about to seize Mr Vole. The young mouse ran, pushing the vole in front of him and calling out: 'Run, keep going, Mr Vole! Try to make it to the woods and hide.'

The vole faltered. 'But my wife – Colin – the rats have got them.'

Matthias pushed him roughly forward. 'They'll get you too, if you don't hurry! Move yourself, Vole. You'll be no good to your family as a prisoner again.'

Taking Matthias's advice, Abram Vole ran as fast as his legs would carry him. Matthias turned and picked up a heavy branch. He faced the oncoming rats.

'Only a dozen of you,' he taunted. 'Let's see what you rats are made of. First come, first served.'

Matthias swung the branch. It whooshed through the

air, causing the rats to stop in their tracks. As he advanced on them flailing the branch, he shouted at the top of his voice, 'Basil, Basil Stag Hare, where are you?'

The rats tried to circle Matthias. One got too near. A hefty blow from the improvised staff sent him crashing to the ground.

'Oh well hit, sir! Jolly well hit!'

It was the hare.

He came bounding up, for all the world as if he were on a Sunday School picnic, grinning from ear to ear. Colin and Mrs Vole came panting in his wake. Matthias gasped with relief.

'Basil, where in heaven's name did you get to?'

The skilful creature dodged a rat, spun round and landed a fierce double-footed kick to its stomach. The rat bowled over, completely winded, all the fight knocked out of its body. Basil chuckled. 'Sorry about that, Matthias my old lad. When these chaps gave up chasing me, I scooted back to my den. Spring cleaning, y'know. A bit late, but I'm only a bachelor in single quarters, what!'

Matthias was flabbergasted. Here he was fighting off a dozen rats, trying to rescue the Vole family, while Basil was dusting out his den! The young mouse could scarcely hold his temper.

'Oh, how nice of you, Mr Hare. So glad you could join us,' he said sarcastically as they beat off rats and hurried the Voles along. 'I don't suppose you put the kettle on for tea?'

Basil bowed to Mrs Vole and offered her his paw.

'Allow me, Ma'am. Why yes, as a matter of fact I did. Nothing like a fresh pot of mint tea after some good healthy exercise, what, what?'

Matthias struck a rat square in the face with the butt of his branch. The hare was obviously insane. Mint tea, indeed!

'Well, I don't suppose you think I'm going to sit in your den drinking tea all afternoon,' he yelled.

Basil had a hammerlock on a rat. He swung him and knocked two more flat on the ground. He winked at Matthias.

'I certainly hope not, old bean. You see, it'd be perishin' awkward, as I've only got a four-piece teaset, and if I'm not mistaken the small gent who took off for the woods like a scalded duck is obviously the husband of this delightful lady vole, so I'll have to invite him too, won't I?'

Matthias tripped a rat with the branch. He was learning to take Basil in his stride.

'Why, of course you will, Mr Hare. What a bore you must think me. I'll probably sit around on the common here and teach the rats to make daisy chains.'

Basil dodged around a rat and laughed approvingly. 'No need to get uppity, young feller. I thought I'd best shelter the Voles and see 'em safe to the Abbey later. Obviously you need to get back to Redwall post haste. A family of voles would only slow you up.'

Matthias grinned ruefully. 'I apologize, sir. I accept your offer of help gratefully, I didn't mean to be rude.'

By now they were at the edge of the common land. The rats had fallen back momentarily.

Basil shook paws with Matthias. 'Good mouse. Right, cut along, young'un. I'll see you when I deliver my charges back to the Abbey.' .

Alone and unencumbered, Matthias struck off into the woods. Travelling doggedly on wearied legs, he realized that his entry to Redwall would have to be from the Mossflower side as the main gate would probably be under attack. Could the defenders hold out? Was Constance organizing that retaliation correctly without him! Had the sentries stayed alert? Was Cornflower safe?

Questions raced through Matthias's brain as he fought his way through the undergrowth. Taking a check on his bearings, he began to worry a little. The Abbey walls should be in sight over towards the north-west. Perhaps he hadn't fully realized the sprawling size of the woodlands. Yes, that was it. Maybe if he kept on trekking the walls would soon come into view.

Somewhere ahead Matthias could hear the trickle and gurgle of a stream. He remembered that it had been some time since he had eaten and drunk. Changing direction he followed the water sounds until he came to the banks of the stream.

Lying face down on a low outcrop of red sandstone Matthias drank his fill of the cool, sweet stream water. Further down the bank he found some young dandelions. Gathering a bunch of tender leaves and buds he made his way back to the sun-warmed sandstone and stretched out on his back, nibbling dandelions and gazing up at the cloudless, blue June sky through the treetops. What an action-packed day it had been!

Matthias was glad of the brief respite after all the excitement. But he told himself that he could not afford to stay long. He must press on to Redwall. He heaved a great sigh; the life of a warrior was very tiring.

Closing his eyes momentarily, he thought of Martin the Warrior. Did he ever feel tired? He must have, defending the Abbey with his large heavy sword, wearing all that armour. Whatever happened to the sword? It had to be somewhere. Legendary weapons didn't rust and wear away to nothing, otherwise they'd never get to be legends.

A dragonfly hovered directly above the young mouse, gently stirring his whiskers. What was this strange creature doing in his territory? He glided a little closer. It was quite safe; the oddly-garbed animal posed no threat to his authority as bailiff of this stretch of water. He was fast asleep, snoring like a squirrel in midwinter, oblivious to all about him.

20

It was late afternoon. There had been one or two minor setbacks, but Cluny and his squad had finally made it up into the elm tree. Some of the rats were really hopeless climbers in Cluny's estimation. There had been quite a bit of jostling and slipping, and as for that idiot Cheesethief, imagine waiting until you were six metres above ground to find out that you were afraid and had no head for heights. Cluny thought angrily that if there hadn't been such an urgent need for silence, he'd have given him what for!

The Warlord began to wish that he had brought along more ferrets and weasels. They possessed good natural climbing ability, and that weasel – what was his name? Scragg – he'd been an enormous help, boosting and encouraging the others, even organizing the lifting up of the plank. Cluny made a mental note for future reference. Officer material that one. Despite all efforts however, they were still below the edge of the parapet. Higher up the elm, branches became thin and whippy, not strong enough to support the plank's weight.

Cluny took stock of the situation. This was really as far as he could go while still retaining some kind of safety factor on their hazardous assignment. He decided to call a halt.

'Right, take a breather. Find somewhere that you won't fall from. In an hour or two it'll be evening; there'll be lots of shadow and less daylight. The mice will have slowed up a bit by then. We'll catch them off guard. Scragg, see this lot keep still and quiet, will you?'

Scragg saluted smartly and offered a helpful comment. 'This branch I'm sitting on, Chief. I've just been testing it and it feels good and strong. Maybe we should mount the plank from here to the wall. It'll reach easily enough. I know it's a bit of an uphill climb, but it shouldn't be too difficult. I don't fancy those branches higher up – they're too thin.'

Cluny climbed across and sat next to Scragg. He spoke in a whisper. 'Good thinking, weasel. Yes, this branch'll do fine. Stick by me, Scragg. You're a useful soldier. With some of the blockheads I've got around me I could be on the lookout for a new Captain soon. You know what that means: extra loot, a bigger share of the plunder. Cluny always rewards initiative, Scragg. Play your cards right and you'll soon get promotion.'

'Thanks, Chief. Don't worry; I won't let you down,' Scragg murmured.

On a lower branch, Cheesethief (who had been eaves-dropping on the conversation) sneered inwardly. Yes, Chief. No, Chief. Three bags full, Chief! Who did that snotty weasel think he was?

And as for Cluny promoting a weasel to captain over rats of his own kind, well Redtooth and Darkclaw and the others might have something to say about that! Upstart weasel, he'd only joined up a day or two ago. If he got half the chance Cheesethief would fix Scragg all right.

Abbot Mortimer looked thankfully up at the sky. Evening had come. They had lasted out well; the rats had not breached the wall in any way. Most of the main fighting had gone into a lull and Cluny's horde were only making spasmodic sallies from the ditch now. Taking advantage of the interval, the defenders hauled up more rocks and rubble to the ramparts. Cornflower and her band of helpers were on top of the walls. Keeping their heads low, they moved from post to post, serving each creature with a bowl of stew, some wild grapes, and a small loaf of honeyed nutbread.

'What a calm, efficient young mouse Cornflower is,' the Abbot remarked to Constance.

The badger passed a bundle of arrows to Ambrose Spike for distribution as she replied, 'Aye, that she is, Father Abbot. But she looks worried. Matthias, do you think?'

'Doubtless,' said the Abbot drily. 'That young mouse is on my mind as well as hers and yours.'

Constance shook her large striped head. 'It's not like Matthias to go off like that. I've searched everywhere in my spare moments, but he's not in the Abbey.'

'Well, wherever he is,' the Abbot replied, 'I'm certain that he is helping our cause, so we'll just have to await his return and trust to Matthias's judgement and good sense.'

The two friends thankfully accepted food from Cornflower and her helpers. Both watched, mystified, as Winifred the otter and the Foremole hoisted and pulled a seesaw into view.

It was a plaything, made in the distant past for the use of infant woodlanders. It had lain near the strawberry patch for as long as anyone could remember. Baby animals played on it throughout the year. As a seesaw it was in perfect working order.

Winifred and Foremole set it down on the parapet. Bent

double, two moles staggered up carrying between them an enormous rock. The Foremole indicated the opposite end of the seesaw. 'Arr, purrum thur, that's a noice bowlder, my beauties.'

When the 'bowlder' was in position, Winifred and Foremole hugged each other tightly. With a nod they jumped heavily on to the near seat.

Whoosh!

The big rock catapulted over the top of the parapet. Several seconds of silence followed, then there was a crash accompanied by screams of pain and shock from the rats packed into the ditch below. Winifred and Foremole gravely shook paws.

'Yurr, oi reckon they pesky varmints got'n an 'eadache,' chuckled the Foremole, as everybody on the ramparts ran to seek cover from the retaliatory missiles hurled by Cluny's horde.

The battle had started again in earnest.

Mouse archers sprang up and loosed their shafts down towards the ditch; otter sling-throwers whipped hard pebbles off with fierce rapidity; long rat javelins flew upwards, causing death and injury in the ranks of the defenders. But now there was a new hazard. Some inventive rat had devised a fearsome weapon: chunks of iron grave-railings from the churchyard, strung to lengths of cord. The rats would swing the cord round and round, gaining momentum until, judging the right direction, they loosed the cord. The missiles sped upwards, two or three times higher than the wall, almost out of sight; then they would plummet downwards, whistling viciously, to burst on the ramparts. Any defender struck by a missile was either instantly killed or horribly maimed. Even if the iron missed its target, the stones and shattered metal fragments ricocheted about dangerously.

Realizing the danger of this new device, Constance

123

ordered all but a chosen few to leave the wall for the safety of the Abbey grounds. However, the strung iron bits soon proved to be a two-edged weapon. Many that were released wrongly came hurtling back down into the ditch, sometimes slaying the very creatures that had hurled them. Even Redtooth, in Cluny's armour, guarding the standard in the meadow, had to make an undignified scurry to avoid being hit, but he could see the demoralizing effect the missiles were having on the defenders, so he ordered the throwers to continue.

Constance bravely stood her ground on the parapet, as did her small band of picked fighters. Whenever one of the missiles landed intact on the rubble pile she would seize it, standing in full view as she whirled the corded iron round and round, releasing it in a blur of speed. Constance was a far more powerful and accurate thrower than any rat. The attackers bared angry fangs at her from the cover of the ditch – of all the Redwall defenders the big badger was the one they most hated and feared.

Seated in the branches of the elm tree at the north wall of the Abbey, Cluny watched the shadows lengthen. To the west, the sky was crimson with sunset. Soon he would raise the plank to the parapet. Then let them beware! No tinpot order of mice was going to stand against the might of Cluny the Scourge.

Methuselah the gatehouse-keeper stood facing the damaged tapestry in the Great Hall of Redwall. Being too old for active battle service he reasoned that the best way he could serve his order was by putting his fertile brain to work.

Somewhere there had to be at least a clue, a single lead that might tell him where the resting place of Martin the Warrior could be found, or where he could regain possession of the ancient sword for his Abbey. But where?

Every now and then over the years Methuselah had searched through Redwall for Martin and his sword. Now he stepped up his questing activities, alas with no success. Vital clues and answers still eluded him. What he needed was a younger, fresher mind to assist him. What a pity that Matthias could not be found. Now *there* was a young mouse with a head on his shoulders. Long years and much mental strain had taken their toll on the ancient mouse. Wearily he swayed on his feet and, putting out a paw to steady himself, he touched the wall – the exact patch of stone over which Martin's likeness had once hung.

Methuselah gave a sigh of satisfaction and allowed a small smile to creep across his features. His search had not been in vain. Beneath his paw there was writing carved into the dust-covered wall.

BOOK TWO

The Quest

1

Matthias came awake slowly. He blinked, yawned, and stretched his body luxuriously. The sun was setting, turning the little stream into a flow of molten red and gold tinged with deep shadow. He lay calm, savouring the peace and quiet of the woodland summer evening.

Reality struck him like a thunderbolt. He sprang to his feet, instantly forgetting the beauty that surrounded him. Lying there snoring and sleeping like a lazy little idiot, and all the while Redwall Abbey and his friends were under attack!

Furious with himself, Matthias strode off angrily into the darkening trees. He could find no words strong enough to express his self-contempt. It was not until he had blundered and crashed along his way for some time, wildly upbraiding himself, that he calmed down with the realization that he was well and truly lost. No tree, path or landmark looked remotely familiar. He despaired of ever seeing Redwall again. Night closed in on the small mouse wandering alone in the depths of Mossflower Woods. Strange, imaginary shapes flitted about in the gloom;

eerie cries pierced the still air; trees and bushes reached out their branches to catch and scratch like living things with claws.

Trembling, Matthias took refuge in an old beech trunk that had once been riven by lightning. Gradually he became critical of himself again: the great warrior, frightened of the dark like a baby churchmouse. From somewhere overhead he heard a scratching noise. Summoning up all his courage he banished his fears. Drawing Shadow's dagger he stepped out into the open, calling aloud in what he hoped was a gruff voice.

'Who's doing all that scratching and scraping? Come out and show yourself if you are a friend. But if it's a rat out there, then you'd best start running, otherwise you'll have to deal with me, Matthias the warrior of Redwall.'

Having spoken his piece Matthias felt his confidence surge back. He stood tense and alert. However, he received no answer, save the mocking echo of his own voice ringing back at him through the dark woodlands.

A slight noise at his back caused Matthias to wheel about with the dagger upraised. He found himself confronted by a baby red squirrel. It gazed up at him curiously, sucking noisily on its paw. Matthias practically dropped the dagger through laughing so much. So, this was the nameless terror that stalked the night?

The tiny creature continued sucking its paw, shifting from foot to foot, its bushy tail curled up over the small back, higher than the tips of its ears.

Matthias stooped, he spoke gently for fear of frightening the infant. 'Hello there. My name's Matthias. What's yours?'

The baby squirrel continued sucking on its paw.

'Do your mummy and daddy know you are out?'

It nodded its head.

'Are you lost, little one?'

It shook its head.

'Do you talk?'

It shook its head.

'Do you often wander about like this at night?'

It nodded.

Matthias smiled disarmingly. He threw his paws open wide. '*I'm* lost!' he said.

The paw-sucking continued without comment.

'I come from Redwall Abbey.'

Suck, suck, suck.

'Do you know where that is?'

The baby squirrel nodded.

Matthias was overjoyed. 'Oh my little friend, please could you show me the way?' he asked.

It nodded.

'Thank you very much.'

The tiny squirrel hopped and shuffled a short way into the woods. Turning to Matthias, it took its paw from its mouth and beckoned him to follow. He needed no second urging.

Suck, suck, suck.

'Well at least,' Matthias thought aloud, 'if I lose sight of this fellow I'll be able to hear him.'

The baby squirrel smiled . . . and nodded . . . and sucked.

2

Abbot Mortimer sat in the grass of the Abbey cloisters. All around him the defenders who had been sent down from the wall lay in slumber. Not knowing when the rats were going to stop fighting, and realizing that they might not, the kindly Abbot advised those who had been relieved to try and get some sleep.

Methuselah came shuffling up. With a sigh and a groan he sat down on the grass alongside his Abbot who greeted him courteously.

'Good evening, Brother Methuselah.'

The old gatehouse-keeper adjusted his spectacles and sniffed the air. 'And a good evening to you, Father Abbot. How goes the battle against the rats?'

The Abbot folded his paws within his wide sleeves. 'It goes well for us, old one, though how I can say that anything goes well which causes death and injury to living creatures is beyond me. We live in strange times, my friend.'

Methuselah grinned and wrinkled his nose. 'But still, it goes well.'

'Indeed it does. But why do you smile, Methuselah?

132

What secret are you keeping from me?'

'Ah, Father Abbot, you read me like a book. I do have a secret, but trust me, all will be made known to you in the fullness of time.'

The Abbot shrugged. 'No doubt it will. But please make it soon. We are not getting any younger, you and I.'

'Come now,' said Methuselah, 'compared with me, you are still a mouse in your prime. Yet like many others that think my senses are failing, you cannot see half the things that my old eyes observe.'

'How so?' inquired the Abbot.

Methuselah touched a paw to his nose knowingly. 'For instance, did you notice that there is a southerly breeze tonight? No, I don't suppose you did. Then look at the top of that old elm tree sticking up above the wall. Yes, that one over by the small door. Tell me what you see.'

The Abbot's eyes followed Methuselah's paw until he saw the tree in question. He studied it for a moment, then turned to the old mouse. 'I see the top of an old elm tree growing out in the woods. But what is unusual about that?'

Methuselah shook his head reprovingly. 'He still cannot see. Dear me! If the breeze is blowing from the south, then the elm tree would move its leaves and branches in a northerly direction as it has always done. But that particular tree is choosing to disobey nature. It is swaying from east to west. This can mean only one thing. Somebody is using that tree for a purpose. At least, that is what I think. Do you agree?'

Without replying or showing any sign of alarm whatsoever, the Abbot arose. Walking calmly over to the gatehouse wall, he beckoned silently to Constance. The badger descended the steps. She held a whispered conference with the Abbot, nodding in the direction of the elm. Less than a minute later, Constance, accompanied by

133

Winifred the otter, Ambrose Spike and a few others, padded carefully along the top of the wall, taking great pains not to be seen.

On the woodland side, Cluny whispered commands to his followers as they pushed the plank towards the wall from their perch in the elm tree. 'Steady now, Cheesethief you moron. Keep your end up! Keep it going upwards, not down!'

Cheesethief struggled to obey. It was all right for the Chief, sitting back there giving out his orders. He didn't have to balance with one claw while pushing a silly plank about with the other. Cheesethief slipped. With a squeak of dismay he let go of the plank. It clattered against a branch.

Fortunately, Scragg the weasel was on the alert. He caught the end of the plank, steadying it. Cheesethief regained his balance and clung miserably to his perch as Cluny hissed in rage at him.

'Clown! Bungling buffoon! Get out of the way! Shift your fat idle carcass and let Scragg take over.'

Burning with resentment, Cheesethief was shoved unceremoniously aside. Cluny aimed a kick at him as the efficient weasel took his place. 'You just sit there and be still,' Cluny snarled. 'And try not to make enough noise to waken the entire Abbey.'

Scragg moved with skill and economy, issuing quiet confident directions to the others. 'Up a bit, left a touch, take it forward steady now, good, hold it.'

The long plank snaked out and upwards, coming to rest gently but firmly on the parapet edge. Scragg saluted Cluny. 'Plank in position and ready, Chief.'

Cheesethief shot Scragg a venomous glance.

Cluny climbed on to the plank and tested it. The improvised bridge wobbled and sprang a bit, but it held.

Cluny turned to the raiding party. 'I'll go first. We'd better have only one at a time on the plank. When I'm on the parapet I'll steady the other end. Scragg, you come next. The rest of you follow.'

Cluny held on to branches for as long as he could. Soon he was out on the middle of the plank with nothing to steady him. Trying hard not to glance downwards at the dizzying drop, he inched his way up the plank, towards the wall.

Cluny was almost in reach of his goal when Constance appeared on the parapet. She gave the plank a mighty kick, sending it off into space!

With a shout of dismay Cluny plunged earthwards, snapping branches as he went. Winifred fired off a pebble from her sling, knocking a ferret clean out of his perch into empty space. Scragg still held one end of the plank. He leaned precariously out from the elm to see where Cluny fell.

Seizing his opportunity for revenge, Cheesethief shoved Scragg hard in the back. The weasel dropped like a stone with the plank on top of him. Cluny's followers were kicking at each other and screaming as they tried to clamber down from the high elm branches.

Leaning across the parapet, Constance and her friends watched the panic-stricken animals descending. Winifred the otter managed to speed up the retreat with a few well-aimed stones from her sling. The defenders viewed their work with grim satisfaction.

Ambrose Spike squinted short-sightedly down at the darkened woodland floor. He tried to assess the casualties.

'How many did we get?' he inquired.

'Hard to tell in this light,' replied Winifred. 'But I'd swear that was Cluny Constance tipped off the plank.'

The badger's brow creased. She shot a quizzical glance at the otter. 'So you saw him too? I'm glad you did. I thought I was seeing double for a moment back there. How could Cluny be in two places at once? I'm sure I saw him standing in the meadow not ten minutes ago.'

Winifred shrugged. 'Well let's just hope that it was Cluny. Personally, I'd like to think that he's lying somewhere down there now, dead as a doornail.'

Constance peered downwards. 'Difficult to say, really. There seem to be around half a dozen or so laid out down there. Can't tell for sure; too much shadow and darkness. Still, I don't think any creature could survive a fall from this height.'

'Maybe we'd better go and see,' suggested Ambrose.

The defenders looked towards Constance.

'Maybe not,' said the badger thoughtfully. 'No, I don't like it. It suddenly strikes me that this could be a diversionary tactic to draw us away from the gatehouse wall. If it was Cluny who fell from the plank, all well and good; but if it wasn't, then he's still around the front. It won't serve any useful purpose counting dead bodies. Let's get back to the main action.'

Led by Constance, the defenders filed hurriedly off.

Cheesethief slunk cautiously out of the undergrowth. It was safe to move now; the woodlanders had gone from the parapet. Behind him, limping and complaining, came the survivors of the ill-fated raiding party. Cheesethief ignored them as he moved among the bodies that had fallen from the high branches: four rats, a ferret, and one weasel. Three of the rats and the ferret were dead. They lay where they had fallen, their limbs in grotesque positions. The survivors immediately pounced upon the bodies of their fallen comrades, plundering weapons and objects of clothing that they had coveted. Cheesethief stood riveted by the single eye.

Cluny was alive!

Beneath the plank Scragg stirred and groaned. Amazingly, he too had survived.

Cheesethief sprang into action, surprised that Scragg still lived but fatalistically accepting that nothing could kill Cluny. 'Quick, get that plank over here, you lot. We've got to get the Chief out of here.'

Using the plank as an improvised stretcher they carefully lifted Cluny on to it. Cheesethief knew Cluny was watching him. Tenderly he lifted the dangling tail and arranged it gently alongside his leader. 'Try not to move, Chief. Lie still, we'll soon get you back to camp.'

The stretcher-bearers moved off slowly through the woods. Cheesethief avoided Cluny's eye. An idea was taking form in his mind. He sniffed piteously, wiping an imaginary tear from his cheek.

'Poor old Scragg! What a good weasel! I think he's still alive. Listen, you lot: carry on and get the Chief home safely, I'll double back and see if I can help Scragg.'

Cheesethief sniggered to himself as the survivors disappeared into the night, carrying Cluny on the plank.

Matthias followed the baby squirrel through bramble and bush. Whenever he tried to communicate, all that he received was a nod or a shake of the tiny creature's head. They had been travelling for quite a long time. As the pale fingers of dawn crept across the sky Matthias was beginning to doubt that his companion knew the way.

Then, suddenly the little fellow pointed to the east with his paw. In the distance Matthias could make out the shape of the Abbey.

'There's no place like home,' he said thankfully. 'What a splendid pathfinder you are, my friend.'

Still sucking his paw, the small squirrel smiled shyly. He took hold of Matthias's tail as they went forwards together, the mouse talking animatedly, the squirrel nodding vigorously.

'I'll take you to Friar Hugo's kitchen and see that he gives you the nicest breakfast you've ever had. Now what do you say to that?'

Suck, suck, nod, nod.

When Matthias arrived at the wall he felt like patting the old red sandstone. He turned to his companion. 'This is where I live.'

A noise nearby caused them both to freeze momentarily. It sounded like some creature groaning. Instinctively Matthias and the squirrel ducked down among the ferns. Cautiously, they crept along in the direction of the sounds.

Silently parting the ferns, they gazed in horror at the dreadful scene around the base of the elm tree. Among the dead animals that lay stretched in unnatural attitudes was a badly injured weasel. He was moaning and twitching fitfully.

Before either of the friends could decide what to do, a rat appeared on the scene. They remained motionless.

Cheesethief was in a cheery mood. He hummed happily under his breath as he prodded Scragg with his foot.

'Scragg, wake up. It's me, Cheesethief. Oh come on now, I'm sure you remember me? The stupid one, the rat whose job you were going to take?'

Scragg's eyes were barely open. He groaned in agony.

Cheesethief cocked a mockingly sympathetic ear. 'What's that, Scragg my old mate? Tired, are you? Yes, you must be, lying there like that. Tell you what, I'll help you to go to sleep, shall I?'

The rat placed his foot on the weasel's throat and began

pressing down. Scragg struggled feebly, fighting for breath, unable to stop his tormentor. Cheesethief took malicious pleasure in his revenge. Cruelly he leaned his full weight upon the weasel's rasping throat. 'Hush now. Go to sleep, Scragg. Dream of the command you never had.'

Scragg made one final gurgling whimper and lay still.

Cheesethief slunk off chuckling with satisfaction.

Hidden in the ferns, Matthias and the baby squirrel held their breath in disbelief. They had seen murder committed!

Matthias and the squirrel waited until they were sure the coast was clear. At last they emerged from the ferns, and Matthias, cupping his paws round his mouth, ventured a low halloo up at the wall. There was no reply.

The little squirrel shook his head. He pointed to the floor with his paw in a gesture that Matthias interpreted as, 'Stop here.'

With breathtaking speed and skill, the tiny creature raced up the trunk of the old elm. Reaching the thin branches above the parapet he ran out along one. Using it as a springboard, he bounced nimbly on to the ramparts and vanished, sucking fiercely at his paw.

Matthias had not long to wait before the small door in the wall nearby grated open on its rusty hinges, and Constance peered cautiously out. Seeing Matthias, she ran to greet him, with the little squirrel perched upon her back.

Matthias was not sure what sort of a reception was in store for him. He need not have worried; Constance hugged him, patted his back and shook him by the paw.

The badger forestalled the explanation that was upon the young mouse's lips. She beckoned Matthias inside, shutting the door behind them. 'You can tell us everything later, Matthias. Right now I insist that you come to the main gate. There's something you must see.'

A minute or two later all three were standing on the gatehouse wall, shoulder to shoulder with countless other defenders. Cluny's horde was retreating, back down the road to their camp at Saint Ninian's church. There was a wild cheering from the ranks of the mice and wood-landers.

Cluny was being borne upon the plank in the midst of his army. Redtooth, who was still disguised in the War-lord's battle-armour, had draped a blanket over Cluny to hide him and keep up the masquerade. But nobody was fooled! Both sides of the wall had heard the tale of mis-adventure in all its gory detail. They knew that the strut-ting rat in armour was not Cluny the Scourge.

Redtooth nevertheless strode proudly along. Cluny might not recover. Besides, he revelled in the respect that he received, dressed as he was in such barbaric finery. He knew that it was only borrowed plumage, but he could always hope that the position might become permanent.

On top of the gatehouse ramparts feelings ran high. The Abbot had issued strict orders that no missiles or weaponry be discharged at the enemy in retreat. Amid the cheering there was quite a bit of resentful grumbling.

Why not smash Cluny's army once and for all?

Now they were on the run, this was the proper time to consolidate a resounding Redwall victory!

But the good Father Abbot would not hear of it. Like a true gentlemouse he believed in tempering triumph with mercy. The jubilatory sounds died away to an eerie silence as the rats toiled raggedly off down the road, raising a column of dust in the early dawn. Dispirited and battleworn, carrying their fallen leader, the maimed and wounded hobbled painfully along at the rear, the bitter ashes of vanquishment and defeat mingling with the dust from their stumbling vanguard.

Even the silent victors began to realize that victory came at a high price. Freshly dug graves and a crowded infirmary bore silent witness to the reality of war.

Matthias felt a gentle paw intertwining with his own. It was Cornflower. Relief showed in her eyes and her voice.

'Oh Matthias, thank goodness you are back safe! It was dreadful, not knowing where you were or what had become of you. I thought you'd never come back.'

'I'm like an old bad penny, I always come back,' Matthias whispered.

'Oh, by the way, how is your father?'

Cornflower brightened up. 'He's made a marvellous recovery. He refused to lie in bed and has been up on the wall helping out. You can't keep a good Fieldmouse down, my dad always says.'

Matthias barely had time to bid Cornflower a hasty goodbye before he was ushered off to the Abbot's room for an early morning conference. He took his seat and looked around the table. There were Constance, Ambrose, Winifred, Foremole, the Abbot, and also his friend the baby squirrel, who stood on a stool, dipping his paw into a bowl of milk and honey, sucking it with noisy enjoyment.

'I think that you would have been in trouble without Silent Sam here, Matthias,' the Abbot said.

The young mouse nodded. 'I certainly would, Father Abbot. So that's his name? Silent Sam? Well, he certainly lives up to it.'

'Indeed he does,' replied the Abbot. 'His mother and father are old friends of mine. They'll pick up his tracks and be along here later to collect him. Do you know, this little chap hasn't spoken since he was born. I've tried every remedy known to Redwall on him, but none has worked, so he was named Silent Sam. But don't let that fool you, he knows Mossflower Woods like the back of his paw, don't you, Sam?'

The tiny squirrel licked his paw and smiled. He indicated a large circle with it, pointing at himself with his unsticky paw.

Matthias reached over and shook the paw heartily. 'My thanks to you, Silent Sam. You are truly a great pathfinder.'

During the meeting there was much useful information exchanged. Matthias told of the rescue at Saint Ninian's, and his encounter with the strange hare.

'Surely you don't mean Basil Stag Hare?' cried Constance. 'Well, I never! Is that old eccentric still bobbing around? I expect we'll see him turn up with the Vole family around about lunch time. I never knew Basil to miss the chance of a free lunch back in the old days.'

The assembled creatures passed on a vote of thanks to Matthias for his resourcefulness and bravery. Matthias blushed. Then he sat listening intently whilst those who had taken part in the battle recounted all they could remember. In the aftermath of that memorable conflict there was much speculation as to what the future held.

Would Cluny recover from his injuries? Had his horde been so soundly defeated that they had learned their lesson? Or would they be back?

It was the Abbot's opinion that Cluny and his rabble would not bother Redwall again. Their leader's injuries would doubtless prove fatal. This statement was strongly opposed by the others, and Constance was elected to speak for them.

'Cluny is still the prime factor,' said the badger. 'That rat is physically tougher than we could ever imagine. It is only a matter of time before he recovers sufficiently to attack us again.'

Constance pounded upon the table with a heavy paw, emphasizing each word. 'And make no mistake about it, Cluny the Scourge will attack Redwall again. I'd stake my life on it! Think for a moment. If Cluny were to give up the idea of conquering this Abbey, he would lose both face and credibility with the army he commands. Furthermore, and most important of all, word would spread across the land that Cluny was not invincible, that he could be beaten by mice!

'This would mean the end of Cluny as a legend of terror; so you see, when Cluny recovers he will be virtually forced to mount a second assault upon Redwall.'

There was a sober silence around the table.

The Abbot arose. He had arrived at a decision.

'So be it. I have listened to your counsel and opinions, my dear and trusted friends. Although I yearn for peace, I feel that I must base my judgement on your words, which I know to be true. Therefore my power as Abbot, and any assistance that I can give are yours for the asking. It is my wish that Constance, Matthias, Winifred, Ambrose, and Foremole take complete command at Redwall in the event of a second invasion. I will concern myself with aiding the injured and feeding the hungry. And now, my friends, I must adjourn this meeting as I have other matters to attend to. Come, Sam. We must wash those sticky little paws before your parents arrive. Oh, and before I forget, Matthias, Brother Methuselah would like to talk with you. He is in the Great Hall.'

3

Cluny the Scourge lay upon his bed, racked with crippling pains. Rat Captains gathered in the corner of the sick room. They sat silent. The terrible injuries would have proved fatal to any other rat on earth, but not to Cluny – a broken arm, a broken leg, numerous cracked ribs, a fractured tail, smashed claws, and other hurts not yet diagnosed.

Redtooth and four of the others might have set upon their leader and finished him off for good.

But the fear of his legendary powers was too strong!

Nobody knew for sure the extent of Cluny's remorseless vitality. Watching him now, the barrel-like chest heaving up and down, the still-strong tail swishing spasmodically, Redtooth marvelled at Cluny's strength. He was not even sure if Cluny was shamming, pretending that his injuries were severe merely as some kind of test or trap that he had set for his Captains.

The twelve sentry rats were locked in the hut they had been set to guard. It was now repaired. They had been soundly flogged for letting the Vole family escape. As a further punishment for concocting lies about a big hare and a young mouse, Redtooth ordered that the twelve be starved until further notice. He had been lenient with them. Cluny would have sentenced them to death and personally killed them with his bare claws.

Outside in the churchyard the leaderless horde did absolutely nothing to reorganize. Sitting about licking their wounds and waiting for the Chief to recover seemed to be the order of the day.

Again the mouse warrior, armed with his ancient sword, returned to haunt Cluny's fevered dreams.

Once more he was falling from the plank on the Abbey wall, falling, falling. Below him waited spectral figures: Ragear, with a blue face bloated to many times its normal size; a rat-skeleton dressed in Cluny's own battle armour; a huge hare with enormous feet, and a thick-bodied, venomous-looking banded snake. He tried to twist away from them as he fell, but, however much he swerved and tried to change direction, Cluny had only to look down and see the fierce-eyed warrior mouse – waiting, always waiting, the sword held point upward for him to be impaled upon. Cluny tried to cry out, but not a sound came; it was as though his throat were being squeezed tightly.

He felt the sharp sword pierce his chest.

Bong!

Once more the sound of the Joseph Bell tolling out across the fields from Redwall wakened the Warlord. Fangburn, who was trying to extract a piece of elm branch from his Chief's chest, leapt backwards in fright as Cluny's eye snapped open inches from his own.

'Get away from me,' Cluny rasped.

Fangburn retreated, mumbling excuses. Cluny eyed him suspiciously – he didn't trust any of them.

'If you really want to help, go and get hold of some of

145

those new recruits who lived locally and bring them here to me,' he gasped.

Within minutes Fangburn had assembled a band of the recruits around Cluny's bed.

'Where's Scragg the weasel?' Cluny growled.

Cheesethief stepped forward, wiping imaginary tears from his face with the back of a filthy claw. 'Don't you remember, Chief? He fell out of the big tree. After I'd taken care of you I went back for him, but when I got to him the poor weasel was dead. What a good, kind—'

'Ah, shut your moaning face,' said Cluny irritably. 'If he's dead, then that's that. Here, you recruits, come closer and listen to me.'

Apprehensively the little group shuffled forwards. Cluny raised himself slightly on one elbow.

'Do any of you know where a healer can be found? I don't mean one like those mice. I need a creature that knows the old ways, a gypsy, one who can cure anything for the right price.'

Killconey the ferret bowed elaborately. 'Ah, 'tis your lucky day, yer honour, for don't I know the very vixen.'

'Foxes?' echoed Cluny.

'Aye, foxes, sir,' the ferret replied. 'Didn't me ould mother always used to say, "there's nothing like a fox to fix"? There's a whole tribe of 'em livin' across the meadow, sir. Old Sela the vixen is the girl you'll be wanting, her and her son Chickenhound. They'll fix you up as right as rain if there's something in it for them. Does yer honour want me to fetch them?'

Slowly Cluny's tail wound itself about the ferret's neck, drawing him in close.

'Get them,' Cluny said hoarsely. 'Find the foxes and bring them here to me.'

Killconey's throat bulged as he tried nervously to

swallow. 'Glug! I will indeed, if you'll just let go of this pore ould ferret's neck, sir, I'll go as fast as if the divvil himself was chasin' me. You lay back now and rest your noble self, sir.'

Cluny released the ferret and lay back with an agonized sigh. Now was the time to think and plan ahead. Next time would be different.

'Redtooth,' he called. 'Take some soldiers and scout around. See if you can find a great hard timber, a big log or tree trunk, something that will serve as a battering ram.'

The mice might have won a battle, but Cluny had not yet lost the war, by the claws of hellthunder!

Those Abbey mice were going to pay with blood for what they had done to Cluny the Scourge.

4

Brother Methuselah was busy with a small brush and a pot of black ink. As he brushed the dust of ages from each letter on the wall, he filled it in with ink. This would make it easier to read the message that had been graven underneath the tapestry.

'Ah, Matthias, there you are,' Methuselah squeaked.

He blinked over the top of his glasses at the young mouse. 'Look, this is something I want you to see. Quite by accident I discovered this writing beneath where Martin's picture once hung.'

Matthias was full of unconcealed excitement.

'What does it say, Brother Methuselah?' he cried.

The old gatehouse-keeper sneezed as he brushed more dust from the lettering on the wall. 'All in good time, young mouse! Here, make yourself useful. You brush the dust off the words while I ink them in. Between us we'll soon get it done.'

Matthias set to work with an energetic goodwill. He scrubbed vigorously, sending up clouds of dust. Between sneezes Methuselah hurried to keep pace with him.

One hour later they both sat on the stone floor, drinking October ale to quench the dust whilst they admired their handiwork.

'It's written in the old hand,' said Methuselah, 'but I can read it clear enough.'

Matthias jostled him boisterously. 'What does it say, old one? Hurry up and read it to me.'

'Patience, you young scallywag,' chided the ancient mouse. 'Be quiet and listen. It takes the form of a poem:

Who says that I am dead
Knows nought at all.
I – am that is,
Two mice within Redwall.
The Warrior sleeps
'Twixt Hall and Cavern Hole.
I – am that is,
Take on my mighty role.
Look for the sword
In moonlight streaming forth,
At night, when day's first hour
Reflects the North.
From o'er the threshold
Seek and you will see:
I – am that is,
My sword will wield for me.'

Matthias blinked and scratched his head. He looked at Methuselah. 'Well, what did all that mean? It's a riddle to me.'

'Precisely,' said the old mouse. 'It is indeed a riddle, but don't worry, Matthias, we will solve it together. I have sent for food and drink. You and I will not move from here until we have the answer.'

Shortly afterwards, Cornflower arrived bearing a tray of breakfast for them both: nutbread, salad, milk, and some of Friar Hugo's special quince pie. She was about to strike up a conversation with Matthias when Methuselah sent her packing.

'Shoo! Away with you, little fieldmouse. I need Matthias with a clear brain to help me solve an important problem, so run along.'

Cornflower winked at Matthias, shook her head at Methuselah and walked off with mock dignity, her nose high in the air. Matthias watched her go until Methuselah tweaked his ear. 'Pay attention now, young mouse. We must study this bit by bit. Let's take the first two lines:

> "Who says that I am dead
> Knows nought at all!" '

Matthias waved a paw. His mouth filled with salad, he mumbled, 'But we know that Martin is dead.'

Methuselah took a sip of milk, pulled a wry face and reached for his October ale. 'Ah but, if we suppose that he is dead, then the words tell us we know nothing at all. So, let us assume that he is alive.'

'What? Do you mean Martin, alive and walking about?' said Matthias. 'We'd recognize him! Unless, that is, he was disguised as someone else.'

The old gatehouse-keeper choked, spluttering ale over his habit. 'Good grief! I never looked at it that way. Very good, young one. Maybe the answer is in the next two lines. What do they say?

> "I – am that is,
> Two mice within Redwall!" '

Matthias repeated the words, but he could make no sense of them. ' "I – am that is". What is? "Two mice within Redwall." Hmm, two mice it tells of.'

'Of two mice in one,' replied Methuselah.

They sat silent awhile, both racking their brains. Matthias mentioned something that was bothering him as he looked at the graven lines. 'What I cannot understand is that sort of dash. Look: "*I – am that is*". Do you see, there is a small dash between the words "I" and "am". In fact the same dash occurs three times throughout the rhyme: here, here and here.' Matthias pointed.

Methuselah adjusted his glasses and peered closely. 'Yes. You may have something there. It could be the key to the whole thing . . . "*I – am that is*". Let's say that the dash separates the line, so that we will look at the last three words, "*am that is*". Suppose we took that part out, then it would read, "*I, two mice within Redwall*".'

Matthias shook his head. 'What do you make of that?'

'Complete nonsense,' replied the old mouse. 'Let's stick with, "*am that is*".'

'Sounds all mixed up to me,' Matthias grumbled.

Methuselah looked up sharply. 'Say that again.'

'Say what again?'

'You mean that it sounds all mixed up to me?'

Methuselah executed a little jig of delight. He patted the wall with his paw, shouting, 'That's it! That's it! Why couldn't I see that? It's all mixed up, of course!'

The old mouse took a great draught of ale. Cackling with glee, he pointed a paw at Matthias. 'I know something that you don't know . . . "*am that is*" . . . Matthias.'

The young mouse frowned. So, the old one had finally cracked. He was in his second infancy.

'Methuselah,' he said kindly, 'hadn't you better lie down awhile?'

But the old gatehouse-keeper kept pointing. He began to chant.

> '*Matthias, I that am,*
> *Matthias, you that are.*'

The young mouse stood tapping his tail in exasperation.

'I wish you'd tell me what you're so excited about,' he said severely.

Methuselah wiped tears of laughter from his eyes as he explained. 'When you said it was all mixed up, that got me thinking. Martin was talking of two mice, himself and another. Ergo, Martin is represented by the word "i". The other mouse is "*am that is*" all mixed up. Now do you see?'

Matthias leaned against the wall. 'I'm afraid I don't follow you.'

'Oh, you young booby,' Methuselah giggled. 'I mixed the letters up and re-arranged them. It's your own name . . . "*am that is*" . . . Matthias.'

'Are you sure?' said Matthias in astonishment.

'Of course I'm sure,' replied Methuselah. 'It couldn't mean anything else! Your name has eight letters in it. So has "*am that is*". An M, two A's, two T's, an H, an I and an S. Whichever way you look at it, Matthias or "*am that is*", it comes out the same.'

'Methuselah, do you realize what this means?'

The old mouse sat down beside him, nodding gravely. 'Oh yes, indeed I do. It means that Martin somehow knew that one day he would live on through you.'

Matthias was staggered. 'He knew about me! Martin the Warrior knew my name! Can you imagine that.'

The enormity of it overwhelmed them both. For several minutes they sat, no word passing between them. Suddenly Matthias leapt to his feet. 'Right, let's get on with it. Look at these lines:

> "*The warrior sleeps*
> '*Twixt Hall and Cavern Hole.*
> *I – am that is,*
> *Take on my mighty role.*" '

'Well, the last two lines are pretty clear,' said Methuselah. 'They mean that Martin, carrying on through you, has a great task to perform.'

'What about the first two lines?' Matthias said. 'They seem fairly obvious, too. Between Great Hall and Cavern Hole there is a flight of stairs. Come on, old mouse.'

In spite of his advanced years, Methuselah gripped Matthias's paw and ran so fast that the younger mouse had difficulty in keeping up.

Between Great Hall and Cavern Hole there were seven stone steps. The problem was, which one held the answer?

'Thinking caps on again,' said the old mouse. 'Let's make a close inspection of these steps.'

Together they examined the stone steps minutely, going back over each one several times. Matthias sat on the bottom step. He shrugged. 'They appear to be seven, ordinary, broad stone steps; nothing special; quite the same as any other set of stairs in the Abbey, wouldn't you say?'

Methuselah was forced to agree. After sitting awhile and letting his eyes roam about, Matthias remarked, 'I've just noticed something. The name of our Abbey is carved into the wall as you go up the steps on the left-hand side, and also as you descend on the right-hand wall. It reads "Redwall", either way.'

Methuselah walked up and down the steps, testing what Matthias had said. 'Yes, so it does. Do you see that each letter is one step's width? Hmmm. Seven letters for seven steps. Surely that must be some kind of a hint?'

Again the two friends sat to ponder the mystery. This time it was Matthias's turn to become excited and point a paw at his companion.

'I know something *you* don't know.'

Methuselah pursed his lips in annoyance. 'You know,

Matthias, for a mouse that claims affinity with Martin the Warrior, you can be singularly foolish sometimes.'

'Huh. No more foolish than you were when you were saying the same thing to me not so long ago,' Matthias retorted.

Methuselah coughed and cleaned his spectacles on his habit. 'Harrumph. Er, yes, well, I apologize. Now please tell me what you have discovered.'

Matthias explained. 'If you place the word "Redwall" running both ways as it does here, you will notice that only one letter occurs in the same place, the letter W. Furthermore, if you were to turn a W upside down it becomes a letter M, which stands for Martin, Matthias, oh, and also for Methuselah, my old friend.'

'Well, curl my whiskers! The young scoundrel has a brain, and it works too. It's got to be the fourth step, the middle one up or down.'

The step in question proved to be as solid and unmoving as its counterparts. Even with their combined strength, the friends could not budge it a fraction.

Matthias wiped sweat from his brow. 'Take a breather, old one. I know who can handle this. The Foremole and his team.'

The moles were not long in arriving. They gathered around the step, sniffing and scratching. The Foremole exercised his authority, clearing them out of his way.

'Yurr moles, get outten loight. Let'n um dog at bone thurr.'

Foremole paced the length of the step then shuffled sideways over it. He tapped it with his great digging claws. He sniffed it, licked it, and rubbed it with his velvet head.

'Ummm, worra you'm gennelbeast know abouten this yurr step?' he asked.

Together they related all the information to the attentive Foremole. He blinked short-sightedly as he ruminated.

'Arr, fourth'n uppards, same down'ards. Yurr, Walt, 'ark, Doby. B'aint that same as your grandmum do foind when she'm rooten about olden toim fortications?'

'What's he saying?' whispered Matthias.

Methuselah translated the curious mole dialect. 'Foremole said, the fourth step upwards is the same as the fourth step down, that much we already know. Then he consulted the two mole brothers, Walt and Doby. It seems the step is the same as one found by their grandmother when she was exploring an old-fashioned castle or fortification. Moles are very sensible creatures, you know, and I think they have the answer to our problem.'

'Good old Foremole,' said Matthias.

'Hush. Let's hear what Walt and Doby have to say,' whispered Methuselah.

The two mole brothers respectfully tugged their noses to the Foremole before answering:

'Urr, that be true, zurr.'

'Our grandmum she'm foind lots o' them.'

'Aye, that she do. Never diggen or breaken, just turn 'em after dustin'.'

Methuselah interpreted to Matthias. 'Apparently their grandmother was somewhat of an authority on steps such as these. The clever old mole would neither dig nor break them. Evidently she could turn the step over, once she had brushed it.'

Matthias addressed the Foremole courteously. 'Excuse me, sir, but do you know how to deal with this step now? If you do, then my friend and I would be only too willing to help you.'

Foremole smiled, his whole face almost vanishing into dark velvet wrinkles. He clapped Matthias on the shoulder in a chummy way. The young mouse was amazed at the weight and strength of Foremole's paw. He was glad that it was a friendly pat.

Foremole chuckled deeply. 'Nay nay, bless your li'l 'eart, Mattwise, you'n owd Methuselam be but mouses, best leave 'er to Foremole, oi'll deal with'n.'

'He says he can cope adequately without either of us,' said Methuselah.

The Foremole produced a thick, fine-haired handbrush from his tunnelling kit. Bending close, he brushed furiously at the upper and lower insteps of the fourth stone. As he swept, he snuffled and blew, following the path of his brush. It soon became apparent that the stone had been cunningly jointed. The dust came away to reveal a continuous hairline crack which ran around the edges of the step.

Next Foremole rummaged in his kit and came up with a tin of grease and a strong thin bar, one end of which was flattened like a spatula. Smearing the grease liberally on top of the third step, Foremole inserted the flat metal tip against the base of the fifth step. He dealt the blunt end of the bar a smart blow, setting it firmly into the crack. With a swift movement he levered the fourth step an inch forward, exposing a long dark gap.

With a grunt of satisfaction Foremole called out to his team, 'Yurr moles, gather round an' set your diggin claws in um crack.'

The mole team dug their claws into the gap, chanting together as they heaved with a will.

'Hurr she come, if'n you please,
Movin' bowlder, sloid on grease.'

To the astonishment of the watching mice, the step slid smoothly outwards on the greased stone. It turned completely over to reveal a dark opening with a downward flight of stairs running off into the blackness below.

5

Old Sela the vixen muttered her charms and spells in a singsong voice. Sometimes she did a hopping little dance around the sick-bed. Cluny was not fooled!

He watched as the fox sprinkled 'magic herbs' on the pillow, reciting another strange spell as she did so.

The old fraud, Cluny thought. All that mumbo-jumbo and magic nonsense. Why does she need it when she knows that she's a perfectly good doctor?

Sela had placed herb poultices and healing salves on all the Warlord's wounds. After bandaging them neatly she had administered a potion that would deaden the pain and induce sleep.

Cluny was satisfied. He had been treated by healers many times before. Sela was the best; all the added muttering, dancing and trickery was done merely to enhance her reputation, to pull the wool over the eyes of stupid ignorant creatures.

She may be a fox, but she'll never outfox me, Cluny thought to himself. Sela had assured him that with three weeks' rest, combined with her healing skills, he would be fighting fit once more.

'Three weeks!' At first the rat leader had raged and

swore. He had never been out of action that long in all his life. But secretly he knew that the fox was right. Without her, Cluny would have been dead or permanently crippled.

Like all of her kind, Sela was a slippery character. What did she expect to gain from all this?

Loot and plunder from Redwall!

Sela had never been allowed past the Abbey gates. She was certain that if Cluny's army overran Redwall, there would be enough treasure to keep even the greediest creature happy for life.

Now, as the potions took effect, Cluny felt himself drifting off to sleep, lulled by the ceaseless chantings and murmurings of Old Sela. He would have come awake like a scorched tiger had he known what the fox was actually up to!

Old Sela had lived on her wits for many years. She was a counterspy by nature – in any dispute or conflict she invariably sold secrets to both sides. It was a dangerous game, but one that she had played well thus far. Her crafty, golden eyes had not been idle for a second since entering Cluny's camp.

Sela knew exactly how many rats, weasels, stoats and ferrets were able-bodied enough for combat. Also, she had seen the working party gnawing industriously at the base of a tall poplar. If that wasn't going to be used as a battering ram then Sela was a trout, and by her own diagnosis of three weeks, she knew to the day when the date of the next attack on Redwall would be.

The vixen watched Cluny's eyes closing under the influence of her medicine. These warlords were all the same – they never gave credit for brains to anyone except themselves. There the big oaf was, snoring like a fox cub in his earth on a winter's night.

She turned to the armed rats who guarded the sick

room. She issued orders to a confidential whisper, 'I want no noise, please. Your Chief must have complete rest. Don't let him exert himself when he wakes. Now you'll have to excuse me.'

She made her way to the door. Fangburn and Redtooth stood barring it.

'Where do you think you are off to, fox?'

Sela licked her lips. She tried to look kindly but earnest. 'Actually I was going back to my den to replenish my stock of herbs, that's if you wish me to treat your leader properly, of course.'

Redtooth prodded her with a spear. 'Cluny gave strict orders that you must stay here until he's better.'

The sly fox blustered. 'But my good rats, surely you must realize that I can do nothing without my stock of herbs? Now please let me pass.'

Fangburn shoved her roughly. 'Sit down. You're not going anywhere.'

Sela seated herself. Her mind was racing. 'Er, then at least let me go out into the churchyard. I've got to have some fresh air. Besides, I can tell my young assistant what herbs I require and he can fetch them for me.'

Redtooth was not convinced. 'But the Chief said you'd got to stay here.'

Sela smiled inwardly. She had them where she wanted them now.

She put on a serious expression, shaking her head gravely. 'Then you had better let me have your names. That way I can tell Cluny when he awakes full of pain with festering wounds. No doubt he'll want to know who it was stopped me trying to cure him.'

This crafty statement did the trick. After a few whispered words between the two rats, Redtooth turned to Sela. 'Listen, fox, you can go out into the churchyard and tell your assistant to run this errand, but Fangburn here

159

will be right beside you with a cutlass in your ribs. One false move out of you, and you'll be a dead healer. Is that clear?'

Sela smiled ingratiatingly. 'By all means. Let your friend come along. I have nothing to hide.'

Out in the churchyard Chickenhound, who was the son of Sela, sat sunning himself upon a tombstone.

Fangburn did not see the secret wink that passed between the two foxes. Chickenhound was as devious as his mother in matters of espionage. His face was the picture of blank innocence as he listened to Sela's instructions.

'Now listen carefully, my son. We have a very sick rat inside that church. He is in urgent need of my special remedies. I want you to run as quickly as you can back to our den. Bring me back some snakewort, cuckoo spit, a medium eelskin, three fine strips of willow bark . . . oh, there's so much to remember, I'd better write it all down for you.'

Sela turned to Fangburn. 'Do you carry any writing materials with you, sir?'

Fangburn spat scornfully at the fox's feet. 'Are you trying to make fun of me, healer? What d'you think I am? Huh, writing materials! The idea of it!'

Sela smiled disarmingly. 'Ah, I thought not. Sorry, no offence. I'll just make do with some bark and a burnt twig. Where could I obtain such things, please?'

Fangburn pointed sullenly with his cutlass. 'Over there by the cooking fire. Be quick about it.'

A few minutes later Sela had presented Chickenhound with a scroll of bark that she had written upon.

'There, that should do it. Now hurry along, my son. Don't stop for anything on the way. Isn't that right, Captain?'

Fangburn puffed out his chest, proud that the fox knew his rank. He pointed a claw at Chickenhound.

'You listen to what your mother tells you, young feller. Get back here with the stuff on that list as soon as possible. Be off with you now.'

The young fox took off like a rocket. Fangburn leaned on his cutlass. 'That's the way to deal with young uns.'

Sela looked at him admiringly. 'Indeed it is, sir. He never goes that fast for me. It's obvious that you've got an air of command about you.'

Fangburn coloured slightly. This vixen wasn't such a bad creature after all. He gestured modestly to the church with his cutlass. 'Er, I think it's time we went back inside. Orders, you know!'

'Oh quite. Can't have you getting in trouble, can we?' said Sela in her best smarmy tone.

As soon as he was out of sight of Cluny's stronghold, Chickenhound slowed to a leisurely walk. He unfastened the bark scroll and read his mother's message.

> To the Abbot of Redwall Abbey
> I know exactly when, where, and how the hordes of Cluny will attack your Abbey. What price will you give me for this important information?
> > Sela the Vixen

Chickenhound sniggered noisily. He knew precisely what his mother required him to do. He recalled Sela's favourite saying: 'I've sold hens their own eggs back and stolen the whiskers from farmyard dogs.' The young fox ambled along the dusty road to Redwall, the hedgerows echoing with the sound of his sly chuckles.

6

Cornflower was having a very busy day.

Having delivered food to Matthias and Methuselah, she went out on the ramparts accompanied by her helpers. They fed the sentries and took back all the dishes. Next she found herself making an extra two trays of food up for Silent Sam's parents. The two squirrels thanked her politely and set to with an appetite. Little Sam stood watching them, sucking his paw. Cornflower had a special soft spot for the baby squirrel; she made up a tray for him too. She had no sooner finished than Constance called to ask a favour of her. Would she mind making up another four trays? Three for the Vole family who had just returned, and an extra large one for Basil Stag Hare. Cornflower cheerfully obliged.

Standing by, her eyes grew wide with amazement. She had never seen anyone shift such vast amounts of food, not even Constance or Ambrose Spike. They were huge eaters, but mere amateurs compared with Basil Stag Hare.

Basil wiped his mouth daintily on a napkin. He had impeccable manners to match his insatiable appetite. He gushed forth praise for the Abbey victuals. 'Oh excellent! Absolutely top hole! D'you know, I'd forgotten how good the old tiffin at Redwall could be. I say, m'dear, would you mind refreshing an old bachelor hare's memory? Another tankard of that fine October ale, and perhaps one more portion of your very good summer salad. Ah, and I think I could manage another few slices of Friar Hugo's quince pie. Superb! Ahem, don't forget the goatsmilk cheese with hazelnuts. I'm very partial to that. Cut along now, you little charmer. My word, what an attractive young fieldmouse gel.'

Cornflower sent two of her helpers. They had to go the long way around to reach the kitchens. Abbot Mortimer had declared the Great Hall and Cavern Hole out of bounds to all creatures, with the exception of those helping Matthias and Methuselah.

Below the newly-discovered steps, a pair of lanterns cast pools of golden light into the inky blackness. The two mice made their way gingerly down the secret staircase. The moles stayed outside, ready to help if they were needed further.

The air was chilly but dry. Deeper and deeper the two friends went until the steps ended at the beginning of a downward-winding corridor. It had been neatly dug and shored up with wooden supports. Matthias suppressed a shudder. How long had it been since any creature trod this silent musty passage? He brushed away cobwebs which disintegrated at the touch of a paw. Methuselah held on to his habit. Now they turned left, now right, then another left turn, left again, then right. Methuselah's voice sounded hollow and eerie. 'The passage was probably dug like this to give it extra strength. Have you noticed, Matthias? We seem to be going downwards still.'

'Yes, we must be nearly underneath the Abbey foundations,' Matthias replied.

The friends pressed onwards. They could not estimate how long they had been following the course of this ancient, winding corridor. Methuselah had ventured slightly ahead. Now he halted.

'Aha, this looks like the end of the line,' he squeaked.

It was a door.

Together they inspected it. Built of stout timber, banded with iron, beset with florin spikes, the door did not appear to be locked. Yet it would not budge.

Matthias held his lantern high. 'Look, there's some writing on the lintel over the door.'

Methuselah read it aloud:

'The same as the steps 'twixt the Hall,
Remember and look to the centre.
My password again is Redwall,
Am that is, you alone are to enter.'

The old mouse did not hide his disappointment. 'Humph! After all the help and assistance that I've given, countless hours of study and valuable time. Really!'

His words fell upon deaf ears. Matthias was already counting the florin spikes that were driven into the door.

Methuselah feigned indifference, but his natural curiosity soon overcame any chagrin he felt at not being allowed to pass the doorway.

'Need any help, young mouse?'

'Forty-two, forty-three, hush! Can't you see I'm trying to count?' came the reply.

The old gatehouse-keeper put on his glasses. 'Well, have you solved the riddle all by yourself?'

Matthias winked at his companion. 'Yes. At least I hope I have. There are three clues in the rhyme you see, the same as the steps. Look to the centre, and the password is Redwall. Now, we must remember that Redwall

164

has seven letters. If you look at these old-fashioned nails—'

'Florin spikes,' Methuselah corrected.

Matthias continued, 'Yes, if you look at these florin spikes, you'll find that they are in rows of seven, the same as the number of letters in Redwall. There are seven rows of spikes going from side to side and seven rows from top to bottom, forty-nine spikes in all. Therefore, the twenty-fifth spike up, down, or across is the exact middle spike. The rhyme says, "*look to the centre*". That's this one here.'

As Matthias placed his paw on the spike in question, the door swung creakingly inwards.

Both mice could feel the hairs standing on their backs as the door opened with agonizing slowness.

When it stood fully open, Matthias put his paw around Methuselah's thin shoulders.

'Come on old friend, we go in together,' he said.

'But the rhyme,' Methuselah protested. 'It says that only you may enter.'

Matthias answered in a strange, full voice. He seemed to grow in years and stature. '*I am that is,* old one. Martin is Matthias. As my trusted friend and faithful companion, I say that you may enter with me.'

Methuselah felt himself in the presence of one many times older than he. Lanterns held high, the two mice advanced through the doorway.

It was a small, low-ceilinged chamber. A stone block rested squarely in the centre.

The tomb of Martin the Warrior!

All around the sides of the stone were detailed carvings, depicting scenes from Martin's life: deeds of valour and works of skilful healing. Lying along the top of the stone was a life-sized effigy of the Warrior. He was clothed in the familiar habit of a Redwall mouse, plain, with no trimmings.

Matthias stood reverently, gazing upon the calm features of his own legendary hero in the silence of the small chamber.

Methuselah whispered in his ear. 'He bears an uncanny resemblance to you, young one.'

As the old mouse spoke, the door behind him creaked shut!

Feeling no panic, Matthias turned to look. On the back of the door hung a shield and a sword belt.

The shield was a plain, round steel thing of the type carried by the warriors of old. The years had not dulled its highly-burnished front. As its centre was a letter M.

The sword belt was in pristine condition, soft and as supple as if it had newly come from the tanner's bench; shiny black leather with a hanging tab to carry sword and scabbard; its broad silver buckle gleamed in the lantern light.

Without a word Matthias undid his novice's cord girdle. Handing it to Methuselah, he took down the sword belt and buckled it about his waist. The belt fitted as if it had been made for him. With great care he lifted the shield from the door and tried it on his arm. It had two grips, one below the elbow, the other for the paw to grasp. It felt oddly familiar to Matthias.

There was more writing where the shield had hung upon the back of the door. Methuselah read it:

'By the moonlight, on the hour,
In my threshold space lay me.
Watch the beam reflect my power,
Unite once more my sword with me.
I – am that is, stand true for all.
O warrior mouse, protect Redwall.'

As in a dream, Matthias gave the door a gentle tug. It

opened. By the lantern lights the two mice made their way back from the lonely chamber. Back to the familiar warmth and cheer of Redwall Abbey. Back to the hot June noonday sun.

7

Constance stood on the ramparts. She leaned over the parapet, watching as a young fox approached along the dusty road, bearing a stick with a white rag of truce tied to it.

The big badger was uneasy. She knew this one, a fox from Old Sela's brood. You needed eyes in the back of your head to watch that lot!

'Stop right there and state your business, fox,' Constance called gruffly.

Chickenhound sniggered, but seeing the badger's stern expression, he quickly took control of himself.

'I want to see your Abbot,' he called.

The reply was abrupt. 'Well, you can't!'

The fox waved his flag, squinting up at Constance. 'But I must see the Abbot! I come in peace. I have important information for sale.'

The badger was unmoved. 'I don't care if you've got the rumbling foxtrot, you aren't getting inside this Abbey. If you want to speak to anyone, then speak to me.'

Constance watched the crestfallen fox, then added as an afterthought: 'And if you don't like it, well, you can sling your brush back up the road.'

Chickenhound was dismayed. This last insult had taken the wind completely out of his sails. He tried to think how Sela would have handled a situation like this. Eventually he unrolled the dark scroll and waved it up at Constance.

'This message is for the Abbot's eyes only. It's important.'

The badger eyed him coldly. 'Then chuck it up here. I'll see that he gets it.'

No amount of wheedling and blandishment would cause the cynical badger to change her mind. She was adamant. In the end, Chickenhound had to throw the scroll up. He made several puny attempts, each one weaker than the last. As the scroll fell back down into the road yet again, Constance called aloud, 'Put some energy into it, you little milksop. I'm not hanging about here all day.'

Chickenhound heaved the scroll with all his strength. He was gratified to see Constance lean out and catch it. Hopefully he called, 'I'll wait right here for an answer.'

The badger grunted noncommitally. She sat down below the parapet out of sight of the fox, and scanned the message. Constance stayed where she was until a reasonable time elapsed, then stood up, panting heavily for effect.

'Tell Sela that the Abbot will see her two days from tonight at ten o'clock in Mossflower Wood. She must come to the old tree stump; and mind you tell her – no tricks!'

Chickenhound waved the flag. He went into a bout of uncontrollable sniggering. 'Right, I've got the message, fat one! Be sure your Abbot brings lots of valuables with him. Goodbye, old greyback.'

Constance poked an angry snout down at the insulting

young fox. 'You'd better get running, frogface! I'm coming down there to put my paw behind you right now!'

Again Constance dropped behind the parapet. She hammered her paws loudly against the stones. Standing up, she watched the terrified Chickenhound racing off down the road in a cloud of dust.

'Snotty-nosed little upstart!' she muttered.

There was no need for the Father Abbot to concern himself with the underhand dealings of traitor foxes. Constance would be well able to deal with the situation herself.

Matthias was famished. He sat down and took his lunch with Mr and Mrs Squirrel, the Vole family, Silent Sam, and Basil the garrulous hare. The young mouse ate mechanically. He did not really want conversation. This latest discovery of a new and baffling rhyme concerning moonlight, the north and an unknown threshold nagged at his brain. Methuselah had gone off to seek the solitude of his gatehouse study, where he claimed he could think more clearly.

Matthias was not the liveliest of table companions. He smiled and nodded, paying little attention to the chatter of the Voles and Squirrels. He was not even distracted by Silent Sam who sat upon his knee, stroking his whiskers with a sticky paw. Basil Stag Hare eyed the food which Matthias had hardly touched.

'Beg pardon, young mouse, old chap, but if you can't finish that blackberry muffin or that redcurrant tart. . . .'

Matthias absently pushed his plate across to the hare. Basil needed no second bidding.

Abbot Mortimer entered. Seeing the look on Matthias's face, he leaned across and murmured in his ear, 'All work and no play makes Matthias a dull mouse.

Cheer up, my son.'

'What! I mean, sorry, Father Abbot, I didn't mean to be rude. I was trying to solve a problem, you see.'

The Abbot patted Matthias indulgently. 'I understand, my son. Methuselah has told me of some of the difficulties facing you both. My advice is, don't let it get on top of you. Relax a little. Time provides all the answers. You've done splendidly so far, Matthias. Meanwhile you must not forget your manners at table with the guests of our Abbey.'

Matthias snapped out of his reverie. Silent Sam was admiring his sword belt. He laughed. 'Do you like that, Sam? It's the sword belt of a famous warrior.'

The little squirrel leaped upon the table. He darted up and down, thrusting out his paw as if he held a sword in it, stabbing away at thin air. He pointed at Matthias. The young mouse gave him a hug. 'No, bless you, Sam. I haven't got a sword of my own yet, but I will have some day.'

Silent Sam pointed to himself, cocking his head on one side. Matthias prodded his fat little stomach. 'A sword for you too, Sam? Well, I don't know about that. Your mum and dad might not want you going about armed to the teeth.'

Basil Stag Hare had the answer. He produced a beautifully made knife. It was very small, encased in a cunningly crafted willow bark sheath. The hare beckoned Sam. 'C'm'ere you dreadful little rogue! I've got the very thing for you. This is a leveret dagger. All young hares carry one. Here, let's try it on you for size, young buccaneer, what, what!'

Basil picked up a worn and discarded sandal. He undid the foot strap. Threading the dagger and sheath along the strap, he fastened it around Sam's waist.

'There, by the left, you look a regular little swashbuckler now,' chuckled the kindly hare.

Bounding up and down with delight, Silent Sam cut a comical figure as he fenced his way along the tabletop, thrusting and parrying at cruets and candlesticks with his new 'sword', sucking furiously on his free paw.

Matthias joined in the laughter as Mr and Mrs Squirrel thanked Basil for the generous gift to their tiny offspring. Forgetting his immediate problems, Matthias passed a happy hour in the company of the friendly woodlanders. He enjoyed it even more when Cornflower appeared. She shared Matthias's seat, glad to be off her feet for a while. Basil nudged Matthias.

'Excellent little filly, that gel! D'you know, she can produce more tuck in the twinklin' of an eye than you could shake a stick at. You mark my words, young feller-my-mouse. A body would be lucky to settle down with her. I say, have you noticed the way she looks at you? Hinds look at stags like that. Noble creatures, stags. It strikes me that you could be just the stag for her. Why, I remember when I was only a young lancejack. . . .'

Cornflower was pulling faces so much that Matthias was about to silence Basil, when Methuselah popped in at the door. He beckoned urgently to Matthias. Hastily the young mouse excused himself and left. Basil leaned closer to Cornflower. He smiled roguishly.

'You didn't know I was a lancejack, did you, m'dear? Ah those were the days of the old Forty-Seventh Hare Border Rangers! That was the first time I ever clapped eyes on a stag! I say, I'm not boring you, am I? Nod's as good as a wink to old bachelor Basil, y'know.'

Methuselah was in a ferment of eagerness as he led his young friend over to the gatehouse.

'Matthias, I've found out where the threshold is!'

The ancient mouse refused to say more until they were

safely inside his gatehouse study with the door firmly shut. Even then he said nothing that made any real sense, shoving Matthias to one side as he delved through old parchments and manuscripts, scattering books left and right.

'Where is it? I had it not five minutes ago. Hullo, what's this? Oh, the treatise on *Bee Folk of Redwall*!' Methuselah hurled the dusty volume to one side, narrowly missing his companion. 'Wait a tick. I think I may have put it down over there.'

Matthias gazed in bewilderment at the overcluttered study. Books, scrolls and manuscripts littered the small room. In his excitement Methuselah opened a desk and practically disappeared under an avalanche of paperwork.

'Hey! Steady on, old mouse! What are you up to?' cried Matthias.

Methuselah emerged jubilant, clutching a yellowed book. 'Eureka! This is it! Sister Germaine's literal translation of Martin the Warrior's Abbey blueprints.'

He flicked swiftly through the dusty pages of the aged volume. 'Let's see: "Gardens", "Cloisters", "Belltowers" . . . ah here it is, "The Great Wall and its Gates".'

The old mouse winked at Matthias gleefully as he adjusted his glasses. 'Listen to this: "On the west wall will be situated a main gate so that creatures may come and go, obtaining entrance to or exit from the Abbey of Redwall. This entrance will be guarded both night and day, for it is the main gatehouse, and as such is the very threshold of our Abbey." '

The two mice hugged each other. They danced around amid the chaos of paper, chanting with joy,

'The gatehouse is the threshold,
The gatehouse is the threshold.'

The Abbot, who was passing by, heard the noise. He shook his head at Ambrose Spike who was coming from the opposite direction.

'Mayhaps they've been at the October ale a little too much, Father Abbot,' said the hedgehog.

The Abbot chuckled at the idea. 'Well, if it helps them on their mission of discovery, Ambrose, perhaps they ought to drink some more, eh?'

'Aye,' Ambrose agreed. ''Tis enough to inspire any creature, good October ale. Perhaps it might inspire you one day to make me keeper of the cellar keys, Father.'

Inside the gatehouse study the two companions were once more at work, trying to break the code of the Great Hall rhyme.

'Well, that's another piece of the puzzle in place,' said Methuselah. 'But we've jumped ahead of ourselves a bit. There are four lines before that to crack yet:

> *"Look for the sword*
> *In moonlight streaming forth,*
> *At night, when day's first hour*
> *Reflects the north."* '

Matthias interrupted. 'Those first two lines sound as if they could only be solved in the darkness. "*Look for the sword in moonlight streaming forth.*" '

'I agree,' replied Methuselah, 'but the next line is of vital importance. It tells exactly when to look; "*at night when day's first hour*".'

'Hmm,' Matthias mused, 'let's look at this logically. Go through it word by word.'

Slowly they repeated the line together, ' "*At night, when day's first hour*".'

Methuselah slumped in his armchair. 'I'm afraid it doesn't mean anything to me—'

'Wait!' cried Matthias. 'Midnight is the last hour of the old day, so by the same token, one o'clock in the morning is the first hour of the new day, but we still tend to class it as night time. It is as the rhyme says, "*at night when day's first hour*".'

'I believe you are right,' said the old mouse. ' "*Day's first hour*" is not when it becomes light. It's one in the morning, still dark.'

Matthias leaned wearily against a stack of books. 'But if the gatehouse is the threshold, where are we supposed to stand to see anything an hour after midnight?'

'That's easy,' grinned Methuselah. 'The rhyme says, "*from o'er the threshold seek and you will see*". It's simple! What is above our heads right now?'

Matthias shrugged. 'The wall, I suppose.'

Methuselah banged his paw down on the arm of the chair. 'Exactly. And where is the only place you can stand on a wall but on top of it.'

Suddenly it became clear to Matthias. 'Oh, I see,' he cried, ' "*From o'er the threshold*", means that we must stand on the wall directly above the gatehouse.'

As fast as they could run, both mice hurried up the steps to the top of the wall. With Matthias in the lead they pounded along the ramparts. Matthias stopped above the gatehouse and stamped his foot upon the stones.

'I'd say about here. Would you agree?'

Methuselah looked a trifle doubtful. 'It looks to be a very rough approximation.'

Matthias had to concede. He looked sheepishly about. The stones where they stood were no different from any other part of the wall. The trail seemed to have gone cold again. Dejectedly Matthias sat down on a heap of rock and rubble that had been there since the invasion.

'Huh, what are we supposed to do now? Hang about up here until after midnight and wait for a miracle?'

The old gatehouse-keeper raised an admonitory paw. 'Patience, young one, patience. Let us take stock and review the facts. Lend me your knife for a moment.'

Matthias drew the Shadow's dagger from his belt and gave it to his friend. He sat watching as the old mouse began writing in the dust from the rubble.

Item one: Martin is Matthias.

Item two: We have found Martin's tomb.

Item three: We have also found his shield and sword belt.

Item four: Our task is to find Martin's sword.

Item five: Where? From here, the top of the gatehouse wall.

Item six: When? At one in the morning when moonlight streams forth.

Item seven: In which direction? To the north.

They sat in silence, digesting the facts on the list; then Matthias spoke: 'Suppose we look to the north.'

Both mice turned their heads northwards.

'Well, what do you see, young one?' queried Methuselah.

Matthias's voice was tinged with disappointment. 'Only the Abbey, part of the bee hives, the north side of this wall, and the treetops beyond. What do your eyes see, old one?'

'Exactly the same as yours do, though perhaps a bit dimmer. Don't give up hope, though. Let us keep looking. Maybe we'll see something.'

The surveillance continued. Apart from retrieving his dagger, Matthias sat very still, peering northwards. Eventually he had to give up, as his eyes were beginning to water and he was getting a crick in his neck. Methuselah had fallen asleep in the afternoon sun.

Angrily Matthias slammed his dagger point deep into the edge of the rubble heap. 'I told you it was a waste of time. Can't you stay awake for five minutes? Must you go to sleep on me?'

The old mouse awoke with a start. 'Eh, what's that! Oh, Matthias, there you are. Dear me, I must have dropped off for a moment. Sorry, it won't happen again.'

Matthias was not listening. He was digging in the rubble with his dagger. Methuselah watched him curiously.

'What in the name of goodness are you up to now?'

The rubble scattered as Matthias dug away madly. 'I think I've found what we're after! There's some sort of shape in the stone down here. Trouble is, there's too much rubbish on top of it. I think we need the Foremole's help again.'

The Foremole and his team arrived panting, with Matthias running ahead. The moles collapsed on the rubble, breathing hard.

'Yurr on'y gotten biddy short legs, us moles do, oi takes it you'm gennelmice needin' our 'elp agin.'

This time Matthias understood. 'Yes please, Mr Foremole. Do you think that you and your team could possibly move this pile of rock and rubble. There's something we need to get at underneath it all.'

Foremole spread his stubby paws wide. He smiled winningly. 'Hurr, no soon as said'n done, young un. Wurr ud you'm loik 'er shiften to?'

Matthias shrugged. 'Oh anywhere, I suppose, as long as it's not in our way.'

The Foremole spat on his paws and rubbed them together. 'Arr roight, mateys, best dumpen this lot whurr it comed from.'

The two mice had to jump aside smartly as the mole team took over. With much 'Hurr-ing and Arr-ing,' they waded busily in, bulldozing the enormous heap of rock and rubble off the top of the ramparts. It tipped downwards in earthy showers, back into the trench in the Abbey grounds from whence it had first come.

Matthias watched admiringly. 'What splendid workers these moles are, Methuselah.'

As the hill dwindled his friend heartily agreed. 'Indeed they are, their skills and knowledge are passed on through families, you know. Earth, rock, shale or root, they can handle it all. Do you know, it was the moles that dug the foundations for this very Abbey. Foremole can claim direct descent from the mole who was in charge of the operation. In fact, it was Martin who bestowed the title Foremole upon his ancestor.'

As the mice conversed, the moles hurled the last of the rubble from the ramparts, then set about brushing the stones clean.

The Foremole tugged his nose in salute. 'Harr, we'm dum now, zurrs, oi'll bid ee g'day.'

Ten seconds later they were all gone.

'Moles aren't too fond of heights,' observed Methuselah. 'Right, let's see what they've uncovered.'

It was a circle cut into the stone.

On one side it was cut shallow, while at the opposite side it was carved deeply. The centre was domed with two slots graven into either slope. At the apex of the dome was the letter M. Beneath it were carved thirteen small circles, each with a smiling face upon it.

Constance came rambling along the wall, checking on the road beneath. 'Hello there, you two! Are you staying up here all day? You'll miss afternoon tea if you don't hurry. There'll be precious little left with three squirrels, three voles, and Basil Stag Hare as guests.'

178

Studying the carvings, Matthias waved absently at the badger.

'You carry on, Constance. We'll be down shortly.'

The badger's natural curiosity was aroused. She came over and stood between the two mice. After a cursory glance she threw up her paws in mock despair. 'Oh no, not more puzzles and riddles?'

Methuselah gave her a severe stare over the top of his glasses. 'My dear Constance, kindly do not pour scorn on things you know nothing of. Leave it to those with specialized knowledge.'

Turning to Matthias, the old mouse continued, 'Yes, most interesting. These thirteen small circles with smiling faces. What do you make of them?'

Matthias could only shake his head. He could not think what the circles might mean.

Constance interrupted. 'What, do'you mean those things? Huh, they're obviously the thirteen full moons of the year.'

Methuselah was distinctly piqued. 'How do you know that? Explain yourself.'

Constance scoffed. 'Ha, any badger worth its salt knows all about the moon. Do you want me to recite all its phases? I can, you know.'

Matthias was suddenly back on the track again. He counted along the moons, stopping at the sixth one.

'That one will be this month, June! When is the full moon due in June, Constance?'

'It's tomorrow night,' came the prompt reply. 'Why, is something supposed to happen then? Some magic or a miracle?'

Methuselah ignored the badger's attempt at levity.

'If we stand up here at one o'clock in the morning on the night of the full moon, we may be able to find the sword of Martin the Warrior,' he said, rather sternly.

Constance scratched her muzzle. 'How are you going to manage that?'

Matthias ran his foot around the edge of the circle. 'We're not quite sure yet, but we are trying to figure it out. You see, it's all linked closely with the rhyme from the wall of Great Hall, Martin's tomb, and the stuff we found in it, this sword belt, a shield, another rhyme on the back of a d—'

Constance interrupted, 'What type of shield?'

'Oh, pretty much the standard kind used by warriors,' Matthias replied. 'A round steel affair with hand- and arm-holds.'

The badger nodded knowingly and continued where Matthias had left off. 'Yes, I've seen that sort of thing before. Not much to look at; in fact, just the type of shield that would fit precisely into this circle. Can't you see the slots for the arm-holds? But then again, if you look at that carved circle, you'll notice that it is cut so that the shield would tilt, probably to reflect the moonlight . . . .'

Both mice stared at the badger. There was awe and respect written upon their faces.

Matthias shook her paw with great ceremony. 'Constance, wonderful badger, old friend. Don't worry about afternoon tea. You just sit yourself down right there, because I, personally, am going to bring you the largest, most delicious tea that has ever been served within the walls of this Abbey.'

The warm, red stone ramparts rang to the echo of the three friends' delighted laughter.

8

Cluny lay with his one good eye half open.

From beneath its slitted lid he watched Sela the vixen.

The sly old devil was definitely up to something, he was certain of it.

Cluny had secretly questioned Fangburn about the conversation that had gone on between Sela and her son. There was no doubt about it, the foxes were trying to dupe the Warlord.

Cluny had cursed Fangburn for twenty different kinds of an idiot. Fancy not being able to read, and allowing Sela to write out a message! Imagine letting Chickenhound go free without first getting the scroll read.

If he had been a little fitter he would have personally slain his oafish captain. But as it was, Cluny kept silent about it all. Even if Sela was playing a double game, he needed the fox's healing powers to regain his health and strength.

Meanwhile, Cluny the Scourge made his own counter-espionage moves. He allowed Sela to minister to his wounds, but he secretly stopped taking the herbs and potions to help him sleep.

Early next morning Chickenhound returned. He carried a bag laden with medicinal ingredients. Cluny feigned sleep, but secretly he observed the foxes closely. They nodded and winked at each other quite a bit. When they were reasonably sure he was asleep, the two held a hurried whispered conversation. And though, unfortunately, he could not hear what they said, their behaviour was secretive enough to make Cluny sure he was right. They were planning a double-cross!

Cluny did not tell any of his officers of his suspicions. He kept everything to himself. This way there could be no possible leak of secrets. Cluny was content to watch and wait, getting a little stronger each day.

Then after a while he came up with a fiendishly simple idea. He ordered that the room be cleared: he wished to be alone so that he could rest. When he was quite sure that he would not be disturbed, Cluny took a quill and parchment from the bedside table. He drew a diagram, complete with pointing arrows, horde positions, lines of attack and defence, together with written instructions. It was a plan for the second full-scale invasion of Redwall Abbey. Cluny made it clear that the success of the attack depended solely on the battering ram breaking through the main gate.

When he had finished writing, Cluny pushed the parchment under his pillow, taking care to leave just a small corner of it jutting out. His officers would be too slow and dull to notice it – a tiny scrap of parchment showing from beneath the pillow. Even if they should, they would attach no importance to it.

But Sela the fox would!

Cluny settled down to wait.

Redtooth and Fangburn returned with their captive guest

an hour later. Cluny stretched himself luxuriously and yawned aloud.

'Aaaah, I had a nice peaceful nap without you three clattering about the room and creating a noise. How's that tree-felling coming along?'

Redtooth leaned upon his spear. 'Shouldn't take much longer now, Chief. I've ordered some of them to get a good blaze going so that the trunk can be fired and hardened.'

Cluny flexed his injured tail slowly. 'Good, make sure that all the large branches are cut off close to the trunk. It'll make it easier to carry. Now, fox, how about changing these bandages and giving me something to make me sleep tonight. That stuff you gave me yesterday wasn't much use. I was tossing and turning for hours before I got any rest.'

Sela made a sweeping servile curtsey. 'Now that my son has brought my new ingredients I can certainly give you medicine to make you sleep, sir. I guarantee you'll go off like a bug in a blanket, if you'll pardon the expression, sir.'

'Just as long as it gets me to sleep,' said Cluny, smiling inwardly.

That night, Cluny allowed Redtooth and Fangburn to guzzle their fill from a cask of barley wine that had been found in the church cellars. He gave Sela permission to drink also. Cluny watched as the fox pretended to drink as much of the barley wine as the rat Captains. While she was doing this, Cluny also pretended to take his sleeping medicine. Cluny and Sela continued with their pantomime, neither letting a drop pass their lips.

It was late night. Cluny joined in the snores of his drunken officers. The room was comfortably warm. A lone candle flickered in its socket. Cluny felt the pillow move slightly.

Sela was taking the bait!

Cluny gave a big imitation snore and smacked his lips contentedly. Some day he must learn to play chess. He betted himself that he would be unbeatable.

Cluny also made a wager with himself that the plans would be back, safely tucked under the pillow, by morning, and that Sela would have an accurate copy of them hidden away somewhere. Now he could catch a few hours' sleep.

No doubt the mice would be interested to learn of his scheme to attack the main gate with a battering ram. They would strengthen the gatehouse and deploy the main body of defenders in the immediate area. Cluny could have laughed out loud.

While they were defending the gate, he would be tunnelling under the south-western angle of the Abbey Wall!

9

The deep, warm, brazen voice of the Joseph Bell tolled across the tranquil meadows, its echoes fading in the leafy depths of Mossflower Wood. It was eleven o'clock on the night of the full moon.

Inside Cavern Hole the candles burned bright. Most of the woodland defenders and Redwall mice had retired to their beds. Those who preferred to stay awake were gathered by invitation of Matthias and Methuselah to a party supper. All who attended wished them well on their quest. Abbot Mortimer took the floor.

'My friends, Redwall mice and honoured guests, we are gathered here tonight, not only to pay tribute, but to add our heartfelt good wishes to Matthias and Brother Methuselah. May they have success and fortune in their venture this night, and may our Abbey soon be enhanced by the restoration of the sword that belonged to Martin the Warrior.'

The Abbot took his seat among cries of, 'Hear, hear.' There was much paw-shaking and fur-patting. Matthias felt deeply honoured, but very impatient. The hourglass had to empty twice more before the crucial time he awaited. He stole a sideways glance at his companion. Methuselah could hardly stop his eyelids from dropping. The hard work they had done, combined with the nervous tension, were beginning to tell upon the old gatehouse-keeper. Matthias nudged him gently.

'Wake up, old one. If you're tired I'll help you to your room. Constance and I can take the shield up to the threshold. You get a good night's sleep. We'll tell you all about it in the morning.'

Methuselah came wide awake with indignation. 'You'll do nothing of the sort! You young scallywag, I could give you a ten-second start and still beat you to the top of the wall! D'you want to try me?'

Constance coughed and spluttered upon a candied chestnut. She roared with laughter. 'Ha ha ha, ho ho ho, I wouldn't attempt it if I were you, Matthias. He's liable to beat you hollow in his present mood.'

The old mouse, seeing the humour of the situation, began to chuckle. 'And don't think I couldn't, you great stripey lump. Here, what do you say we put this young mouse up in the dormitory? It's way past his bedtime. You and I could go to the threshold together.'

Constance and Methuselah collapsed against each other, laughing helplessly. It was all Matthias could do to keep a straight face. He pretended to take offence at Methuselah's statement.

'Why, you old pair of relics! It wouldn't take me two ticks to bring you some warm milk and tuck you in your own beds. Then I'd be free to get on with the job myself.'

The three friends laughed until tears streamed down their cheeks. Methuselah held his sides as he spoke between gusts of merriment. 'I say, Constance – ha ha ha – you old fogey – oh ha ha ha tee hee! – you'd better come along with us – ha ha ho ho oooh! – Matthias is a bit old for this sort of thing! Hahahahahahaha.'

Matthias had fallen off his chair. He waved his paws, pleading for the joking to stop, as he rolled about on the floor, exploding from bouts of giggling to fits of laughter.

Basil Stag Hare tut-tutted severely as he remarked to Ambrose Spike, 'Tch, tch. Dreadful table manners. Just look at those three wallahs, kicking up a hullaballoo like that! Eating's a serious business. They haven't touched a bite of supper, y'know.'

'Aye, so I see,' grunted the hedgehog. 'Here, you don't suppose they'd mind, do you?'

'Not at all, not at all, dear fellow,' said Basil regally, as he shared the contents of the three plates between himself and Ambrose. 'Saves it all going to waste, what, what?'

It was fifteen minutes before one o'clock in the morning. Three figures crossed the Abbey gardens as the moon broke from behind a drifting cloudbank. The nearby pond was bathed in a silver sheen, parts of the sandstone wall reflecting back a wavery bluish light. Constance and Methuselah carried lanterns; Matthias bore the warrior's shield upon his arm. They ascended the wall steps in single file, acknowledging the murmured good-wishes of those on sentry duty.

Matthias had decided against trying the shield in its niche before the appointed hour. He felt somehow that they must abide by the rules of the verse, waiting until day's first hour on the night of the full moon. It just had to be so. No use tempting fickle Dame Fortune.

Solemnly the three friends gathered around the carving upon the ramparts. Matthias clutched the shield tightly, waiting for the stroke of one. High above the small world of Redwall the moon also waited, suspended in velvety space like a pale, gold coin. It seemed that the minutes stretched into an eternity in which silence reigned over all.

187

The great Joseph Bell boomed out once. It was one o'clock – day's first hour. Slowly, reverently, Matthias lowered the shield of Martin, down on to the stone circle that had been carved many long years before to receive it. The shield made a mild clanking sound as it was laid to rest in its niche. It fitted perfectly into the stone receptacle. All three creatures stood back a pace to see what might happen. Matthias was first to cry out.

'Look! The shield is reflecting the moonlight back into the sky!'

Moonlight seemed to concentrate upon the highly-polished steel dome in its designated position, sending an intense beam of white light back off into the night sky.

Methuselah blinked. Holding his paw across his eyebrows, he stared into space, trying to follow the path of the reflected moonlight. 'Truly it is a most beautiful, wondrous sight,' he breathed. 'Alas, my old eyes are not what they were. All I see is a light shooting off into infinity.'

'Look at the Abbey roof,' Constance murmured. 'The beam cuts right across the top gable. I can see the weather vane as clearly as if it were day.'

'Good heavens,' Matthia squeaked. 'You're right! The Abbey weather vane, it's the one thing that's caught in the path of the light.'

'The North! The North!' Methuselah shouted. 'It's the weather vane arm that points north! That's where the sword must be!'

Solemnly the three friends placed their paws one on top of the other. At long last the mystery was solved. They knew now where the sword of Martin the Warrior had lain for countless years.

On the arm of a weather vane, pointing north!

However, it was three rather disconsolate creatures that

sat down to early breakfast after a few hours' fitful sleep. They had encountered a major problem: how to get the sword down?

'What a pity we haven't got about thirty or forty extra-long ladders that we could tie together to reach the roof,' muttered Constance.

'Oh, do be quiet, Constance,' Matthias grumbled. 'That must be the tenth time you've said that in the last hour.'

'Sorry, only trying to help,' she mumbled.

Methuselah pushed his porridge aside. 'There are only two ways that you could help, my friend. One, by keeping silent. Two, by turning yourself into some creature that could climb all the way up to that roof. A bird, or a squirrel or something.'

They sat and stared at Methuselah in amazement. A solution of stunning simplicity had been found.

'I do hope that Mrs Squirrel hasn't decided to have a lie-in,' said Matthias. 'She'll need an early start if she's going to make it back by lunchtime.'

Mrs Squirrel (or Jess as she liked to be called) was only too pleased to oblige her friends from Redwall.

Having been given full instructions by Matthias, Jess stood at the base of the immense Abbey building. The squirrel performed what looked like an intricate acrobatic dance, followed by several cartwheels at lightning speed.

'She's just limbering up,' Mr Squirrel explained to Matthias.

A large crowd of mice and woodlanders had gathered to witness the epic ascent. Not even in the oldest recorded writings was there any mention of a creature venturing to climb as high as the Abbey roof. It was a most formidable task, for the roof soared to nearly twice the height of the bell tower.

Jess elbowed her way through the throng. She kissed Mr Squirrel, patted her son Silent Sam upon the head, then shook paws with Constance, Matthias and Methuselah. With a brisk, cheery manner she scooped up a handful of soil, rubbing it into her paws to give some extra gripping power.

'Lovely day for a climb,' she remarked off-handedly.

Then away she went, paw over paw, up the massive Abbey face.

The lower wall with its arched sandstone window frames held no difficulties for the tough squirrel. She climbed with speed and alacrity. Lifting herself over the gutter with a neat flick of her bushy tail, Jess clattered across to a small slate side roof. She was temporarily lost to view at the start of the second stage. As she came into sight again, the watchers below could not help but notice that the climb was more difficult, progress was slower.

Mr Squirrel cupped his paws and called up, 'Are you all right there, Jess?'

Latching her tail around a projecting gargoyle, Jess shouted back, 'Well, I'm making headway, m'dear. This stone though – it's a bit rough on the old paws and claws. Not like good old wood or tree bark.'

Chins went up, heads tilted back, the crowd below followed the ascent of the plucky Jess Squirrel. By this time she seemed to the watchers to be rapidly diminishing in size as she forged upwards.

The Foremole (who was never too keen on heights) covered his eyes with a paw. 'Gurr, moi dearie, dearie me. She'm loiken an owlyburd allaways up thurr. Nay, oi'm afeared to look.'

Although Matthias had to agree with Foremole, he continued looking upwards. Jess was reduced to a mere speck now. The young mouse gritted his teeth, willing the brave squirrel onwards. 'Go on Jess, you can do it!

Not far to the gable now!'

The crowd fell silent. All that could be heard was Silent Sam sucking his tiny paw as he clutched on to his father's tail.

Suddenly Winifred the otter broke the quiet: 'Look, Jess has made it over the gutter! She's on the roof.'

A mass cheer went up. The squirrel was on the last lap. Now she would have to call into play all of her climbing ability to keep going up the treacherously steep smooth slates.

Methuselah polished agitatedly at his spectacles. 'Where is she now? Will someone please enlighten me?'

'She's on top of the roof, walking with a foot either side of the apex towards the gable,' yelled Abbot Mortimer.

Methuselah sniffed. 'No need to shout, Father Abbot. I'm only hard of sight, not hearing.'

Mr Squirrel clapped his paws joyfully. 'Oh she's made it! My Jess has made it!'

Amid the riot of jubilation Matthias watched. The weather vane moved slightly, indicating that Jess, actually out upon the north pointer, must be trying to retrieve the sword.

What a daring climb! What a courageous creature! Jess Squirrel would surely take her place in the annals of Redwall Abbey.

Mr Squirrel held Silent Sam up in his arms. 'Look, Sam. Mum's done it! She's on the way back down now.'

Silent Sam clenched his little paws over his head. He shook them like a tiny champion. Nobody in all the world was a better climber than his mum.

Jess was nearly halfway down when a shout of consternation arose from the crowd below.

'Look out, she's being attacked by sparrows!'

Sure enough, the fierce birds were whirling in close to the intrepid Jess. They tried to peck at her, seeking to dislodge her, or distract her enough to make her fall. It was a fearsome, sickening drop should she lose her grip.

Matthias took command. He acted swiftly.

'Hurry, get the six best field and harvest mouse archers! Those birds have got to be stopped immediately.'

The angry sparrows persisted with their savage assault. Jess kept on descending resolutely. She had no way of defending herself.

The Abbot and Constance had to leap forward to restrain Silent Sam. He had left his father and was trying to scramble up the base of the Abbey Wall with the small dagger clenched in his teeth.

Constance attempted to reason with Sam. 'Stay clear, little one. You'll only distract your mum. Look, she's doing splendidly! An old bunch of sparrows can't bother her. Stand back now; here come the bowmice!'

Speedily notching shafts to their strings, the archers angled their bows upwards.

'Do not aim to kill any of the birds,' the Abbot cried. 'Shoot to frighten them off.'

'Shoot,' Matthias yelled.

The first volley of arrows was launched. They fell short of the sparrows. Jess carried on scrambling downwards, beating off attackers whenever she had a free paw.

'They're getting within range now,' shouted Matthias. 'Aim, fire!'

The mouse archers sent off a hail of arrows that came close enough to cause a scatter among the sparrows. Taking advantage of their brief confusion, Jess clambered down on to the small side roof.

The tenacious birds regrouped and came at her again. Below, the bowmice stood ready.

'She'll make it down,' Ambrose Spike yelled. 'One more good volley should scare them off.'

'Ready, fire!' called Matthias.

The deadly shafts hissed upwards, causing a mad flurry among the attackers. Purely by accident a stray arrow struck one young sparrow. It came tumbling down the slope of the small roof, dropping to earth like a stone, the arrow sticking in its leg just above the knee joint. Cheated of their intended victim, the sparrows flew off, chirping bad-temperedly.

Constance snatched up a woven rush washing basket. Holding the small sparrow firmly with her paw, she gripped the arrow in her teeth and yanked it clear from the bird's leg. The badger then upended the basket, imprisoning the maddened sparrow beneath it.

Shouts of joy mingled with relief greeted Jess Squirrel as she dropped wearily to the grass.

'Phew!' she gasped. 'What a wild bunch of savages those sparrows are! I thought they had me once or twice back there.'

Before the heroic squirrel could be united with her family, Matthias came dashing across.

'Jess! Did you get the sword?' he panted.

The squirrel shrugged and shook her head. 'It wasn't there, Matthias. I climbed out along the north pointer and actually saw the shape of the sword in the holder where it was supposed to rest. There were even some loose rusty wires that may have held it in position at one time or another. But there was definitely no sword. I'm sorry, Matthias, I tried my best.'

'Of course you did, Jess,' said Matthias, hiding his disappointment. 'Thank you very much for your valiant efforts.'

Half an hour later, the crowd had dispersed and gone about their business. Matthias sat with his back against the Abbey wall, his mind in a turmoil. All that hard work, solving the clues, burning midnight oil, endangering the lives of his friends, it had all come to nothing. He beat his paws against the stones of the Abbey, a tear of frustration gleaming in his eye.

'Why, Martin, why?' he moaned.

The captive sparrow fluttered her wings against the upturned basket. 'I killee you!' she chattered angrily at Matthias. 'I killee mouse, lettum Warbeak free, you um dirty worm.'

Matthias peered through the cracks at the insulting prisoner.

'Oh, shut your beak, you little monster!' he muttered. 'You're in no position to kill anyone.'

The sparrow's venomous temper increased. 'King Bull Sparra, he killee you. Makum dead quickfast.'

Matthias laughed mirthlessly. 'Will he indeed? Well, you tell King Thingummy if you should bump into him again, that you've met Matthias the Warrior, and I don't kill that easily, my bad-tempered little friend.'

This last statement sent the young sparrow off into a veritable dance of rage. 'Mouse no friend of Warbeak! Killee, killee!'

Matthias tapped the basket with his foot. 'Listen, Warbeak, if that's your name. You'd better improve your temper, or you'll find yourself without food to eat or any medical attention. So if I were you, I'd sit quietly for a while and think about that.'

Matthias spun on his heel and marched off, the enemy sparrow's chirps still ringing in his ears: 'No wanna food, no needa 'tenshun. Warbeak Sparra, all brave, killee.'

Matthias sighed wearily.

There was just no talking to some creatures.

10

Sela the fox continued to complain. She must have a certain type of herb that was not in her kit. It could only be found in Mossflower Wood at the dark of night.

Cluny listened to the fox's pleas, knowing that they were merely an excuse to gain her freedom. He paused as if to deliberate, watching the hopeful expression on Sela's face.

'Hmm, I can see that you need this herb, so why don't you send your son Chickenhound to get it?'

Sela was never stuck for a ready answer. 'No no, I'm afraid that's useless, sir. He's too young and inexperienced. Chickenhound wouldn't know where to start looking.'

Cluny nodded sympathetically. 'Aye, you're probably right. I suppose I'll have to stretch a point. You can go off to the woods to search for this vital herb. But be warned, fox! There will be two rats with you all the time. One false move and I'll have that bushy tail of yours to trim the collar of my war cloak. Is that understood?'

Sela's head bobbed vigorously. 'Of course, sir. What reason would I have to play you false? I'm looking forward to a good share of plunder, once I've healed you and Redwall is conquered.'

The huge tail snaked out and caressed the fox. 'Of course you are, my friend. How silly of me.'

Cluny actually smiled. Sela shuddered.

That evening Sela left the church, accompanied by Redtooth and Fangburn. Secretly she could have danced with delight. Only two guards! With her knowledge of Mossflower, Sela could quite easily give them the slip for fifteen minutes or so.

Back at the church Cluny had risen from his bed. He attempted an exploratory walk, leaning on his banner as he stumped gingerly around the room.

Good! In a short while he would be back to his old self again.

Cluny spoke aloud to the picture of Martin, bound to his standard: 'Ha, that fox should easily give those idiots of mine the slip. Then she can deliver my false plans to your Abbot. It's all going along quite smoothly. Bit of a blow for your side, eh, mouse?'

Twilight tinged Mossflower Wood. Sela sniffed the breeze. She glanced up at the sky. It would soon be dark and she could keep her rendezvous with the mouse Abbot at the old stump.

Redtooth and Fangburn were both unhappy and uncomfortable. For the last hour Sela had led them through stinging nettles, swarms of midges and marshy ground. They blundered along, hacking at the undergrowth with cutlass and spear.

'I think we must be somewhere near the mouse Abbey,' Fangburn said.

'Stow the gab! Keep your eyes on the fox,' Redtooth snarled.

'I wish I'd brought some lanterns along with us,' Fangburn whined.

Redtooth's already dangerously-thin patience snapped. He grabbed hold of his snivelling crony and started shaking him. 'Listen, thickhead! If you don't stop your moaning I'll chop your tongue out with my cutlass! D'you hear me?'

Fangburn struggled free. Angrily he jabbed at Redtooth with his spear. 'You dare try anything with that blunt old breadknife, and I'll spear your gizzard before you can blink an eye!'

'Oh you will, will you?'

'Yes, I will, smarty rat!'

'Then take that, big mouth!'

'Ouch! Punch me, would you? I'll soon show you!'

Together the rats crashed into a prickly bush, kicking, biting and pummelling each other. Claws, tails and teeth came into play. They went at it hammer and tongs for several minutes until Redtooth emerged the victor. His nose was bleeding and he had lost a tooth, but he was in better shape than his opponent.

Fangburn crawled miserably out of the wrecked bush. Both eyes were blacked, a chunk of his left ear was missing, and his whole body was covered in long raking claw marks and prickles. He bent painfully to retrieve his spear. Seizing the opportunity Redtooth landed him a mighty kick on the bottom. His nose ploughed up a furrow of soil.

Panting furiously, Redtooth berated Fangburn: 'You half-witted fool! Now see what you've done! While you were busy assaulting a superior officer, you let the fox escape.'

Fangburn sat up. He winced through discoloured eyes. '*I* let the fox escape? Me? Oh no. You're the one in charge! *You* let her get away, not me. Wait'll I report this to Cluny. I'll tell him that you—'

'Will you shut up?' Redtooth yelled. 'It's no use us standing here arguing. We'd better get searching for the fox. I'll go this way and you go that way. The first one to find her keeps shouting until the other arrives. Have you got that? Now get moving.'

The two rats stumbled off through the woods in different directions.

Meanwhile, in another part of Mossflower Wood, Sela sneaked along looking from left to right. There was the three-topped oak, there was the Abbey Wall. Ah, here it was, the old stump.

The moonlight illuminated the scene clearly. She was alone. Where was the mouse Abbot?

A heavy paw clamped itself around Sela's neck from behind. Her tongue shot out. Struggling uselessly, she gagged and choked.

Constance's gruff voice growled into her ear, 'Be still, fox, or I'll snap your neck like a dead twig!'

Sela froze. There was nothing more dangerous than a fully-grown badger. Their strength and ferocity were renowned.

Constance's free paw snapped the herb pouch from the fox's belt. She shook the contents out on to the stump. Grabbing the copy of Cluny's invasion plans she studied it briefly, then stuffed it into her belt.

'Your Abbot was supposed to meet me with a reward,' Sela whispered.

The badger's eyes blazed with contempt as she spun the vixen around. 'Here's your reward, traitor!'

Whump!

Constance dealt Sela a sharp blow between the ears. The fox fell in a senseless heap. Constance ducked behind a tree and called out in a high-pitched voice, 'Over here! I've got the fox! Quick, over here!'

Redtooth was first to arrive. He came dashing through the bushes and halted at the sight of the unconscious fox among the ferns.

'Hell's teeth, fox. Where's Fangburn? What the devil do you mean slinking off like that? Get up on your feet and answer me.'

Constance emerged from behind the tree. 'I don't think she'll wake up for a while yet. Fancy meeting you here, rat.'

Redtooth got over his surprise quickly. Seeing the badger unarmed, he swished his cutlass through the air and smiled menacingly.

'Well, well. It's the friend of the mice! So, we meet again, badger!'

Constance stood tall, her huge paws folded. 'Redtooth, isn't it? I see you still remember me from your defeat at the wall. I told you then we had a score to settle.'

Redtooth bared his teeth and snarled. 'I'm going to enjoy this, badger. I'll make sure you die slowly.'

The rat leaped at Constance, swinging his cutlass expertly, but for a heavy badger, his adversary moved light and skilfully. Neatly sidestepping a cutlass-thrust, she cuffed the rat smartly on the point of the nose. Stung into retaliation, Redtooth charged Constance with the point of his blade.

A fierce kick in the ribs and a swift chop to the claw sent the rat and the cutlass in opposite directions. Redtooth lay winded upon the ground. Constance leaned over him.

'Get up and retrieve your weapon,' the badger growled.

As Redtooth stood, he grabbed a handful of earth and

flung it into Constance's eyes. The big badger staggered back, rubbing at the grit which clogged her vision. The rat picked up the cutlass and swung it, slashing wildly at his enemy's thick fur. He scored several hits.

Suddenly panic gripped him. The wounded badger had seized the blade regardless of its keen edge. Constance pulled Redtooth in close. She gave a sideways push, snapping the cutlass blade in two pieces. Kicking the rat over on his back, she flung the broken blade away and grabbed the rodent's tail tightly with both paws.

Redtooth screamed in terror as he felt himself leave the ground to go spinning aloft over the badger's head. With his tail pulled taut and the wind whistling through his fangs, Redtooth howled as the trees went by in a green blur. Like an athlete throwing the hammer, Constance whirled on her hind legs, faster and faster, until suddenly she threw her burden with a colossal heave.

Redtooth would have flown a record distance had there not been a stout sycamore tree several metres away. . . .

Ignoring her injuries Constance called into the surrounding woods, 'Over here, he's over here!'

Then she limped swiftly off in the direction of Redwall with the captured plans.

Only moments later Fangburn came blundering through the ferns. He tripped upon the groaning fox who was just coming round.

'Here, what's happened? Where's Redtooth?' he asked anxiously.

Sela sat up, rubbing her head, trying to recognize her surroundings. She saw the old stump littered with her herbs and potions. The pouch lay nearby. Holding her head with both paws she tried to halt the thumping ache.

Damn that badger's hide! She'd taken the plans from

Sela as if she were confiscating acorns from a baby mouse. So much for the 'rich rewards'.

Fangburn prodded Sela with the spear. 'Hey you, pay attention! I asked you where Redtooth is.'

Sela probed a loosened tooth with her tongue. 'Leave me alone. How should I know?'

Fangburn persisted. 'Now listen, fox. I want to know what's been going on here. I'm sure I heard Redtooth calling out. Hell's whiskers, wait until Cluny gets to hear about this!'

Sela pointed a shaky paw. 'There's your rat, by that big sycamore yonder. Huh, looks like he's had a spot of bother, too.'

Fangburn touched Redtooth with his foot. 'Aaaaargh! He's dead. Look, this sword's been broken in two.'

The fox and the rat stood looking at each other, their thoughts running on parallel lines. It was fairly obvious what must be done if they were to save their skins.

'Right,' said Sela. 'We'd better work out a good story to tell Cluny when we get back. He's not stupid, so we'd better get it right.'

The unlucky pair stumbled off through the night-time woodland, gesticulating and muttering together, weaving a fabric of lies that they hoped would satisfy Cluny the Scourge.

11

Once again the Abbot's room was the scene of a late repast. The news that Constance had brought showed without a doubt that Cluny would soon be on the track again.

Abbot Mortimer was the first to admit that he had been mistaken. 'The intelligence brought to us by our friend Constance is conclusive. Cluny will never rest until he has Redwall under his heel, therefore I feel that I must apologize for my misjudgement of the situation. You, my commanders, were right, and now, thanks to Cluny, we know the secret details of the enemy horde's next attack.'

The Abbot slapped a paw down on the plans. 'It is all here, but as I have said before, I will not concern myself with the fighting of a war. It is my task to heal the injured and give sustenance to the defenders. It is the duty of you, my generals, to plan the repulse of this invasion.'

Matthias held up a paw. 'Father Abbot, it is our duty not only to defend but to retaliate.'

There was a strong murmur of agreement from around the table.

The Abbot bowed and placed his paws within his wide

habit sleeves. 'So be it,' he said with great solemnity. 'I leave the salvation of Redwall to you, my commanders.'

The Abbot bowed once more then retired for the night, leaving Matthias, Constance, Winifred, Foremole and Ambrose Spike.

The meeting continued. They were joined by Basil Stag Hare and Jess Squirrel. Methuselah also attended to act as mediator and counsellor, approving some ideas whilst discouraging others, calming the hothead and encouraging the timid. Much good sense was talked and the tone of the meeting was that of creatures who were determined to win at all costs. The discussion, running on sensible lines, went on until it was nearly dawn. It was a confident and satisfied group of friends who shook paws as the meeting ended.

Basil insisted on taking Constance to the infirmary to have her wounds treated. The badger tried to shrug him off.

'Pah! Such a fuss over a few minor scratches,' she grumbled.

The hare chuckled admiringly. 'A few minor scratches! Will you listen to the heroine? Why, my dear badger, those are honourable wounds, gained on the field of combat. I say, Jess, lend a paw here. Have you seen the dreadful gashes that friend Constance has collected? By the left, old gel, you should be *hors de combat*. Not even a stag could put up with slashes like that. Come on now, let's have you, there's a sensible bod.'

Constance was led off muttering by Basil and Jess. All the rest retired to their beds, with the exception of Matthias and Methuselah. They strolled around the cloisters, savouring the peace of the midnight hours.

'You know, old one, I can't help thinking that a victory would be assured if only we had the Warrior's sword,' Matthias said.

Methuselah nodded wistful agreement. 'Indeed it would. But, alas for all our efforts, the trail is as cold as a midwinter night. I'm afraid we must resign ourselves to the fact that the sword is lost or hidden somewhere forever.'

The old gatehouse-keeper leaned upon the young mouse's arm as they walked along, talking of this and that. Eventually the conversation came around to the sparrows' attack upon Jess.

Methuselah shook a warning paw. 'Extremely dangerous birds, sparrows. Very warlike and quarrelsome. Luckily they keep to themselves and will only attack if their territory is intruded upon as you saw today. By the way, did you see that young one who was brought down by the archers?'

'I certainly did,' Matthias replied. 'Constance has got the bad-tempered little wretch imprisoned under a wash basket. What a nasty young villain. The arrow only scratched her really. It was shock more than anything else that brought her down. Says her name is Warbeak.'

Methuselah was taken aback. 'Do you mean to tell me you've talked with her? Remarkable! The sparrow language, or "Sparra" as it is called, is very difficult to comprehend.'

'Oh, I don't know,' said Matthias casually. 'I didn't find it too hard, and at least the little hooligan seems to understand what I'm saying to her.'

Methuselah's curiosity was aroused. 'And what has she been saying to you, this, er, Warbeak?'

'Pretty much what you'd expect,' Matthias replied. 'Either she, or the leader King Bull Sparra, is going to kill me. Evidently she looks on anything that can't fly as an enemy.'

They strayed over by the gatehouse. The old mouse invited Matthias in for a late nightcap. Methuselah appeared very interested in sparrows. He leafed through his record books.

'Let me see, "Summer of the Big Drought" . . . "Winter of the Deep Drifts" . . . yes, I thought I'd find it here. Do you remember I told you of a sparrowhawk who I treated about four years back? Well, here is my report, some small notes I made at the time. This hawk talked of the sparrows. She called them winged mice, though for the life of me I cannot see any comparison between highly civilized mice and those primitive savages. Point was, though, this sparrow-hawk said she'd been told that the sparrows once stole an object of great value to our Abbey. She didn't say what it was. I thought the bird was merely trying to impress me with idle gossip: I should have questioned her further. We may have found out just what the object was.'

Matthias looked pensive. 'Then you think as I do. It could have been the sword.'

The old mouse sat tapping his paw upon the record book. 'It could have been, Matthias, it could have been. You see, the sparrows never communicate or bother with us. They never fly into our Abbey. But, up on the roof, well, that's a different matter. They consider that to be their territory. As I see it, the sword was the only object of value we had up there, although we did not know it at the time. So who else but another bird would know that the sparrows had stolen it?'

'By the whiskers, old one,' Matthias said excitedly, 'I think you've hit the nail on the head. Do you think that our bad-tempered captive might know something about the rumour?'

Methuselah grinned mischievously. 'Lend me your dagger. I have a simple experiment that I wish to try on our prisoner. Come on.'

Matthias escorted his friend to where the basket lay by the Abbey walls. There was no sound from within. Methuselah tapped the basket sharply with the blade of the dagger.

Warbeak had been caught napping. She came to life in an irate mood. 'Worms, all worms, you old mouseworm! Stay 'way, Warbeak killee!'

Methuselah tried his level best to act tough. 'Be silent, you little baggage, or I'll spike you on this dagger, and your King too, if he dares to come down.'

In a fury, Warbeak smashed her small body against the sides of the basket, causing the old mouse to take a step back.

'Ha, go on, you killee Warbeak with um dagger! Wait see! You not get King Bull Sparra with little worm knife. King have a big sword! Chop all mouses up! Killee pretty quick, you betcha.'

Methuselah laughed with delight. 'You see! The Sparrow King owns a big sword!'

Matthias did a cartwheel. He whooped with joy. 'Methuselah, you're a magician, an ancient wizard.'

The old mouse shook his head modestly. 'Oh, dear me no. I like to think of myself as an aged but extremely erudite scholar.'

12

Sitting comfortably propped up upon pillows, Cluny sipped a beaker of barley wine as he listened to the improbable tale spun by Sela and Fangburn. They both fidgeted nervously during the course of their deceitful narrative, trying desperately not to contradict one another, while at the same time avoiding the cold, impassive eye of the Warlord.

'Er, it was like this, Chief,' Fangburn stammered. 'Me and old Redtooth were keeping our eyes on the fox here, when suddenly Redtooth hears a noise in the woods, so off he goes to investigate.'

'Where was the noise coming from?' snapped Cluny.

The deceivers spoke together.

'North,' said Sela.

'West,' said Fangburn, simultaneously.

'Er, er, it was sort of north-west,' Sela gulped, realizing how foolish she sounded. Knowing that Cluny was smarter than either of them, she wished she didn't have this big dumb rat to corroborate the story.

'So Redtooth went off to see what the noise was,' Sela faltered. 'We told him not to go, sir, but he insisted.'

Cluny watched Sela's legs shaking.

'Go on, what happened then?' he murmured.

Fangburn took up the tale again. 'Well, you see, Chief, he was gone an awful long time. We both called out to him but there was no answer.'

'So we both went to look for him,' said Sela.

Cluny toyed with the beaker. His eye bored into the fox.

'We searched and searched, sir,' Sela mumbled, 'but all we could find was this big stretch of marshland and bog. . . .'

'Which poor old Redtooth had wandered into and been sucked down never to be seen again,' Cluny supplemented.

Sela kept wishing the floor would open up and swallow her.

Fangburn sobbed brokenly. 'Our poor friend Redtooth, gone forever!'

'Yes, our poor friend Redtooth,' Cluny agreed sympathetically. Suddenly his voice hardened as he shot a question at Fangburn: 'You! How did your face get knocked about, and where did you get those long scratches from?'

Sela jumped in hastily. 'Er, er, he walked into a big thorn tree, didn't you, Fangburn?'

'What? Oh, yes. I was dashing about and I didn't see it, Chief. The fox can tell you. She saw it, and if she didn't, well, I already told her,' said Fangburn, his voice trailing off miserably.

Cluny laughed mirthlessly, his fangs showing yellow and sharp. 'So, you walked into a big thorn tree and got two black eyes, a torn ear and your whole hide covered in long scratches?'

Fangburn stared at the floor. He had to swallow twice

before he could answer, his voice subdued, 'That's what happened, Chief.'

Cluny's tone was laden with sarcasm. 'And then I suppose that three little pigs with wings flew down and gave you a toffee apple each?'

'Er, yes. Er, I mean, what was that, Chief? . . . Oouch!' Fangburn hopped on one leg as Sela kicked his ankle to silence him.

'You, fox!' Cluny snarled. 'Where's the special herb you went to search for?'

Sela was completely nonplussed. 'Special herb? I—'

Cluny hurled the beaker. It bounced off Fangburn's nose, splashing barley wine over them both.

'Get out! Out of my sight, before I have you tortured and roasted!' Cluny roared at the unlucky pair.

There was an undignified scramble. The door slammed shut behind the conspirators. Cluny lay back and smirked; everything was going according to plan. He had lost Redtooth, but what the devil? Redtooth had been an ambitious rat. Cluny only admired ambition in one rodent – himself.

Far off in Mossflower Wood, the night breezes stirred the treetops gently. The moon rode in a cloudless sky; its pale light filtered through the waving foliage to create the beautiful but strange effect of a shimmering, swaying carpet on the woodland floor.

'Asmodeus, Asmodeusssssss.'

The covering of dead moonlit vegetation on the ground trembled and rustled. What better cover than a light breeze and a hunter's moon? Glittering black eyes searched the night, a forked tongue tasted the air, the small living plants appeared to shudder as the long, scaly body brushed by them, trailing its way along.

'Asmodeus, Asmodeusssssssss.'

Softly rustling, deceptive as the speckled shadows, the huge adder roamed his domain. Patience and stealth were acquired by long experience. Sometimes the serpent would lie totally inert, awaiting the unsuspecting paw that trod too close. Other times it would raise itself, uncoiling to look into bushes for eggs and birds on the nest. Some nights it was lean hunting: many creatures sensed the approach of the slithering evil, or scented its dry, musty, deathlike odour. The snake had often gone hungry at times like these. But, patience and stealth, patience and stealth; a lesson soon learned is a meal soon earned. At the foot of the sycamore the adder stretched itself alongside the still form of Redtooth. Well, an unexpected bonus! This was another rat that could not scurry off. No expenditure of venom or hypnosis needed – how fortunate! The huge reptile coiled itself languorously around the dead rodent.

'Asmodeus, Asmodeusssssssssss.'

No need of burial parties. Nature and the woodlands took care of their own funeral arrangements. There was but one efficient undertaker. The adder's jaws opened in something resembling the nightmare of a smile. The pathway to eternity was open.

13

Matthias was excused duties at the gatehouse fortifications. The council had agreed that both he and Methuselah, plus any creature they chose to help them, were to be left to their own devices. The majority of the Redwall mice thought that Matthias was acting a little oddly, but the young mouse knew exactly what he was about. He strolled slowly through the Abbey grounds. Behind him hopped Warbeak on a lead with a collar about her neck. On the sparrow's uninjured leg Matthias had tied a brick; not a very big brick, but one large enough to stop the bird getting airborne or trying any sneak attacks upon its captor. Thoroughly disgruntled, the sparrow hopped along like a feathered convict with a ball and chain, forced to follow the young mouse wherever he chose to wander.

At first, Warbeak had raved and threatened. Death was too good for Matthias! Warbeak was going to kill him twice, then cut him up and drop him from the top of a high tree for the worms to feed upon! Matthias had merely tugged the lead sharply and quickened his pace. When the savage young sparrow showed signs of good behaviour, Matthias would feed her morsels of candied chestnut.

The treatment was working.

Outside the gatehouse Matthias rested. He fed the sparrow some more of the candied nut.

'There now, you good bird, well done,' he said, approvingly.

Warbeak scowled fiercely, but she munched the nut readily.

Methuselah popped his head out briefly and beckoned. 'Come into the study, Matthias. Oh, and bring that little horror too.'

In the cluttered study the old mouse produced a yellowed volume. 'Our old friend Sister Germaine's translation of the original Redwall Abbey blueprints. I think I've found what we are looking for in the main diagram. See.'

Matthias studied the blueprint carefully.

'Brilliant!' he exclaimed. 'You've done it again, my friend! A route to the Abbey roof from the inside.'

Methuselah breathed upon his glasses, polishing them on his fur. 'Really, it's thanks to Sister Germaine for keeping such fastidious records, young mouse. Now, here's where you'll start.'

An hour later Matthias left the gatehouse with Warbeak bobbing behind. As they went the young mouse muttered to himself, 'I'll need five or six strong climbing ropes, some spikes, oh, and a hammer. Must have a hammer. Now let's see, a good haversack to carry it all, enough food and drink, ah, and some candied chestnuts for you, my friend.'

Warbeak uttered a stream of curses as she stumbled on the brick. Matthias waited as she picked herself up. 'Tut tut, such language for a young sparrow.'

Constance and Ambrose Spike watched the odd pair pass by. The badger tapped the side of her head with a paw.

'Bats in the belfry.'

'Or sparrows,' giggled the hedgehog.

Basil Stag Hare superintended the willing creatures who carried logs and filling to shore up the gatehouse entrance. The hare had brought a touch of military efficiency to bear upon the exercise. He had formed the volunteers into a living chain which constantly passed the defence materials along.

Basil brought his good-natured authority into play. 'You there! Fourth from the end chappie! Liven your ideas up, laddie buck. That's the third time you've spilled a basket of soil. Here, let me show you how.'

The timid mice smiled among themselves. The blustering hare was quite a kindly creature really, all bark and no bite at all. He shared the tasks with them, working as hard as anyone.

'No, no, Brother Whatsyourname. You pass logs along like this. Look, you go and get a bite to eat. Come on, the rest of you beautiful dreamers! Stir your stumps or I'll have your whiskers for bootlaces.'

The helpers laughed and did the best they could. Now and again there would be barely stifled giggles as they watched the performance of Silent Sam. He stood behind Basil, pantomiming the hare's every movement, puffing up his tiny chest and strutting about importantly.

In the Abbey kitchens, Cornflower carefully wrapped Matthias's food in fresh dock leaves. Matthias sidled up, helping himself to a candied chestnut. Cornflower rapped his paw with a wooden ladle.

'Those nuts are for that poor little sparrow. Leave them

213

alone, you great glutton,' she scolded.

Matthias snorted indignantly. 'Poor little sparrow, my eye! Listen, Miss, if I let that young hussy off her lead for five minutes, we'd all be murdered in our beds.'

The young fieldmouse helped Matthias with the haversack straps. She tried not to let her concern for him show. 'Matthias, I know you won't tell me where you are going, but wherever it is, please take care of yourself.'

Matthias adjusted the dagger in the black sword belt. He stood framed in the doorway, smiling confidently. 'Don't worry, Cornflower. I fully intend to take care of myself, for the safety of Redwall Abbey . . . and for you.'

A moment later he was gone.

Halfway along the top dormitory passage, Matthias halted. A stepladder was set up underneath a wooden loft door in the ceiling. Methuselah came along, leading Warbeak. The sparrow was still wearing the collar, lead and brick shackle.

Matthias looked up at the door. 'So, that's where we're going, eh.'

The old gatehouse-keeper gave him a neatly-drawn map. 'You'll find it all marked down there, Matthias. That door leads to a loft. Turn to your right and keep walking until you touch the wall. To your right you will find a gap in the wall. On the other side of that gap you will come out about halfway up the wall of Great Hall on a ledge between the arches of the sandstone columns. From there you must climb up to a higher row of ledges alongside the stained glass windows. Scale the rib in the centre of the first window to the left and you will find yourself on a wooden ridge that runs along parallel to the curve of the roof. Further along that ridge there is another wooden loft door. I'm sorry, but I cannot locate it exactly; you must find it yourself. When you do, go through it and you should be directly underneath the top roof attic. From there on you are on your own. I cannot help you, Matthias.'

The ancient mouse placed his paws on his young friend's shoulders. His voice trembled as he bade good-bye. 'Good fortune go with you, Matthias. I wish that I were young and agile once again so that I could accompany you.'

Methuselah embraced the young mouse as if he were his own son, and as Matthias ascended the ladder, the old mouse called out final instructions to him.

'If that sparrow causes you any trouble, don't hesitate to kick her off into thin air. She'll come down as fast as the brick she's tied to!'

Warbeak scowled but made no comment. She knew Methuselah spoke the truth: the brick was like an anchor against her leg.

Matthias gave the loft door a strong shove upwards and slid it to one side. He covered his eyes and coughed as the dust of ages poured down upon his head.

Tugging the sparrow behind him, he climbed into the loft.

It was very dark and gloomy. Matthias peered over to his right; faintly he could make out a strip of wan, greyish light filtering in.

'Him be gap in um wall like old worm mouse say about,' Warbeak chimed.

'Hey, keep a civil tongue in your head, sparrow! That's my friend you're talking about,' gritted Matthias as he strode off to the right, tugging the lead. His concentration broken, he stepped awkwardly upon a joist and tripped heavily into the thick dust.

Warbeak was upon the young mouse in a flash!

The sparrow scratched hard at Matthias's neck and

pecked at the back of his head, forcing it down to the floor.

Matthias felt the suffocating dust clog his mouth as he struggled to turn his body over. Warbeak pecked and scratched frantically, her target obscured by the bulky haversack. Reaching up behind himself, the mouse felt around until he grasped the sparrow's leg. Giving it a hard pull, he rolled over, plucking out his dagger in the same movement. Matthias lay across Warbeak, pinning her to the floor, the point of his dagger pricking the sparrow's throat.

'Listen, Warbeak,' Matthias panted. 'One more move like that and it will be your last. Do you hear me?'

Both creatures lay still awhile, their faces close together, breathing heavily. The sparrow was still defiant. 'I gettum chance, Warbeak killee mouse. Sparra not give up, you see!'

Matthias sprang to his feet, tugging the lead viciously. He dragged the sparrow stumbling and tripping to the crack of light. Swinging the bird forwards, Matthias pushed her through the narrow aperture, squeezing through after her with great difficulty.

They were on the first ledge, high above Great Hall.

Without warning, Matthias shoved Warbeak roughly off the ledge.

The startled sparrow shot downwards and stopped with a jerk, only thick neck feathers saving her from strangulation. Matthias held the lead tightly with both paws, straining backwards as the sparrow dangled and fluttered over Great Hall.

'Now, you promise to behave yourself, or down you go, my friend,' Matthias shouted.

With her heart hammering at the surprise attack and her predicament, Warbeak realized that she was completely at the mercy of her captor. Burdened with the brick, she had no chance of flying. As she hung flapping uselessly, Matthias called down, 'Make up your mind! My paws are getting tired. This lead's beginning to slip.'

A forlorn little voice answered. 'Warbeak not wantum die. Mouse win. Pull sparra up. Be good. Give um word.'

Bracing himself against a stone arch, Matthias pulled the sparrow back to safety. Together they sat on the ledge sharing a canteen of water, both weary and dusty. Matthias was still wary of his prisoner.

'How good is the word of a sparrow?' he asked.

Warbeak puffed out her chest. 'Sparra word always good. Warbeak no say um lie. Me swear by mother's egg. That big swear.'

Matthias reflected that he had used desperate measures to secure a promise, but with justification. He was being uncompromising with himself as well as his captive. No more could he afford to be the silly little novice that had bumbled about the Abbey before the start of the present troubles. He was maturing, learning the warrior's way. This mission was vital: Redwall depended upon him, just as it had once depended upon Martin the Warrior.

Warbeak cocked her head quizzically to one side. 'What um Matthias think about?'

The young mouse repacked the water canteen into his haversack. 'Oh, nothing much, Warbeak. Come on, we'd better get on.'

With an odd feeling, Matthias realized that he and Warbeak were now on first name terms.

Cluny might be making promotions. There were now three rat officers on the list of the dead.

First it had been Skullface, killed beneath the wheels of the cart. Next to go was Ragear: there was talk of a serpent; he was never seen again. Now Redtooth, Cluny's first officer, was missing, presumed dead.

Most of Cluny's army had an eye to promotion; not only for prestige – there were the extra shares of loot to be considered.

Killconey the ferret extolled the virtues of his weasel friend, Scragg, who had met his death at the foot of the big elm tree. 'Aye, let me tell you, buckos. Scragg: now there was a weasel with a head on his shoulders! Officer material he was, definitely. D'you know, I still can't figure how a smart boyo like that could let himself be killed in a fall from some old tree.'

Cheesethief sneered. 'Clumsiness, I'd say. I was there and saw it all. Besides, Cluny wouldn't have a weasel officer ordering rats about.'

'And why not?' challenged the ferret. 'I'd wager the Chief would promote any creature that showed good sense and a fightin' spirit. Will you look at me now? I'm a fine figure of a ferret. Why, if I was the Chief I'd make me a Captain just like that!' The ferret snapped his claws.

Cheesethief spat upon the ground in contempt of Killconey, knowing there was not much chance of promotion for himself. He was only rated as a minor sort of officer. If it came to a decision, Darkclaw was the natural choice. Fangburn had fallen from favour since the incident with Sela and Redtooth. Nevertheless the weasels, and their brethren the stoats and ferrets, argued their case hotly. Why shouldn't others be promoted? What was so superior about rats? Mangefur, Scumnose, and Frogblood considered rats to be the élite of Cluny's horde. Darkclaw sided with them while trying to placate the others, attempting to keep a foot in either camp should it come to a vote. One never knew!

Little chance there was of anything democratic being allowed by Cluny the Scourge, who lay on the bed with his eye closed, ignoring the whispered bickering and backbiting around him. He would promote only when he was good and ready. Meanwhile, just let any of his horde dare try to press the issue!

Sela and her son skulked in a corner. They felt trapped. Nobody had spoken to them since the demise of Redtooth. It was as if they were being blamed.

Suddenly, Cluny called over to Sela, 'Hey, fox, take that brat of yours outside for a bit! Get some fresh air, and remember, no wandering off! Send Darkclaw in here to me, and that gabby ferret, whatsisname, Killconey.'

The foxes hastened to do as they were told, glad to be out of the oppressive atmosphere of the sick room.

Darkclaw and the ferret came marching in, not knowing whether to be confident or apprehensive. You never knew with Cluny.

They both saluted. 'Chief?'

Cluny got out of bed. He paced back and forth, testing his legs. Each day they grew a bit stronger. He walked past the pair and spoke without turning to face them, 'Who knows anything about tunnelling?'

Killconey stepped smartly forward. 'Ah, the tunnels, yer honour. You're talkin' to the very creature.'

Cluny rested upon his standard. 'You?'

'Who else but meself, sir?' the ferret wheedled. 'And don't I know some grand ould animals that could help? Ferrets like me, stoats and weasels; why, sure, we're as good as any mole when it comes to the tunnelin', so we are; shorin' and bankin', sinkin' shafts and galleries—'

Cluny banged the standard against the floor. 'Enough! Where are these others that you mentioned?'

Killconey cocked a claw over his shoulder. 'Sure, they're all outside, your worship. Shall I go and fetch them?'

Killconey threw a fancy salute and departed. Cluny pulled Darkclaw close to him. He spoke confidentially,

'Don't you know anything about tunnels, Darkclaw?'

The rat shook his head unhappily. Cluny put his claw around Darkclaw's shoulder. 'Well, never mind, I've got other work for you. We can't let ferrets, stoats and weasels take all the glory, can we? You've always been a good solid rat, Darkclaw. You help me and I'll see that you get a rich reward when the time comes.'

Darkclaw nodded obediently.

Some time later, Cluny was deep in conference with Killconey and his squad. It was interrupted by a scuffle and commotion from outside. Cheesethief strode in, dragging Chickenhound and prodding Sela ahead of him with a spear.

'What's going on here?' Cluny demanded.

Cheesethief smirked triumphantly. 'It's these two foxes, Chief. I caught them with their ears against the door; they were listening in.'

He skilfully tripped Sela and Chickenhound with the spear butt. They fell in a heap at Cluny's feet, where they lay shivering and protesting their innocence.

'Not us, sir. We weren't eavesdropping.'

'We were just leaning there for a rest. We're only simple healers.'

Cluny nodded understandingly. 'I see. You just wanted to help with the digging, is that it?'

Eager to please and panic-stricken, Chickenhound blurted out, 'Yes, that's right, sir. Give us a chance and we'll tunnel with the best of them.'

Sela groaned despairingly as Cluny kicked her son viciously. 'Who said anything about tunnelling, fox? I only mentioned digging.'

Sela attempted to save the situation. 'Please, sir, take no notice of the young fool. All he meant was that when you said dig—'

A whack from the bannerstaff silenced Sela. Cluny's voice was icy with condemnation. 'Traitors! All that he meant was that you slipped up when you copied my plans for an attack with a battering ram. So now you know that I intend to tunnel into Redwall.'

Sela licked dry lips. She stared pleadingly at the Warlord; but there was no mercy in the single eye.

'You know too much, vixen. You and your son played a dangerous game. Nobody outsmarts Cluny. I've won, and you have both lost.'

The foxes clasped their claws. They knelt, whimpering pitifully. Cluny stood over them, enjoying his power as judge. He signalled to Cheesethief and Darkclaw.

'Take these miserable turncoats out of my sight. You know what to do.'

Shrieking and screaming for mercy, the foxes were dragged away. Cluny turned back to the ferrets, weasels and stoats.

'Now, about this tunnel.'

14

Matthias and Warbeak had made slow progress. The climb up to the arches and stained-glass windows was long and arduous. Matthias had relieved the sparrow of her brick to make the going easier, pinioning her wings instead. At intervals the young mouse drove spikes into the joints of the stone. He was careful not to look down: it was a terrifyingly impressive distance down to the Abbey floor. Only once did he risk a quick glance, not certain if the dark spot on the ground might be Methuselah watching them.

There was real peril negotiating the curve at the top of the arch. Hanging tightly to the spikes he had fixed, Matthias leaned out dangerously; there was nothing but determination and the strength in his paws to stop him from plunging down to a frightening death. Gritting his teeth, he made it to the apex of the arch. He reached over the stone ledge which divided the arch from the stained-glass windows above and, taking a firm grip, propelled himself upwards and sideways. His legs landed further along the ledge. With his cheek resting on the stone, he gave one last heave and rolled on to the safety of the ledge.

Sitting up, Matthias knotted two ropes together. He lowered them to Warbeak, who was waiting below at the base of the arch. The sparrow looped the rope about herself. As she climbed she aided Matthias by finding clawholds and making use of the spikes.

Leaning back against the stained-glass windows they ate lunch. Warbeak gave a twittering laugh.

'Matthias um all red mouse.'

'Ha, you should talk, Warbeak!' Matthias replied. 'Look at yourself. You're blue all over.'

The bizarre effect was created by sunlight shining through the stained glass. As they ate, Warbeak would dodge her head from side to side, changing colour as she did so. 'Lookee! Now me green, blue again, now red like um Matthias mouse.'

'If you don't sit still you'll be white with fright, because you'll fall,' Matthias warned.

When they were sufficiently recovered to start again, Matthias tried the sandstone centre rib of the window. It was carved into a profusion of curlicues and niches which made the climb considerably easier. Soon they reached the wooden ridge at the bottom of the roof curvature. It was perilously narrow. Together they edged along it, their backs bent unsafely forward with the curve of the ceiling behind.

Neither of them was aware of the inquisitive, beaked face of a sparrow who watched them from the corner of a stained-glass window. It noted the would-be intruders, then flew off.

Matthias drew his dagger. He stuck it into the wooden ceiling to steady himself as they halted to look for the next loft door.

'I can see it,' said Matthias, 'there, along to your left. You'll have to lead, Warbeak.'

223

Gingerly the sparrow slid her claws along the smooth wooden ridge. Suddenly Matthias felt the dagger come free from the wood. He lost his grip and leaned outwards, teetering and waving his paws. Warbeak stopped him falling by pulling him back. The dagger went spinning down – it was a considerable time before they heard the faint clatter as it hit the Abbey floor.

'Gosh!' said Matthias in an awed voice. 'I thought I'd had it then. I was certain I'd fall. Thanks for saving me, Warbeak.'

Gradually they inched their way along until they arrived beneath the loft door. It was too high and difficult for either of them to reach. Matthias made several attempts before he had to admit defeat. He sat upon the ridge, kicking his legs and feeling quite angry with himself, failure staring him in the face.

'A fool, that's what I am! A little fool, climbing all this way to be beaten by an old loft door.'

The sparrow tapped him with her claw. 'Why not Matthias cut Warbeak free? Then fly with Sparra wings and open little worm door.'

Matthias looked blank. 'Beg pardon?'

Warbeak explained again. 'You no listen. Warbeak say, cut wings free, fly up and open door.'

'Give me your sparrow's word that you won't fly off.'

'Is good. Give Sparra word. Promise no 'scape.'

'Swear by your mother's egg.'

'By mother's egg. Warbeak swear.'

Matthias undid the twine that pinioned the sparrow's wings, and Warbeak flapped her wings experimentally. 'Long time no fly. Me good, you see.'

The young sparrow launched herself off the ridge. She went into a series of zooming circles and performed a few acrobatic turns for her friend's benefit.

Matthias grinned. 'Righto, I'm impressed. Now get

back here, you little showoff, and open this door.'

Warbeak sped back, hovering level with the loft door as she set her claws into the latch. 'Watch out, . . . Door open, fall on um mouse.'

The young mouse backed away as the sparrow released the door. It banged down hard, flapping on its hinges.

This time Matthias was aware that there would be a shower of falling dust when the door opened downwards. Wisely he had edged far enough along the ridge to avoid both the heavy door and the dust shower.

With Warbeak flying behind him as a backup in case he fell, Matthias used the open door as a ladder. He was soon up through the opening. Though the inside was dull and gloomy, he could see they were in a long trench-like defile, one side of which was a fairly straight wall while the other side was a high curving slope, the reverse side of the arched wooden ceiling.

Matthias called Warbeak to him. He undid the collar and lead from the sparrow's neck, and packed them away in the haversack. He patted his flying friend. 'Warbeak, I can no longer keep you collared. You are a free sparrow and a very good friend.'

The young sparrow blinked her fierce little eyes. 'Matthias, my mouse friend. I no leave um. Stay with you.'

Together they spent several minutes searching the high ceiling above. Warbeak, having the advantage of flight, was first to find the final trapdoor which they had guessed must exist.

It was not a hard climb for Matthias, merely an excited and rather undignified scramble up the curving wooden roof back. This time they found that the door opened inwards. It was really heavy. The two companions strained together until it creaked loudly and opened.

Matthias scrambled through, followed by Warbeak. They found themselves completely surrounded by sparrows as the door slammed shut behind them. The birds argued and chattered aloud as they sprang upon Matthias, pinning him to the lid of the door with many claws. He was unable to move a single whisker. As quickly as it had started, the noise ceased. The flock of birds parted. Matthias found himself staring straight into the bold, aggressive face of a big, strong-looking male sparrow. The bird glared at him with a crazy light in its bright, mad eyes.

'Mouse worm, you um my prisoner! This um court of Sparra! Me King Bull Sparra!'

15

The bodies of Sela and Chickenhound, the two traitor foxes, lay limp in the ditch that ran alongside the road. The rats of Cluny's horde had executed them with spears and tossed them there. Sela lay still, her once bright, cunning eyes glazed over in death.

But gradually Chickenhound began to twitch and groan.

He was still alive!

The fox's entire body was afire with pain. Twice they had stabbed him, once in the back leg, and again right through the loose skin and fur at the scruff of his neck. Chickenhound had screamed and fallen into the ditch, helped by the feet of the rat executioners. He had immediately blacked out. Sela's carcass landed on top of her son's body in the shallow, muddy water.

The rats were satisfied that both foxes were dead, and if they were not, well, who was going to climb down through those stinging nettles into the slippery ooze to find out? They hurled clods of earth at the prone forms in the ditch and stood watching them for a time. When flies began to gather on the foxes, the rodents lost interest and wandered off.

Chickenhound regained his senses. He lay quite still with Sela's body draped across him. When he was satisfied that the coast was clear he struggled painfully clear of the grisly carcass that had once been his mother.

Old fool! She would never have been in this mess if she'd let a much younger and smarter fox handle things.

With a total lack of sorrow for his deceased parent, Chickenhound began figuring out his next move. He would have to lie low in this stinking ditch until darkness fell. Even though he was severely hurt, the irony of the situation caused the young fox a silent snigger. It was he, not his mother, who had outwitted Cluny. Now he would soon be free with the revised plans of the attack upon Redwall Abbey. Surely that would be worth something?

As soon as it was dark, Chickenhound made his move. He was only too glad to do so. Flies, wasps, worms, and all manner of crawlies had been thoroughly investigating him all afternoon. Slowly and carefully he rolled about in the thick mud until it formed a poultice, cooling the wounds in his leg and neck, preventing further blood loss. Under the cover of night he wobbled unsteadily to his feet, limping away up the bed of the ditch towards Redwall.

The going was painfully slow, but Chickenhound consoled himself on the long journey by boosting his own ego. 'Maybe a silly bunch of rats could put one over on Sela. Huh, she was old and had lost a lot of her guile. Not like me! They hadn't reckoned with a smart intelligent young fox like I am. I'll show them! Revenge will be mine! They'll see what it's like to be up against an expert in espionage.'

Hours later, within sight of the Abbey walls, Chickenhound discovered a slope that was not too steep and started to pull himself up out of the ditch. He gasped and cried out in agony as he climbed. Using some creepers and an overhanging bush, the young fox finally made it to the road.

Completely exhausted, he lay in the dust. How long he had been dragging his wounded body along the ditch bed he could not tell. In his present weakened condition he could not go a step further, but fell into a state halfway between unconsciousness and sleep.

Silent Sam was Cornflower's bodyguard on her nightly round of the ramparts. He marched solemnly by her side as she gave out mugs of hot soup to the grateful sentries that watched through the night hours. Ambrose Spike watched hungrily as she poured him a steaming mug of the delicious soup. The hedgehog thanked her profusely, hoping that there might be seconds after the others had been served.

'What a thoughtful little body you are, Miss Cornflower. I always say there's nothing like some good home-made vegetable soup to keep the life in my old spines. It's a fair night, but mark you, it gets a bit chill 'twixt dark and dawn, m'dear.'

Whilst the hedgehog and the mouse were chatting, Silent Sam was never still for a second. He trotted about on the parapet, always sucking his paw, leaping from stone to stone, fighting off imaginary foes with his tiny dagger.

At first Cornflower thought he was play-acting as usual. The baby squirrel stood on top of the gatehouse threshold. Pointing down to the road with his knife, he beckoned Cornflower and Ambrose with his well-sucked paw to come and see something.

The young fieldmouse wagged her ladle. 'Put that

dagger away and stop your climbing, you little scamp.'

Silent Sam remained as he was, like a well-trained pointer dog.

'P'raps he's trying to tell us summat, Miss?' grunted Ambrose. He waddled over to the parapet and looked down to where Sam pointed.

'Well, bless m'soul, Miss Cornflower. I do believe that our little soldier 'ere has spotted a hobject. There's a creature a layin' down there, but I'm blowed if it's fish or fowl, there's so much mud and dust plastered on it,' whispered the hedgehog. 'You stay put, Missy. I'll go and fetch help.'

Cornflower and Silent Sam stood looking down from the parapet. Ambrose, aided by Jess Squirrel and the Foremole, ventured out into the road to investigate. At their back stood a dozen stout mice guarding the gatehouse door under the command of Basil Stag Hare.

'Steady in the ranks there,' said the hare quietly. 'Keep your eyes peeled for signs of ambush, and no talking now.'

Chickenhound was lugged inside as rapidly as possible. Unable to contain their curiosity, the defenders questioned the limp, half-awake fox as they carried him across the Abbey grounds.

'Did your friends the rats do this?'

'I suppose it's sanctuary you want now?'

'Harr, warra you'm be about, a layin' in yon road?'

Chickenhound's head flopped from side to side as he was borne along. He would only say one thing. 'The Abbot. I must see the Abbot. Keep that badger away from me, or you'll learn nothing.'

Basil dismissed the rearguard and caught up with Ambrose. 'I say, you'd best get that rascal straight to the jolly old Abbot. Let him make his statement before he pegs out, don'cha know.'

Chickenhound was hauled into the Abbey building and laid out on a bench. Abbot Mortimer shuffled up in his nightshirt, rubbing sleep from his eyes. He inspected the fox's wounds with a critical, practised look and spoke dispassionately, 'Well, fox, what do you want from us? No doubt Cluny your master has sent you here to spy.'

Chickenhound shook his head in weak denial. 'Please, I must have some water.'

Jess Squirrel picked up the water jug but withheld it.

'Tell the Father Abbot what you want, sly one,' she rasped sternly.

The fox reached out feebly for the water jug. Much to the Abbot's dismay, Jess still held it at a distance.

'Speak first. You'll get water when we get information,' she insisted.

The sight of an injured animal distressed the Abbot, but he decided wisely to leave matters to Jess. The squirrel knew what she was doing.

'Cluny's horde did this to me,' croaked the fox. 'My mother, Sela . . . they killed her. I know of Cluny's new plans. Care for me and I will tell you all.'

Chickenhound fainted clean away.

'Huh, I certainly wouldn't waste good time and medicine on this one,' said Jess coldly.

Ambrose Spike scratched his stomach speculatively. 'True, Jess, neither would I. But mayhap he has vital information, otherwise why would he drag himself 'ere in this state?'

The Abbot inspected the fox's neck-wound beneath the muddied fur. 'What Ambrose says makes sense. Would you lift the wretched creature up and carry him to the sick bay, please?'

Cornflower and Silent Sam watched the fox being carried away. Sam stood in front of her, his dagger drawn

231

to protect them both. She ruffled his pointed ears.

'It's all right now, Sam,' she said, gently. 'The fox cannot hurt us. Thank you for protecting me.'

The little squirrel sheathed his knife and resumed paw-sucking.

Winifred and Abbot Mortimer sat by the bed in the sick bay. They kept up their vigil until Chickenhound regained consciousness. The fox whimpered. He gazed around at the homely little room.

'Oh my neck! What is this place? Where am I?' he groaned.

Winifred pushed the patient gently back on to the pillows and held a bowl of water to the cracked, dry lips.

'Please drink this and lie still,' she ordered.

Chickenhound slurped and gulped greedily at the water as the Abbot enlightened him. 'You are in the infirmary at Redwall Abbey. As yet I do not know the full extent of your injuries. When you have rested my friends will cleanse you and dress your wounds.'

Chickenhound could hardly believe his ears. 'You mean I can stay! But I haven't told you of the new plans yet.'

The Abbot wiped driblets of water from the patient's chin. 'Listen to me, my son. We would not turn you away from our gates, unless you were an enemy that meant us harm. All creatures are cared for at Redwall Abbey and it is my task to care for the sick and injured. You are my responsibility. Whether or not you choose to give information is a matter that your own heart must deal with. Meanwhile you will receive our hospitality and sanctuary until you are fully recovered.'

Chickenhound lay thinking about what the kindly old mouse had said. Suddenly he blurted out. 'The battering ram is only a decoy. Cluny means to use it as a diversion so that he can tunnel underneath your Abbey walls. I don't know exactly where he plans to start digging, but I do know that he will come at you from under the ground.'

The Abbot shook his head reprovingly as Winifred lowered the lamp flame and drew the curtains. 'Cluny is surely the spawn of darkness. He will stop at nothing, my son. Now I realize this and I believe what you tell me is true. But why did you crawl all the way to Redwall with this information – almost at the cost of your life?'

Chickenhound did his best to look sorrowful and out-raged as he lied. 'Because they killed old Sela, sir. She was my mother. I will not rest until justice is done to her murderers.'

The Abbot patted the young fox's paw. 'Thank you for entrusting your confidence in us, young one. Close your eyes now, and try to get some rest.'

When the Abbot had departed, Chickenhound snuggled his filthy body down against the clean white sheets. He felt a little better already, well enough to have a quiet snigger.

There was no fool like an old fool!

This mouse was as stupid as Sela had been. Let the mice fight the rats and the rats fight the mice; what did he care? Redwall must be a veritable treasure house to a clever young fox.

16

Dunwing was the widowed mother of Warbeak. She was also sister to the mighty King Bull Sparra. When her daughter had been shot down by the arrow, she had given her up as dead. Now that she was back safe and sound she stroked and scolded her at the same time with relief. When she could get a chirp in edgeways, Warbeak related the strange story to her mother in the rapid Sparra dialect.

As she was doing this, Matthias lay pinned to the floor by the claws of many fierce Sparra warriors. As far as he could tell, the place was one enormous loft. This was the court of King Bull Sparra, whose wrath seemed about to descend upon him.

The sparrows lived higgledy-piggledy here in one great untidy tribe. The roof above met in the shape of an upturned 'V', thus making the court a long triangular structure. Under the eaves at either edge were countless scruffy-looking nets, all of which appeared to be filled to overflowing with shrieking baby sparrows. At one end the loft was blocked off by roofing slates and old nesting materials. This was the King's own private chamber. Matthias estimated that it was probably underneath the spot where the weather vane was situated.

King Bull Sparra was not a bird to be trifled with. He
noticed the young mouse's evident interest in his surroundings and quickly diverted his attention with a
savage kick at the helpless figure.

'What um mouseworm want in court of King?' he
snapped.

Matthias, realizing that this was no time for idle chit-
chat, promptly shouted out in a loud, courtly manner, 'O
King, I come to return one of your brave young warriors!'

The statement caused an immediate hullaballoo. Bull
Sparra flapped his wings once and quiet descended. He
cocked his head to one side, assessing this bold young
intruder.

'You lie, mouseworm. Not helpum Sparra! Mouse
enemy,' he shrieked. 'King Bull Sparra say killee um
enemy, killee!'

Instantly Matthias found himself fighting for his life. The
Sparra soldiers piled in on him, jabbering, clawing and
pecking. He managed to get a paw free and struck out left
and right, dealing hefty blows to several of the sparrows.
Matthias realized that he would soon be overwhelmed as
more sparrows pressed in one him, urged on by the mad
exhortations of their King. 'Killee, killee, make um
mouse dead, killee!'

As Matthias battled to free his other paw he felt himself
enveloped by two pairs of wings. Warbeak and Dunwing
were attempting to shelter him. The mother sparrow was
crying out, 'No killee! Mouse good! Save um my egg
Sparra.'

The King was not convinced. 'Mouse enemy, gotta
make um dead.'

King Bull Sparra had no fledglings of his own.

235

Warbeak, who was his favourite niece, called out to her uncle, appealing for mercy. 'No, no, King Bull. Not killee Matthias mouse! Him save Warbeak! Give Sparra word to mouse that you no killee.'

The King sprang in among his warriors, scattering them like chaff. They cowered before him as he shouted out a new edict. 'Foolworms! Stop! King say no killee mouse! We have Sparra word of my sister's eggchick.'

The Sparra warriors backed off. Matthias picked himself up. Luckily, he had not come to much harm. He dusted his habit off. 'Whew! Thank you once again, Warbeak my friend. I owe you my life.'

The King issued orders to two Sparra warriors. 'Battlehawk, Windplume! Gettum bag. Find out what mouse carry.'

Matthias stood firm as the haversack was pulled from his back. The two warriors could not figure out how to open it. They tore at the material with beak and claw until it gave way. The contents scattered upon the floor. Matthias stood respectfully to one side as the King rummaged through his meagre possessions.

King Bull Sparra drank some water from the canteen. He spat it out.

'No worms, only um mousefood,' he commented.

Warbeak sighed wistfully. She looked longingly on as her uncle found the package of candied chestnuts and ripped it open. Bull Sparra dubiously sampled one. His face lit up with pleasure. 'This good food for Sparra King. Not good for mouseworm. Me keep.'

He tucked the candied chestnuts under his wing, then picked up the collar and lead and beckoned to Matthias. 'Mouseworm, come here. You lucky. King lettum live.'

The young mouse approached the sparrow with trepidation, not wanting to antagonize the moody, dangerous bird. The Sparra King buckled the collar tightly about

Matthias's neck, scarcely leaving him room to breathe. He attached the lead and laughed aloud. Dutifully the other sparrows laughed with him.

Matthias felt his blood boil. He tried to contain his rising temper; the court of the Sparra King was no place to have tantrums. Mentally he promised himself that he would never again use a collar on any living creature. The indignity was unspeakable.

Bull Sparra handed the lead to Warbeak. Turning to his subjects, he chuckled insanely and pointed at Matthias. 'King Bull Sparra spare um mouse. How you like him for pet, my niece? Mouse, you obey my sister and her egg-chick, funny ha?'

All the sparrows laughed loud and long, vying with each other to show the most merriment. The King was a completely unpredictable tyrant. When he made a joke it was always funny.

Warbeak gave the lead a tug and whispered to her friend, 'Matthias, you see Warbeak and um mother not make laugh. Sorry.'

The young captive winked at his warder. He was beginning to hatch a plan. 'Don't worry, my friend. At least I'm alive.'

Warbeak handed the lead to her mother. 'This Dunwing; she mother. Um good Sparra; not hurt mouse. See!'

Dunwing gave the lead a light pull. She gave Matthias a smile and a nod. He decided that he liked Warbeak's mother.

The King issued his orders to Warbeak and Dunwing. 'You keep um mouseworm on um lead. No wander, no stray. Give um plenty work. Much kick, like this.'

Bull Sparra raised a kick at Matthias, who dodged nimbly and started to dance and sing with a silly expression on his face.

The King stood with his head cocked to one side, amazed at the performance of this strange mouse.

Matthias pranced comically about, improvising a song as he went:

> 'Up higher than before,
> I'm near the roof indeed,
> The King gave me a collar,
> His sister holds the lead.'

Round and round he skipped, repeating the verse over and over.

Bull Sparra flapped his wings and laughed hysterically. 'Hahahahahahaha! Look, Battlehawk! See, Windplume! Mouseworm be hurt in um headbrain. He crazy! Hahaha-hahahaha.'

Obediently everybody laughed with the mad monarch.

After a while the sparrows drifted off, some to their nests, others to hunt worms. A chosen few went with the King to play three feathers, a popular Sparra gambling game of which Bull Sparra was very fond. Dunwing and her daughter led the dancing mouse off to their nest at the rear of the court under the farthest eaves.

Despite its outward untidy appearance, the nest was neat and cosy on the inside. Warbeak had gathered Matthias's gear together. Repacking it into the torn haversack, she returned it to her mouse friend, eyeing him in an apprehensive manner.

'Matthias be sick in um head?' she inquired.

The young mouse lay back gratefully in Dunwing's nest and smiled reassuringly at them both. 'Not at all. I'm as sane as you are. However, if I act as if I'm mad then maybe your King and his warriors will not regard me as a threat. Perhaps they will leave me alone and forget about me.'

Dunwing looked up from the meal she was preparing. Her eyes were serious.

'Matthias mouse do right thing,' she said. 'Bull Sparra be wicked; bad temper. Sometimes Dunwing think Bull Sparra mad. Best he thinks you um no-harm mouse.'

Matthias bowed deferentially to her. 'Thank you, Dunwing. You are a very brave sparrow. You put yourself and Warbeak in great peril, saving me as you did.'

Dunwing served them both some food. Thankfully Matthias noted that she refrained from putting worms and dead insects on his portion. The mother sparrow watched him with soft, intelligent eyes. The mouse was about the same age as her daughter.

'Matthias save um my Warbeak,' she said. 'We have no Sparra warrior to look after us. Warbeak brave like um father was. Now um father, he dead. I learn to stand up for us 'til Warbeak grow into um great warrior some day.'

The hours slipped by as the three conversed. Matthias learned much of the Sparra customs and way of life.

Dunwing, being the King's sister, was of royal blood. Her husband had been killed the previous spring in a battle with some starlings. He had saved the life of the King, whereupon Bull Sparra had vowed to care for her and her daughter: but he had instantly forgotten his promises, leaving the pair to fend for themselves. Only in moments of urgency would Dunwing remind him of his vow, knowing that Bull Sparra was a dangerous despot. So normally Dunwing maintained a diplomatic silence in his presence.

Sometimes Bull Sparra would retire to his private chamber. He would remain in there brooding for days, suddenly emerging to fire his warriors with grandiose schemes and wild ideas. No one dared to disobey him, even though half an hour later he had forgotten his previous foolhardy notions and wandered off to hunt worms. Later he would return to find that his plans had not been carried out. In a furious squabble of accusation and recrimination he would demote officers and promote the most unlikely soldiers from the ranks. Next day he had forgotten it all again and was hatching more crazy plans. Matthias was constantly amazed at the mode of life in the Sparra court. The sparrows showed no kindness or civility to one another, often fighting savagely among themselves on the slightest pretext. Warriors, and even fledglings joined in. The injuries they inflicted upon each other were appalling.

Sparra folk knew nothing of the firemaker's art. By day the court was illuminated by sunlight that streamed in through the cracked and broken slates and slanted up through the eaves. All food was eaten uncooked, worms and small insects providing the main diet. The Sparra did not discriminate between different species of insects. All came under the general heading of 'worm'. Thus a sparrow might make a meal of a butterfly or a grasshopper and refer to it as 'wormfeed'. 'Worm' was also used to denote an enemy or a coward or anything alien to the Sparra. Fresh flowers and tender shoots of vegetation were used to supplement the worm diet, also berries and whatever fruit a Sparra could carry in flight. Matthias was grateful for this. He abhorred the idea of eating live worms or dead insects.

There was no strict routine or chores ever carried out. Apart from parents feeding fledglings, everything was left undone until tomorrow, which meant it never was done. The evidence of this lay all about the court; dirt, dust, filth and general chaos prevailed.

Matthias gradually found that once he could keep pace with the speedy delivery of Sparra language it was relatively simple. The use of the term 'um', was indiscrimate, thrown in wherever the speaker fancied. It was quite basic. Often ordinary words were joined together or elongated by adding 'ee'. Some of the Sparra chattered with such rapidity that Matthias was sure they could not understand themselves.

Matthias was not sure whether Warbeak knew of his mission to bring back Martin's sword; certainly Dunwing did not. The young mouse had had a good look round most of the court, but the sword was not to be seen. Matthias reasoned that it must be in the one place he had not yet explored: the private chamber of the King. He thought long and hard about how he might obtain access to the royal apartment. He did not want to cause trouble for his friends, nor did he want them to suspect what he had come for. And supposing he ever did regain the sword, the next problem would be how to take it safely back down to the floor of the Abbey and his own kind.

Matthias figured that he had been in his new surroundings for a night and a day. Towards the evening of that day, he was sitting outside the nest, repairing his torn haversack and taking stock of his personal effects. Each time a sparrow passed by he would grin vacantly and strike up his song. No one bothered to take much heed of him.

Warbeak flew in from a lone wormhunt. She stood watching Matthias.

'Me hunt um worms,' she chirped. 'Bring um dandelions for Matthias. Mouse like eatum flowers.'

Matthias replied in Sparra language. 'Warbeak um good hunter. Mouse like flower. Makum good wormfood. Where be Dunwing mother?'

Warbeak pointed to the King's chamber. 'Dunwing gettum Bull Sparra wormfood ready. King have no wife to makee food.'

Matthias acted unconcerned. He pulled at the collar to loosen it.

'Um collar hurt mouseneck,' he grinned.

Warbeak shrugged sympathetically. 'King say you wear um. No can takee off. Me sorry.'

Matthias continued sorting through his belongings. He came across an unopened package. What a stroke of luck! It was candied chestnuts. Hastily he slipped them into the haversack, hiding the nuts from Warbeak. Under normal circumstances he would gladly have given them to his friend, but this was different. Matthias needed them as bait.

They continued gossiping until Dunwing returned. After a decent interval the young mouse spoke to her, 'You go to um King's room all um lotta time.'

Dunwing nodded.

'Me um only Sparra King Bull lettum into there,' she laughed. 'He lazy Sparra. Not makum own wormfood.'

Matthias shared her laughter.

'Betcha um King not know how to makum own wormfood,' he chuckled. 'What you think, Dunwing? Matthias findum gift for King?'

The Sparra mother looked up sharply. 'What um mouse mean. Gift?'

Matthias drew close and whispered conspiratorially. 'You 'member how King Bull like um mouse candy nuts? Me findum more. You takee me. We give nuts to um King.'

Dunwing looked doubtful. 'What for mouse wanna give um nuts to King?'

Matthias spread his paws as if stating the obvious. 'So um King lettum mouse free. Wanna go back to um mousehome.'

Matthias held his breath and watched Dunwing. Finally her face softened. She smiled sympathetically. 'All right, Matthias. We try um. Not do much harm, but 'member, not makum Bull Sparra bad temper. He killee sure.'

With an inward sigh of relief Matthias swept up the packet of nuts.

'Thank you, Sparra mother,' he said. 'Mouse not makum trouble for you. Nuts makum King happy, you see.'

With Matthias trailing behind her on his lead, Dunwing tapped on the slates which formed King Bull Sparra's wall. An irate voice came from within.

'Fly 'way, Sparra! King wantum sleep.'

Dunwing realized they had chosen a bad moment. Nevertheless she persisted, this time tapping harder. 'Lettum in, King brother. It Dunwing and crazy mouseworm. Gottum gift for great King.'

A sleepy head poked round the door opening. Bull Sparra blinked owlishly at them and yawned in their faces.

'Better be 'portant, um Majesty no like to be woked,' he grumbled.

As they entered the room, Matthias skipped about and sang his ditty. Whipping out the packet he selected a nut and popped it straight into the open beak of the astonished ruler.

'Mouseworm findum more candynuts for big King Sparra,' Matthias giggled. 'Fetchum here quick. Maybe mouse givum King all nuts. King lettum mouse go home free.'

The King munched and chomped greedily on the sweet nut, eyeing the packet covetously. 'Ha, mouseworm givum King all nuts. Majesty have great things on um mind. Me thinka bout, hmmm, lettum mouse go free-home.'

Matthias capered about. He went down on one knee, offering the nuts. Bull Sparra snatched the parcel. Hoggishly he stuffed far more of the nuts into his beak than it could cope with. Closing his eyes in ecstasy he gobbled furiously. Pieces of nut falling from his beak littered his breast feathers.

Matthias's eyes roved about the chamber, searching. It was nothing special as Sparra habitations went: a straw palliasse, some butterfly wings stuck to the wall by way of decoration. In one corner there was a huge overstuffed old chair. How it got there would forever remain a mystery. Matthias's attention was held by something that protruded out of the back of the chair. It was an old-fashioned-looking object made from black leather with lots of silver trimming, identical to the belt he was wearing.

The scabbard of Martin's sword!

Surely the sword must be somewhere close by?

Matthias wished that he could see around the back of the chair to confirm his discovery, but he had to bring himself back to the issue at hand.

King Bull Sparra crammed the last candied chestnuts into his beak and chomped with evident enjoyment.

Dunwing attempted to press for justice. 'King eatum gift. Now mouse go free?'

The King held out a grasping claw. 'More! Mouse-worm got more candynut gift for um Majesty?'

Matthias remained kneeling. He appealed to the gluttonish ruler.

'O King, um mouse have no got more candynuts. Give um all to great Majesty. Now you let mouse go free-home,' he said hopefully.

Bull Sparra pecked nut morsels from his feathers, his eyes gleaming craftily.

'Ah! Now King give um Sparra word. I say if mouse-worm give um more candynuts then go free, but must give lot.' The King spread his wings wide apart. 'This many lot!'

The young mouse bowed his head. 'But Majesty, me gottum no more nut.'

Unexpectedly Bull Sparra's mood changed for the worse. He crumpled the empty dock-leaf packet and hurled it into Matthias's face.

'Mouseworm get more! More, you hear?' His eyes shone madly as the feathered hackles rose around his neck. 'King not argue with crazy mouseworm. You gettum gone now, plenty quick or me killee. Go now. Majesty sleep.'

Sensing that the King had become dangerous, Dunwing did not hesitate. Roughly she dragged the mouse by the lead from the chamber.

Matthias spluttered with uncontrollable rage. 'Dunwing, how you lettum stupid oaf be King of Sparra?' he choked.

The mother sparrow shushed soothingly and dragged Matthias off to the safety of her nest.

Warbeak had gone off hunting again. Dunwing sat down and tried to reason with the angry young mouse. 'Matthias not let King Bull hearsay him stupid oaf. You be dead wormbait much soon.'

Matthias opened his mouth to protest. The sparrow silenced him with an upraised wing. 'All birds know that King Bull mighty fighter. Him save Sparra tribe many time from um enemy. He sometime lazy, sometime bad temper, but not stupid. Bull Sparra sly like hum fox, only pretend to be stupid, just like Matthias.'

Dunwing had guessed that Matthias had gone to the

King's chamber for other reasons than to gain his freedom. This was a very wise mother bird. He decided to put all of his cards on the table.

'Dunwing, listen. I want to tell you a story,' he said. 'It is all about the mice who live in the Abbey beneath us, and of one mouse in particular called Martin the Warrior . . . .'

The sparrow listened intently as the young mouse unfolded the story of Redwall Abbey and the part that he was playing in its hour of need. When Matthias had finished his tale, Dunwing saw the truth of it in his open face. She drew close and said quietly, 'Matthias, Dunwing knew! Um first day you come here I see um belt you wear. It all same as thing behind chair in King's room.'

'But why——?' Matthias interjected. Again Dunwing silenced him.

'Young mouse sittum still,' she said. 'Now me tell you um story. Many time ago, before my mother was egg, King named Bloodfeather. He stealum sword from northpoint. Sword make Sparra folk proud, brave fighters, strong egg-chicks, much wormfood to eat. Sword hang in court of Sparra. Bloodfeather die, who know how? Bull Sparra become um King. My husband Greytail tellum me this 'fore he die. Bull Sparra wear um warrior sword. Case be too heavy. Leave case behind in room backa chair. Carry sword in clawfeet. King Bull he much showoff. Dig worm with sword. My husband go longa with him. One day they hunt in Mossflower trees, giantworm come, one with poisonteeth. Alla time say "Asmodeusss", like that. Bull Sparra droppum big sword. Even he scared of poisonteeth. Giantworm curl round um swordhandle. Bull Sparra, he order my husband Greytail gettum sword back. Greytail try, but worm bite um with poisonteeth. He hurt bad, but fly back to court with um Bull Sparra. They leave sword in

Mossflower with giantworm. My husband die. Bull Sparra say hurt in starling fight. Not true. Greytail tell me all 'fore he die. Warbeak still egg; not know how father die.'

Matthias watched sympathetically as Dunwing fought back her tears. Gently he patted the widowed sparrow. 'Greytail be um mighty warrior to face poisonteeth alone. You glad um Warbeak be his eggchick.'

Dunwing smiled through her tears. 'Matthias be good mouse.'

There followed an embarrassed silence. Matthias spoke half aloud. 'So, it seems my quest has been in vain. But what of the scabbard?'

'Scabbard mean um sword case?' Dunwing inquired. Matthias nodded.

'Me tellum 'bout sword case,' Dunwing said bitterly. 'King Bull Sparra be frighten to tellum rest of Sparra that he lose sword. Huh, he not know um Greytail tell me, but I watchum King, Dunwing know. Bull Sparra still pretend um sword in case. That way he stay King. If I tell, he killee me and Warbeak, this I know. Someday Warbeak my eggchick be Queen. She have royal blood, then Sparra folk be better, be happy. Bull Sparra rule for now, huh, lose heart, lose sword. Um no good crazy bird, Bull Sparra.'

That night as he settled down to sleep in Dunwing's nest, Matthias had a good deal to reflect upon. So, King Bull had lost the sword to a giantworm with poisonteeth. Matthias knew the description fitted only one thing: a snake!

Poison probably meant it was an adder. He had never seen an adder, nor any other type of snake. At Redwall he had learned of snakes from the talk of others. They spoke of the adder as if it were reptile that was half legend, half nightmare. It was said that even the Father Abbot himself would flatly refuse to treat a snake, no matter how bad its condition might be. Luckily there had never been cause to. There had never been reports of an adder in the area of Mossflower, that was why most creatures tended to treat it as a mythical reptile; but wise ones like Constance, the Abbot and old Methuselah assured everyone that the adder was cold, deadly fact. They said that in all the world there was nothing more feared; the strong coils, hypnotic eyes, and poison fangs.

Matthias shuddered. It sounded even more fearsome than Cluny the Scourge! How could a mere mouse take the sword from this adder that Dunwing had described? The one that said 'Asmodeusss'? Matthias tried to put it from his mind. Gradually sleep overtook him.

'You come quick, mouseworm. Um King wanta see you.'

Rough claws seized Matthias, dragging him from the nest only half awake. It was the two Sparra warriors, Battlehawk and Windplume. They lugged Matthias off without further explanation, tugging cruelly on his lead. The last things he saw before he was pulled off into the darkness of the court were the pale, worried faces of Dunwing and Warbeak.

He shouted to reassure them: 'Don't worry, I'll be all right. Take care of yourselves.'

Battlehawk hit Matthias in the face with a stiff, bony wing. 'Mouseworm, shuttum beak or me killee.'

'Not before I see your King you won't,' the young mouse retorted.

Battlehawk aimed a kick at him, but Windplume deflected it. 'Leave mouse alone. You killee him, King killee us.'

Windplume grinned at Matthias. 'Mouse cheeky, but

248

brave like um Sparra warrior.'

King Bull Sparra had finished napping. Something was disturbing him about the captive mouse. He had been too busy guzzling candied chestnuts to let it bother him. But now that he was wide awake it hit him like a ton of bricks.

The mouseworm's belt!

What had taken Dunwing a single glance to recognize had finally dawned on the King. Matthias's belt was the same as the sword case behind his own chair!

A broken piece of mirror reflecting the moonlight was the only illumination in the King's chamber. He dismissed his two warriors to wait outside. The King of the Sparra folk sat staring at the young mouse in silence.

Matthias stood his ground bravely, not knowing what to expect. Bull Sparra stood up. He strutted about in front of Matthias, then around behind him. Matthias felt his belt gripped from behind by strong claws. The crazed King whispered close in his ear.

'Where mouseworm gettum belt?'

Matthias swallowed hard. He tried to act casually.

'Belt? Oh, you mean this belt? Mouse always have um belt for many long time. Not know where me gettum.'

Thump!

Matthias hit the floor as the King shoved him fiercely in the back. 'Mouse lie. King Bull not um wormfool! Where you gettum? Tell, tell.'

As he shouted madly, the sparrow pulled at the belt. Matthias knew he was facing death with the insane ruler in one of his lunatic rages: he must think fast.

'No gottum more candynuts,' the young mouse cried. 'Please, Majesty, give um mouseword, no more candynuts. Me give um great King this belt, then he lettum mouse go freehome.'

249

Matthias's plea had the desired effect upon the mad King. He sat in the big chair, his eyes glinting cunningly.

'Sparra law say King must killee mouseworm, but me um good Majesty. No killee mouse. Give um belt to King.'

Matthias unbuckled the belt and handed it over. King Bull fondled it, then fastened it on himself. As he admired the belt, strutting in front of the broken mirror, the sparrow spoke in a normal voice.

'Nice, good belt. Mouse know of great sword?'

Instantly Matthias was on his guard. One wrong word might spell death for Dunwing and Warbeak. He must affect ignorance to allay the King's suspicions.

'Oh, Majesty, that um good belt. Make King look fine, like mighty warrior. Not lookum so good on mouse.'

Bull Sparra appeared flattered. He preened himself then asked the question again, this time in a coaxing tone. 'Surely Matthias know of um great sword?'

In spite of his dangerous predicament Matthias was inwardly amused at the King's use of his name. Slumping to the floor, he sat with his head between his paws, the picture of dejected innocence.

'Oh mighty King, mouse not have um more candy-nuts. Not know 'bout um sword thing, not even have belt now. Me die if not soon go free. Please lettum poor mouseworm go home.'

Matthias's show of pathos seemed to cheer the King. He tucked his wingtips into the belt that he had fooled the mouseworm into giving him. Ha, he had eaten all the mouse's nuts too! Feeling no end of a fine bird, he gave a sharp whistle that brought his two warriors on the double.

'Looka this mouseworm,' he scoffed. 'He not happy that I spare um. You take um mouse back to my sister Dunwing. Tell her King say, take care of um mouseworm. He give me good gifts, candynut, belt. Maybe mouse find more gift for good Majesty, who lettum live. Take 'way now. Must get more sleep. Go.'

As Matthias was dragged off once more, he pretended to cry out in distress. This caused Bull Sparra much amusement. He waved a wing in farewell, calling out to the prisoner, 'Gettum good sleep, mouseworm. Thinkum way to get more gift for Majesty, hahahahaha!'

The two warriors and a nearby fledgling who was half awake laughed obediently with their King.

Matthias thanked his lucky stars that he had once more come out alive. Had he refused to give the belt he would surely have died. Anyhow, he reflected, it was only a temporary loan. As he planned on stealing the scabbard from Bull Sparra, why not the belt to go with it?

17

Basil Stag Hare and Jess Squirrel were as thick as thieves. When they were not helping with the defences, they could be found in odd corners whispering together. Nobody knew what their conversations were about, or what exactly they were plotting. But with the fastest runner and the champion climber of Mossflower, it was sure to be something spectacular!

Cornflower and Silent Sam watched them stealing off at lunchtime to continue their conspiracy beneath the trees in the orchard where they would not be disturbed.

'What do you suppose your mum and Basil are up to, Sam?' asked the young fieldmouse, whose curiosity was aroused.

Silent Sam shrugged his tiny shoulders and buried his head in the lunch-time milkbowl. He drank in a noisy, enjoyable infant fashion. Whatever Jess was planning had Sam's complete approval, simply because his mum could do no wrong as far as he was concerned.

Basil stretched comfortably in the shade while Jess sat out

in the sunlight, her tail, curled overhead, acting as a sunshade.

'Ah, this is the life, Jess me old climber.' Basil yawned cavernously as he fed crumbs to the ants. 'Plenty to keep the inner creature satisfied. Scorching June weather, and a top-hole billet for snoozin', what, what.'

Jess nibbled on a wedge of cheese. 'Aye, and it's up to woodlanders like us to keep it that way, Basil. What sort of a neighbourhood would this be for young uns like my Sam to grow up in if Cluny and his lot were to take over?'

Basil humphed through his military-style whiskers. 'Good grief, doesn't bear thinkin' about, old gel! Those rats and vermin, an absolute shower of yahoos and cads! Bad influence, y'know.'

They both sat nodding in agreement, faces full of grim righteousness, uttering dire home truths and generally working themselves up into a fine old state of indignation.

'Huh, Cluny the Scourge! A bully and a braggart if ever I clapped eyes on one.'

'Yes, and a robber to boot. Fancy stealing Martin's tapestry from the mice! What harm have they ever done to him?'

'Y'know, it strikes me that it'd do the Father Abbot's heart good to see that tapestry back in its rightful place again.'

'Indeed it would, and the troops would take new heart.'

'Ha, what a blow it would be to that feller Cluny and his filthy band of robbers.'

Basil bounded up and ate the last of Jess's cheese decisively. 'Well, what are we waiting for then? Come on, Jess you old hazelnut woffler. Up and at 'em. Forward the fur!'

Jess flexed her climbing claws and bared her teeth angrily.

'Just you try and stop me,' she chattered fiercely.

Without telling anyone of their intentions, the two expert campaigners slid out secretly by one of the small doors in the Abbey walls. Soon they were stealing through the green, noontide depths of Mossflower Wood.

Cluny was up and about. His first decision was to put the horde through their paces. He had decided that they had become fat and lazy from lying about in the church grounds while he was confined to bed, but now he was on the mend they were going to do some drill. Standing on a tombstone, he leaned slightly upon his standard and viewed the army in training.

Panting and sweating, a large mob of rats dashed to and fro burdened by the battering ram. The captains, hoping to curry favour with Cluny, harangued the hapless runners: 'Pick your feet up, you lily-livered scum! Come on, lift that ram properly, you idle devils.'

Practice tunnels were being dug willy-nilly owing to the lack of communication between rats and other species. Ferrets, weasels, and stoats, their faces smeared with moist, dark earth, popped out of the ground in the oddest of places. Unaccustomed to such strenuous labour, they would stop digging as they pleased, basking in the sun until they were trodden on by columns of marching rats. A squabble would ensue until they all became aware of the watchful eye of Cluny. Then it would be heads down, resume marching, get back to tunnelling.

Either side of Cluny on the tombstone stood Darkclaw and Killconey. Scornfully watching the chaotic manoeuvres, the Warlord would criticize first one then the other for the shortcomings of the creatures they represented. Both squirmed under the lash of the Chief's tongue.

'Darkclaw, look at the way those rats are marching! Idiots! They look like a flock of lambs at a village school outing! Haven't you taught them anything?

'Oh hellfire! That stupid lot with the battering ram have just marched straight into a tunnel! Killconey, tell those morons of yours not to tunnel into the parade ground. Just a minute, that weasel there, the one grinning all over his face like a drunken duck: lock him up without food or water for three days! That'll wipe the daft smile off his face. Well, what a fine pair of commanders you two turned out to be. I can't turn my back a minute and you've got all hands behaving like mad frogs in a bucket.'

Cluny ranted and fumed at the animals under his banner. They were going to march, sweat, dig, carry, drill and tunnel, until they performed to his satisfaction. Sloppy idle lot! He'd show them now that he was back; he'd keep them at it all day and all night if need be. Cluny had taken a vow whilst he lay injured: never again would he allow himself to be thwarted by mice and woodland creatures.

At that precise moment, two of those very creatures stood on the fringe of Mossflower Wood, spying across the common land to where Cluny's army was exercising.

But for the gravity of the situation, Basil and Jess would have seen the chance for many a good laugh. What a difference between the antics of this rabble and the way in which the Abbey defenders went about their business of training! Jess observed that it was the contrast between slaving under a tyrant and voluntary cooperation arising from determination and good fellowship.

The plans of the two comrades were well laid. Basil decided that now was as good a time as any to put them into operation. He turned to Jess.

'Well, you old tree-jumper. Let's see if we can't baffle

255

the blighters with science!'

They shook paws and ventured out on to the common land: Basil Stag Hare, camouflage-expert and foot-fighter, in the lead; Jess Squirrel, champion climber and pathfinder, close behind him. They were like twin cloud-shadows drifting silently across the land.

Cluny had climbed down from his perch on the tomb-stone. He stood by the churchyard fence, intent on trying out the whipping powers of his fearsome tail upon a few rats that he had dubbed 'the awkward squad'. Flexing his long scourgelike tail he gave a few experimental swishes and cracks as he shouted commands.

'Left wheel! I said *left* wheel, you buffoons! You there, don't you know the difference between your left and your right? Hold out your left paw.'

The frightened rat stuck out what he fervently hoped was his left paw.

Swish. Crack!

The unfortunate rodent screamed and danced about with the stinging pain of the thick, whiplike tail. Cluny foamed with ill-temper.

'Blockhead! That was your right paw. Now hold out your left, stupid! I'm going to make an example of you this lot won't forget.'

A voice interrupted him. 'Tut tut, officer striking an enlisted creature! Bad form, old chap, thumping bad form!'

Cluny whirled round. Just out of reach across the fence on the common land stood Basil Stag Hare, in the 'at ease' position.

Cluny goggled in thunderstruck silence at the auda-cious Basil, who merely scowled in mock censure.

'Not the sort of thing one expects from a horde commander, what! Personally I'd have you blackballed from the church premises.'

Cluny's voice was a strangled yell: 'Get him! Grab that spy! I want his head!'

Basil chuckled. 'What's the matter? Isn't your own head good enough? No, I don't suppose it is. Ugly-looking brute, aren't you?'

A mob of rats had scrambled through the fence to catch Basil, but it was like trying to catch smoke upon the wind. He was there and gone. From her hiding place Jess tried hard to stifle her giggles.

After several exhausting minutes it became apparent that neither the rats nor the dozen or so panting ferrets, weasels, and stoats who had joined the chase on Cluny's orders, were remotely close to apprehending the strange hare.

Gripping the standard in bloodless claws, Cluny climbed over the fence to the common land.

The comrades' scheme was beginning to work.

Basil bobbed up alongside Cluny. 'What ho, old rat! Showing a bit of initiative? Never ask the troops to do what you can't do yourself and all that! Splendid!'

He dodged playfully out of reach. Cluny snarled and went after him. Basil ducked and weaved, drawing Cluny further out on to the common. All eyes were upon the two figures. This made it easier for Jess to change hiding places as she followed them.

Cluny pursued doggedly, making no sudden moves, waiting for the hare to get over-confident so that he could strike. His soldiers moved about twenty paces behind the action. Cluny had warned them off – he wanted a one-to-one confrontation.

Cluny jabbed out with the banner at Basil. The hare

inwardly rejoiced. They were getting closer to Moss-flower Wood. Soon Jess would make her move. Meanwhile, he must draw the rat further out. Avoiding the stabs of the banner pole and the swift whiplike slashes of the tail, Basil realized that this was no clumsy rat he faced. He chanced a sudden glance to check if Jess was nearby, and as he did, his back left leg shot down into a pothole. It twisted and Basil fell heavily to the ground.

Cluny charged in. He lifted the banner and slammed it down on the hare's unprotected head. Basil twisted quickly to one side.

'Now Jess. Now!' he yelled.

As Basil shouted, several things happened at once.

Jess came blasting out of nowhere like a red whirlwind. The banner thudded into the soft earth where Basil's head had been a fraction of a second before. Basil freed his leg as Jess leaped like a salmon. In mid-air she ripped the tapestry clean off the standard in one go.

Cluny bellowed with rage. His followers came surging across the common to aid him. Basil leapt to his feet and hobbled gamely in front of Cluny, shielding Jess. The squirrel raced about trying to distract Cluny.

Basil winced as he called out to his friend: 'Run for it, Jess. I'll hold 'em off!'

Jess ducked a blow from Cluny's tail. 'Not likely! If you stay, then so do I.'

Basil limped about, keeping himself between Cluny and Jess.

'You stubborn beast,' he yelled. '*Will* you get going?'

The horde was almost upon them. Quick as a flash, Jess grabbed the end of Cluny's tail. She swung him with all of her might, throwing him off balance and sending him crashing into the front-runners of the horde. Jess threw Basil's paw about her shoulder.

'Come on, Basil, head for the woods. We'll make it together.'

Both creatures dashed from the common into the depths of Mossflower. Behind them, Cluny's horde was in headlong pursuit, yelling and shouting. As they ran, Jess panted, 'Here, take this and give me the decoy! Hurry.'

Basil snatched the tapestry and reached beneath his tunic. He gave Jess the crude replica they had prepared, which was in reality an old dishcloth from Friar Hugo's kitchen.

The sounds of the pursuers grew louder. They were gaining.

'Now, you drop out of sight,' Jess gasped. 'I'll draw them off, then you can double back through the churchyard and up the road to Redwall. They'll never think of searching along that way.'

As suddenly as she had spoken, Jess glanced to one side. Basil was no longer there. A breathless military voice whispered from the undergrowth, 'Will do, old chum. See you back at the Abbey. Have a good chase now, cheerio.'

Basil Stag Hare, camouflage expert, had gone to earth.

Jess could see Cluny and the horde coming through the trees. She stood and waited until they caught sight of her. She saw Cluny point and shout:

'Over there! The squirrel! She's the one who's got the tapestry. Get her! Take her alive if you can.'

Coolly Jess stood her ground until they were almost upon her. Right at the last second she went like a blur up the side of a horse-chestnut tree, stopping just out of reach. Some of the more agile ones tried climbing to get at her. Jess merely scampered further upwards.

'Get down, you nincompoops,' Cluny hissed. 'Don't

try to outclimb a squirrel. See if you can keep her near the ground while I think what to do.'

The rats climbed down. As they did, Jess returned to the lower trunk. She had to buy as much time as possible to allow Basil's escape.

Cluny lounged nonchalantly against the tree. 'Well done, squirrel. Very clever indeed. I could use someone like you in my army. Somebody smart, with brains like yours.'

Killconey also demonstrated his persuasive powers. 'Ah, you take the Chief's word. He's lookin' for a good first officer. Why don't you come down now and talk it over? Sure, the loot will be grand when we conquer the Ab – Ouch!'

A small, green spiky chestnut still in its husk bounced off the vociferous ferret's head. Jess moved higher to a branch with a more plentiful supply. She waved the decoy tapestry at Cluny.

'Is this what you're after, Ratface?'

Cluny battled to keep his temper. Darkclaw nudged him and whispered, 'What about the other one, Chief? Shall I take some troops and start searching for him?'

'No, I'll deal with the hare another time. Right now I want you all here in case there's a chance of trapping this one,' Cluny murmured.

Jess's keen ears caught every word the Warlord had said. The plan had worked! She threw a hard spiky nut and called to Cluny: 'Hey, Ratface! Do you actually think that you've got "this one" trapped? Ha, I'm about as trapped as a skylark in the air on a clear day! There's not one of you can get near me.'

'I know that, squirrel,' Cluny answered. 'But just think for a moment. If I win the war against the mice – and I will, you know – I've made a vow to kill everyone inside Redwall. Now suppose that you've got someone dear to you in there; you know what I mean: a mate, a little baby, some family—'

Cluny dodged about as a shower of spiky chestnuts hurtled down.

'You filthy murdering scum!' shouted Jess. 'You rotten loathsome slime! If you come near my family, I'll rip that evil eye of yours right out of your stinking face!'

Cluny knew that he was succeeding with his scheme against the squirrel as more hard chestnuts pelted down.

'Throwing things won't do you much good. Listen, I'm a reasonable creature. All I'm asking you to do is to think of your family. You haven't got to join us if you don't want to. Stay up in that tree forever if you want, it doesn't bother me. All I need is that little scrap of tapestry. It isn't much to ask, is it? Your loved ones will be safe if you hand it over.'

Jess was about to hurl more nuts and insulting remarks when the form of Cluny's plan dawned on her. The rat was trying to do exactly as she and Basil had done. It was a trap to make her become careless. Two can play at that game, Jess thought to herself. The horde of soldiers watching the squirrel noticed a change come over her. She appeared agitated, gnawing upon her lip and rubbing her paws together. In anguish she clutched the tapestry, hugging it to her body.

'I don't care about the others at Redwall, but I've got a husband and a small son. You wouldn't hurt them, would you, Cluny?'

The Warlord detected a sob in the squirrel's voice.

'No, no, of course I wouldn't,' he said soothingly. 'All you have to do is let go of that scrap of cloth and let it drift down here to me. The moment you do, your loved ones' safety is assured, believe me, squirrel. I give you my word of honour.'

Jess wiped her eyes on the decoy cloth and sniffed piteously as she answered. 'Well, all right then. If I have your promise that my family will be safe, then you can have this old thing. It means nothing to me.'

Jess released the piece of material. It drifted down through the branches – Cluny could scarcely restrain himself from leaping for it. Killconey hurried forward, his eyes shining with reverence. He picked the dishrag up gently, offering it to Cluny.

'Here you are, yer honour, the lovely thing itself, safe and sound.'

Avidly Cluny snatched the cloth. His eyes narrowed. Something was wrong. He gave a scream of terrible rage. Instantly his followers scrambled into the bushes as their Chief ripped the tapestry into shreds, his mighty claws rending and tearing as he roared madly: 'It's a fake, a copy, worthless trash. Aaaaaarrgh!'

From her perch in the tree, Jess watched with grim satisfaction. 'Aye, worthless trash, rat, just as you are. The real tapestry is back at Redwall by now. You've been fooled.'

'Kill her! Kill the dirty little swindler!' Cluny's cry rang out. But before a spear or a missile could be thrown, Jess had gone. She darted from tree to tree with artistic speed. Far above Mossflower ground in the upmost terraces of foliage, the champion squirrel turned her flight in the direction of Redwall Abbey.

Some time around early evening Jess arrived back, springing lightly from a high elm branch to the parapet of the Abbey wall. She could tell by the sound of happy chattering and general jubilation that once more the picture of Martin was safely back.

Bounding down into the grounds she was surrounded by cheering friends, not the least of whom was Mr Squirrel, who smothered her with kisses, while their son Silent Sam sat upon her shoulder and dampened her head by patting it lovingly with a well-sucked paw.

The woodlanders carried Jess shoulder-high into the

dining hall, where sat another celebrated hero, Basil Stag Hare. He looked up momentarily at his comrade from behind a staggering mountain of scrumptious food, and pointed to his leg, which was swathed in a hugely exaggerated bandage.

'War wound,' Basil muttered as he demolished a plateful of quince and elderberry pie. 'Got to keep the old strength up, y'know. Lashings of nourishment; only way to heal an honourable injury. Feed it, what, what!'

Silent Sam hopped upon the table. He showed Basil a tiny scratch on his unsucked paw. The kindly hare inspected it gravely. 'Egad, looks like another serious war wound! Better sit here by me, little warrior. Feed it well, that's the ticket.'

They both tucked in voraciously. Friar Hugo came waddling up, his face a picture of delight.

'Good creatures,' he chuckled. 'The late rose is starting to flourish anew. Eat to your heart's content.'

Jess placed her paws on the fat mouse's shoulders. The squirrel's face was a mixture of sadness and concern.

'Friar Hugo, old friend, brace yourself. I am the bearer of tragic news!'

Alarm spread across Hugo's pudgy features. 'Tell me, Jess. What dreadful thing has happened?'

Jess spoke haltingly in a broken voice. 'I fear that Cluny tore up one of your oldest and most venerable dishrags. Alas, Redwall will never see it wipe another plate!'

Behind the Friar's back Basil and Sam almost choked with laughter in the middle of an apple cream pudding.

Shafts of evening sunlight flooded Great Hall as old Methuselah worked painstakingly away with needle and thread. He was sewing Martin the Warrior back in his former position on the corner of the magnificent Redwall tapestry.

263

18

Matthias huddled deep into Dunwing's nest. He shuddered comfortably, wriggling to get further into the dried moss, downfeather and soft grass. During the night a wind had sprung up. He peeped over the rim of the nest. It was a grey day of the kind often found at the too-brilliant start of early summer. Clouds scudded nose to tail across the sky, though it was not raining and the wind was quite warm. Nevertheless, the eaves and the roof cracks magnified the sighing and moaning of the vagrant wind, driving the young mouse back to snuggle up once more as he had often done in his own bed in the dormitory. Matthias thought of the neat, cosy little bed and a wave of homesickness swept over him. Would he ever sleep in it again?

A busy flutter of wings announced the mother sparrow's arrival.

'Matthias mouse um sleepyhead! Gettee up! Things to be done this day.'

Matthias stretched, yawned, and scratched under the collar.

'Good morning, Dunwing,' he said politely. 'What

things are to be done today?'

The sparrow settled herself. She looked gravely at the young mouse. 'Today Matthias escape Sparra court. Me makum plan, King not right to keepum mouse prisoner.'

Matthias was suddenly wide awake. The sparrow had his undivided attention. 'A plan? What sort of plan? Oh, please tell me, Dunwing!'

The mother sparrow explained. 'First, no can go back through um loft door. King much angry, have many great slate pile on um door. Stoppum intruders. Door not open again, me think.'

Matthias whistled. 'Well, the crafty old sparrow! But how am I going to get back down? Do you think you could fly me down in some way? You are bigger than Warbeak—'

Dunwing immediately squashed the idea. 'Matthias talk crazy. Even Warbeak and Dunwing together not able to do that. Sparra very light, maybe strong beak, claws, but wings small, not like great birds, fall like stone carrying mouse. Huh, sometimes even worm too heavy, carry in bits, two, three journeys.'

Matthias began to apologize for his ignorance, but the mother sparrow cut him short. 'Dunwing thinkum plan; pay 'tention now. Me sendum Warbeak to tellum old gatemouse, how you call? 'Athuselah? Good. My egg-chick she tellum old mouse to gettum big red squirrel; bring plenty climbrope; when she see you on um roof she climbee up, help Matthias mouse down.'

'Why, of course!' cried Matthias. 'What a splendid idea! I wouldn't be a bit afraid with Jess there to help me down. But what about the King and his warriors? If they see me, I won't stand a chance.'

Dunwing waved impatiently. 'Thattum next part of plan. Pretty soon Warbeak come back. She tell what time um squirrel meet you, good. Then Dunwing whisper um big lie fib to other Sparra. It soon spread.'

Matthias was puzzled. 'Spreading lies; what good will that do?'

Dunwing preened her feathers, smiling craftily. 'Um great fibba lie. Me whisper um bit here, there, about giant Poisonteeth. Say him lying hurtee down in Mossflower trees, look to die, Poisonteeth havum sword withum, you see.'

Matthias gazed in admiration at Warbeak's mother. 'Well, I never! You are going to spread a rumour that the snake has the sword and is dying down in the woods. Amazing; I can picture it now. Bull Sparra will go chasing straight down there with his warriors. Meanwhile I will escape out on to the roof. Correct?'

Dunwing nodded. 'Matthias stealee belt, sword case, quickfast. Climb down off roof withum red squirrel.'

The young mouse could not meet the mother sparrow's eyes. He was overcome with guilt and shame. 'Dunwing, I'm sorry. How did you guess?'

The sparrow placed a claw upon his paw. 'Me know alla time. Matthias mouse not come to bringum my egg-chick safehome. Come for sword. Not gettee sword. Alla same, belt-case belong mice. You must takee away. These things trouble for um Sparra. Husband dead because of um sword.'

Dunwing clasped Matthias's paw warmly. 'Dunwing likeum mouse. You good friend to my Warbeak. Me thinkum she dead 'til you bringum back. Me help you stealee case, belt.'

Matthias was lost for words. He laid his head against the mother sparrow's soft feathers, brushing a tear from his cheek.

Warbeak came fluttering and bustling in. 'Wind much strongblow. Old mouse say he tellum squirreljess, you be out on um roof when Josabell ring lunchworm. Squirreljess meetum there with climbrope.'

Matthias scarcely tasted the food that Warbeak had brought back; his mind was focused on the plan. It was extremely hazardous. There would be great danger, not only for himself but also for his Sparra friends.

Supposing Bull Sparra took the belt and sword case with him?

What if the King left them behind but hid them in a new place?

Would Jess be able to catch sight of him?

If he did not make it out on the roof, what then?

There were so many things that could go wrong. What would Martin the Warrior have done in a situation like this? Matthias decided that Martin would have put on a brave face and trusted to a warrior's luck. And that was precisely what he was going to do.

Dunwing left the nest an hour before the Joseph Bell tolled lunchtime: she had to start spreading the tale of the snake. Rumours were often circulated among the Sparra folk. All it took was a few chosen whispers in the right places. Pretty soon the Court of King Bull Sparra would be in uproar. Later, when it all turned out to be nothing, nobody would remember who started spreading the rumour – it had always been the same with the Sparra.

Matthias passed a miserable few minutes in the nest with Warbeak. When the false news broke, the young sparrow would have to fly along with King Bull and the other Sparra warriors. The two friends might never see each other again.

However, there was little time for emotional farewells. Outside the nest pandemonium was sweeping the Sparra Court.

Dunwing had performed her task well. A loud drumming like the beating of many wings against the wooden floor filled the air.

'King call alla warrior,' Warbeak murmured. 'Gotta go now. Me meetum Matthias mouse again one day.'

Warbeak undid the collar. It fell from Matthias's neck. 'Mousefriend settum me free. Now me settum you free. Warbeak go now, Matthias. Good wormhunt.'

They shook paw to claw. The young mouse said his farewell in the Sparra language: 'Matthias look for Warbeak. See um someday. You go now. Be um brave eggchick. Mighty Sparra warrior. Great friend.'

A swift rush of wings and Warbeak was gone.

Matthis kept his head well down inside the nest. He listened as the flapping of wings and chirping of sparrows grew less and less. Finally there was silence. Dunwing popped her head over the rim of the nest.

'Matthias come quick, not lose um time!'

Together they hurried through the deserted Sparra court. Dunwing knew there were mothers in every nest with small chicks. These birds remained quietly out of sight when there were no warriors about to defend them. Matthias and Dunwing pushed hastily past the scrap of sacking that served as a door to the King's chamber and began their search.

The scabbard had gone from the back of the chair.

'Oh, I just knew it!' Matthias cried. 'That sly old Bull Sparra has taken them with him.'

Dunwing shook her head. 'No, me see um King go. He not takeum belt or case. Search hard, we must findum plenty quick.'

The chamber was so sparsely furnished that it required very little searching. Dunwing fluttered about but Matthias became discouraged.

'Oh, what's the use?' he cried. 'It's gone, all gone! There's only bits of half-finished food, old slates, butterfly wings, and this stupid old chair.'

In his frustration, Matthias gave the sagging armchair a hefty shove. One of the legs collapsed and it fell backwards, revealing crossed lattice strips of hessian on its underside.

Dunwing hopped on the upturned chair, twittering with elation. 'Look see! Look see! King hide stuff under um old wormchair!'

Through the crossed latticework Matthias could see the shine of black leather and silver. Hastily they ripped and tore with beak, claw, and paw. Dust and aged stuffing flew everywhere. Matthias triumphantly pulled the scabbard and sword belt free of the wreckage.

There it was, supple, shining black leather, chased and trimmed with the purest silver. The scabbard fitted prefectly into the well-made holder on the belt. This was truly the equipment which had belonged personally to Martin the Warrior of Redwall Abbey!

'No time for um mousedream! You hurry, quick!'

Matthias paid full heed to Dunwing's plea. Sweeping the belt and scabbard up, he slung them across his shoulder.

'I'm with you, Dunwing! What next?'

The usual way for sparrows to leave the Court was to fly out from under the eaves. Not being a sparrow, Matthias felt his stomach turn a cartwheel at the prospect of what he must do next. He would have to go on his back under the eaves and, with nothing beneath him but a heart-stopping void of space, negotiate his way out and around the curving gutter to reach the steep upward sweep of the roof.

The first mistake he made was to peep over the edge of the eaves. Far, far, below, the Abbey grounds looked like a spread-out pocket handkerchief, the great wall representing its border. With the blustery howling wind pinning flat his ears, and forcing the breath back down his throat, Matthias giddily covered his eyes with a paw. He felt physically sick at the mere thought of it all.

'It's no good, Dunwing. I'll never be able to do it,' he gulped.

The mother sparrow pecked him sharply upon his paw. 'Matthias mouse got to do it. You no go you um mouseworm. King Bull come back. He killee you. Huh, me thought you warrior.'

'So did I until I saw how high this lot is,' Matthias wailed.

Dunwing patted him with a reassuring claw. 'You go gettum climb rope. Bring here. I showum how.'

The young mouse rushed headlong back to the nest, rummaged in the haversack and found a stout climbing rope.

Dunwing was waiting for him. She tied it firmly around his waist. Matthias tested the knot apprehensively as the sparrow told him what she proposed to do.

'Me fly out on to um roof. Holdum other end of rope plenty tight. You swingum out. No worry, me pullee up.'

Grasping the rope in her beak, Dunwing flew out on to the roof and braced herself.

'Matthias come now, me ready,' she called.

'Don't think about it,' Matthias told himself aloud. 'Just do it!' Clinging for dear life to the rope he launched himself over the edge of the eaves.

Matthias closed his eyes. His heart seemed to stop as he dropped. The rope went taut and he came to a sudden halt. The boisterous wind buffeted him about like a feather. Gritting his teeth, he began pulling himself up

vane. There was the accursed mousewor
d shouting with the sword case and belt slu
. He saw it all now. He had been tricked, dup
ed by his own berserk rage, Bull Sparra fl
wards. When he was high above the you
dropped like a stone, right on target.

screamed aloud in agonized terror as
k buried itself into his shoulder. Instinctiv
ut with his free paw and struck Bull Sparra
e furious claws almost lifted Matthias from
e as the King gripped the belt, trying to d
Letting go of the vane, Matthias battere
s head with both paws. He felt his feet le
the maddened sparrow heaved away at
g the scabbard to become disarranged
n across the young mouse's face.

ng fury, Matthias grabbed the scabbard.
sword, smashing it mercilessly once, tw
e Sparra King's face. The force of the bl
ghty sword case knocked Bull Sparra se
led from the roof out into space. Matt
anic. The King's claws were still caught
belt.

quirrel clamped a paw across her mout
eard the scream and saw Matthias and
d from the roof, locked together by
hey fell outwards into space from the t
the Abbey roof.

paw over paw, unable to reach the wall for help as the rope was held outward by the projecting gutter.

'Climb good. Dunwing have um rope plenty tight hold,' the sparrow called out from the roof, her voice muffled by the wind.

Matthias's paws quivered with the strain of hauling up his own body weight. He strove gallantly upwards, reaching the gutter. It took all the young mouse's courage to let go of the rope and grab for the thin curing edge. Nerving himself he did it in one clean move, clamping his paws heavily into the weatherworn, sandstone groove. Under the unexpected weight it crumbled and broke!

Matthias plunged downwards, his feet now where his head had been a second before. A chunk of stone hurtled past him on its flight to earth. The rope went taut with a jolt that drove the breath from him. Matthias dangled on the rope's end for a moment, then he started to slip slowly down.

Above him on the roof. Dunwing had lost her footing. The sparrow's claws screeched and grated on the roofing slates as the weighted rope pulled her downwards on the steep slope. Dunwing leaned back, trying to dig her claws in somewhere to check the inexorable slide. The broken gutter edge loomed up, surprisingly bringing with it a desperate chance. With lightning speed, Dunwing tugged hard on the rope, gaining a little slack. Giving a skilful flick, she jammed the rope in the niche of the broken stone edge. It slipped for a moment, then held. Flying out, Dunwing took a few extra turns upon the rope, locking it firmly off on the projecting edge. Letting go of her end, the sparrow flew down underneath Matthias. She started pushing him upwards.

Matthias climbed as he had never done before. Aided by Dunwing, he made it. He grabbed for the gutter just as the sharp, newly-broken stone sawed through the rope.

Snap! Grab!

As the rope parted, Matthias clung to the gutter. With Dunwing pushing as she flew upwards, he scrambled over the edge of the gutter and rolled inwards to safety.

Dunwing joined him. They both lay completely exhausted as the wind howled around them, stunned by the danger they had come through.

The mother sparrow was first to recover. She drove her mouse friend relentlessly to his feet. 'Matthias, come hurry! We waste um time.'

The climb of the sloping roof was extremely treacherous. Slightly unhinged by the perilous events, Matthias giggled to his friend, 'It's all in the average day's work of a warrior. No use of a warrior worrying, ha ha ha.'

Taking into account loose slates, buffeting wind, and the occasional slide backwards, Matthias reckoned he had done pretty well as he gained the roof ridge. He straddled it with both feet, gazing straight ahead at the north point of the weather vane.

Dunwing fluttered above him. She saw the look of achievement upon his face and ruffled his ears with her claws. 'Matthias mouse, me gotta go now, no can helpee anymore. Takum care. Good wormhunt.'

Dunwing flew off to her nest back at the court of King Bull Sparra. Matthias pressed forwards along the roof ridge.

He would never forget Dunwing and her eggchick Warbeak. Friends in need are friends indeed.

Bracing himself against the weather vane, Matthias shielded his eyes and peered down into the Abbey grounds. Starting from there he began a systematic search upwards. Most of it was too far below him to make out anything clearly.

The Joseph Bell boomed out the lunch hour.

At first Matthias could no[t]
and looked hard. A small da[rt]
its way up. He waited with [
It was Jess Squirrel!
Clinging to the vane wi[th]
up and down in a frenzy. [
at the top of his voice. 'Hi[
O please hurry!'

Jess was trying her best, [
handicapped by her big [
winds swept it about pl[
own tail from draggin[g]
thither.

The champion squi[rrel]
Normally she would n[ot]
such blowy conditions[
Matthias's voice had n[
wind, but someone ha[d]
King Bull Sparra!

Having found neithe[r]
become peeved and ba[
search party that the[
woods until they fou[
go back to the Spar[
important matters t[
from the woods secr[
fancy a second m[
whether it was aliv[e]
teeth often did. [
himself, the King [
roof.

'Jess, up here! L[
Bull Sparra's m[

weather
waving a[
about him[
Madde[n]
straight u[
mouse, he[
Matthias[
King's bea[
he lashed o[
the eye. Th[
weather va[
it off him. [
Bull Sparra[
the roof as [
belt, causin[
flapped dow[n]
In a fighti[
used it like a[
thrice, into t[
from the we[
less. He top[
screamed in [
in the sword[

Below, Jess S[
horror. She h[
Sparra topple[
sword belt. T[
most point of[

19

Chickenhound was having one of his sniggering fits, even attempting to dance a little jig. He had been left to his own devices.

The old fool of an Abbot and his stupid devoted band of creatures were all outside, shoring up gatehouses, drilling, fetching, carrying, and generally being good and useful.

What a crowd of ninnies!

With a sack upon his back the wily fox roamed from room to room. The Abbey was his oyster.

'Hmm, this is a nice green glass vase.'

'Why hello, what a lovely little silver plate.'

'My my, fancy leaving a beautiful gold chain like you all on your own.'

'There now, I'll just pop you all into my sack. Don't worry, Uncle Chickenhound will take care of you!'

Sniggering delightedly, the fox trotted along the corridor into the next room. More and more small valuables and family keepsakes belonging to the mice and their woodland guests vanished into the thief's sack. He sniggered uncontrollably. Imagine all the hard work and fighting that Cluny was going to do, just to get at all this, and here was he having first choice.

He was Chickenhound, master burglar. He had outlived Sela, outwitted Cluny, and pulled the wool over the eyes of an Abbeyful of mice. One day they would speak his name as the Foxprince of Thieves! Chickenhound paused to admire a handsome pair of brass nutcrackers. Oh yes, very elegant indeed! Into the sack they went. He trotted down the stairs into Cavern Hole. The tables had been laid for afternoon tea. Stuffing and gorging, he moved from place to place, choosing only the tastiest morsels. On his tour of the dining hall he collected a good quantity of cutlery and some fine antique cruets. Anything that did not suit the young fox's taste was smashed or vandalized. Milk was spilt upon the floor and bread trampled into it; candles were broken and vegetables squashed across the walls.

Chickenhound shouldered his sack and turned his attentions to the kitchen. He booted the door open and walked straight in, slap bang into Friar Hugo. The fat old mouse was bowled completely over.

The unexpected fright sent Chickenhound dashing back through Cavern Hole with the outraged Friar's shouts ringing in his ears.

'Stop thief! Stop the fox!'

Chickenhound bounded up the stairs into Great Hall. Behind him the Friar, having regained his feet, puffed along raising the hue and cry.

'Stop thief! Come back here, you villain!'

With great love and care, Methuselah was putting the final touches to his repair of the tapestry. Only a very sharp-eyed observer would be able to tell that it had once been torn. The warning shouts caused him to stop what he was doing. he turned to see the fox racing towards the paw over paw, unable to reach the wall for help as the rope was held outward by the projecting gutter.

'Climb good. Dunwing have um rope plenty tight hold,' the sparrow called out from the roof, her voice muffled by the wind.

Matthias's paws quivered with the strain of hauling up his own body weight. He strove gallantly upwards, reaching the gutter. It took all the young mouse's courage to let go of the rope and grab for the thin curing edge. Nerving himself he did it in one clean move, clamping his paws heavily into the weatherworn, sandstone groove. Under the unexpected weight it crumbled and broke!

Matthias plunged downwards, his feet now where his head had been a second before. A chunk of stone hurtled past him on its flight to earth. The rope went taut with a jolt that drove the breath from him. Matthias dangled on the rope's end for a moment, then he started to slip slowly down.

Above him on the roof. Dunwing had lost her footing. The sparrow's claws screeched and grated on the roofing slates as the weighted rope pulled her downwards on the steep slope. Dunwing leaned back, trying to dig her claws in somewhere to check the inexorable slide. The broken gutter edge loomed up, surprisingly bringing with it a desperate chance. With lightning speed, Dunwing tugged hard on the rope, gaining a little slack. Giving a skilful flick, she jammed the rope in the niche of the broken stone edge. It slipped for a moment, then held. Flying out, Dunwing took a few extra turns upon the rope, locking it firmly off on the projecting edge. Letting go of her end, the sparrow flew down underneath Matthias. She started pushing him upwards.

Matthias climbed as he had never done before. Aided by Dunwing, he made it. He grabbed for the gutter just as the sharp, newly-broken stone sawed through the rope.

Snap! Grab!

As the rope parted, Matthias clung to the gutter. With Dunwing pushing as she flew upwards, he scrambled over the edge of the gutter and rolled inwards to safety.

Dunwing joined him. They both lay completely exhausted as the wind howled around them, stunned by the danger they had come through.

The mother sparrow was first to recover. She drove her mouse friend relentlessly to his feet. 'Matthias, come hurry! We waste um time.'

The climb of the sloping roof was extremely treacherous. Slightly unhinged by the perilous events, Matthias giggled to his friend, 'It's all in the average day's work of a warrior. No use of a warrior worrying, ha ha ha.'

Taking into account loose slates, buffeting wind, and the occasional slide backwards, Matthias reckoned he had done pretty well as he gained the roof ridge. He straddled it with both feet, gazing straight ahead at the north point of the weather vane.

Dunwing fluttered above him. She saw the look of achievement upon his face and ruffled his ears with her claws. 'Matthias mouse, me gotta go now, no can helpee anymore. Takum care. Good wormhunt.'

Dunwing flew off to her nest back at the court of King Bull Sparra. Matthias pressed forwards along the roof ridge.

He would never forget Dunwing and her eggchick Warbeak. Friends in need are friends indeed.

Bracing himself against the weather vane, Matthias shielded his eyes and peered down into the Abbey grounds. Starting from there he began a systematic search upwards. Most of it was too far below him to make out anything clearly.

The Joseph Bell boomed out the lunch hour.

At first Matthias could not be certain. He slitted his eyes and looked hard. A small dark blob was definitely making its way up. He waited with bated breath as it came nearer.

It was Jess Squirrel!

Clinging to the vane with one paw, Matthias jumped up and down in a frenzy. He waved frantically, shouting at the top of his voice. 'Hi Jess! It's me, Matthias. Hurry. O please hurry!'

Jess was trying her best, but from the start she had been handicapped by her big curling bush of a tail. The rude winds swept it about playfully. She could not stop her own tail from dragging and pushing her hither and thither.

The champion squirrel climbed gamely onwards. Normally she would not have attempted the climb under such blowy conditions. She concentrated on the ascent. Matthias's voice had not reached her across the vagrant wind, but someone had heard the young mouse's shouts: King Bull Sparra!

Having found neither sword nor snake, the King had become peeved and bad tempered. He issued orders to the search party that they were to stay on the floor of the woods until they found something. Meanwhile, he must go back to the Sparra court, where he said there were important matters to attend to. Bull Sparra flew away from the woods secretly relieved. On reflection he did not fancy a second meeting with the giant Poisonteeth whether it was alive, dead, or just pretending, as Poisonteeth often did. Muttering and grumbling to justify himself, the King flew upwards to his court under the roof.

'Jess, up here! Look, I've got the scabbard!'

Bull Sparra's mad bright eyes glanced upwards to the

weather vane. There was the accursed mouseworm, waving and shouting with the sword case and belt slung about him. He saw it all now. He had been tricked, duped!

Maddened by his own berserk rage, Bull Sparra flew straight upwards. When he was high above the young mouse, he dropped like a stone, right on target.

Matthias screamed aloud in agonized terror as the King's beak buried itself into his shoulder. Instinctively he lashed out with his free paw and struck Bull Sparra in the eye. The furious claws almost lifted Matthias from the weather vane as the King gripped the belt, trying to drag it off him. Letting go of the vane, Matthias battered at Bull Sparra's head with both paws. He felt his feet leave the roof as the maddened sparrow heaved away at the belt, causing the scabbard to become disarranged. It flapped down across the young mouse's face.

In a fighting fury, Matthias grabbed the scabbard. He used it like a sword, smashing it mercilessly once, twice, thrice, into the Sparra King's face. The force of the blows from the weighty sword case knocked Bull Sparra senseless. He toppled from the roof out into space. Matthias screamed in panic. The King's claws were still caught fast in the sword belt.

Below, Jess Squirrel clamped a paw across her mouth in horror. She heard the scream and saw Matthias and Bull Sparra toppled from the roof, locked together by the sword belt. They fell outwards into space from the topmost point of the Abbey roof.

19

Chickenhound was having one of his sniggering fits, even attempting to dance a little jig. He had been left to his own devices.

The old fool of an Abbot and his stupid devoted band of creatures were all outside, shoring up gatehouses, drilling, fetching, carrying, and generally being good and useful.

What a crowd of ninnies!

With a sack upon his back the wily fox roamed from room to room. The Abbey was his oyster.

'Hmm, this is a nice green glass vase.'

'Why hello, what a lovely little silver plate.'

'My my, fancy leaving a beautiful gold chain like you all on your own.'

'There now, I'll just pop you all into my sack. Don't worry, Uncle Chickenhound will take care of you!'

Sniggering delightedly, the fox trotted along the corridor into the next room. More and more small valuables and family keepsakes belonging to the mice and their woodland guests vanished into the thief's sack. He sniggered uncontrollably. Imagine all the hard work and fighting that Cluny was going to do, just to get at all this, and here was he having first choice.

He was Chickenhound, master burglar. He had out-lived Sela, outwitted Cluny, and pulled the wool over the eyes of an Abbeyful of mice. One day they would speak his name as the Foxprince of Thieves! Chickenhound paused to admire a handsome pair of brass nutcrackers. Oh yes, very elegant indeed! Into the sack they went. He trotted down the stairs into Cavern Hole. The tables had been laid for afternoon tea. Stuffing and gorging, he moved from place to place, choosing only the tastiest morsels. On his tour of the dining hall he collected a good quantity of cutlery and some fine antique cruets. Any-thing that did not suit the young fox's taste was smashed or vandalized. Milk was spilt upon the floor and bread trampled into it; candles were broken and vegetables squashed across the walls.

Chickenhound shouldered his sack and turned his at-tentions to the kitchen. He booted the door open and walked straight in, slap bang into Friar Hugo. The fat old mouse was bowled completely over.

The unexpected fright sent Chickenhound dashing back through Cavern Hole with the outraged Friar's shouts ringing in his ears.

'Stop thief! Stop the fox!'

Chickenhound bounded up the stairs into Great Hall. Behind him the Friar, having regained his feet, puffed along raising the hue and cry.

'Stop thief! Come back here, you villain!'

With great love and care, Methuselah was putting the final touches to his repair of the tapestry. Only a very sharp-eyed observer would be able to tell that it had once been torn. The warning shouts caused him to stop what he was doing. he turned to see the fox racing towards the

276

door with Friar Hugo trailing far behind, shouting for all he was worth.

Methuselah had only to move a few paces and he was blocking the doorway. Bravely he held up a frail paw at the oncoming fox.

'You young blaggard! So this is how you repay our kindness. You are far worse than your wicked mother!'

Chickenhound swung the loaded sack with both paws at the old gatehouse-keeper's head.

'Out of my way, you doddering old fool,' he panted.

The heavily-laden sack struck Methuselah a crushing blow. He collapsed instantly on the floor and lay still.

Chickenhound froze momentarily. The sack of loot clattered from his nerveless paws. Friar Hugo halted in his tracks. The fox stared down at the pitiful crumpled figure, he had not meant to hit him so hard.

'Murderer! Oh, you barbarous creature! You have killed Brother Methuselah!'

Friar Hugo's cry galvanized the fox into action. He grabbed the sack and fled from the Abbey.

The fat little Friar fell to his knees; tears coursing openly down his plump face. He cradled the sad, small bundle that had once been the wisest and oldest mouse of Red-wall.

Chickenhound sneaked along, keeping close to the Abbey. He slunk swiftly across the grounds to one of the small doors in the massive outer wall. The murderer had to get out into the woods before Hugo regained his senses enough to raise the alarm. Wrestling wildly with the stout bars and bolts, he managed somehow to open the small iron door. Without a backward glance the fox bolted off into the Mossflower woodland. As he ran the Joseph Bell began tolling out the alarm.

277

Chickenhound's confidence grew as he raced through the woods. He sniggered. Daft old fool! Served him right, he should have got out of the way. Hadn't he realized that he was facing Chickenhound, the overlord of all criminals?

Pressing deeper into Mossflower he paused and listened upon the wind for sounds of pursuit. Faintly he could distinguish certain noises. Whoever it was seemed to be travelling at a breakneck pace with little regard to obstructing bush or foliage. The sound of snapping branches and undergrowth being trampled grew nearer. The fox's finely-attuned sense of smell told him that there were two creatures on his trail. One of them was a hedgehog, but the other? Chickenhound's legs began to tremble. His heartbeats echoed in his ears. There was only one creature in all the wood with that heavy unmistakable scent . . . Constance the badger!

Instinctively, the terrified fox looked wildly about for a place to hide, running was out of the question in his present state of panic. It was as if some dark force had heard his silent plea. Not ten metres from where he stood was the ideal refuge, a hollow in the base of a dead oak. There was a space between two thick roots, partially covered by ferns, and Chickenhound slung the sack down the hole and dived in after it.

To his surprise he found it quite large and dry with a thick carpet of dead grass and leaves. It was dismally dark, but still, it was the best place at a moment's notice. He would be quite invisible and safe from detection. Let them try and find him now!

With Ambrose Spike trailing in her wake, Constance crashed through the woods. So great was the badger's anger and grief that she was oblivious to any notion of stalking or tracking. She barged along straight through anything that stood in her way, the heavy striped face a mask of cold fury. The hedgehog stayed behind Constance. Those huge blunt paws were ready to tear some creature into dollrags; no power on earth would save the murderous fox if Constance caught him. But the badger's retribution was not to be.

Quaking with fear, Chickenhound held his breath as the woodland juggernaut thundered by within a couple of metres of the hideout. He listened hopefully as the path of destruction trailed off into the distance of Mossflower. Once more the woods grew quiet.

Chickenhound finally exhaled a long sigh of relief.

Once again the newly self-titled overlord of crime had outsmarted a couple of mere animals.

Who on earth did they think they were?

When word got around of his daring exploits other creatures would come to him, foxes perhaps. Yes, he could see it all, Chickenhound at the head of a band of robber foxes, plundering and thieving wherever the whim took him. Of course he would change his name to a title more fitted to his position: Redflash, or Nightfang, or maybe Mousedeath. Yes, he liked the sound of that, Mousedeath! His band of minions would admire him, telling each other tales of his astonishing deeds, convinced that the mysterious Mousedeath had always been an infamous thief, unaware of his humble beginnings as Chickenhound, son of Old Sela.

As he crouched in the darkness the young fox decided that the coast was now clear. He could venture out again. Reaching behind, he felt for the sack that contained his first solo haul. Before he left he wanted to fondle his treasures once more, to reassure himself that they were an auspicious start to his new venture. In the gloomy hideout his paw reached out and felt something.

It was not the sack of loot.

'Asmodeusssssssssss!'

That evening the Joseph Bell rang out a message of sadness and grief to Redwall Abbey.

Mice and woodlanders sat about on the stone floor of Great Hall, each creature with its own sorrowful thoughts.

Two Redwall mice dead upon the same day.

Jess Squirrel sat with her head between her paws. Mr Squirrel had taken the inconsolable Silent Sam off to bed. Jess had explained fully to the Abbot and the Council how she had witnessed Matthias's fall from the roof with the sparrow. Instead of falling straight down, both creatures had been swept out of Jess's line of vision by huge gusts of wind. Where Matthias's body lay now nobody knew.

As soon as her feet touched ground the squirrel had gone about organizing search parties. They had scoured the area until the light became too bad to continue, returning after fruitless hours spent searching Redwall grounds and Mossflower Wood.

The compassionate Father Abbot consoled the sad squirrel: 'Jess, it's no fault of yours. There was not a thing that you could have done, my friend. The fall was so great that no creature could have survived it. Tomorrow we will search again, then we must bury my old companion Methuselah. Poor mouse, he never did anything to deserve such a cruel fate.'

The Abbot pointed to the tapestry, shaking his head. 'See, my old gatehouse-keeper's last good work. He restored Martin to his place of honour. Methuselah was the gentlest mouse I ever knew. Oh what a tragic waste of two lives: one who spent his years in search of knowledge, the other cut down before his tree of youth had chance to blossom!'

Cornflower spoke up. She was dry-eyed and pale, her paws tightly clenched. 'Father Abbot, the loss of Matthias's life was not a waste; it was a tremendous act of bravery and self-sacrifice. He died trying to aid Redwall and all of us in the struggle against the forces of evil, as did his friend Methuselah. I am sure that this is the way they would wish to be remembered in our hearts, as warriors and heroes.'

There was an instant murmur of approval from all present. Overcome by the sad events, the defenders left the hall, some to do guard duty, others to their beds.

Constance remained sitting upon the floor, her face expressionless, the mighty paws clenching and unclenching. Brother Alf rose and stretched.

'You'd best get some sleep, Constance.'

The badger stood up wearily and rubbed her eyes.

'No thank you, Brother. I couldn't sleep a wink at a time like this. You know how it is.'

Brother Alf sighed deeply. He knew, having watched Matthias since the first day he arrived at the Abbey gates, a woodland orphan, always polite, willing, and cheerful. But now . . . .

'Come with me then,' said Alf. 'I've got work to do. There's all the fishing nets to be laid for the night. Perhaps you'd like to come along and help me?'

Glad of the chance to do something, the badger agreed. She and Alf strode off, talking of old times.

'D'you remember that big grayling that you and Matthias caught?' Constance said.

Brother Alf chuckled. 'Do I! Matthias wouldn't be satisfied until that fish was landed on the bank. I was all for giving up, but not him.'

Constance nodded admiringly. 'Aye, that fish fed the whole Abbey! I remember, because I had three helpings, two less than that spiky wastebin Ambrose.'

Strolling leisurely around the bank of the Abbey pond the two companions gathered up the nets preparatory to spreading them upon the water. Brother Alf went further along the bank looking for floats. Constance was about to sit down at the water's edge when she heard Alf calling: 'Constance, look! Down here! There's a sparrow!'

The badger ran and joined the mouse, looking to where he pointed. Sure enough, half in and half out of the water was the body of King Bull Sparra. With a great splash Constance waded into the shallows and dragged the corpse up on to the mossy bank.

'It looks as if he's been drowned, Brother. Quick, get some help and bring lanterns. Hurry!'

The badger thrashed about in the water. Why, oh why hadn't the search party thought of looking in the Abbey pond?

Help arrived swiftly.

'Out of the way, Constance! The rest of you keep those lanterns high.' With hardly a ripple, Winifred and three of her otters slid into the water. As she swam Winifred issued orders. 'Spread out and dive deep. We'll quarter the pond between us. I'll take the south corner.'

Tense moments ticked by. A crowd of creatures lined the banks. All that could be seen was the still dark water, broken at intervals as the sleek form of an otter surfaced and dived again.

A cry went up as Winifred appeared, towing a still shape. Willing paws dragged the otter's burden up on to the bank.

Shaking herself like a dog, Winifred panted, 'Look what I found half-sunk in the water over there. It's a good job the rushes held him up.'

Creatures crowded around, all asking the same questions.

'Is it Matthias?'

'Is he dead or alive?'

Constance pushed her way through to the limp, sodden figure. The Abbot and Cornflower were close behind her.

Abbot Mortimer appealed to the onlookers, 'Give us room there! If you really want to help, then stand back, please. Someone give Cornflower a lantern. Good mouse, hold it up.'

Obediently the crowd fell back. More lanterns were brought forward. The Abbot worked feverishly, resuscitating, levering and pounding the prone form of Matthias.

Cornflower voiced the question that was on the mind of every creature there. 'Oh Father Abbot! Is he alive? He doesn't seem to be moving.'

The otter clamped a damp paw about her shoulders. 'Hush now, the Abbot is doing everything in his power. We will know soon enough.'

Brother Alf pushed through, carrying something. 'Winifred, one of your otters has just come up with this sword belt and scabbard. He found them near where Matthias was.'

'Bring them forward,' said Constance. 'They may be of some help if Matthias opens his eyes. You never know.'

The Abbot beckoned urgently. 'Cornflower, give me that lantern, child. Quickly!'

Holding the lantern-glass close to Matthias's nose and mouth, the Abbot was rewarded by the sight of the faint mist that appeared on it. 'He lives! Cornflower, Matthias is alive! Bring blankets, get a stretcher, we must get him inside the Abbey . . . .'

Without a word to anyone, Constance lifted Matthias

gently as if he weighed no more than a feather. Carefully the big badger clasped the young mouse close into the warmth of her rough coat. The crowd formed an aisle either side of her as she strode swiftly to the Abbey. Lanterns bobbed about in the darkness like fireflies as the great Joseph Bell tolled out a message of joy and hope to Mossflower.

20

The new day dawned in a haze of soft sunlight. It crept across the countryside suddenly to expand and burst forth over all the peaceful woods and meadowland. Blue gold tinged with pink, each dewdrop turned into a scintillating jewel; spiders' webs became glittering filigree, birdsong rang out as if there had never been a day as fresh and beautiful as this one.

The extravaganza of nature's glory was completely lost upon Cluny the Scourge. His one good eye squinted upwards through the smoke of the morning campfires.

'Huh, it's going to be as hot as the hell's furnace, but at least it won't rain,' he muttered aloud to himself.

Under the impatient eye of the Warlord, Cluny's horde gulped down a hasty meal and scurried about picking up weapons. Suitably geared for battle, they quickly fell into ranks.

Cluny's personal armourer put the final touches to his Chief's war apparel. With the tip of the standard Cluny signalled his captains. Darkclaw, Frogblood, Fangburn,

Cheesethief, Scumnose, and Mangefur scrambled into their positions.

As yet Cluny had not chosen a new second-in-command, though he had let it be known that any of his followers who distinguished himself in the coming battle would receive immediate promotion in the field. Killconey the ferret stood alongside his Chief with a drum that he had made from an old water butt. He had unofficially appointed himself drummer-cum-soothsayer. The ferret watched Cluny intently; the Chief was going to speak. He banged the drum, calling the horde to silence. Cluny lifted the visor of his war helmet and stared out across the waiting horde.

'This time there will be no mistakes!' he yelled. 'And there will be no retreat! We stay, even if it means putting Redwall to siege. We stand firm! Anyone who takes one backward step is dead. Anyone who disobeys orders is dead. Anyone who does not fight tooth and claw with all of his might is also dead.

'That is my promise, and Cluny always keeps his word. Hear me! All we face is a lot of peaceful mice and some local woodland creatures. Defeat them and I will give you rewards you never dreamed of. The enemy are not trained fighters like we are, not natural killers. There is not one among them who can lead as I lead you.'

At the centre of the front rank stood a rat who had been wounded in the first encounter at the Abbey. He whispered out of the corner of his mouth to his comrade-in-arms alongside him, 'Huh, leads us my foot! Last time we attacked he stood well out of the way, back in some meadow.'

The sharp ears of Cluny had caught what the unfortunate soldier had said. The Warlord leaped down from his rostrum and seized the trembling miscreant, booting him forward into plain view of the army.

'See this traitor?' Cluny shouted. 'Here's a rat who doesn't think I lead my horde. Cluny the Scourge sees and hears all. Watch now, and let this be a lesson to anyone that dares doubt me.'

The wretched rat soldier lay shaking on the churchyard path. A hush fell across the entire horde. He stared beseechingly into the merciless eye of Cluny.

'Oh please, Chief, it was only a joke, I didn't mean to—'

Crack!

The powerful tail whipped expertly out, slashing across the rat's face with its poisoned metal war barb. The army looked on in horror as the stricken victim shuddered and lay dead at Cluny's feet. Ignoring the slain soldier, Cluny the Scourge pushed his way roughly through the horde until he reached the cemetery gates. It was going to be a long march to Redwall, burdened as they were with the battering ram and all the paraphernalia of destruction. They would have to camp overnight by the roadside, and the great attack upon Redwall would take place early the next day. There was to be no secrecy. For maximum effect the army must be seen marching boldly up to the very gates of the Abbey in full array.

Cluny shook his standard. As the ferret's drum thundered out he roared madly. 'On to Redwall! Smash the gates! Kill, kill!'

The shimmering heat waves from the road reverberated to the shouts of the horde: 'Cluny, Cluny, kill, kill, kill!'

21

In his fevered dreams the young mouse wandered through dark caverns. Somewhere a voice was calling out to him.

'Matthias, Matthias.'

It sounded vaguely familiar, but he had other things to do than identify the voice. He must find the sword. In the stygian gloom he saw the late rose; it was bathed in a pale blue light. What was it doing here in this dark netherworld?

Matthias saw that all the tiny thorns on the rose stems resembled small swords. He felt he should speak to the rose.

'Please tell me, late rose, where will I find the sword?'

The topmost rose quivered. He watched it blossom before his eyes. At the centre of the blooming petals was the face of Methuselah. 'Matthias, my friend, I can help you no more. Seek out the aid of Martin. I must go now.'

The face of the old gatehouse-keeper faded. Slowly, his feet hardly touching the floor, Matthias travelled a long corridor. At its end were two figures. He halted by the first figure, unable to distinguish who it was, but feeling an aura of friendly kinship emanating from it. Matthias looked to the second figure. Here was something he had never before encountered. It had neither arms nor legs. With a hissing sound the spectral thing opened wide its mouth. Inside there were two sharp fangs and a flickering tongue which quivered and turned into a sword. With a cry of joy the young mouse started running forward, only to be restrained by the phantom figure of the first apparition. Matthias was not surprised to see that it was Martin the Warrior.

'Martin, why do you stop me from getting the sword?' he asked.

Martin's voice was warm and friendly. 'Matthias, I am that is. Stay! Beware of Asmodeus.'

Martin took hold of Matthias's shoulder. The young mouse tried to wrench himself free.

'Let me go, Martin! I fear no creature that lives.'

Martin tightened his hold relentlessly upon Matthias's shoulder. Pain shot through him like a red hot lance. Martin cried out, 'Hold him still now, hold him still!'

It was the Father Abbot. He was saying the same words as Martin had said. Brother Alf held tight to Matthias's shoulder as the Abbot dug deep with a probe. He extracted a dark pointed object which he tossed into a bowl that Cornflower was holding.

'Ouch! That hurt, Father,' Matthias said weakly.

The Abbot wiped his paws upon a clean cloth.

'Well, my son, you are back with us at last,' he said. 'That must have hurt. There was half of a sparrow's beak lodged in your shoulder.'

Matthias blinked and looked about. 'Hello, Cornflower. You see, I got back in one piece. Oh hello, Brother Alf. I say, is that Basil in the next bed?'

'Hush now, Matthias, and lie still,' Cornflower chided him. 'You're lucky to be alive. It was touch and go right through the night.'

Abbot Mortimer pointed at the first rays of sun streaming in through the window. 'Yes, but you are back now; and see, you've brought with you a magnificent June summer morning.'

The young mouse lay back upon the crisp white pillows. Aside from a bursting headache and the pain in his shoulder it felt good to be alive.

'But what's Basil doing asleep in the next bed?' he persisted.

'Oh him,' Cornflower chuckled. 'He says that he has an honourable war wound that requires a lot of food and rest, the old rogue.'

'That may be,' replied the Abbot. 'But it would be churlish to begrudge Basil's requests. After all, he did recapture our tapestry from Cluny. It was a very daring deed.'

Matthias was delighted. 'Martin's tapestry, back here at the Abbey? How marvellous! I'll bet old Methuselah is over the moon to have it back once more.'

There was a moment's silence. The Abbot turned to Brother Alf and Cornflower. 'Please, would you leave us alone for now? I have something to tell Matthias. You may visit him tomorrow. He still needs a lot of rest.'

The two mice nodded understandingly and left.

Half an hour later, after unfolding the sad tale of Methuselah, the Abbot also took his leave.

Matthias turned his face to the wall, bereft of any tears or lamentation after the stresses of the experience he had recently come through. The death of his old and valued friend left a feeling like a large leaden lump inside his chest. He curled up and tried to hide within himself.

How long he lay there, racked by grief and misery, he had no way of knowing. Basil Stag Hare awakened and called across, 'What ho! Well, bless me medals if it ain't young Matthias! How are you, laddie buck?'

Matthias replied in a small sad voice, 'Please, Basil, leave me alone. I've lost Methuselah. I don't want to speak to anyone.'

Basil hopped nimbly across and perched on Matthias's bed. 'There, there, young feller m'lad. Don't you think I know how you feel? Good grief, an old campaigner like me? When I think of the chums I lost in bygone battles . . . Good and true friends they were, but I taught meself to keep a stiff upper whisker, y'know.'

Matthias remained with his back turned upon the hare.

'But you don't understand, Basil.'

The soldier hare snorted. He grabbed Matthias and turned him over so they were face to face.

'Don't understand? I'll tell you what I don't understand, young chip. I don't understand how a chappie like yourself who is supposed to be a great warrior can lie there moping. You're like an old lady otter who's just lost a fish. If old Methuselah were here now, he'd chuck a jug of water over you and turf you right out of that bed on your fat little head!'

Matthias sat up and sniffed.

'D'you think so, Basil?'

The hare slapped his 'injured' leg, winced, then laughed aloud. 'Think so? I know so! Do you imagine that old mouse sacrificed his life so that you could lie about feeling sorry for yourself all day? Huh, he'd have told you himself. That's not the way of a warrior. Get up, sir, stir yourself, make Methuselah proud of you!'

Matthias's eyes gleamed with a new determination.

'By golly, you're right, Basil! That's exactly what my old friend would have wanted! I'm sorry; you must think I've behaved like a dreadful young fool.'

The hare's ears flopped comically as he shook his head.

'Not at all, m'dear feller; think nothing of it. I must confess that I was a bit like you when I was a leveret, y'know. Now, what d'you say we get about the business of living properly again? I say, I'm positively famished; what about you?'

Matthias could not help laughing at the irrepressible hare.

'Well, I am a bit peckish, now you come to mention it.'

'Capital,' cried Basil. 'I could eat a stag, antlers and all. I say, they do a wonderful nosebag for us wounded heroes, y'know. Just watch this, m'lad.'

The hare tinkled a small brass bell on the bedside table. Within seconds Friar Hugo and Cornflower appeared.

'Ah yes, the catering staff,' said Basil. 'Er, harrumph! The other injured warrior here and myself would be greatly obliged for a little sustenance. Nothing too grand, y'know; just something for our poor wounded teeth to nibble on. Got to keep body and fur together, what, what?'

Cornflower was pleased to see Matthias looking so much better. She exchanged winks with him and Friar Hugo. The fat friar bowed in a servile manner as he answered the hare. 'Very good, Mr Stag, sir. Two bowls of gruel coming up.'

Matthias and Cornflower struggled not to laugh aloud. Basil exploded. 'Gruel! What the devil do you mean by gruel? What sort of slop is that to give renowned warriors, eh? We want to be cured, not killed! Now listen to me, you pair of scullery fusiliers, I want a decent brunch: half a dozen boiled eggs, some crisp summer salad, two loaves of hot bread, two hazelnut cream junkets, two – no, better make it four – oven-baked apple pies, oh, and chuck in some of those medium-sized quince tarts if you see any lying about. Well, don't stand there with your great jaw flapping! Cut along now, quick as y'like.'

Cornflower curtsied with mock solemnity. Friar Hugo held up a paw. 'You forgot the October nutbrown ale, sir.'

Basil thumped the bed. 'Good Lord, so I did! Er, just four flagons, thank you, my good mouse.'

Cornflower and Friar Hugo exited leaning upon each other, their faces crimson with suppressed laughter.

'Strange creatures,' Basil mused. 'Blowed if I can see anything funny about a couple of heroes wanting to be fed so that they can stay alive. Takes all kinds to make a world, young feller, other ranks included.'

Later, as they made a hearty meal, Matthias set about pumping the hare for information.

'Basil, what's a viper?'

'Hmm, a viper? Well, it's an old poisonteeth worm y'know, an adder. Never had a lot of truck with the slimy fellers meself. You'd do best to stay away from them, old chum.'

Matthias continued probing the hare's knowledge. 'Are there any adders around the Mossflower region, Basil? I mean, if there were, then you'd be the very creature to know about them, being an expert and all that.'

Basil puffed out his narrow chest as he absentmindedly ate one of Matthias's quince tarts. 'Adders in Mossflower? Now let me see. No, I don't suppose there are nowadays. There was talk of one a long time back, but I shouldn't think he's around any more. Filthy reptiles, adders. Nothing like stags, y'know. Now what the devil was that adder chap's name? No, I can't remember it for the life of me.'

'Could it be Asmodeus?' Matthias inquired innocently.

Basil Stag Hare dropped a half-eaten apple pie on the bedside table. He was suddenly very serious.

'Asmodeus? Where did you hear that name?'

'A little bird told me,' Matthias replied.

Basil retrieved his apple pie. He munched thoughtfully.

'Your sparrows, eh? Savage little wallahs. No discipline of course. Darn good fighters, though. But tell me, what do jolly old sparrows know about Asmodeus?'

'It all has to do with Martin's sword,' Matthias explained. 'You see, one of their kings stole the sword from the north point of the vane on the Abbey roof. That was many years ago. From there the sword had been passed down through sparrow kings until it came into the claws of the late King Bull Sparra.'

'Not the silly ass who managed to get himself drowned yesterday?' said Basil through a mouthful of hazelnut junket.

'The same one,' Matthias replied. 'But to cut a long story short, the adder stole the sword from him. That's why I want to know about Asmodeus, you see.'

'Play with fire, you'll get yourself burned,' warned the hare.

Matthias knew Basil could be manipulated. He was insistent: 'Oh please, Basil, you must tell me all you know. It was Methuselah's life-work trying to find that sword. I must continue for his sake.'

The hare gnawed thoughtfully on some bread and salad. 'Well, if you put it that way, young fellah, anything I can do to help I will. You'll need a good guide—'

Matthias interrupted: 'I must find the sword by myself, Basil. Just tell me all you know about the adder called Asmodeus.'

The hare lay back on his bed. He took a long draught of October ale before answering. 'Quite frankly, old chap, I know nothing about the bally snake. I thought the blighter had died years ago.'

Matthias groaned aloud, but Basil cut him short. 'Mind you, having said that I think I have a pretty fair idea who *will* know. Listen, if you strike out north-east across Mossflower Wood, you'll find a deserted farmhouse beyond the far edge. Now, the chap you want to see is a whopping great snowy owl that patrols between the fringes of the wood and the old sandstone quarry. His name is Captain Snow. Bear in mind though, he'll eat you on sight if he gets the chance! Military bird, but a real bounder.'

'Then how do I get to talk with him?' said Matthias abruptly.

'Temper, temper, m'lad,' Basil chuckled. Reaching down to his bedside locker he dug out his dress tunic. It was covered in medals and decorations from a hundred campaigns. The hare selected a medal. Detaching it from the jacket, he tossed it across to Matthias.

'Here, catch! That's a medal, donch'a know. Captain Snow gave it to me for saving his life.'

'You saved the owl's life?' said Matthias.

'I should say I did,' Basil laughed at the memory. 'Feathery old fool went to sleep in a rotten dead tree. It got blown down in a gale and trapped the blighter underneath. He'd have died if I hadn't come along, dug under the thing and pulled him out. Popped out like a shuttlecock under a door. Fellow officer, you understand. Couldn't leave him there to get flattened; his face is flat enough as it is.'

'So all I do is show him this medal?' asked the young mouse.

Basil laughed at his friend's naiveté. 'Yes that's all, but if you don't want to be scoffed, make sure he sees the medal before he sees you. Tell the old buffer that Basil

Stag Hare sent you. And mind your manners! Make sure you call him by his proper rank, "Cap'n". Oh, and I'd like that medal back sometime. Spoils the look of me number-one dress tunic, missing decoration.'

Matthias studied the medal. It was a silver cross embellished with a spread-winged owl. The ribbon was of faded white silk. Though it was old, it shone bright in the sunlight.

'Thank you, Basil,' he said. 'I'll see you get it back. Is there anything else I should know?'

'Not much. Just remember what I've said, old chap. This Captain Snow is a night hunter, by the way. He probably sleeps in some old tree all day with one eye open. You mark my words, laddie, old Snow doesn't miss a thing. He knows all the creatures in his territory; where they live, what trails they use and so on. Ha, they don't call owls wise for nothing. Bit of a duffer all the same, letting a tree fall on him. Keep your eye on him though. If he catches you napping he'll chomp you up, medal and all.'

Basil finished his ale and yawned. 'Now get some sleep, Matthias. I'm fagged out after that snack. My old honourable war wound is beginning to play me up. I must have a bit of a snooze.'

With that Basil closed his eyes. He was soon snoring gently. Matthias realized there was no more to be said, so he decided to have a rest too. Basil Stag Hare: what an amazing old campaigner, the young mouse thought, as he drifted off to sleep.

Shortly after twelve o'clock Matthias awakened. The noontime sunlight flooded the room. Basil was flat on his back snoring stentoriously. Although his shoulder still throbbed, Matthias felt fit and refreshed – well enough to travel. He knew, however, that he must act with stealth and secrecy. If the Abbot or Cornflower or any of his friends knew of his scheme he would have no chance at all. They would make certain he was confined to bed until further notice.

Quietly he arose and dressed himself, hanging his sandals around his neck by their thongs. Taking a clean pillowslip he stocked it with the remainder of the food from the table. Someone had thoughtfully placed his dagger on the bedside locker. It must have been found on the floor of Great Hall. Searching around, Matthias came upon a good stout pole, probably used as a window or curtain opener. He decided it would come in handy.

Carefully he inched the door open, closing it again swiftly as the Abbot and Brother Alf padded by. Matthias listened to Alf's voice. 'I looked in on them about ten minutes ago, Father. They're both sleeping like hibernating squirrels. It's not likely that they'll wake until evening.'

The footsteps receded down the passage. Matthias crept from the room, and stole off in the opposite direction.

He was surprised at the ease with which he left the Abbey, slipping off into Mossflower through the side door in the wall, where unknown to him Methuselah's murderer had also passed on the previous day.

Alone in the woods, Matthias felt a bit wobbly upon his legs. He sat down against a beech tree until the feeling passed. Tying the pillowcase bundle to his pole, he hefted it across his good shoulder and struck off boldly through Mossflower towards the north-east.

22

Matthias judged by the sun that it was past mid-afternoon. He had made steady progress through the woods. Nothing untoward had occurred. He had stopped and had a light snack, gained his second wind and pressed forward, taking care not to create too much noise lest he disturb any predators. The young mouse had discovered a path of sorts, skirting the dense underbrush and avoiding patches of marshland. Always keeping the tree moss on his left, he continued eastwards.

Matthias pinned the medal to his habit, telling himself that he might stumble into Captain Snow's territory at any moment. Lulled by the warm sun, cool shade, and birdsong, he trekked onwards, thinking of nothing in particular and enjoying the sense of freedom amid so much beauty.

Seemingly from out of nowhere a mouse leaped, barring Matthias's path! He halted, sizing the strange mouse up. It was an odd-looking wild thing. Matthias was not even too sure it really was a mouse.

The creature had spiky fur which stuck out at odd angles all over. Around its brow was bound a brightly-coloured scarf. The stranger was fully a head shorter than Matthias. It stood defiantly blocking his way, glaring at him with the maddest looking eyes he had ever encountered.

Matthias smiled politely and addressed the odd mouse, 'Hello there! Beautiful afternoon, isn't it?'

'Never mind that nonsense,' it replied in a gruff voice. 'Who are you? Why are you trespassing on shrew land?'

Matthias paused. So this was what a shrew looked like? He had never seen one before, but he had been told of their bad tempers.

The young mouse decided to fight fire with fire. No point being good mannered with this little hooligan. He snarled in what he hoped was an aggressive manner, 'Never mind who I am! Who do you think you are, you little raghead?'

The shrew seemed uncertain for a moment, then she stormed back in her low gruff voice, 'I am Guosim, and you still haven't told me what you want in shrew territory.'

'Guosim,' echoed Matthias. 'What sort of a name is that? And anyhow, if you don't want creatures coming across your land, then you should put signs up. As far as I'm concerned Mossflower has always been free to all.'

'Except this part,' snapped the shrew. 'Don't you know anything? Guosim stands for Guerrilla Union of Shrews in Mossflower.'

Matthias laughed scornfully, 'I couldn't care less what it stands for! Make way for a Redwall Abbey Warrior. I'm coming through!'

Immediately Matthias took a step forward, Guosim stuck her paws between her lips and emitted a sharp whistle. There was a swift rustle in the undergrowth. Matthias found himself surrounded by at least fifty shrews.

They packed around him, creating an angry hubbub in their deep rough tones. All of them wore coloured head-bands, all carried short rapier-like swords. Guosim had difficulty in calling them to order.

'Comrades,' she shouted. 'Tell this mouse what happens to a trespasser.'

The replies that came back were varied.

'Break his paws.'

'Skin him alive.'

'Chop off his nose.'

'Hang him by the tail.'

'Stuff his whiskers down his ears.'

A stern-looking old shrew barged Guosim out of the way and whistled sharply. He produced a round, black pebble and held it up.

'Any comrade who wants to speak must hold the pebble. Otherwise, shut up!'

Complete silence fell. He handed the pebble to Matthias.

'Now, explain yourself, mouse.'

There were one or two murmurs of dissent. Why should a stranger who was not a shrew have first say? The old shrew danced with rage. 'Will you lot shut up? The mouse has the stone; shut your traps!'

Silence fell once more. Matthias cleared his throat. 'Er, ahem. Guerrilla Union of Shrews in Mossflower, forgive me: as you see, I am a stranger in these parts. I do not intentionally trespass on your land. Had I known I would have taken a different route. You have probably noticed by my habit that I come from Redwall Abbey. Though I am a warrior, we are a healing and helping order. It is usual for all creatures to allow a Redwall mouse to pass in peace. This is the unwritten law.'

The older shrew (whose name was Log-a-Log) took the pebble from Matthias and addressed the others.

'Right, comrades. Now we know a bit more about things, let's have a show of paws. All those in favour of letting the mouse go free.'

Paws went up: Log-a-Log counted them. Exactly half of those present. He called for those against, and took another count.

'Half one way, half the other. The casting vote is mine. Now let me tell you, I know we take care of our own, but the Redwall mice are a legend in Mossflower. They do no harm to any creature. In fact they do a lot of good.' Log-a-Log raised his paw. 'Therefore, comrades, I vote that the mouse goes free!'

There followed an equal number of cheers and boos, a squabble ensued and fighting broke out. Guosim snatched the stone from Log-a-Log and waved it about.

'Listen to me,' she roared. 'I know that Log-a-Log is a wise elder, but I am president of our union, comrades. The mouse hasn't told us where he is going.'

There was a brief silence. Another shrew snatched hold of the stone. 'Aye, that's right! Where are you off to, mouse?'

The stone was thrust at Matthias.

'I'll tell you,' he said. 'But my name is not "mouse". It's Matthias. Redwall Abbey is in danger from Cluny the Scourge and his horde—'

There was immediate shouting and gruff oaths. Matthias knew the drill; it was surprising how the stone-holder could gain quiet among such a noisy quarrelsome gathering. Matthias continued, 'As I was saying before I was so rudely interrupted, we at Redwall are under attack by Cluny and his horde. Evidently you have heard his name before. Well, I believe that I have the solution to Cluny. It is an ancient sword that once belonged to a great mouse named Martin the Warrior. To find the sword I must ask Captain Snow the whereabouts of Asmodeus.'

301

The shrews made a frenzied rush into the undergrowth; Matthias found he was standing alone. After a few minutes Log-a-Log and Guosim ventured stealthily out again. Forgetting the stone, Guosim spoke in a awed voice, 'D'you mean you actually intend to walk right up and speak to Snow?'

Matthias nodded. Log-a-Log continued where his comrade had left off: 'You're going to ask the Cap'n where you can find Giant Poisonteeth, mouse? Er, I mean, Matthias. You are either very brave or raving mad.'

'A little bit of both, I suppose,' said the young mouse. 'Do you know much about Captain Snow and Asmodeus?'

Both shrews trembled visibly. Guosim's voice had risen an octave. 'Matthias, you must be crazy! Don't you know what you're walking into? Captain Snow . . . why, you'd be just a snack to him. And as for the other one – Giant Ice Eyes – who could even go near him? He eats as many shrews as he wants. No living creature can stop the poisonteeth!'

A heart-rending moan arose from the shrews in the undergrowth.

Matthias still had the stone. He held it up and addressed them boldly. 'Guerrilla Shrew Comrades, I do not ask you to do my fighting. Merely point me in the direction of Captain Snow. Who knows? If I finally get the sword I may be able to liberate you.'

Log-a-Log took the stone. 'Matthias of Redwall, you are on our land. We will escort you. The Guerilla Union of Shrews in Mossflower would never live down the shame of having a stranger fight their battles for them. You may not always see us, but we will be close by. Come now.'

Matthias moved north-eastwards with the company of

shrews whose numbers seemed to swell as they went along. At nightfall there were upwards of four hundred members of the Shrew Union seated around the campfire breaking bread with the warrior from Redwall. That night Matthias slept inside a long hollow log with both ends disguised to make it appear solid.

Like Basil, the shrews were masters of camouflage. Their very survival depended upon it.

Half an hour before dawn the young mouse was roused by a shrew who gave him an acorn cup full of sweet berry juice, a farl of rough nutbread and some tasty fresh roots that he could not identify. By dawn's first light they were on the move again, marching until mid-morning. Matthias saw the edge of Mossflower Wood. The tall trees thinned out, bush and undergrowth were sparse. Before them lay an open field of long, lush grass dotted with buttercup and sorrel. In the distance he could see the abandoned farmhouse that Basil had spoken of. All the shrews had disappeared with the exception of Guosim and Log-a-Log. The latter pointed to the barn adjoining the farmhouse.

'You might find Captain Snow in there taking a nap. Now is the best time to approach him, after he has a full stomach from the night hunt.'

The two guerrilla shrews melted back into the woods. Alone now, Matthias crossed the sunny field leading to the barn, just as Basil had taught him: zig-zag, crouch, wriggle, and weave.

He tiptoed into the barn. There was no sign of an owl. In the semi-darkness Matthias could make out various old farming implements rusted with disuse. On one wall there was a huge stack of musty, dry straw bales. He decided to climb up the bales, in the hope of getting near

Captain Snow, who most probably would be sleeping perched in the rafters.

Matthias scaled the packed straw. He stood on top and looked about. Nothing. He ventured forwards, and suddenly slipped and fell down a hidden gap between the bales. Scrambling and clutching, he plunged down to the floor.

Matthias's feet never touched the earth. He landed clean in the gaping mouth of a huge marmalade cat!

23

Constance stood on the parapet overlooking the road; dawn was breaking behind her, in the east. However, more important things troubled the badger's mind. The Abbot came bustling up with Basil limping in the rear. Both creatures looked extremely concerned.

'Have you seen Matthias?' the Abbot asked. 'He's been missing from his room since yesterday afternoon.'

Basil looked rather shamefaced. 'All my fault, I'm afraid. Should have kept my eye on the little rascal. We'll have to organize another search party.'

'No time for that,' snapped the badger. 'Look!'

Down the road in the distance, a long column of dust was rising. The three creatures sniffed the faint breeze. It was unmistakable. Cluny's army was coming to Redwall!

'We'll need every available defender,' Constance murmured. 'No need to cause a panic, but this looks like a full-scale assault. The fox's warning was true.'

Jess, Winifred, Foremole and Ambrose were sent for. Together they leaned over the parapet, watching the dust-cloud draw nearer. The beat of a drum was audible, and individual rats could be picked out.

'They're heading right for us,' said Jess grimly. 'Better get all defenders to battle stations.'

At a given signal, John Churchmouse began tolling the attack warning upon the Joseph Bell. All through the Abbey and its grounds creatures stopped what they were doing. Picking up weapons that lay close to paw they assembled at their appointed posts to await further orders.

Cluny waved his standard above the sun-flecked dust rising from the road. Gradually the horde ground to a halt.

Shading his eye against the sun, he stared up at the walls.

'Surrender to Cluny the Scourge,' he bellowed harshly.

'Go and boil your head, rat!' came Constance's gruff reply.

Cluny took a pace back, letting his standard dip low. Two score of sling-rats ran forward, whirling their stone-laden weapons. They let fly a volley at the ramparts, shouting bloodcurdling war cries. The stones clattered harmlessly off the wall and fell back to the road.

Cluny cursed inwardly. For all his show of force and arrogance, he had made a strategical error.

The sun was in his army's eyes!

The defenders had the advantage. This soon became clear when a platoon of otters on the ramparts unloosed a rattling fusillade of heavy pebbles. Pandemonium broke out in the vanguard of Cluny's horde, with cries of agony as the pebbles found their marks. One stone actually struck Cluny's helmet.

'Back to the ditch and the meadow! Stay out of their range!' Cluny did his best to keep his voice even. As the army retreated to safety he was the last to go, willing himself to walk slowly as if that was the way he had planned it.

Four rats lay dead near the wall, and Killconey's drum stood unattended in the road. Basil Stag Hare sniffed drily.

'Not a very well organized initial sortie for the invincible horde. Our chaps took the wind out their sales, what?'

'Hurr, they do 'ave to wait 'til sun moves round,' commented Foremole.

'But we don't,' cried Jess. 'Bring the archers! Keep the slings going! Let's give that mob in the ditch something to think about.'

Out in the safety of the meadow, Killconey attempted to soothe Cluny's ego. 'Ah, what a sly ould move of yours, sir, lullin' them into a false sense of security! Make 'em think they're winnin', that's the game.'

Unexpectedly Killconey received his reward for flattery at the wrong time – a thwack over his head from the standard.

'Shut your mouth, ferret,' Cluny said sourly. 'Get me some sort of a command post rigged up here. Cheesethief, where are the gangs with that battering ram?'

'Coming up right away, Chief,' called Cheesethief as he trotted off to find where the ram carriers had got to.

It was not long before the tiny harvest-mouse archers were bending their bows, sending small pointed shafts darting into the ditch. These, supplemented by the stouter arrows of the fieldmice, and the otter slingers, caused many wounds and great discomfort to the would-be attackers, pinning a good number of them down. Morale was low because Cluny had ordered no retaliation until after midday.

Jess Squirrel abseiled swiftly down to the road on a rope.

Looping the rope's end around the old water-butt that had been the ferret's drum, she sprang inside, calling up to the parapet, 'Haul away, Constance.'

The barrel fairly flew up under the badger's strong paws. Jess was quite pleased with herself. She had plans for the drum to beat the rats! Basil Stag Hare strode the parapet with a swagger-stick tucked beneath his arm. He dodged around the squirrel, who was rolling the barrel along. Retaining the dignity befitting his rank, Basil kept up a constant stream of orders, 'Fire at will, you mouse types! Otters, pick out your targets! Any moles here? Report to the Foremole down in the grounds right away.'

The hare had cast off his leg bandage. Now that he was back in active service the 'honourable war wound' was completely forgotten.

Meanwhile back at the meadow Cluny sat brooding under a makeshift tent.

Cheesethief came hurrying up, urging on the contingent of battering ram carriers. Hoping to find favour with Cluny he had put himself at the head of the party, helping them to carry the cumbersome object.

'Come on, mates,' he cried. 'Let's knock on the Abbey door!'

Having negotiated the ditch, they charged across the road. Once they had passed a certain point it created a difficult angle for the defenders on the wall to fire at them.

The massive ram shuddered as it smashed against the gatehouse door. With Cheesethief shouting encouragement, the ram carriers took a short run back and battered the door again.

Cluny was heartened to see things going right for a change. There was more to Cheesethief than he had at first thought.

The door was rammed a third time. Now creatures on the wall stood up in full view as they retaliated by firing down on the ram carriers. Cluny called up his best slingers and archers, ordering them to pick off the defenders. Fortunately for him, the sun was starting to move southwards, and the otters and mice on the ramparts were clearly visible. Cluny's archers caused numerous casualties, forcing the defenders to drop below the parapet. The battering ram continued, although as yet it had made no lasting impression upon the solid construction.

Missiles from the wall had slackened off, giving Cluny's horde a chance to desert the ditch for the relative safety of the meadows. Cluny appeared well satisfied for the moment. He called Killconey to his side.

'This is more like it, ferret. Right, get the tunnel gangs! Gather your weasels, stoats and ferrets. Take them back along the ditch to the south-east corner of the Abbey wall. When it is dark I'll send you a signal, then you can start tunnelling through the ditch wall, across the road and under the Abbey wall. Is that clear?'

Killconey threw an elaborate salute. 'Sure, it's clear as the mornin' dew, yer honour!'

Cluny closed his eyes, intent upon keeping his present good mood. 'Then get going, and try to get it right this time.'

The battle continued sporadically all day and into the evening. The ram carriers kept up their attack, but somehow the great door withstood them. When the last vestiges of twilight were gone, Constance called the Captains together. They squatted beneath the parapet in darkness as the badger outlined the situation.

'Listen, we're all right for the moment, but sooner or

later something will have to be done about the battering ram. Has anyone got a good idea? I'm open to sensible suggestions.'

Below them the ram kept up its remorseless battering. Ambrose Spike had reported some minor splintering at the top inside edges of the door, but the shoring of earthworks was holding out. Foremole had assured them that any attempted tunnelling would take at least a few days before signs showed. Meanwhile, he and his moles were carefully monitoring the earth in the Abbey grounds.

Throughout the day-long battle, the animals not directly involved in the fighting had been busy too. The Father Abbot was tending the wounded in Great Hall, Friar Hugo was constantly sending Cornflower and her helpers back and forth to the ramparts with food and drink. Mrs Churchmouse and Mrs Vole were making bandages from old clean sheets. Silent Sam had been left with Tim and Tess the Churchmouse twins. He had played with the infants until they fell asleep in a heap of bandages.

Sam wanted to go up on the wall, but his parents had forbidden it. Slipping out of Great Hall, he passed the time for a bit, listening with an ear to the ground in the company of the moles. But Sam soon became bored. He stabbed at the earth with his tiny dagger, imagining that rats were popping up from make-believe tunnels. After a while he wandered over to the foot of the wall and sat sharing some food with Jess. The little squirrel signalled to his parent, asking her what she wanted the big barrel for.

Jess Squirrel took her little son upon her knee and explained. She had an idea that the barrel, filled with something or other, could be dropped down upon the ram carriers. But she was not too sure what it would be best to fill the barrel with.

Sam jumped down from his mother's knee. The barrel was lying on its side. He sprang up on it and walked it about, rolling it very skilfully under his feet. All the time he was sucking hard on his paw, trying to think how he could help.

The tunnel gangs lounged about, leaning on the sides of the ditch. Killconey stretched full length on a mossy patch.

'Ah, I tell you, this is the life! Better than gettin' shot at! Me ould mother always said, get a good job and keep yer head down.'

Scumnose came creeping along in the darkness. He nudged the ferret. 'Cluny says you can begin tunnelling now.'

Killconey marked a cross on the ditch wall with his claw. 'Right you are! We'll start about here, buckoes. Come on now, dig for victory.'

BOOK THREE

The Warrior

1

The invasion at Redwall continued throughout the night, the whole scene illuminated by a bright summer moon. Neither side gave the other any quarter. When the main action went into a lull, sporadic sniping would break out: bow, lance, sling and spear all coming into play with deadly effect. One thing that remained constant throughout the battle was the sound of the battering ram pounding away remorselessly at the Abbey gatehouse.

Cluny made it his duty to assess personally the progress at the tunnel workings. He was scathingly critical of the small hole that had been gouged into the side of the ditch, roundly cursing any creature who dared to complain of difficult obstacles.

'Can't get past the rocks and tree roots my eye!' he snarled. 'Idle stupid laziness, that's what is holding up the progress of this tunnel! I'll be around first thing tomorrow to see how much further you lot have dug, and if it's not to my liking, I'll cave it in and bury the whole shirking crowd of you!'

However, the battering ram pleased Cluny much

more. He knew it was worrying the Abbey defenders. The rat crews that manned the heavy object were changed every hour by Cheesethief, who stayed with the ram the whole time, encouraging the carriers on to greater efforts.

Cluny had gained a new respect for Cheesethief. Mentally, he had already promoted him to second-in-command. Sensing this had made Cheesethief redouble his efforts. He worked the rat crews like a slave driver. No rodent dared complain about one whom the Chief held in such high regard.

Constance stood on the wall with her Captains. The badger's brow was furrowed with anxiety. Basil Stag Hare, the most seasoned campaigner among them, was the only one who apparently took it all quite lightly.

''Pon my word,' he chuckled, 'the way those blighters down there are carrying on with the jolly old ram, they won't need to tunnel in soon. I'll give it half a day at most, then we'll have rats piling in over the shoring, what!'

Ambrose Spike positively bristled at the nonchalant hare. 'Well, I must say that *is* a comforting thing to know! Any more little gems of information to cheer us up, eh?'

Basil strode off in high dudgeon, re-emphasizing his previously forgotten limp. 'Dearie me, old lad, no need to be so touchy! Merely making a military observation, y'know.'

Constance called the two old friends together. 'Look, it's no use quarrelling among ourselves. We should be thinking of a solution. Come on, you two, stop sulking and be pals again.'

Smiling sheepishly, Basil and Ambrose shook paws. Winifred the otter pounded the stones of the parapet in frustration.

'I say there's got to be a way to stop that confounded

ram! We've lost far too many defenders. They get picked off every time they stand up to retaliate. It's got to be a very simple solution; a small obvious thing that we've all missed.'

Jess Squirrel, aided by Silent Sam, manoeuvred the barrel up on to the ramparts. She patted it. 'Something simple – like this!'

The Captains gathered around the barrel, examining it. The top had been covered over with gauze. A strange noise issued from within.

'Well, Jess. Don't keep us in suspense. What's in the barrel?' the badger growled.

'Shall we tell them, Sam?' grinned Jess.

Silent Sam gave a broad wink and tapped a well-sucked paw against his nose. He and his mum were enjoying this.

'What we have here, my good comrades in arms,' said Jess grandly, 'is stage one of our anti-battering ram scheme, thanks to my small offspring here who found the hornets' nest.'

Basil clapped the two squirrels soundly upon their backs. 'Of course, that's the ticket! A hornets' nest in a barrel. Just chuck it down on the beastly old enemy, what?'

Jess and Sam smiled with wicked delight.

'Ha, but that's only the first stage,' said Jess. 'Here's the second.'

She and Sam ducked out of sight. A moment later they were back with two buckets.

'Two pails of good, fine, slick vegetable oil,' Jess announced. 'The minute they drop the battering ram, we'll tip this down all over it. Let's see them try to break a door with it then!'

Jess and Sam were congratulated heartily by all. Smiles appeared on faces that had been gloomy shortly before.

Sam bowed graciously each time he was thanked. Nobody was refusing him permission to be up on the wall now.

Down below, the scrabbling of rats' feet and the monotonous thud of the ram continued. Winifred and Constance lifted the barrel on to the parapet edge. They angled and tipped it until a fine delicate balance had been achieved. The badger peeped over at the activity below, waiting for the best moment. She beckoned Silent Sam to her. The time was exactly right.

'Pray, would you do us the honour, Master Samuel?' said Constance with mock courtliness.

Feigning an equal gravity, Sam made an elegant leg, and delivered a short, sharp kick to the barrel. Buzzing angrily, it dropped out of sight over the edge of the Abbey wall.

There was a crash and a yell, followed by the shocked screams of agonized rats. They milled about in the roadway dancing in pain as myriads of maddened hornets attacked furiously. Some rats ran off down the road, others hurled themselves into the ditch pursued by the relentless, stinging insects.

The long battering ram lay unguarded, conveniently spotlighted by the rats' abandoned torches. Two well-aimed buckets full of vegetable oil were hurled down. They smashed directly on target, saturating the entire length of the ram.

Before the hornets could seek out new victims, Basil ordered the defenders down to the gatehouse study where they had a celebration snack.

Cluny stooped inside the tunnel workings surrounded by as many of his followers as could pack in without causing mass suffocation. Killconey held Cluny's cloak over the entrance hole. Outside the air resounded with buzzing and pitiful screams.

The ferret gingerly touched the tip of his swollen nose. Cluny stooped in stony silence. He did not sit or attempt to touch his own injuries. The others might laugh. Dumbly, he endured the pain of the fiery stings. Further across the meadows there was a mass scramble of bodies into a small mere. The hornets zinged about waiting for snouts to break the surface.

Dawn revealed a sadly-disorganized horde. Cluny wisely held back his temper. Many of his soldiers looked so demoralized that they were liable to make a run for it and desert. He reasoned that there was little to be gained by adding insult to injury. Seven rats, two ferrets, and a stoat lay dead in the ditch. Unable to escape the main body of hornets, they had been stung so many times it had proved fatal.

Cheesethief limped slowly up, covered in ugly lumps. 'Chief, they've poured some stuff over the battering ram! We can't hold on to it. We tried, but it's like trying to pick up a wet eel. The blasted thing slid right out of our claws. One of the bearers had both legs broken when it slipped and fell. Sorry, Chief, but we didn't expect them to think anything up like that. Hornets and slippery stuff; it's not fair!'

Cluny pointed across the meadow. 'Regroup the army over there. Let them feed and rest. Send someone scouting for dock leaves to rub on those stings. I'm going into my tent to do some serious planning. We're not beaten yet, not by a long chalk. They can't produce a hornets' nest every day.'

Cluny stumped off dejectedly, rubbing his backside with one claw.

*

There were one or two insect-sting casualties to be treated at the Abbey Infirmary. Fortunately, Brother Rufus had a specific compound that he had invented some years back to deal with such emergencies as summer stings.

Silent Sam was re-enacting the entire episode in panto-mime for the benefit of Tim and Tess and some other infant creatures. They were in tucks of laughter at his antics as Sam slapped at his fur and performed somer-saults with a comical expression on his face.

Constance and the Captains assembled back on the wall after a few hours' rest. They could see no immediate threat from the horde licking their wounds across the meadow. This gave ample opportunity to assess the damage caused to the gatehouse door.

Jess Squirrel was lowered over the ramparts on a rope. She went swiftly down and inspected the door. In a short while she was back up again to report that although there were many deep dents and at least two long cracks, the old gatehouse door was still holding well.

Constance decided that later on they could lower some carpenters and smiths to deal with the repairs. Of late the badger had become preoccupied with an idea that was rapidly turning into an obsession. Cut off the head and the body would die. By some means she must kill Cluny the Scourge!

Out across the meadow she could plainly see the War-lord's tent. In the strong sunlight the badger watched the silhouette of the big rat moving about behind the canvas. The main problem was that the tent had been pitched too far out of range for sling or bow. Unless the weapon was big and powerful enough to reach that far . . . . That was it!

A large powerful bow, something along the lines of a crossbow. What if it could be mounted upon the ramparts unknown to Cluny and his horde? At a given time, say mid-afternoon, Cluny's shadow would be clearly visible through the tent fabric in the bright June sunlight. A big arrow or bolt properly aimed from the bow, and *twang!*

Exit Cluny.

Delighted with the plan, Constance shared her knowledge with only one other creature, the solitary beaver. Enlisting the aid of the beaver's highly capable molars, the badger left him gnawing away at a yew sapling in the orchard while she went off to find an arrow that would fit her brainchild. An ash staff that had seen service as a candle-snuffer proved to be ideal. With a heavy stone Constance flattened the conical brass extinguisher fitted to the top of the staff until it resembled a vicious-looking spear. She flighted it with duck feathers. A thin plaited climbing rope rubbed with beeswax made an excellent bowstring. With the help of the beaver, Constance bent the yew sapling against the Abbey wall and strung it to the right tension. Together they mounted it upon a dining table with nails and strapping, and bore it up to the ramparts. Constance would only grunt brusquely at anyone inquiring what the strange contraption was for; only she and the beaver needed to know that. The two creatures sat out upon the ramparts sharing lunch, conversing in low secretive tones.

'That should do the trick!'

'Aye, let's keep our paws crossed that it does. We'll only get one shot.'

'Ha, one shot is all we'll need.'

'Shall we wait until the sun has passed its zenith? That way we can see him clearer.'

'Good idea. When the Joseph Bell tolls mid-afternoon should be best.'

Having finished lunch, the pair lay out like old watchdogs on the sun-warmed stones.

Half an hour later they were snoring.

*

Cluny was a resourceful rat. He often wished that his army thought as he did instead of being just a mob of incompetents. But then, if the horde were as clever as he was, there would be no need of a leader. Such was life, he reflected. Nobody could think up a new strategy as he could.

And this time Cluny reckoned that he had hit upon a foolproof plan! He strode across the meadow and hand-picked thirty-odd rats.

'Follow me,' Cluny rapped. 'Cheesethief, I'm leaving you in charge until I get back.'

Without another word Cluny marched off with his selected rodents, first to the upturned hay cart in the ditch down the road, then a quick circle around into Moss-flower Wood.

Like his predecessor Redtooth, Cheesethief was ambitious. He interpreted Cluny's order as the much-coveted promotion to second-in-command. The Chief had not even acknowledged Darkclaw. In his elation, Cheesethief even forgot the painful hornet stings. He strutted about asserting his new-found authority.

'Darkclaw, send those ferrets out for more dockleaves, will you?' he ordered. 'Oh, and see that no one else strays too far. I'll be in the tent if you need me for anything, but try not to disturb me.'

Darkclaw scowled resentfully. Nevertheless he carried out the orders. If he didn't, he was certain that Cheesethief would report him to Cluny for insubordination.

Cheesethief swaggered into the tent and glanced around. Cluny had left the better part of a wood pigeon, some cheese, and there was still a handsome measure of best Saint Ninian barley wine in the Chief's canteen.

Cheesethief tucked in with satisfaction. Redtooth used

'Oh get up you disgusting little beast! I know you're not dead.'

Slowly the young mouse rose to his feet. The cat seemed uninterested in him as a possible food source. Matthias's legs were shaking so much that he had to sit down again.

They stared at each other. Matthias could think of nothing to say. The cat spoke again. This time its voice was indignant. 'Well, have you nothing to say for yourself, mouse? Where are your manners? Don't you think you should apologize for leaping into my mouth like that?'

Matthias managed to stand again. He bowed shakily. 'I beg your pardon, sir. It was purely accidental. I fell, you see. Please accept my humble apologies. I am Matthias of Redwall and I sincerely hope I have not disturbed you in any way.'

The cat sniffed distantly. 'Yes, at least you seem to have some sort of decent upbringing, Matthias of Redwall. I accept your apology. Allow me to introduce myself. I am Squire Julian Gingivere.'

'Pleased to mee you, Squire Julian,' said Matthias politely.

The cat yawned regally. 'You may call me Julian. The title is hereditary. I never wanted it, Squire of what? A broken-down ramshackle farm building and a stretch of river over yonder! One has no real friends, no trusty servants, not even a mate for that matter. Hmmm, I suppose the Gingivere line will become extinct when I die.'

Matthias could not help feeling a certain amount of sympathy for the lonely aristocrat.

'At least you seem to lead a peaceful life,' he said hopefully.

'Oh, spare me your platitudes, mouse,' Julian replied in

a world-weary voice. 'What would you know about loneliness and trying to preserve one's standards in a decaying world? I say, do you think you could manage to clean yourself up a bit? You look an absolute fright, standing there all covered in dust and straw. And while you're doing that maybe you'd like to explain how you came to be sneaking around my barn.'

As Matthias brushed himself down, he related the object of his mission. Julian looked down at him in surprise.

'Captain Snow eh? That old maniac! I've forbidden him the use of my barn, you know. What a thoroughly dreadful bird! He eats anything that moves or crawls. Atrocious table manners, too. All that regurgitating of bone and fur. Ugh!'

'Could you tell me where I might find him, please?' Matthias asked.

'Certainly,' replied Julian. 'Snow lives in a hollow tree these days. I'll stretch a point and take you there. But please don't expect me to introduce you or even talk to him. When I barred Snow from here we had a dreadful quarrel. Things were said that cannot be rescinded. I vowed that day never to speak to that old owl for as long as I live.'

Matthias sensed that Julian and Snow had once been good friends. Maybe the rift in their relationship was the cause of Julian's present state of fatalism and gloom. He decided wisely not to pursue the matter further at the moment.

Riding upon a cat's back was a new and unusual experience for Matthias. Although he took great care to disguise it, Julian was quite an observant creature. As he strode with an easy grace across the farmyard he remarked idly, 'Your friends the shrews are out in force today. Ignorant

326

little things! They think I can't see them. Give Log-a-Log and Guosim a message from me, will you? Tell them it is quite safe to come into the barn for hay and other items. Snow doesn't roost there any more. Goodness knows, I certainly won't hurt them. My diet consists of herbs, grasses and an occasional fish from the river. I gave up red meat years ago. You might also mention that if they must come to my barn, would they please desist from arguing and fighting so much? There's nothing quite as upsetting as quarrelsome little shrews disturbing one's meditations.'

Matthias agreed to convey the message to the Guerrilla Shrews. They had arrived at a small overgrown orchard. Julian halted within twenty paces of a stunted oak. As he bade Matthias climb down he cautioned him, 'You probably can't see Captain Snow, but he's watching us. I can tell when he's at home. Be extra careful, Matthias. The old glutton will more than likely eat you on sight – typical of an owl. Well, I'm off now. If you get the chance, say Squire Gingivere said that he must surely admit he was in the wrong and apologize. Only then can we resume our friendship and live together in the barn. Goodbye, Matthias, and do take care.'

'Goodbye, Julian, and thank you!' Matthias called after the retreating figure of the last survivor in the Gingivere dynasty.

The young mouse unpinned Basil's medal from his tunic. He ventured cautiously forwards, holding it aloft. If Julian said that Captain Snow was about, then it must be so.

An unearthly screech shattered the silence, followed by a rush of wings. The owl swooped out of nowhere straight for Matthias.

Ducking and weaving as Basil had taught him,

Matthias waved the medal and yelled at the top of his voice, 'Truce! Basil Stag Hare sent me. I claim a truce!'

He was knocked flat upon his back. Massive needle-pointed talons tore the medal from his grasp. Captain Snow landed in front of Matthias, raising the dust with his vast wings. The young mouse found it hard to believe that such an awesome and impressive bird existed.

Captain Snow stood hugely tall with an incredible wing-span. The owl's pure-white plumage was broken only by a few brown bars on the wing and some dark spots on the crown. He had six dangerous talons in front, two at the back of his legs and a sharp heavily-curved beak. His eyes were colossal; twin golden orbs with circular black centres.

Matthias continued ducking and weaving, conscious that his life hung by a thread. Captain Snow flicked out a talon. Matthias dodged nimbly aside.

'State your name and rank. Who gave you my medal?' snapped the owl in a flat hard voice.

Still moving quickly, and panting for breath, the young mouse gasped, 'Matthias mouse, Warrior of Redwall Abbey. The medal belongs to my friend Basil Stag Hare. He sends his compliments, Cap'n Sir.'

'Stand fast,' snapped the Captain.

Matthias stood rigid. The owl's talons started to inch forwards as if they had a life of their own. The young mouse moved steadily backwards away from the talons. Captain Snow licked saliva from the edges of his beak; it was plain that he desperately wanted to eat Matthias.

'What did the cat say to you, mouse?' he rasped. 'Did he mention me?'

Matthias repeated the message from Julian. 'Squire Gingivere says, sir, that if you were to admit yourself in the wrong and apologize to him, then you could both be friends and live in the barn again.'

As he spoke, Matthias had been moving away from the seeking talons. On a sudden instinct he dived to one side as the owl pounced. He skipped and ran on a zig-zag course, away from the murderous bird. Bilked of his target, Captain Snow madly tore at the grass and scattered dust. All at once he wheeled about and flew upwards, perching at the entrance to his nest-hole in the stunted oak. 'All right, you can stop running away now, little warrior. Come back here. I want to talk to you.'

Matthias stood a safe distance away from the tree. Captain Snow shifted from one foot to the other, muttering huffily, 'Me, in the wrong? Never. I won't apologize to that cat! I refuse to!'

When the owl had finished arguing with himself, Matthias called out, 'Cap'n Snow, sir, there is a question that I must ask you.'

The great snowy owl beckoned towards his hole with a sweeping wing. 'Listen, mouse, you can't stand down there shouting up at me. Why not come into my lair, er, nest. Then we can chat together in comfort.'

Standing on tiptoe Matthias could catch a glimpse of the 'nest'. The walls were lined with all types of fur, shrew, mouse, vole, even rat. The skulls and bones of small creatures were hung up as macabre decorations. Matthias smiled nervously. 'Er, if you don't mind, Cap'n, I think I'd prefer to stay where I am.'

The Captain cackled raucously and pointed a talon. 'So, you'd prefer to stay where you are, sir? Well, I don't blame you. Right, out with it. What's this question you want to ask me?'

'Do you know of Asmodeus the giant adder, and where might I find him, sir?' Matthias called boldly.

The owl preened his breast feathers. He cocked his head on one side. 'I know of everything that moves within my territory, mouse. Yes, I do know of Asmodeus. I also know where he calls home. Why do you ask?'

'Because the adder has something that belongs to our Abbey; an ancient sword, sir,' Matthias replied.

'Ah, the sword,' said the owl. 'I remember the night he passed here carrying it. You'll never get that sword from Asmodeus, a puny little mouse like you! The adder has magic in his eye that would freeze you like a statue. Huh, I wish mine could.'

Matthias felt his temper rising. He shouted angrily at the self-opinionated bird, 'I don't care if he's got magic eyes, poison teeth, coils of steel, or whatever! I mean to have that sword! I'll steal it from the snake or fight him for it. If I have to I'll—'

The rest of Matthias's words were drowned out by the hysterical screeching laughter of the owl, who nearly fell from his perch with merriment. He blinked tears from his huge eyes.

'You'll what? Did I hear you say that you'd fight Asmodeus? You! Oh little mouse, run away and play before I crack a wing laughing. Ha ha ha hee hee oh hohohoho! Oh, dearie me! Are you sure you haven't been drinking old apple brandy? A mouse fighting an adder! Oh my, now I've heard everything!'

Captain Snow laughed helplessly. Matthias yelled up challengingly, 'Ha, I'll bet *you* couldn't fight Asmodeus!'

The owl wiped tears from his eyes with a snowy wing as he hooted. 'I've never tried. And I wouldn't relish the prospect, little one! The snake and I would probably both end up dead.'

Matthias called mockingly, 'That's because you're afraid. Look, I bet I'll fight Asmodeus and win too.'

'Bet you won't.'

'Bet I will.'

'Bet you anything you won't.'

Matthias pointed at the medal in Captain Snow's talons. 'Bet you that medal that I will!'

The Captain flung the medal backwards into his nest. 'Done!'

'Hold on, owl,' Matthias shouted. 'What are you putting up as a wager? The medal is not yours. You gave it to Basil Stag Hare.'

Spreading his wings to their incredible length, Snow screeched, 'I'll bet anything. Whatever you say, mouse.'

Matthias nodded cunningly. 'Oh, I don't want to take everything you own. Let's just say that you guarantee to return my medal and make a few little promises.'

Again the owl had difficulty in controlling his unbridled hilarity. 'Ha ha ha! The nerve of him! All right, my little warrior! It's a bet. Name your promises.'

'Right,' said Matthias solemnly. 'You must promise on your oath that if I win you will never eat another mouse or shrew of any type.'

'Agreed,' chortled the owl. 'In fact I'll go even further. I promise you that if you defeat the snake, I'll admit I was wrong to that stuffy old cat. I'll even apologize to him on bended knees, so there!'

'On your word as a captain,' Matthias pressed.

The owl held out a wing and a leg as he recited: 'I swear by my captaincy and by my illustrious ancestors Nyctea and Glacier, that I, Captain Snow, will return the medal and cleave to my oath if you should win against Asmodeus.' The owl broke into laughter again: 'Oh, hahahaheeheeheehohoho! This is the easiest bet I ever made! It'll be like taking the wings off a dead butterfly.'

'Maybe to you, sir, but not to me,' Matthias countered. 'Now, tell me where I may find Asmodeus, Cap'n.'

'In the old sandstone quarry,' the owl replied. 'You'll have to cross the river. There are caves in the quarry, passages too. Explore them. You won't find Asmodeus until you are least expecting him. By then it will be too late. You'll be deader than an icicle in hell. Goodbye, mouse.'

331

Matthias turned his back upon the snowy owl and strode off with a string of taunts ringing in his ears.

'Nice to have my silver medal back!' jeered the owl. 'I'll think of you when I wear it. You should have let me eat you. It'd save you a journey to the quarry . . . . Oh, I almost forgot. You won't be able to give the hare my best wishes . . . . You'll be snug inside the snake!'

Matthias walked onwards, ignoring the cruel jibes of the owl, through the farmyard and across the grassland, not stopping until he arrived at the fringe of Mossflower Wood. The shrews broke cover and milled about noisily with their endless questions.

'Ha, so you got back then?'

'Why didn't Snow eat you?'

'Bet you've never seen an owl that size before, eh?'

'What news of Poisonteeth?'

'Did you find out where he is?'

'Don't just stand there! Tell us, tell us!'

Fierce quarrelling broke out. Swords were being drawn as Matthias sought out Log-a-Log and took the black stone from him.

'Shut up and stop fighting, you hooligans, or you'll get to know nothing!' Matthias bellowed.

An expectant hush descended upon the Union members of the Guerrilla Shrews of Mossflower. Matthias found it hard to keep the contempt out of his voice. 'I found Captain Snow. Actually I was led to him by Squire Julian Gingivere. Does that name ring any bells?'

There was an embarrassed shuffling in the ranks of the listeners. Many turned their eyes to the ground, particularly Guosim and Log-a-Log.

Matthias folded his paws. He stared about in disgust. 'Oh, yes. I'd just like to thank you all! Especially you, Guosim, and Log-a-Log. What a sly, nasty, despicable thing to do, sending me into that barn without a single word of warning about the cat.'

Log-a-Log ripped the cloth band from his brow and flung it down. He took the stone up in his paw. 'Matthias, I speak not only for myself but for all the Guerrilla Union. We are very sorry, you must believe that. It completely slipped our minds. We forgot about the cat. You see, we are shrews, not only by name but also by nature. We argue, quarrel, bicker and fight so much among ourselves that we lose sight of the important issues. That is the way it is with us. Please accept our apologies, friend.'

Matthias retrieved the stone. 'I forgive you this once. You say you are shrews and you call me friend. You tell me that you forget. Let me tell you, I am a Redwall warrior. I always remember who my friends are, and I never forget an injury done to me! However, we will say no more of this. You must listen to me now. What I have to tell you is of great importance. It can change the life of every shrew here. Captain Snow has told me that Asmodeus lives in the old sandstone quarry across the river. He has given me his promise on oath: if I defeat Asmodeus, the owl will never again take the life of a shrew.'

When the astonished hubbub had died down the young mouse continued, 'Think about it, Guerrilla Shrews! It would be a double blessing for you. With Asmodeus dead and Captain Snow held to his oath you could live in safety from both. And while I'm on the subject, my friend Julian the cat is quite harmless. He will not hunt you. Any time you need something from the barn, you have his permission to take it, providing you do so quietly, with no fighting or arguing. That is all I have to say to you, save for one thing. Lead me to the quarry.'

Matthias stood patiently waiting as subdued conversation went on all about him. Surely they could not refuse so generous an offer? He tried hard to pick up the threads of talk. Some seemed all for it but others were apparently reluctant to trust his word. Finally, a small militant-looking shrew came forward and picked up the stone. He addressed Matthias in a very official manner. 'Our rules say that the quarry across the river is not in shrew territory, mouse. Therefore, we cannot go with you!'

Log-a-Log sprang forward and dealt the speaker a mighty blow, laying him flat out on his back.

'You cowardly, ungrateful little fool!' cried Log-a-Log. 'How can you say such a thing after all this warrior is trying to do for us?'

Guosim grabbed the stone from the ground. 'Stop, Log-a-Log! You have no right to strike a comrade! He was only stating the facts. Our Guerrilla Union rules clearly state that no member can be forced to venture beyond official shrew boundaries.'

Before Log-a-Log had chance to reply, a riot broke out. Shrews began kicking, punching, arguing, screaming, wrestling, and shouting. The edge of Mossflower Wood was in pandemonium.

Matthias held up the stone and tried shouting above the mêlée. His voice was lost in the uproar. Angrily, he grabbed the nearest shrew and shouted at him, 'Listen, you! Tell me which direction the river is in, or else—'

The struggling creature pointed a paw to the north-east before wriggling from Matthias's grasp to dive headlong into the fray.

Fury took hold of the young mouse. He waved the stone and cried out, 'Go on, fight, you stupid idiots! I don't need any of you! I'll go it alone, and here's what I think of your bossy little union and rotten old stone!'

He hurled the stone with a mighty effort. It flew off over the heads of the rioters, disappearing into the wood.

Matthias turned on his heel and stormed off towards the river.

3

An air of apprehension lay across the camp in the meadow. Cheesethief was dead. Pierced by an immense arrow and dressed in Cluny's best battle armour, he lay amid the wreckage of the leader's tent. Not one of the horde dared to go near the gruesome scene lest they be found in a position of blame upon Cluny's return.

Constance peered agitatedly over the parapet. Something was not quite right, she felt it in her nostrils. The badger's worst suspicions were confirmed by the sight of Cluny crossing the road and heading back into the meadow. Constance watched him leap across the ditch. There could be no doubt about it, that rat was definitely Cluny the Scourge. She had killed the wrong rat!

Cluny had left his picked band back in the woodlands. They knew what they had to do. It would take a bit of time, but it was a sound, workable plan. Striding swiftly over the meadow, some sixth sense told Cuny that all was not right. His one eye scoured the area. There was the horde, gathered together at the far end, but what had happened to his tent?

Cluny could vaguely discern a huddled figure tangled in the wreckage. Speculation was useless; he speeded up his pace.

Fangburn met him halfway. Cluny held up a claw, silencing him. He would get to the bottom of things without stuttering excuses. He kicked the tent folds aside, revealing Cheesethief's stricken face. The great arrow-shaft protruded from the ruined armour, his war gear.

Cluny glanced backwards and forwards from the Abbey to the body. He took in at a quick rate all that had happened. The big badger was peering over the wall. It was her doing!

Cluny's brain raced ahead. On the far edge of the meadow the horde were looking decidedly uneasy. A mistake had been made, the arrow was meant for him. The Warlord's fertile mind suddenly came up with an idea of how to turn the situation to his own advantage.

Fangburn was, to say the least, surprised. Cluny clapped him heartily on the back and led him across to where the rest of the horde waited apprehensively. Cluny laughed aloud to put them at their ease. He winked his eye roguishly.

'Well, I see my little scheme worked out just fine. We got the dirty traitor, didn't we, Fangburn, my old mate?'

Fangburn was completely baffled, but he knew better than to disagree.

'What? Oh, er, of course we did, Chief.'

Cluny nodded over at where the body lay.

'Do you see that? Well, let it be a warning to you all. Ha, I knew what was going on with Cheesethief. Didn't anyone see him at the battering ram last night acting all high and mighty?'

There was a general murmur of agreement. Most of the

rats had been pressed into volunteering as ram carriers by the ambitious Cheesethief.

'Aye, we saw him, Chief.'

'Chucking his weight about, shouting orders.'

'He kept me on that ram for two hours.'

'Yes, you'd have thought that he was the commander of the horde.'

'Exactly!' Cluny shouted. 'I'd had my eye on Cheesethief for quite a while! He was doing a fair piece of ordering about without my permission. Why, I bet he ordered some of you lads around while I was gone.'

'He started shoving me around, Chief,' volunteered Darkclaw indignantly. 'It was "do this", "fetch that", "jump to it", "I'm using the Chief's tent". I think Cheesethief was getting too big for his boots, Chief.'

Cluny threw a claw around the speaker's shoulder. 'Thank you, Darkclaw. You're an intelligent Captain. You could see as well as I did that Cheesethief was planning to take control of my trusted horde. Why else would he start using my tent and dressing up in my battle armour?'

The soldiers nodded sagely to each other. Cluny was right. There was no fondness in the ranks for the dead, power-hungry bully.

Cluny continued, 'You see, I knew the badger and her friends were planning to kill me, so I thought I'd kill two birds with one stone: fool them, and save myself the trouble of having to execute Cheesethief. In fact I let the Redwall crowd do the dirty work for me. I didn't want any of my loyal soldiers put to any trouble. I gave the traitor enough rope and let our enemies hang him!'

Cluny slapped his thigh and burst out laughing. The horde joined him, falling about with merriment at their Chief's black joke. What a cunning idea! There was no doubt about it, the Scourge didn't miss a single trick.

Cluny waved cheerfully to the distant figure of Constance on the wall.

'My thanks to you, badger!' he shouted. 'You did a fine job!'

Constance could not hear a thing from the distance of the ramparts, which was just as well in the circumstances.

Cluny was almost jovial as he turned to the horde. 'Well, my good warriors. Has anything else happened while I was away?'

Killconey performed one of his most elaborate salutes. 'The tunnel is goin' very well, yer honour.'

'Good, good,' said Cluny. 'Anything else to report?'

Mangefur and Scumnose piped up jointly. 'We was out searching for dockleaves, Chief, way out across those fields over there—'

Cluny halted them. He nodded to Scumnose.

'You tell me.'

'Well, we was rootin' about by some hedges, Chief,' said Scumnose, 'and we found a whole tribe of dormice fast asleep. So we pounced on 'em and tied them up in a bunch. Nice big fat ones they are, Chief.'

Cluny interrupted. 'Dormice, eh? You haven't killed them yet, I hope?'

Scumnose shook his head vigorously. 'Oh no, Chief. We're keeping 'em nice and fresh in the ditch there. D'you want to see 'em? I think there's about twenty all told.'

'Good. You did well. I want them kept alive,' muttered Cluny as he walked across to the ditch and peered down at the captives.

The dormice were huddled miserably together, their necks looped cruelly together on a rope. They whimpered fearfully at the sinister sight of Cluny the Scourge.

'Which one of you is the leader?' he snarled.

A bedraggled youngish mouse held up a timid paw. 'I am, sir. My name is Plumpen. Please let us go free. We

338

have done no harm to any living creature. Violence is against our nature. We—'

'Silence,' Cluny snapped. 'Or I'll teach you what violence means.'

An anguished moan arose from the dormice lying in the ditch. Cluny cracked his tail.

'Cut out that cringing,' he said contemptuously. 'You are my prisoners to do with as I like. Oh don't worry. I won't let them kill you yet. I've got other more useful things in mind. You, Plumpen, or whatever your name is, tell your tribe that they won't be harmed as long as you do what I say. For the present you are to stay down there under guard. Scumnose, Mangefur!'

'Yes Chief?'

'You two are responsible for these prisoners,' said Cluny. 'See that no creature goes near them. Stand guard night and day. If just one of these dormice goes missing, you'll both end up on a roasting spit. Is that clear?'

After Cheesethief's carcass had been disposed of, Cluny sat beneath an awning that had been improvised from the damaged tent. He watched the armourer diligently repairing his prized war gear and fumed inwardly. His equipment had been battered – and he had lost a valuable Captain. The Redwall contingent had stolen a march upon him, and the battering ram had failed miserably. Once again the thinking was left to him. The horde were more concerned with licking wounds and feeding their stomachs. Strategy was not their responsibility. However, on reflection the balance was beginning to swing in his favour again. He now had three possible keys to the Abbey. One was the tunnel; the rats in Mossflower Wood were attending to his second scheme; and the third – Cluny glanced over to the ditch. The capture of the dormice would prove an even more devious avenue to the conquest of Redwall, provided he played his cards right.

Early evening saw the attack upon the Abbey get under way once more. Jess Squirrel and Ambrose Spike had joined the ranks of archers. They popped up and down selecting random targets.

'I don't like it,' Jess remarked.

Ambrose grunted as he released a feathered shaft at the ditch. 'Don't like what, Jess?'

The squirrel put aside her bow and sat down under cover of the parapet. 'They seem to have slackened off somehow, and we haven't seen much of Cluny lately. It's not like the horde to behave in this way. Personally, I think there's something afoot that we don't know about.'

Winifred the otter was standing nearby. She slung a stone hard, nodded in satisfaction at the resultant scream, and joined the two friends. 'Aye, I'm inclined to agree with you, Jess. The Scourge has probably figured some new move. This attack may only be a cover. By the way, is there any word from the Foremole and his crew?'

'Oh they've still got their ears to the ground,' Ambrose said gruffly. 'Foremole says they've heard the odd echo, nothing definite though. South-west corner is where he thinks they might surface, eventually.'

'Yes, I've heard that, too,' Jess agreed. 'We'll have to arrange a warm reception for those filthy vermin when they show up!'

'What baffles me,' Winifred mused, 'is where young Matthias has got to. It's not like him to miss the chance of a battle.'

Abbot Mortimer was on his rounds with food. He had been eavesdropping on the conversation and could not help commenting, 'D'you know, I was just thinking that same thing myself, but we must give Matthias the benefit of the doubt and trust in his judgement. I've a feeling that he could be the salvation of us all. One thing you may rest assured of, wherever that young mouse is he'll be concerned with the survival of Redwall in one way or another, I'm sure.'

'Ah, well,' Jess sighed as she picked up her bow and notched an arrow to it. 'We'd better make sure he has a home to come back to. On with the war, friends.'

The squirrel drew the bow full stretch and stood up. She paused a moment peering along the yew shaft then released the string with a vibrant twang. Below on the edge of the meadow a creature fell transfixed. One stoat less to carry out Cluny's commands!

4

Matthias set up a solitary makeshift camp that night. After a frugal meal he wrapped his habit tight about his body to ward off the chill breeze and settled down to sleep. Alone with his bitter thoughts about the ungrateful shrews, the young mouse finally dozed off.

Sometime before dawn he became aware of movements and sound nearby. Carefully, Matthias slitted one eyelid open. His feet were warm. He felt the extra weight of a blanket that had been draped over him while he was asleep.

The Guerrilla Union of Shrews in Mossflower had returned!

Small campfires had been lighted, and breakfast was being prepared. Matthias decided that it must be nearly daybreak. Turning on his side he kept up the pretence of sleep. Ignoring the presence of the shrews he drifted back into a warm slumber.

It was fully daylight when he reawakened. The sun beat down through the trees, mixing its rays in the pale blue smoke of the cooking fires. Log-a-Log brought toasted

342

wheatcake and a bowl of herb tea. Sitting up, Matthias accepted them noncommittally. He ate and drank in silence while Log-a-Log folded the blanket and packed it away. The shrew stood beside him and gave a short, nervous cough.

'Ahem, er, Matthias; I'm sorry about what happened yesterday. As you can see, we've decided by majority vote to come along with you.'

The young mouse continued to ignore him. Log-a-Log slumped down.

'Matthias, listen. We shrews of the Union try to run our lives along democratic lines. You must not think too harshly of us. The shrew who spoke out against accompanying you was only stating chapter and verse of the act. I was wrong to hit him. Guisom did right to uphold his argument.'

Matthias arose and shouldered his bundle. 'Look, Log-a-Log. Don't talk to me about your silly rules: subsection three, paragraph four and all that nonsense. You are either with me or against me. I haven't got valuable time to waste on a lot of Shrew Union rules and disputes.'

Log-a-Log picked up his pack and smiled broadly at the young mouse. 'Matthias, my friend, we are with you to a shrew. Tooth, claw, and nail! Lead on, bold warrior.'

Matthias laughed in open relief. 'Well, let's get started, friend Log-a-Log. We've got an adder to fight and a sword to win!'

Surrounded by a band of shrews which had started quarrelling over the best route to the quarry. Matthias marched stolidly forward. They trekked through the trees leaving Mossflower Wood far behind; across open ground, giving the farmhouse a carefully wide berth; breeching hawthorn hedges and spanning dried-out ditches; through several fields that lay fallow in the summer stillness.

A halt was called at lunchtime on the banks of a slow, broad river.

Matthias sat next to Guosim during the midday meal. It would be the last cooked food they would get. Stealth and secrecy would be the order of the day upon the other side of the river. No fires, no noise. Matthias flicked a pebble into the water.

'How are we supposed to cross this lot?' he asked.

Guosim spoke through a mouthful of bread. 'Log-a-Log. How else? That's how he got his name, you know. His father and his father's father before him were all called Log-a-Log. The whole family were all ferryshrews on this river. If you needed to cross the water you stood on the bank and shouted "Log-a-Log". Here, let's see if it still works.'

Guosim walked to the river's edge. Cupping her paws around her mouth she called in an ululating voice: 'Loga-logalogalogalog!'

The older shrew appeared out of a reed bed, balanced upon a large floating tree trunk which he propelled skilfully with a long pole into the side of the bank. Angrily he sprang ashore, upbraiding Guosim. 'Puddenheaded shrew! D'you have to broadcast the fact we're here? Shouting out like a great foghorn! We'd better strike camp and get across now, before someone comes.'

'I was only showing Matthias how to call for the ferry-shrew,' Guosim muttered surlily.

'Is that all!' said Log-a-Log heatedly. 'Then why don't you show him the snake tracks in the mud there? Or didn't you notice them? Asmodeus passed through here not four hours ago. He's probably gone hunting in Moss-flower Wood. It's a mercy we didn't bump into him. He might come back this way before the day is through.'

Matthias stared in horrified fascination at the broad

slimy path that had been left in the mud by the snake. The shrews had all clambered hastily aboard the strange craft.

'Hurry along, Matthias! All hands on deck!' Log-a-Log hissed.

Despite the danger of the enterprise, the young mouse actually enjoyed the ride across the river on the tree trunk. Several of the shrews dug lines out of their packs and fished successfully, amassing quite a tidy little catch before the ferry nosed into the opposite bank with a gentle bump. The shrews disembarked and Matthias helped Log-a-Log to conceal the ferry in some bulrushes.

'I was thinking,' Matthias mused. 'Do you suppose we could all hide somewhere? That way we might see Asmodeus return and track him to his lair.'

'That's exactly what I had planned myself,' the shrew replied. 'If we spread out along the bank and remain hidden, then we'll stand a good chance of spotting Poisonteeth. It's a good idea, but I can see a drawback. Supposing the adder catches the scent of shrews? There's so many of us that it's a distinct danger.'

'Then again,' Matthias argued, 'would it not be better if we made our way to the quarry and waited there? Asmodeus is bound to head for home.'

'I wish it were that simple, my friend,' Log-a-Log replied. 'The land around the quarry offers no concealment; too flat and bare. Poisonteeth is full of ancient cunning too. He may have a secret entrance outside the quarry itself. I think it is best we wait here. I'll spread the comrades out in a line. We'll all keep watch.'

Throughout the long afternoon, Matthias lay hidden at the base of a lilac bush. He was within calling distance of shrews secreted a short distance away, as they were of their neighbours further along. Fully a kilometre of the bank was covered in this fashion. Whoever spotted

Asmodeus was to report, after letting one minute elapse, to Matthias, who was positioned roughly at the centre of the line. Guosim and Log-a-Log were stationed on either flank.

The blazing sun hung over the watchers like a fiery disc. Matthias kept his sights on the river and the ground in front of him, not daring to move, whether to eat, drink or scratch. He was forced to endure the unwelcome attention of inquisitive flies and insects that buzzed about and walked across him at their leisure. Often he would focus so hard that his imagination played tricks. A slight ripple upon the water, or a vagrant breeze through the grass, became Asmodeus. He would blink and reassure himself that it was only a product of his tensed mind.

The young mouse lost track of time until he became aware of the sun starting to sink in a reddening sky heralding the twilight. Surely the snake must pass this way soon!

As complete darkness descended, a shrew sneaked up through the grass and tapped Matthias's shoulder.

'What's the matter? Has Asmodeus been sighted?' Matthias asked.

The shrew pointed out along the flank that Guisom headed. 'I don't know, mouse. You'd better come and see for yourself. I'll go and get Log-a-Log.'

Matthias scrambled out from beneath the lilac. Something must have gone wrong! Throwing caution to the winds he dashed along the river bank. Other shrews left their hiding places and followed him.

Guosim was seated upon the open ground, her eyes wide with fright, teeth chattering madly, her whole body trembling like a leaf.

Log-a-Log came racing up. Matthias shouted to him, 'Guosim's in a state of shock! Help me, let's get her into the water.'

Grabbing Guosim between them they rushed her into the shallows and ducked her under the surface of the river. She came up spluttering but coherent.

'Giant Poisonteeth, the snake, Asmodeus, he was here! I didn't spot him until it was too late. He's taken Mingo. Gave him the magic eyes, then bit him and dragged him off! Poor Mingo. Ugh! It was horrible, horrible, I tell you, the rotten filthy reptile!' Guiosim flung herself down sobbing into the grass.

Log-a-Log pulled her roughly to her feet. 'Come on, don't lie there crying, shrew! The adder probably left a good wet trail for us to follow. Where did it happen?'

Guosim ran shakily some distance to the left. She pointed to the ground. 'Right here! You can see the great slithering marks! Look!'

The evidence was quite clear. The wet path in the dry grass gleamed in the dark.

They followed the trail with Matthias and Log-a-Log in the lead. It twisted and turned tortuously, over small hillocks, through hedges and across fields. Even when the wetness stopped there was the musty odour of death clinging to the ground.

At the top of a small rise Matthias dropped into a crouch. Signalling everyone to do likewise, he pointed downwards.

'Look, Log-a-Log! There!'

Spread out beneath them was a vast disused quarry. It was as if some gigantic hand had scooped a great hole in the landscape. The shape was roughly oval. The steep, red sandstone sides were terraced half way around into long flat shelves. Piles of fallen stone were dotted about amidst the defunct workings. The scant vegetation lent the quarry an air of stark desolation.

They lay on the edge of the pit straining their eyes into

the dark floor area below. Steadily, Log-a-Log gave orders to the Guerrilla shrews to retire back across the field where they could rest up and eat a much-needed meal. Only he and Guosim remained at the edge of the quarry with Matthias, who settled any further debate by saying, 'I'm going down there for a look around as soon as it's light.'

'If you must go, then we will come with you,' murmured Log-a-Log.

Matthias shook his head. 'No. I cannot allow it. It's far too dangerous.'

Guosim, who was fully recovered, spoke out courageously, 'You cannot stop us, Matthias. You are not a Union member, therefore we are not under your command. The rules clearly state this, so the decision is out of your paws. We go! You and Log-a-Log get some sleep. I'll take first sentry duty.'

The three friends slept in turns, relieving one another through the long watches of the night hours. Matthias was on duty when the first fingers of dawn probed the quarry. What a difference daylight made to the sinister night-time appearance of the scene below!

The sandstone ranged through a spectrum of pale sunlight gold, banded through every shade of yellow, fawn, umber, brown, down to the dusty red sandstone that must have been hewn out in distant ages to provide the masons with material to build Redwall Abbey.

He roused his companions to view the awesome spectacle.

'To think that all this peaceful beauty should hide such cold evil,' he breathed wonderingly.

In silent Indian file they began the descent. The going was not too hard. There were lots of handholds and steps and the sandy rock was quite firm, not at all slippery. It took less than an hour for the three friends to climb down.

They stood together on the flat quarry floor gazing around.

'Supposing Poisonteeth decides to hunt today,' whispered Guosim.

'I have a feeling he won't,' Log-a-Log replied. 'Asmodeus got a full day's hunt in yesterday. With the unexpected bonus of poor old Mingo on his way home he'll probably sleep through today and go out to hunt tonight.'

'So that gives us all day to find out where he is,' added Matthias. 'Shall we look together, or split up?'

'Stick together,' said Guosim as she and Log-a-Log drew their short rapiers. Matthias took out his dagger. They started searching the quarry for a possible hole or concealed entrance.

The trio scoured the lower slopes, looking and probing. They inspected underneath stunted bushes, turned over chunks of rock, crawled beneath huge slabs, always watching keenly for the telltale single winding track of the adder. The silence was oppressive. There was neither birdsong nor the hum of insects inside the sunken arena. Having crisscrossed the floor they progressed to the middle terraces, but the results were equally disappointing. All morning they had searched the quarry without any success.

At midday Log-a-Log called a halt. They sat on a flat table-shaped rock halfway up and shared hard tack lunch followed by a canteen of water. It was not a cheerful meal. They each sat with their own thoughts. Finally Guosim stood up, dusting her fur off. She clapped her paws together in a brisk manner, urging her companions to resume the task.

'Right, come on, you two, we've only got half a day left.'

Matthias and Log-a-Log gathered up their packs and

weapons as Guosim leaned on the side of a narrow slab and continued her summary.

'If we search around the top lip this afternoon, that only leaves us the heeeeeeeee . . . !'

The echo of the cry hung upon the still air. Guosim was gone. The narrow slab she had been leaning against swung loosely on a pivot. They had found the entrance to the lair of Asmodeus Poisonteeth.

5

Cluny the Scourge anxiously awaited the arrival of darkness. One of his three plans had reached fruition a lot earlier than he had expected.

Killconey had proved an invaluable help. He had been across to the woods to satisfy his curiosity about what the rats were doing there. It came as no surprise to the ferret to see a large siege tower under construction. However, there was a problem. The cart still lay upturned in the ditch. Try as they would, the rats had not been able to remove a set of wheels and an axle from it.

Killconey had a word with Cluny and was immediately sent down to supervise the operation. The garrulous ferret showed the rats that he possessed a sound knowledge of the principles of fulcrum and leverage. He rigged a block and tackle to supplement a dead tree limb that they were using as a lever. Ignoring wheels and axles he roped the cart to the block. With all rats, and a great deal of luck, he managed to lift the hay cart until it was halfway out of the ditch. Further pressure on the lever sent the hay cart past its own point of balance. The block and tackle parted under the strain, sending the ferret and the rats on the level shooting down into the ditch. By mistake it did the trick. With a crash the cart landed upright in the road.

They pushed it into the woods. Killconey oversaw the lifting of the tower on to the bed of the cart. Delighted by his own ingenuity he added the final touches. In a short time the siege tower, its wheels muffled with sacking, stood completed, ready for use.

Cluny gathered his Captains about him and outlined his strategy. Tonight, when it was dark, Fangburn would step up the attack on the gatehouse wall as a diversionary measure. Cluny would command a picked band of the best fighters. They would bring the siege tower from out of the cover of Mossflower Wood and wheel it to a part of the wall where the defence appeared weakest. Under cover of darkness they would filter from the top of the tower on to the ramparts. A quick slaughter of the defenders would leave Redwall wide open to them.

Cluny watched the evening sky anxiously. It would not be long now. He signalled Fangburn to begin the diversionary assault.

Yelling and shouting fearsome war cries, the attackers leapt from the ditch, peppering the ramparts with a hail of arrows, spears and stones.

'Redwall to me! Come on, mice!' cried Constance. 'Let's give better than we get. Redwall to me!'

Basil Stag Hare had formed three lines of bowmice on top of the wall. They worked with military efficiency as the hare rapped out orders.

'First rank fire! Drop back, kneel and reload!'
'Second rank fire! Drop back, kneel and reload!'
'Third rank fire! Drop back, kneel and reload!'
'First rank forward again. Fire!'
The commands continued unabated. Enemy soldiers

fell stricken on the road, Darkclaw rushed about bringing up reinforcements.

'Keep those slings throwing! Bring up extra spears! Close up that line! Don't fire until you see them stand!'

John Churchmouse, Mr Vole and Friar Hugo ran about bending low. They collected up all the arrows, spears, and stones hurled by the horde, issuing them to the defenders.

'Come on, otters! Give them back a taste of their own medicine!' Winifred urged her slingers on while directing fresh archers into the ranks of the bowmice.

Constance and the beaver shared a stack of enemy spears. They returned them with frightening power and devastating aim.

Ferret archers at the edge of the meadow found the range of Basil's bowmice. Several were felled before Jess Squirrel and Winifred, along with some crack otter slingers, sent down a barrage so swift and accurate that it decimated the ferrets within minutes.

While the battle went ahead, ranging from the heights of the parapet to the depths of the ditch, the Joseph Bell rang out over the carnage.

Cluny snapped the battered visor down on his war helmet. He rapped Killconey on his shoulder.

'Good! Now is the time! Come on, ferret!'

Together they slunk off down the ditch, running crouched over to the south-east corner of the wall where it was relatively quiet. Keeping noise down to a minimum, Cluny ordered his troops to bring forward the siege tower. Straining and pushing, the rat soldiers trundled the tall contraption from its woodland hiding place. The going was even harder across the short space of soft meadow ground. Cluny himself lent a claw, pulling on one of the lead ropes. He tugged mightily, causing the cumbersome tower to sway dangerously as it bumped over grassy hillocks.

'Bring it up close to the wall,' he whispered urgently. 'That's it! Now make sure it's on an even keel! I don't want the top wobbling all over the place.'

Stones and soil were tamped around the wheels, wedging them still. The great tower stood ready for use.

When Friar Hugo hurried off to join the defenders he left Cornflower in charge of the kitchens. She had busied herself with setting pans of oatmeal and oven bread ready for the next morning's breakfast. Cornflower then thought of the sentries up on the wall, and she set about making a large pan of vegetable soup. It was a great favourite with the defenders at night time, especially when she made it to her own recipe.

Helped by Mrs Vole and Mr Squirrel she ladled it into three big earthenware jugs. Taking up a jug each, with a small basket of fresh loaves and some goat cheese, they set off, with Cornflower in the lead carrying a lantern. The first stop was the south-east corner, where Foremole and his crew had a monotonous task: night and day they monitored the grounds for sounds of tunnelling. They were glad of a short respite and some hot food while they chatted to the caterers in their gruff polite tones.

Cornflower was never quite sure of what the Foremole was saying, but she loved listening to his funny, coun-trified-mole dialect.

'Yurr, missie, they ratten varments be a-comin up'n two days, oi'll reckern. Gar! we'm give em owd 'arry if'n they shows thurr 'eads.'

Cornflower was only picking up one word in three, but by the fierce scowl on Foremole's face, she was certain that the rats would not find it a pleasant experience being given 'owed 'arry'.

The Foremole tugged his nose graciously at her. 'Wurr! Thankee kindly. Nought loik vedgible soop to keep'n loif in uz moles.'

Mr Squirrel chuckled to Cornflower and Mrs Vole. 'Well, I take it the moles are quite fond of home-made vegetable soup. I know my Jess'll be ready for some.'

'Yes, and so would Sam if he weren't fast asleep in bed,' Cornflower replied. 'Look, you and Mrs Vole start serving along by the gatehouse. Keep your heads low and be careful. I'll start up here at the corner and see you back at the kitchen later.'

With the lantern and basket in one paw and the jug in the other, Cornflower ascended the steps at the south-east corner of the wall. Brother Rufus assisted her up on to the ramparts.

'Ah, the young fieldmouse with the magic soup! Nice to see you, Cornflower. It gets lonely up this end where there's no action.'

Brother Rufus held out his mug. He watched gratefully through the cloud of steam that arose from the jug. 'Mmm, that smells good! Vegetable soup, my favourite!'

Cornflower was not listening. She was staring open-mouthed across Brother Rufus's shoulder. The soup was overflowing from the mug and spattering on the stones as she continued to pour.

Across the top of the parapet a ramshackle wooden platform had appeared as if from nowhere. Perched on top of it, ready to spring, was a villainous-looking rat with a cutlass clenched between his teeth.

Cornflower shrieked aloud.

More by accident than design, Brother Rufus spun around and sent the scalding contents of his mug splashing full into the rat's eyes. With a piercing wail of agony the rat fell from the top of the platform. Scarcely aware

355

of what she was doing, Cornflower threw the lantern. It shattered on top of the siege tower, drenching the dead wood in lamp oil. Instantly the flames licked hungrily over the platform, turning it into an inferno.

Attracted by the flaring blaze that lit the night, defenders rushed from all quarters to see what was happening. Over thirty rats were in the high reaches of the burning tower. Many more were in the middle and still more on the lower frames. Rats were kicking and fighting each other to get down from the blazing tower. They bit and trampled and slashed. Some jumped while others were pushed, screaming as they fell to the field far below.

Cluny ran about in a berserk rage. Temporarily bereft of his senses, he seized hold of smouldering, injured rats, some with their fur alight.

'Get back up there, you cowards! Jump on to the wall!' he screamed in his madness.

The rats who had been attacking the gatehouse left off fighting and ran down the road to the fiery holocaust. Sparks crackled and shot off into the night sky. Cluny lashed out at all and sundry with his tail, foaming at the mouth and cursing wildly, his face a terrifying mask of insanity in the glare from the tower.

'It's only a bit of fire! Get back up there, you blundering fools! Kill the mice!'

Darkclaw and Fangburn grabbed hold of Cluny's smouldering cloak. They dragged him backwards.

'Get out the way, Chief! It's starting to fall!'

With a roaring crackle and snap of blazing timber the siege tower leaned crazily to one side. It tottered, then collapsed in a flaring sheet of flame and sparks. The hay wagon listed drunkenly and was pulled over on its side where it lay burning furiously.

*

The incident put an end to that night's fighting. On top of the wall cheering broke out. Cornflower was the heroine of the hour. She blushed as Foremole nodded admiringly.

'Arr, you'm looken more 'andsome in this loight, missy! Yurr, you gotten any vedgible soop left? Didn't give it all to those varments did ee?'

Below the wall was a scene of mass carnage. The ground was littered with the bodies of attackers who had fallen prey to the flames in the ill-starred venture of the siege tower. Surrounded by his Captains, Cluny was led down to the safety of the ditch. Apparently unaware of anything about him, he muttered dark words to himself, strange things that others could not comprehend.

Behind the Warlord's back the Captains looked at each other in a puzzled fashion.

Had the mind of Cluny the Scourge finally snapped?

The fire had dwindled to smouldering embers by the next morning. Constance and the Abbot looked at the results from the ramparts. A wide area of the meadowland was burned black and scorched flat. Even now parts of it sizzled in the morning dew.

'Thank goodness it did not spread to the woods,' said the Abbot, 'otherwise all of Mossflower might have gone up in flames.'

The badger stared sadly at the scorched earth. 'True, no side uses fire as a weapon, not even Cluny. It is the one thing that spells certain death to creatures on both sides. We must look on it as an accident, Father Abbot.'

'Accident or not, we owe Cornflower a debt of gratitude,' replied the Abbot. 'She is a very brave young fieldmouse. But for her swift action we would all have been under the heel of the tyrant today.'

In the Abbey kitchens Cornflower stirred the oatmeal and checked on the bread baking in the oven. She smiled to herself. What would Matthias have thought of it all?

Last night's heroine. This morning's cook!

6

Whilst Log-a-Log held the rock from closing, Matthias peered into the hole. It was a long dark tunnel sloping down the side of the quarrystone.

There was neither sight nor sound of Guosim.

They called her name in loud whispers, not wanting to shout for fear of disturbing the snake. Matthias became impatient.

'Come on, Log-a-Log. We'll have to go in there. Be as quiet as you can.'

'Wait a tick,' the shrew replied. Taking a small boulder he jammed the entrance slab from swinging shut. 'I'm ready now. Lead on, Matthias.'

They ventured cautiously into the long sloping passage, digging in their heels to prevent themselves sliding right down as Guosim probably had done. On reaching the bottom they stood awhile to let their eyes become accustomed to the gloom. The floor levelled out. The tunnel was high and broad enough to allow them to walk side by side without stooping. As they walked further, Log-a-Log pointed at strange symbols and weird signs that had been scraped into the surface of the soft stone.

Though the quarry tunnels were natural, they had obviously been the lairs of generations of serpents; most of the signs were of a reptilian nature. The friends pressed onwards until the passage broadened out into a small chamber with two more tunnels leading from it.

'You take the left and I'll take the right,' Matthias whispered. 'Mark an arrow on the wall with your sword at intervals. I'll do the same with my dagger. That way we won't get lost. Should you find Asmodeus, come straight back to this chamber. If he finds you, then the best thing to do is run as fast as you can and shout like mad.'

'Take care, warrior. I'll see you later,' said Log-a-Log.

Gripping his dagger in readiness, Matthias crept into the right-hand tunnel. It was slightly narrower than the first, but just as high. The walls were yellow stone, so soft that it was almost like damp sand. Scarcely daring to breathe and glad that his feet made no sound on the sandy floor, Matthias went ahead, remembering to mark an arrow every few metres. From somewhere up ahead the young mouse could hear the sound of dripping water; the musical echoing plops made an eerie noise in the sinister stillness of the passage.

His paw encountered a space in the left wall. It turned out to be a rectangular anteroom. Matthias was horrified to discover that it was full of cast-off snake skins. They lay about on the floor, dry and withered. He shuddered at the thought of their former occupants, the hairs rising on the nape of his neck as he swiftly abandoned the repulisve scene and hurried along the passage.

It was more than twice as long as the entrance tunnel. As Matthias cut another arrow into the wall he noticed that the carved symbols looked older, more primitive. This place had been a serpent's den long before it had been a quarry. The passage ended abruptly. Matthias walked out into an immense cavern.

The Great Hall of Redwall would have fitted into a corner of this colossal structure. At its centre was a vast shimmering lake that glowed with a pale phosphorescent light. The droplets of water came from somewhere high up in the dark recesses of the roof; they dripped steadily down and broke the surface of the subterranean lake, causing a continuous ripple. Matthias noticed that there were numerous other caverns and tunnels leading from this large cave.

'Asmodeussssssss!'

The sound froze the very blood in his veins. The adder was close by: where he could not tell. The deadly hiss echoed all around him.

'Asmodeussssssssssss!'

Matthias bravely tried to quell the panic that welled up inside him.

'If the snake knew where I was he wouldn't waste his time trying to scare me,' he reasoned. 'He would have got me by now.'

Feeling slightly reassured, but still very uneasy, Matthias circled the pool trying hard to ignore the loathsome hissing sound.

'Asmodeussssssssssss!'

Summoning up his courage, he stole silently into the nearest cave. In the glow that reflected from the pool, Matthias saw a sight that gladdened his heart.

There was Guosim seated with her back against the wall!

Matthias ran across and seized the Guerrilla Shrew by her paw. 'Guosim, how did you get here, you little nuisance? We've been sear—'

Guosim toppled on her side, dead!

With a strangled sob the young mouse recoiled. He

could see the poison fang marks clearly upon the shrew's chest. Guosim's face was bloated, the eyes screwed shut, the lips blackened.

'Asmodeussssssssssssssss!'

Matthias stumbled from the gruesome death-larder of the adder, out into the main cavern. He sat for a while shuddering with horror at what he had seen, hardly believing that the still body had been a warm, living, breathing creature not long ago. Forcing himself to rise and carry on, Matthias continued his explorations.

The next entrance was a tiny hole in the wall, scarcely worth bothering about. Nevertheless, he decided to investigate it. Crouching on all fours, Matthias forced his way into the hole which proved to be another tunnel. He began forcing his way along its narrow length.

'Asmodeussssssssssssssss!'

The dreadful sound was much closer now! Struggling and pushing forward, he came to the end of the tunnel.

Suddenly Matthias was face to face with the giant adder.

'Asmodeussssssssssssssss!'

The huge reptile was sleeping. With every breath it expelled, the snake's tongue flickered out, repeating the vile name: 'Asmodeussssssssssssssss!'

Matthias stared in mute fascination. The snake's eyes were not shut but filmed over in sleep. It was breathing slowly and regularly. The huge muscular scaly body was coiled in no recognizable pattern. At odd intervals the immense coils would shift lazily with a dry scaly rustle; the head, however, remained fixed in the same position. Across the jumble of banded coils Matthias thought he could catch a glimpse of the tapering tail.

There were other things in the lair of the snake; a fox's tail, wood pigeon wings, the head of a big fish, and fur pelts of many species of creatures.

But Matthias saw only the sword of Martin the Warrior!

It hung from the fork of a tree-root at the back of the viper's den. A large red pommel-stone was set into the top of the hilt. The handle was of black leather and silver to match the belt and scabbard. Below a heavy silver crosspiece was the blade. Made from the finest steel, its double edges tapered to a ruthlessly-sharp tip. Down the centre of the blade ran a blood channel, either side of which there were symbols which Matthias could not make out.

This was truly the Sword of Redwall Abbey! It was his duty to get it. Matthias moved more stealthily than he had ever done in all his life. Inch by careful inch, paw by whisker, slowly, painstakingly trying to make his body as small as possible, he flattened himself against the wall to get by the huge spadelike head. The tongue almost slithered across his face as it slid in and out, constantly repeating the dreaded name.

'Asmodeussssssssssssssssss!'

He felt the adder breathing, its cold exhalations carrying the sweet musty odour of death stirring his whiskers. A coil moved and faintly touched his leg. Matthias sucked in his breath and squeezed closer to the wall. The snake blinked, sending the opaque tissue upwards. The young mouse was confronted by the wide-open eye of the monster staring directly at him.

'Asmodeussssssssssssssssss!'

The eye filmed over again as the snake carried on with whatever evil vision it was dreaming. Sweat like ice water drenched Matthias's fur. Asmodeus had opened his eye while still remaining asleep. There was no other explanation possible.

The moments of suspense ticked by for what seemed ages

until Matthias managed to squeeze past the serpent's head. Avoiding the gigantic coils he walked quickly and quietly over to where the sword hung from the tree roots on the cave wall.

Matthias lifted the ancient sword down. Reverently he placed both paws around the handle. Tighter and tighter he gripped it until the point lifted from the floor and the bright blade stood out level in front of him. He sensed how Martin must have felt each time he had held this beautiful weapon. The young mouse knew that he had been born for this moment, his grip causing the tremor of the steel to run through his entire body. It was part of him!

Matthias's main concern was to get safely away with the sword. In the confined space of the snake's den there was no room to wield the fabled blade. If he struck at Asmodeus he would be crushed to death against the walls by the powerful lashing coils of the adder in its death throes. Nothing would be accomplished by such a foolhardy action. Like a seasoned fighter, the young mouse chose to nominate the time and place of combat. He looked around the den. The hole he had come through was obviously too small for the adder to have used for the same purpose. It served as a breathing hole for Asmodeus, also as amplification to echo the dreaded name through the caves and tunnels as a warning to intruders.

Near the snake's tail which lay directly across his path, he saw the skins and pelts on the cave wall tremble slightly. They were covering the only possible entrance and exit for a reptile of such enormous girth. Emboldened by his ownership of Martin's weapon, Matthias tickled the tail lightly with the sword point. It had the desired effect. The long, scale-encrusted coils rippled as the serpent changed position in its sleep. Speedily he slipped through the curtain of skins into the passage. It curved in a crescent-shaped arc, bringing Matthias back into the main cavern with its luminous lake.

Log-a-Log came dashing, pale-faced, out of the cave that contained Guosim's body. Eyes wide with terror he ran straight into the paws of his mouse friend, narrowly missing injury on the sword blade.

Before he could be silenced he yelled out in a panic-stricken shout, 'Matthias, Guosim's dead! I've just seen her in that cave! She's dead! Guosim is dead!'

In his den down the tunnel, Asmodeus came awake.

7

The Captains of Redwall looked to Constance for guidance. There was no question of overriding her commands. Of all the woodlanders she was the oldest and wisest creature within the walls. The badger was slow-thinking and deliberate, but straight as a die. Her knowledge was born of vast experience, the natural cunning of a survivor.

Jess, Winifred and Basil stood solidly behind Constance. They had just related to her the latest piece of intelligence received. The attackers would emerge from their completed tunnel sometime around mid-afternoon.

The badger thanked them and shook her striped head knowingly. She had not been caught off guard, thanks to Foremole. Now she would need the aid and specialized knowhow of the mole leader to stave off this latest threat to the Abbey.

Cluny the Scourge was still acting strangely. He sat in his patched-up tent at the far edge of the meadow and said nothing. Even when Killconey marched jubilantly up with the news that the tunnel was within a fraction of being completed, Cluny sat and stared at the ground. He did not appear in the least moved by the good tidings.

The ferret stood awkwardly, ill at ease, awaiting orders. Cluny sat unmoving as if he had forgotten Killconey's presence. The ferret tried once more.

'It's the tunnel, Chief. We'll have it ready by this afternoon!'

The Warlord looked up blankly.

'Oh yes, the tunnel! Well, carry on. Er, you know what to do. I've got things to think about,' he muttered absently.

Outside in the meadow, Fangburn and Darkclaw listened in disbelief to the ferret.

'I tell you, he's off his rocker,' said Killconey. 'Sittin' there like a stuffed dummy, ha! Things to think about if you please! Meanwhile, we've got the whole horde to go through that there tunnel and take the Abbey. What're we supposed to do?'

'There's only one thing we can do,' replied the stolid Darkclaw. 'We've got to carry it through ourselves while the Chief's not well.'

'Darkclaw's right,' agreed Fangburn. 'The three of us will take charge of the whole business.'

They both looked at the ferret, waiting for him to express an opinion.

'I suppose you're right,' Killconey said. 'But listen. The rest of the army mustn't get to know about the Chief, otherwise they'll desert. Y'know, I can't seriously believe that Cluny's out of his mind. Just you wait and see. It's probably just another grand ould plan he's thinking up.'

The trio of self-appointed Generals marched down to the tunnel. They climbed inside to check upon progress. It was long, dark and smelly. Weasels and stoats jostled past them carrying baskets of earth or dragging rocks and roots. Killconey pointed out the finer details to his fellow commanders.

'Sure, we're right underneath the road now. The ground is good and hard. It didn't need any shoring at all. Now, see the footings of the wall! Mind your heads! From here I've had some props put in to hold the weight. Further on the going gets really soft, but we've run out of decent timber. Still, I don't reckon it'll make a great deal of difference. If we move the army along fast enough we should all be inside the Abbey before they know what's hit them.'

Above ground, a mole leaning his ear against a thinly-beaten copper basin that was upturned on the earth listened carefully to every word the ferret was saying. He repeated it to Brother Walter, who wrote everything down word for word.

Constance scanned the report and picked up her heavy cudgel.

'Before we know what's hit us, eh?' she growled. 'We'll be doing some hitting of our own before the day is through!'

From the south-west corner of the wall, moles had marked the exact run of the tunnel with two lines of cord and pegs. The Foremole and his team knew all there was to know about the diggings: depth, approximate dimensions, the placement of shoring, even where the first rat's head was likely to break ground. The plan that Constance and Foremole had jointly worked out would require very little hand-to-hand combat, much to the badger's displeasure.

Two outsize cauldrons of boiling water stood ready on tripods with slow fires burning beneath them to keep up the temperature. Constance and the beaver positioned themselves behind these, tipstaves at the ready. All available mice and woodland defenders were gathered in two groups, on either side of the cord-marked aisle. They waited, looking to the badger for further instructions. To a passing stranger it might have looked like some strange Abbey ritual: two fires, two parallel cords, and all the serious-faced creatures gathered in two groups on the grass in the hot June afternoon, waiting silently.

The armed ranks of the horde were formed up in the ditch. Fangburn marched up and down, issuing final instructions. It had not been an easy task getting them in line without Cluny there, but the persuasive tongue of Killconey had assured them that the Chief was aware of their every move and would deal with malcontents and troublemakers later on.

'Pay attention now,' Fangburn called. 'Darkclaw is up at the end of the tunnel. When the diggers break through he will leap up into the Abbey grounds. Four soldiers are with him. They'll hold off any attack while the rest of us get above ground. Now, once you are up don't hang about. Make straight for the Abbey building. Try to capture the mouse Abbot. Darkclaw won't be with you; he'll take some warriors and fight his way through to the gate. Once it's open the others will be able to get in. I don't need to tell you, these are not peaceful creatures we are up against. You've seen for yourselves; they've had a certain amount of luck to date, but they are determined fighters, so when you get up there Cluny wants you to show them what a horde of trained soldiers can really do! Don't forget, the Chief knows how to reward good fighters when it comes to splitting up plunder.'

Cluny had fallen asleep in his tent. He needed peace to clear his troubled mind. But peace was not easy to come by when the mouse warrior visited his dreams once more.

Try as he would, Cluny could not evade the grim avenger with the sword. Shades of creatures that he had slain through the years came back to mock him. They got in his way, tripping him so that he stumbled and fell. Each time he would rise wearily and start to run again, the nemesis at his back pursuing, striding unhurriedly, never changing pace as the wraiths of his dead Captains, Skullface, Redtooth, Ragear, and Cheesethief hovered about, urging him to turn and face the warrior mouse. But he dared not turn. He kept running.

The two weasel diggers thrust upwards in the narrow confines of the tunnel. They sprang aside as earth showered down and daylight poured in. With a seething press of soldiers behind him, Darkclaw stepped up to the waiting diggers. They boosted him upwards. He grabbed at the grass, his spear tucked under one claw. He stopped suddenly, his body halfway out of the hole.

The first things he saw were two huddled crowds of small creatures. They stood either side of a double line of pegs and rope. Darkclaw grinned wolfishly. They were obviously playing some kind of silly little country game. He had caught them unarmed.

A noise from behind distracted the rat. He swivelled around. He found himself facing two huge cauldrons which bubbled and simmered ominously over twin fires. Behind them stood the big badger and another strange-looking creature, equally well built.

Darkclaw set his claws against the ground to lever his body out of the hole. Before he could do anything to stop them the badger and her companion tipped the bulky pots over.

Darkclaw did not even get a chance to scream out a

370

death cry. Boiling water cascaded down over his head in a hissing, steaming deluge. The force of the rushing water sent his body plummeting back down the hole. Endless gallons of scalding water hit the rats in the tunnel like a hellish tidal wave. The tightly packed rodents were instantly slain.

On the surface, Constance cried out to the waiting defenders. 'Jump in between the ropes. Now!'

The weight of combined bodies hit the ground between the lines.

Constance began a steady chant: 'Jump-two-three! Jump-two-three! Jump-two-three!'

Under the constant pounding of countless feet the whole area that had been marked out by the moles suddenly sank into a trench. The tunnel had collapsed.

The defenders stood and cheered in the depression directly above what had once been Killconey's tunnel. The badger gave the order to stop. Foremole and his crew moved in to block off the hole with rocks and rubble. Friar Hugo ordered the cauldrons to be carried back inside to his kitchens. The Abbey creatures fell silent and drifted away from the heap of stones which blocked the hole, a fitting headstone for a mass grave of the enemy.

At the tunnel entrance in the ditch, Fangburn and Killconey were madly thrust aside as rats, weasels, ferrets, and stoats fought their way out of the tunnel.

'Hey, what's happened?' Fangburn shouted. 'Come back here this minute! Where d'you think you're all going?'

The defeated warriors ignored him. Caked with filthy mud and trailing broken spears they dashed off along the ditch.

Killconey peered into the tunnel. All he saw was the

battered body of a stoat being borne towards him on what appeared to be a boiling wave of ooze. The ferret jumped backwards as the shoring burst and the tunnel workings caved in with a dull rumble of earth.

As Cluny ran, another spectre appeared in his fevered dream, it was a hideous-looking thing covered in a dark steaming substance. It stood barring his way with its arms stretched wide as if to embrace him. Cluny pushed it savagely from him. It moaned piteously: 'Chief, it's me, Darkclaw. Look what they did to me.'

Outside the tent Killconey and Fangburn exchanged uneasy glances.

'You dug the tunnel, so you go in first.'

'No fear, I'm only a ferret. You're a naturally superior rat. You'd better go first.'

'Shall we go in together, then?'

'Better not. It looks like the Chief's asleep. He might not thank us for waking him up out of a nice dream.'

'Aye, that's true. Let's leave it until later.'

8

Asmodeus's eyes glared through the narrow hole in front of him. There were two creatures standing together in the big cavern, a shrew and a mouse. He hissed in anger. The mouse was holding his sword, his own beautiful sword!

The adder bunched his sinewy coils and shot through the skin-hung opening. He bared his evil poisoned fangs. No mouse was going to steal the sword of the serpent.

Matthias seized the frightened Guerrilla Shrew by his paw, pulling him along at a swift run.

'Asmodeus must know we're here by now. Come on, Log-a-Log! Let's get out of this place, quick!'

They hurried down the nearest opening, immediately spinning around and racing back. Asmodeus was in the passage sliding towards them. They paushed momentarily in the big cavern. With the shrew on one paw and the sword in the other, Matthias looked wildly about.

'Over there, Log-a-Log! Move!'

Skirting the edges of the shimmering pool, the two friends dashed into a smallish tunnel at the other side.

Behind them in the cavern the giant adder settled down

to a leisurely slither, his tongue flickered wickedly.

'Asmodeusssssssss! No hurry now, they are not going anywhere!'

With a cry of dismay the fleeing pair saw the blank wall ahead. They had run into a cul-de-sac!

Log-a-Log had stopped. His teeth were beginning to chatter. 'Th . . . th . . . th . . . there's no way out! We're trapped!'

Matthias continued running to the dead end. He felt the surface of the wall, and ran his paws up and down it.

'We must do something,' he panted. 'There must be some way to escape the snake. Get hold of yourself, shrew. Think!'

Asmodeus poked his head into the entrance. His sibilant voice called in to them: 'Stay where you are, little ones. I will come to you, Asmodeussss!'

Log-a-Log had gone rigid with fright. He stood petrified. Matthias had begun digging furiously at the wall with its sword point. He gouged and thrusted, muttering to himself. 'At least we've got nothing to lose but a sword and our lives. There might be something on the other side of this lot.'

The sword struck a tree root. He dug around it, probing, probing busily until the soft half-formed sandstone gave beneath the blade. Frantically, Matthias redoubled his efforts.

Log-a-Log gave a strangled sob. In the dim distance of the tunnel, Asmodeus could be seen advancing slowly but surely towards them.

Matthias felt the sword of Martin break through the stone. He looked back over his shoulder. The giant adder was slithering closer with each passing second. He hacked madly to widen the opening he had made. Sticking the sword in the ground, he grabbed Log-a-Log and shook him soundly.

'Here, shrew! You are smaller than I am! Climb through, then see if you can tug me backwards by my feet. Come on, move yourself if you want to live!'

Log-a-Log came out of his trance. Leaping quickly into the hole he scratched the damp sandy grit left and right. Ducking beneath the tree root he scrabbled awkwardly through into a tiny cell-like space on the other side.

Asmodeus was close to Matthias now. Wielding the sword the young mouse backed off. He felt the hole behind him and scrambled into it sideways, still facing his enemy. Taking care not to let the sword-point drop, he shouted to his companion, 'Log-a-Log, can you see my feet? Grab hold of them, pull me through.'

Matthias hung uncomfortably. He tightened his paws on the sword-handle and moved it from side to side with the sway of the big viper's head. Suddenly he felt the shrew pulling on his feet. Wriggling his body Matthias started to move backwards. Asmodeus bared his fangs. He moved forward at the struggling mouse. Matthias swung the blade at the snake's open mouth. It hissed and recoiled. As Matthias contorted himself to negotiate the tree root, he poked the point of the blade at the enemy's head.

'Stay back, evil one, or I'll kill you!' he shouted.

Asmodeus gave a low, soothing hiss. 'Come to me, little mouse. Let me wrap myself around you. I will give you the kiss of eternal sleep.'

With a triumphant shout the young mouse disappeared completely into the hole. He fell on top of Log-a-Log at the other side. Forcefully the snake launched his great body at the opening, crumbling earth and rock as he pushed his coils through the aperture.

'He's coming!' Log-a-Log screamed in terror.

Matthias shoved his friend behind him. Planting his feet wide apart he hefted the great sword in both paws.

'Stay out of the way, shrew. There's no more retreating. All ends here!'

The gigantic spadelike head of the snake thrust itself through into the small space.

'Give me my sword, mouse, and I will make your dying easy!' he hissed.

Matthias laughed in the face of the adder. 'Come and get it, Poisonteeth.'

Asmodeus tried forcing his body through with one swift thrust. He found his bunched coils jammed firmly in the tree root. Relaxing, he allowed his head to wave from side to side.

'Look at me, my little friend. I can see that you are a great warrior. You are not afraid to gaze into my eyes. Look at me.'

The eyes seemed to expand and dilate until they filled the whole of Matthias's vision. They dominated him. He could not tear his gaze away. Asmodeus continued in a persuasive undertone.

'See, they are the twin pools of eternity. Sink into them, and you will find darkness and rest.'

Log-a-Log was completely hypnotized. Matthias, too, felt overcome by an immense lethargy. The adder's voice was a cold, dark, green velvet fog that threatened to envelop him. He stared deep into the deadly eyes, his lids began to droop heavily . . . .

Martin the Warrior strode boldly up through the dark mist.

I am that is! Matthias, why do you sleep? There is a warrior's work to be done here! Pick up your sword, Matthias! The evil one shall not have it. Strike out for me now, my brave young champion!

Asmodeus was working his body free, pushing forward.

Matthias's eyes were shut, his lips moved with one
word.

'Strike.'

Suddenly the spell of the snake was broken. The young
mouse's eyes snapped open, clear and bright. He swung
the ancient sword high and struck at the giant adder.

He struck for Redwall!

He struck against evil!

He struck for Martin!

He struck for Log-a-Log and his shrews!

He struck for dead Guosim!

He struck as Methuselah would have wanted him to!

He struck against Cluny the Scourge and tyranny!

He struck out against Captain Snow's ridicule!

He struck for the world of light and freedom!

He struck until his paws ached and the sword fell from
them!

When Log-a-Log awoke from out of the trance he saw his
friend, Matthias the Warrior.

He stood shaking. His chest heaved with exertion. His
paws hung limp at his sides. The great sword lay against
the warrior's blood-flecked habit, its long, deadly blade
crimsoned in victory.

And the head of Asmodeus Poisonteeth, the giant
adder, lay severed upon the ground, its eyes dulled in
death, never again to hypnotize another living creature!

9

It was the afternoon of the following day. Matthias marched into the farmyard at the head of all the Guerrilla Union of Shrews in Mossflower. He halted the entire regiment outside the barn and turned to Log-a-Log.

'Wait here, my friend. There's someone I have to see.'

The young mouse stood in the gloom of the barn, knowing he was being watched. Without turning or looking around he addressed the cat.

'Julian, it is Matthias. I have returned.'

The marmalade cat loomed up out of the half-light. 'So I see. Welcome, little friend! Is that the sword you told me of?'

Matthias proffered the blade for inspection. 'It is indeed. Asmodeus the snake lies dead. I slew him with this very weapon. It is the great sword of Martin the Warrior!'

Squire Julian Gingivere handled the sword with care. He laid it on a hay bale. Sitting next to it he folded his paws under him and half shut his eyes.

'Matthias, let me give you some good advice. I am much older than you and have seen far more life. There are not many illusions left to me, and I do not want to shatter your dreams or blight your ambitions, my friend; but I must say what I have to.

'We Squires of Gingivere are an ancient line. In the past I have seen many such tokens as this weapon. My Grandsires owned a vast armoury full of magnificent and valued battle equipment. No doubt your sword is indeed a beautiful thing. It is a tribute to whoever forged it in bygone ages. There are very few such swords as this one left in the world: but remember, it is only a sword, Matthias!

'It contains no secret spell, nor holds within its blade any magical power. This sword is made for only one purpose, to kill. It will only be as good or evil as the one who wields it. I know that you intend to use it only for the good of your Abbey, Matthias; do so, but never allow yourself to be tempted into using it in a careless or idle way. It would inevitably cost you your life, or that of your dear ones.

'Martin the Warrior used the sword only for right and good. This is why it has become a symbol of power to Redwall. Knowledge is gained through wisdom, my friend. Use the sword wisely.'

Matthias picked up his weapon. He was surprised at Julian's words. They were an echo of something that his old companion Methuselah had once said to him.

'Thank you, Julian,' he said. 'I will remember your lesson well. Now I must ask a favour of you. Would you come with me? I want you to be present when I speak to Captain Snow.'

The cat sniffed disdainfully. 'You ask quite a lot. I wouldn't do this for anyone else, you know.'

Reluctantly Julian stalked out into the sunlight with Matthias. There was an immediate spate of loud, frightened chatter from the regiment of Guerrilla Shrews. Squire Julian Gingivere merely nodded, and addressed them in a regal but distant manner: 'Good afternoon. Very clement weather for the time of year, don't you think?'

For the first time since the formation of their union, the shrews stood in slack-jawed silence, completely lost for an answer!

As they strolled along, Julian protested to his companion, 'Really, Matthias, I think you are asking a bit much of one. Does one have to stand around listening to that befeathered regimental bore giving air to his hidebound militaristic views? Oh, it's too much!'

Matthias stroked the sulky cat's forepaw. 'Come on, Julian. I think you'll be pleasantly surprised.'

The marmalade cat stifled a yawn. 'You don't say. Has another tree fallen upon the pompous old fool?'

Captain Snow paced around the base of his nest tree. He glared at the cat, then at the mouse holding the sword. He snorted, hunching his neck into ruffles and folding his wings behind him.

'Listen, mouse. I don't want to hear how you did it. Probably wouldn't believe you anyhow. But here you are, and I suppose that's that?'

Matthias hid a smile; he tapped his foot in mock impatience. 'I'm waiting, Cap'n Snow, sir. Remember your promises on oath?'

The owl's eyes bulged with ill temper. He flung Basil's medal at the young mouse's feet.

'There! Take your medal back, you insolent little pup. I'm not saying another word while that salad-eating cat is within hearing range.'

Matthias traced patterns in the dust with the swordpoint and spoke civilly to the owl. 'Well, Cap'n Snow, sir. I never took you for a bad sport. Besides, I've got an entire regiment of shrews hidden all about. They're waiting to hear you honour your wager.'

The owl spread his wide, snowy wings and flapped upwards to perch on the edge of his den. Folding the wings and shutting his eyes tightly he shouted out with bad grace, 'I promise never to kill or eat another mouse or shrew of any type as long as I live, so there!'

He hooted and vanished swiftly into his den.

Instantly the shrews broke cover, dancing and whooping with delight.

Captain Snow popped his head out of the nest. 'Go away! Begone! I can't stand it, all those little dinners dancing around. It's too much, I tell you!'

'Excuse me mentioning it, sir,' Matthias shouted over the hubbub. 'But what about your promise regarding our friend the Squire?'

The owl emerged grumpy and ruffled. Thoroughly humiliated, he called out to his former friend the cat, 'It was all my fault. I apologize to you, Squire Julian.'

He was completely taken aback by the cat's reply. 'Not at all, my dear friend. It is I that must apologize to you. The whole incident was entirely due to my priggishness and lack of manners.'

Captain Snow swooped down and perched near the cat. 'D'you really think so? Oh, come on, Julian old chap. I must share the blame. It was my barrack-room feeding habits that started the whole thing. You mustn't blame yourself, old friend.'

A rare smile covered the features of the normally laconic Julian. He purred comfortingly. 'No, no. I insist that we share the blame fifty-fifty. Besides, the question won't arise now that you've sworn off shrews and mice. I say, have you ever tried a fresh trout salad with mustard and cress? Why don't you come over to the barn? I'm sure there'll be enough for two. I mean, trout's not exactly a vegetable, is it?'

Wing in paw, the reunited comrades strolled off to the barn, chatting amiably as if there had never been a cross word between them. Julian was last to enter the barn. He gave Matthias a broad wink.

'Who knows, my friend? Maybe the sword does possess some magic. Personally, I think it's the warrior who wields it.'

For the first time in many days. Matthias laughed heartily. He felt so good within himself. After all the action and mental strain, travel and grief, he felt suddenly reborn, larger than life and brimming with new-found self-confidence. Certainly there were great difficulties and hard tasks ahead of him; when the time came he would handle them. For the present he was satisfied with this feeling of immense happiness.

Holding the sword lightly, he balanced its point against the earth and laughed freely. It was infectious: Log-a-Log joined in; then one Guerrilla Shrew; then another, and still yet more, until the whole regiment and their warrior mouse friend set the countryside ringing from river to woods to farm and field with the happy sounds of their honest joy.

10

The Cluny that emerged from the ragged tent in the meadow was far from being sick in the head.

The members of the horde watched the way he strode purposefully about. The old glint was back in his single eye. His orders were crisp and concise. Even the long tail had a fresh crack about it. The Chief seemed sharper than he had been before.

In the aftermath of the tunnel disaster, Cluny had called off the attack for a full day, withdrawing all his followers well back across the meadow. The Warlord gave his horde time to recuperate from the fiasco; a whole day's leisure, with no recriminations and hardly any orders.

The Captains of Redwall wasted no time in making use of the temporary respite. Repairs were started upon the gatehouse door. Teams of woodland carpenters, Abbey smiths and labourers, plus any creatures that felt the need to help were lowered down to the road in large wicker-work baskets. Should the enemy in the meadow decide to make any sudden move, the workmen could be speedily hauled back up to the ramparts. All that day the rope gangs were kept busy sending down wood, spikes, cordage, tools, and repair materials.

Cluny sat and watched them from the distance as he talked aloud to himself. 'Good work, mice, strengthen my gates. I wouldn't want to rule a fortress with broken doors.'

Fangburn was passing. He overheard Cluny conversing with himself. Not sure whether the remarks were addressed to him, he stopped.

'Eh, are you feeling all right, Chief?'

'Never better!' Cluny replied. He pointed at the repair crews. 'See that, Fangburn? Honest industrious work, and what for, eh?'

Fangburn hazarded a guess. 'To keep us out, Chief?'

'No, to stop us getting in,' Cluny chuckled. 'Get some soldiers and light a fire down in the ditch. Make it a proper blaze, good and hot.'

Fangburn knew better than to question the reason for his Chief's order, no matter how strange it sounded.

'A big fire? Right you are, Chief. I'll get them going right away.'

Fangburn hurried off, aware that Cluny was watching him.

Shortly after there was a huge fire burning in the ditch. The horde gathered close by to see what Cluny was up to. The crackling flames gave off waves of heat, causing everyone to step back. Above the ditch the air shimmered and danced.

Cluny stood in the ditch, claws on hips. He cracked his tail.

'Scumnose, Mangefur! Bring up those dormice prisoners!'

The twenty dormice were dragged forward in a pitiable condition. They cowered on the ground in front of the

Warlord, half starved and dull eyed.

Cluny pointed. 'You, leader mouse! What's your name again?'

'Plumpen, sir,' the bedraggled mouse replied.

Cluny grabbed Plumpen roughly, dragging him away from his fellow captives on the ground.

'What are these other miserable creatures to you, Plumpen?' he snapped.

The dormouse explained in a shaky voice: 'My family, sir. My mother, father, brothers, sisters, and my wife and two little ones. Oh please, sir, spare them, I beg you!'

Cluny laughed cruelly. His eye was devoid of pity. He leaned close to Plumpen and whispered harshly, 'What would you do to save them?'

The dormouse watched Cluny's eye rove lazily from his family to the blazing inferno.

'Anything! Anything you say! What do you want of me?' he screamed in his fear and anxiety.

Cluny cracked his tail triumphantly, pulling Plumpen forward until their noses touched. The big rat's voice was as foul and evil as his breath.

'Listen carefully. You are going to open the Abbey door for me, my friend. If you fail, your precious little family will pay the penalty! Now, here is what you must do.'

Constance hauled upon her rope. It was no hard task for a fully grown badger. On the other ropes there were creatures that could not compare with her for strength, but they hauled and pulled with an equally good will. Cornflower and Silent Sam kept busy supplying cool drinks and sweat cloths. The repair work went ahead at a steady pace.

No one noticed that there was an extra mouse labouring among the workers in the roadway.

Plumpen!

Cluny had supplied him with a habit taken from the body of one who had fallen slain from the ramparts. Plumpen had concealed himself in the ditch and travelled under cover until he was level with the gatehouse. At the appropriate moment he slipped out with a plank upon his shoulder and joined the work force. They toiled away industriously until Jess Squirrel, who was acting as overseer, decided that the work was completed, as indeed it was. The old gatehouse door looked as good as new. All the tools and spare timber were gathered up and the roadway was swept. Satisfied with a job well done, the work crews stacked up their materials, and were hauled up to the ramparts in the large grain basket. Plumpen sat between Brother Alf and Brother Rufus. Across the meadow he could see Cluny, watching, always watching.

Plumpen cursed the fate that had put him and his family in the hands of the rats. What a happy friendly lot the Redwall creatures were. He was served afternoon tea sitting on the grass in the cloisters. The dormouse felt the good food turn to ashes in his mouth at the thought of his betrayal of fellow mice, but there was no alternative if he wanted to save his family. After tea he wandered off on the pretence of carrying out some fictitious task. When there was nobody about he hid himself in the old gatehouse den which had once been Methuselah's study. Locking the door, Plumpen lay down lonely and miserable to await nightfall.

Inside Cavern Hole the Father Abbot addressed a morale-boosting speech to his Captains.

'Friends, it will avail Cluny little to put the Abbey under state of siege. As you know, Redwall is virtually self-supporting. All we require to sustain life and comfort is here within these walls. Therefore, I suggest we carry on as normally as possible.

'However, the walls must always be guarded. I leave it to you, my Captains. Stay ever vigilant against Cluny and his horde. I know that with your counsel and good judgement, we will soon see the day when the enemy are forced to go elsewhere and leave Redwall in peace.'

There was loud applause for the Abbot's heartening words, but Constance was not convinced. She whispered her thoughts to Basil and Jess. 'Never. Cluny won't leave us alone until either we are dead, or he is!'

Basil Stag Hare nodded in agreement. 'I know, old scout. But the Abbot's such a decent old buffer that he believes there's good in everyone, even Cluny. What?'

'And so do I,' Jess muttered. 'I believe Cluny *will* be good some day. Good and dead!'

Gradually the day drew to a close. Lights dimmed as Redwall prepared for a well-deserved night's rest. The meadowland and woods grew quiet and peaceful. On top of the walls, sentries leaned on the parapet listening to the evening birdsongs. Across the meadows the enemy campfires burned low into the soft June night.

Plumpen waited another hour as Cluny had instructed: then it was time to make his move. Stealing quietly out of the gatehouse study the dormouse headed north, staying well within the deep shadow of the wall. At the small north wall gate, Plumpen drew a scarlet cloth from his habit. Smearing the bolts with grease from the cloth he silently worked them loose.

Killconey lay watching the gate from behind a sycamore in the woods. Near to every other entrance one of Cluny's most trusted soldiers was concealed, awaiting the signal. It was the ferret who was rewarded by the sight of the scarlet cloth being shoved through the door jam. He hurried away to tell Cluny.

It was dead of night when Cluny's horde moved out of the meadow. Around the embers of each campfire bundles of grass and twigs had been wrapped in blankets. To the unsuspecting sentries on the wall the bundles looked like sleeping forms: they sensed nothing amiss. The horde circled northwards through the meadowlands until Cluny judged they were far enough from Redwall to escape detection. He crossed the road at the head of his army.

They filtered back through the leafy cover of night-time Mossflower towards the Abbey. Now that his goal was in sight, Cluny used all the stealth of a stalking hunter, waiting until the entire horde was in position. Each soldier crouching quietly among the ferns and bushes knew the penalty for making any sound that would betray their presence; not death from the defenders, but death at the claws of their own Chieftain.

Cluny could wait. He gave it another half-hour, until he could actually see some of the guards on top of the wall nodding off at their posts. What was thirty minutes after he had waited so long for this moment? With practised skill he slid from his hiding place and crossed to the wall door. One gentle push and the small iron door swung slowly open on its greased hinges. Cluny stood in the doorway as his soldiers filed past him on their way to the Abbey building. There was little need to worry about the wall guards. Those who were awake would be watching the road or the enemy camp, their backs turned on the secret invaders.

Plumpen stood by, anxiously watching the Warlord. At least his family would be safe now. The dormouse had faithfully carried out his part in the dreadful scheme;

Cluny must surely keep to his word. He did not see the look that passed between Cluny and Fangburn.

Fangburn swung the heavy club and brought it crashing down on the back of Plumpen's head from behind. The unlucky dormouse crumpled to the ground without a sound.

Cluny the Scourge bared his fangs, grinning wickedly into the dark. He had finally brought his horde into Redwall!

11

The last rays of the sinking sun streamed through the open barn doorway, lighting up formerly darkened corners. Matthias lay on the hay amidst the remnants of an epic celebration feast. The Guerrilla Union of Shrews in Mossflower had really outdone themselves laying out this spread. He picked up a truffle and tossed it away with a sigh of satisfaction, fearing he might burst if he forced another bite into his mouth.

On one side of the young mouse the gifts from Squire Julian Gingivere, Captain Snow, and the shrews were piled high; on the other was his sword, reflecting the rays of the afternoon sun. The Guerrilla Shrew regiment had chosen to sleep off the effects of the party outside in the sun. They lay about the farmyard, too full even to argue.

Log-a-Log shuffled lazily in and flopped down beside his mouse friend.

'Greetings, oh mighty warrior,' he giggled. 'Saviour of the shrews; slayer of Poisonteeth; he who speaks with cats; friendmaker of owls and uniter of—'

'Oh shut up, you noisy little devil!' Matthias chuckled as he kicked Log-a-Log off the hay into the dust.

'D'you know much about birds?' Log-a-Log said. 'What about sparrows?'

Matthias yawned. 'Well, what about sparrows? I've had some dealings with 'em. What do you need to know?'

'Nothing really,' the shrew murmured sleepily. 'But there's been one reported over at the edge of the woods. Of course, no one can understand a single word that the savage heathen is saying. She's screeching away back there, hopping and dancing about, working herself up into a right old tizzwozz, or so I've been told.'

Matthias sprang up, grabbing his sword. 'Come on, Log-a-Log. I speak the Sparra language. We'd best get over there and find out what's upsetting her.'

With a score of Guerrilla Shrews in their wake the two companions set off for Mossflower at the double.

Above the long grass in front of the woods the Sparra warrior could be seen. She fluttered up and down creating a raucous din. Log-a-Log and the shrews were taken aback when Matthias ran ahead of them, shouting at the top of his voice, 'Warbeak Sparra, thattum you, old worm warrior!'

Joyfully the two friends reunited. They rolled about in the grass like a pair of mad creatures, pounding each other on the back.

'Matthias mouse! Um old wormfriend! Biggee fat brave now! How are you?'

The shrews were completely baffled. They sat about scratching their heads at the strange behaviour of the sparrow and the mouse. Matthias chattered to Warbeak in the rapid Sparra tongue, telling of all that had happened since they last parted. Warbeak for her part told Matthias of her fortunes to date.

Upon the death of King Bull Sparra, Warbeak had been crowned Queen. Dunwing, her mother, had wished it to be so. The tribe were happy under the wise rule of their youngest–ever Queen. No more would sparrows have to live under the claw of an unpredictable maniac.

After Warbeak had related her story she became grave. 'Matthias, um Redwall have big trouble. We watch, see from um roof. Ratworm makum lotta plans, um mice brave warriors. Alla time fight back, beatum ratworms plenty. But Warbeak watchum ratworm King. He um badworse than King Bull. Him make bad plan, catchum Abbey. Ratworm soon be inside Redwall. Matthias mouse come quick. Bringum sword.'

An icy claw of fear gripped Matthias's stomach. He sat down hard in the grass.

Log-a-Log shook his friend. 'What's she saying, Matthias? You look as if you've seen the ghost of Poisonteeth. For goodness' sake, what's going on?'

'It's my home, Redwall,' Matthias said in a hollow voice. 'Cluny the Scourge is about to capture it!'

Log-a-Log spoke urgently to the shrews. 'Quick, get the regiment ready as fast as you can. We're off to the Abbey at Redwall. Tell them to catch us up. I want no argument or votes! Tell every shrew to be fully armed. We must march night and day if we are to save Matthias's friends.'

Matthias picked up the sword of Martin. 'By thunder, Log-a-Log! You're right! I fought hard for this sword in order to save Redwall! Come on!'

'Shrewmouse helpum you. How many warrior him got?' Warbeak chimed.

'A full complement,' Log-a-Log answered. 'About five hundred shrews.'

Warbeak spread her wings. 'I bring alla tribe Sparra warrior. We come, help.'

Matthis shook Warbeak's claw warmly. 'Thank you, Queen Warbeak my friend. Now we must go. A strategy can be worked out on the way to the Abbey. Let's hurry. There's no time to lose. It's do or die now!'

The mouse, the shrew and the sparrow plunged off into the green wooded world of Mossflower together.

One thing Matthias was certain of as he strode swiftly through the trees; it would be he and he alone who faced Cluny the Scourge at the bitter end.

12

The Father Abbot was awakened by a swordpoint at his throat. He was completely surrounded by snarling rats. Jess, Basil, Winifred and Foremole all found themselves in similar situations. The iron claw of Cluny's discipline was strongly evident throughout the manoeuvre. Complete silence had been observed. Only those held captive were aware of the horde's presence.

The main danger to the attackers was Constance. As always, she slept out upon the grass in the Abbey grounds. More than two score of rodents carrying a strong rope net between them had stolen up on the sleeping badger. They threw the net over Constance, fixing it into the ground with long stakes and bludgeoning her senseless before she was properly awake. Cluny watched the proceedings with grim satisfaction. Redwall was his!

Small creatures rubbing sleep from their eyes in confusion were dragged out into the Abbey grounds. Woodland infants wept fitfully as they clung to their parents: bullying rats pushed and harried everyone out into the open where they made them sit on the grass. Abbot Mortimer in his homespun nightshirt was kept to one side with his Captains. Their paws were cruelly bound behind them. They stood in stolid silence as sniggering rats referred to them as 'The Ringleaders'.

Cluny the Scourge stood in the Great Hall, surveying the marvellous tapestry. He did not need to steal scraps of it now; it belonged solely to him. Fangburn, Frogblood, Scumnose, Mangefur and Killconey came marching smartly up. They saluted him.

'The Abbey is yours now, Chief.'

'We've got all hands outside, Chief.'

'Any further orders, Chief?'

Cluny ran his tail reflectively through his long claws. 'Yes. Bring the Abbot's chair out of the place they call Cavern Hole. Have it set up for me on a platform by the gatehouse. I've got some judgements to deliver.'

The horde Captains swaggered off jauntily. Cluny addressed the picture of Martin upon the tapestry.

'Well, warrior mouse. What do you think of your brave Redwall defenders now? Huh, not much, I imagine! I'm going to let you stay up there and witness some drastic changes.'

Cluny jabbed a claw at Martin, his voice laden with menace, 'No more will you haunt my dreams! A voice inside me spoke as I waited in the woods tonight outside your precious Redwall. It said that before sunset this day I would be free of my nightmares forever. What do you think of that?'

Martin continued to smile fearlessly down upon Cluny. The Warlord cracked his tail, shattering the silence of Great Hall. He seemed driven to great anger by the apparent unconcern of the Warrior.

'Henceforth this place shall be known as the Hall of the Scourge,' he shouted insanely. 'No more will the Abbey be known as Redwall, it shall be called Cluny's Castle!

Everything will change!'

The Warlord went off into a berserk rage, stamping about the Hall, slashing and whipping at the shadows with his tail as he invented new titles, screaming them out as the echoes bounced back off the walls at him.

'The Great Rodent Wall!'

'The Lake of Drowning!'

'The Field of Dead Mice!'

'Ferret Gate, Stoat Orchard, Weasel Bell. Hahahahahahaha!'

Outside upon the grass the woodland captives heard Cluny's crazed laughter ringing from the Abbey. They shivered at the thought of their inevitable fate. He was making them wait, drawing out the tension, revelling in their misery, savouring his evil victory.

Abbot Mortimer looked up at the sky.

'It will soon be dawn,' he said sadly.

A rat pushed him heavily to the ground.

'Shut your doddering mouth, old one,' he snarled nastily.

Jess Squirrel knocked the rat flat with both her feet, and sank her teeth into the bully's back. A pack of rats leaped upon Jess. They dragged her off their screaming companion and beat at her with their spear butts and cutlass handles.

'Leave her alone, you cowards!' Mr Squirrel shouted as he struggled to hold back Silent Sam. 'You're very brave in a gang, but you wouldn't face my Jess if her paws were free, you scum, not if there were twice as many of you!'

The Father Abbot struggled to his knees. 'Please, I beg of you, do not fight on my account. They have the advantage. You'll only get hurt.'

'Aye, sensible words, your honour,' Killconey said, as he made way for the Abbot's chair to be carried through.

'Take my tip and sit quiet until the Chief comes out. Don't make it harder on yourselves than it's going to be. That's what me ould mother always used to say.'

'Good grief, shouldn't think a blaggard like you ever had a mother,' Basil sniffed disdainfully.

Killconey cackled and slapped his thigh. 'Well now, aren't you the big comical rabbit? Let me tell you, my fine gentleman bucko, you won't be half so funny when the Scourge is done with you. No sir!'

The prisoners slumped dejectedly upon the Abbey grass, awaiting the break of dawn and the coming of Cluny the Scourge.

13

Warbeak and Log-a-Log had to force Matthias to take a rest. The young mouse had set a scorching pace, marching through the night from the far borders of Mossflower Wood. The Guerrilla Shrew had trouble keeping up. He was smaller than Matthias and did not have the advantage of flight like the sparrow. Always several metres behind, he panted for breath as he stumbled gamely on. Even Warbeak was beginning to feel the effects of prolonged low night-time fluttering, through the woodlands, around trees, over bushes; it was not the same as a clear clean flight through the upper atmosphere. Only Matthias kept going at a dogged headlong dash. He stopped for nothing. The heavy sword hanging from his shoulders by a length of cord thumped against him as he urged his legs forward: the breath rose ragged in his throat. His companions realized the urgency of the situation, but they saw that if Matthias continued to drive himself at this rate, he would soon collapse.

The matter was solved when Matthias tripped upon a tree root and went sprawling flat. His two friends pinned him down and held on while they tried to talk sense to him.

Finally convinced, Matthias sat among the ferns with his allies. It was not wasted time: they held a council of war.

'You carry on to Redwall, Matthias,' Log-a-Log said. 'I will wait here for my band. We'll force march most of the way, don't worry. The Guerrilla Shrews won't be far behind you. We'll make good time in this cool night air.'

The young mouse was assailed by gnawing doubts. 'That's all very well, but how are we going to scale the wall into the Abbey grounds? If Cluny has captured Redwall, he's bound to have sentries posted upon the ramparts.'

'What for um ratworm want sentry?' Warbeak shrugged her wings. 'Him catchum Abbey, not know we come to catchum back.'

'Warbeak, you're right! But it still doesn't solve the problem of how we get in,' Matthias replied.

The young Sparra Queen winked cheekily. 'Is easy. Me gettum Sparras to open um little wormdoors in um wall; east, south, north; you see, they do good. Warbeak go now, see um friend Matthias mouse at Redwall.'

The Sparra Queen shot off into the air like an arrow from a bow. Matthias arose to continue his journey. Log-a-Log stayed behind and waited for his warriors to catch up.

Beside the north wall gate, Plumpen stirred. He groaned and rolled over. There was a bad wound on the back of his head, but he was still very much alive. The first sight that greeted the dormouse's hazy vision was three sparrows standing over him. They were Dunwing, Battlehawk and Windplume. Silently they slid Plumpen out of the open door into the woods.

Dunwing gave orders to the two Sparra warriors:

'Take um red rag and grease. Bring many Sparra. Fly quiet, greasum other little wormdoors. Wait 'til Queen Warbeak come. No let ratworms see warriors, go now.'

Throughout the night hours many sparrows worked secretly on the locks, bolts and hinges of the small wall-gates.

Somewhere in Mossflower, Matthias was still pressing on to Redwall. Log-a-Log and the regiment of Guerrilla Shrews were hot on his trail. A thousand Sparra warriors perched in the branches of the trees all around the Abbey, waiting.

14

The light of dawn began to appear in the sky. The sun's rays tinged the sandstone walls to a dull pink and clouded red. Dew was upon the late rose.

Despite the blessing of a glorious summer day, the whole of Mossflower was doom-laden with an awful tension that threatened to burst upon the captives seated on the grass.

Horde Captains came stamping out of the Abbey. They prodded the prisoners with cutlass points and slapped out with flat blades at the helpless defenders.

'Come on, you lot! On your feet! Stand up straight, you mice! Step aside there! Make way for Cluny the Scourge!'

Reluctantly the Redwall contingent complied. They turned. All eyes were on the door of Great Hall.

The silence was broken as the door slammed back upon its hinges. Cluny strode out. Behind him, bearing the horde standard and lighted torch, came Fangburn and Killconey. The victorious horde soldiers cheered wildly. Cluny was the picture of barbaric power, geared for a war from his poison tail tip to the frightening battle helmet.

He looked every inch the conqueror.

Regally he swept through the ranks of both sides, looking neither to right nor left. Mounting the dais which had been set up for his use, he swirled the sinister cloak about him and sat down in the Abbot's chair. All that could be heard was the crackle of the torch and the unhappy whimper of one of the infant captives. He sat impassively, claws gripping the chair arms, visor lowered.

Slowly lifting the visor, Cluny allowed his single eye to rove around. It came to rest on the Abbey leader.

'You, Abbot Mouse, come here!'

With two rats flanking him, the Father Abbot stepped forward in a slow, dignified manner. Even clad in his nightwear he radiated calm and fortitude. Cluny sat back sneering openly.

'Ha! So this is your leader? A little fat mouse in his nightshirt! What a fearsome warrior he looks! Well, what now, mouse? Are you going to go down on your knees and beg for your life, old one?'

Abbot Mortimer stared calmly into Cluny's savage eye. 'I will never bend my knee on my own behalf. However, if I thought I could save the life of one of my friends I would gladly fall down on both knees. But I know you, Cluny, better than you know yourself. There is not a scrap of pity or mercy in your heart, only a burning desire for vengeance. Therefore, I will not kneel to one who is consumed by evil.'

Cluny sprang to his feet trembling with rage.

'Kneel to me, mouse! Kneel or I will kill you,' he stormed.

Angry growls and the rending of grass from beneath the net on the ground heralded Constance's awakening. She began to heave and push. The net started to work loose. She called out to Cluny in a gruff, insulting voice.

'Hey you! You scruffy, one-eyed vermin! Remove this net and face me alone! We'll see who ends up on their knees!'

At a signal from the Warlord a gang of rats leaped upon Constance and beat her back into unconsciousness with their weapons. They drove the securing stakes deeper around the net.

Basil Stag Hare kicked out at them. When he had driven the rats off he faced Cluny boldly.

'You, sir, are not fit to command any creature! You are a coward and an evil maniac. Even if my paws were not tied I would think twice before soiling them upon the likes of you. Tcha! You are beneath contempt, you . . . you . . . Rat!'

A stinging blow from a weasel's club sent Basil limping and tripping to the ground. The weasel struck him again and again upon the legs. He doubled up in pain as the horde jeered and laughed.

Cluny pointed at the hare. 'Remember your tricks on the common behind the church? Before this day is done you'll never run and dodge again!'

His eyes blazing with madness, Cluny flung his claws wide. 'All of you, defenders of Redwall, listen to me! When I first came to the Abbey I gave you a choice: surrender or die. You chose to fight me. Me, Cluny the Scourge! I lost battles, I lost skirmishes, I lost soldiers, but I have won the war. You are the losers. Now you must pay with your lives!'

As the Warlord spoke, something seemed to snap deep within the Abbot. He rushed forward and tried to grasp Cluny.

'No, no, you dare not harm these creatures!' he cried. 'It would be murder.'

Cluny grabbed the Father Abbot and threw him to the ground. Lashing the frail figure with his poison-barbed tail, he shouted, 'Who are you to tell me what to do? There is only one law, my word! There is none to stop me; not badgers or hares or otters or mice. I will kill you all. Kill, kill, kill!'

Suddenly a thunderous voice was heard. 'Cluny the Scourge, I have come to settle with you!'

A gasp arose from the crowd. Cluny's tail fell from his grasp as both victors and vanquished turned towards the Abbey whence the voice had issued.

There in the open doorway of Great Hall stood the warrior mouse!

It was as if he had stepped out of the tapestry upon the wall. On his arm was a burnished shield, at his waist was a sword belt of black leather and silver. From the scabbard at his side he drew forth a mighty sword.

Cluny's voice shook as he addressed the nightmare visitor.

'Who are you?'

The warrior stepped forward into the daylight. Sunrays glinted diamond-like off his sword.

'I am that is!'

Unable to take his eyes from the warrior, Cluny stumbled backwards.

He cowered behind the Abbot's chair, his mouth working convulsively. 'You are something out of my dreams. Go away, I'm not asleep!'

The warrior mouse strode out into the crowd. He pointed his blade at the quivering Warlord.

'I am that is! Martin, Matthias, call me what you will. It was long ago written that you and I would meet, rat.'

'Seize him!' Cluny screamed.

Frogblood sprang forward, brandishing a spear. Before he could raise it, the ancient sword flashed in the warrior's grip and hewed him lifeless to the ground.

'I will slay any invader that moves,' Matthias shouted.

'Cluny, this is between you and me. Your army will not interfere.'

Suddenly the Joseph Bell began tolling. Sparra warriors appeared in swarms that almost obscured the sky above the Abbey. They landed in droves around the parapet edges. The grounds came to life with teeming swarms of Guerrilla Shrews armed to the teeth with rapiers, cudgels, and slings. Matthias whirled the sword above his head as he roared out his battle cry.

'Redwall, Redwall. Strike for Redwall!'

The final conflict had begun.

Shrews struck down the enemy guards as Sparra braves released the prisoners' bonds with short slashes of their sharp beaks. The freed defenders grabbed up anything that would serve as weapons. They hurled themselves upon the enemy, sparrows and shrews siding them against their larger adversaries. Rats, ferrets, weasels, and stoats fought with the ferocity born of desperation. Their very lives depended on the outcome.

Cluny plucked the blazing torch from Killconey's grasp. He flung it at the face of the oncoming warrior. Matthias deflected it with his shield in a cascade of sparks and went after the horde leader. To gain a brief respite, Cluny pushed Killconey into Matthias. The ferret grappled vainly but was cloven in two with one swift stroke. Matthias stepped over the slain ferret, whirling his sword expertly as he pursued Cluny.

Ignoring his unprotected back, Matthias failed to see Fangburn stealing up behind him. The rat raised his cutlass in both claws, but, before he could strike, Constance had hurled the net over him. Fangburn struggled like a landed fish as the big badger picked up the net and swung it several times against the gatehouse wall. Dropping the lifeless thing, Constance plunged with a terrifying roar into a pack of weasels.

The thick tail of the Warlord flicked out venomously at Matthias's face. He covered swiftly with his shield as the poisoned metal barb clanged harmlessly off it. Cluny tried again, this time whipping the tail speedily at the young mouse's unprotected legs. Matthias leaped nimbly to one side and swung the sword in a flashing arc. Cluny roared with pain as it severed the tip of his tail. The bloodied stub lay on the grass with the barb still attached. Hurling the Abbot's chair at his adversary, the rat seized an iron spike. Metal clashed on metal as the warrior mouse parried Cluny's thrusts.

They battled across the green Abbey lawns, right through the centre of the maelstrom of warring creatures. Oblivious to the fighting around them they sought to destroy each other, hacking, stabbing, lunging, and swinging in mortal combat.

Meanwhile, teams of Sparra warriors were jointly lifting struggling rats and flying high to drop them into the middle of the Abbey pond. Ferrets had cornered a band of shrews and were threatening to massacre them when a column of otters sprang to the rescue. Keeping heavy pebbles locked in their slings they battered continuously at the ferrets. Besieged by fierce sparrows, rat sentries leaped in panic from the top of the ramparts; those who stayed were dealt with by Jess Squirrel who swung a heavy iron chain around like a deadly flail. Down below, Ambrose Spike was rolling about like a whirling ball of needles. Silent Sam acted as his eyes, propelling him into each fresh bunch of rats with a long stick.

Matthias and Cluny continued battling savagely. Iron smashed upon steel as Cluny called up reserves from his vast strength and cunning to defeat his opponent. Twice he had hurled clawfuls of soil at Matthias's eyes, but each time the shield rose swiftly and deflected them. The warrior mouse hacked away stoically. He was beginning to feel his paws numbed by the jarring blows of the hefty iron railing against the sword blade. Cluny too felt the vibrations each time the sword clanged upon his weapon. The pain shot right through him, down to the tip of his injured tail. Along the ramparts they fought, blinded by sweat, panting and blowing, neither asking nor giving quarter; down the stairs and across the grass once more, they slashed and struck at each other right up to the entrance of Great Hall.

Cluny dodged behind the half-open Abbey door and hit out at his attacker. Matthias's sword point lodged deep in the wood. Seizing his chance, the rat dodged nimbly into the open, and battered madly at Matthias's upheld shield until he was forced to drop it. Cluny's iron spike drove cruelly into the mouse's unguarded paw. Matthias cried out and instinctively kicked the shield upwards at his adversary. It struck Cluny squarely under the chin, the sharp metal edge causing a long slash.

As the rat reeled away clutching at his throat, Matthias freed the sword from the door. Ignoring their wounds they immediately clashed again, going at it hammer and tongs. Cluny lashed out with his bleeding tail and tripped Matthias. As the warrior mouse lay upon the ground the rat roared and stabbed downwards with the spiked railing. Matthias rolled to one side; the point sank deep into the earth. He struggled to his feet, striking out and scoring Cluny heavily down the side. But the long tail whipped out, lashing the warrior mouse several times across the face.

Cluny staggered into the entrance to the bell tower, where Friar Hugo had been tolling the Joseph Bell. At the sight of the rat Warlord, he released the rope and scuttled underneath the stairs where he hid trembling. Matthias came thundering in. Cluny dodged around him and slammed the door, locking them in together. If only he could get the mouse at close quarters and stop him from using the sword, Cluny thought, then he could win with his superior strength.

They locked in combat again. Cluny barred the railing across the sword blade. Pushing with both claws he drove Matthias backwards. Now he could see victory in sight. If only he could pin the warrior mouse against the wall he would be able to throttle him with the edge of the railing. Cluny braced his feet and strained. He could feel the breath labouring raggedly within his chest; he must win! The voices had told him he would never again see the warrior after the sun set upon this day. The prophecy had to be fulfilled once and for all.

Remorselessly he used his greater strength to drive the young mouse backwards. They were only inches from the wall now. Matthias realized what Cluny was doing. He would be finished once he was pinned against the wall. There was only one thing to do, Mathias suddenly swerved aside and collapsed on his back. Kicking his legs out rigid, he sent Cluny crashing into the wall. Matthias leaped over Cluny, and bounded up the spiral stairs into the darkness of the belfry.

Cluny lay against the wall, panting heavily. He managed an evil, wheezing laugh.

'There's no way out up there, mouse,' he called. 'I'm coming up after you. You're as good as dead now.'

Matthias didn't reply. He sat exhausted up in the dark belfry with his legs dangling over the stout timber bell axle. Down below, Cluny squatted against the wall, glad of the chance to take a breather. Beneath the dusty stairs, Friar Hugo sneezed.

Laughing triumphantly, Cluny seized the little fat friar

by his tail and dragged him from his hiding place.

'Look, mouse!' he called. 'See, I've got your little fat friend. Ha, I won't have to climb those stairs after all. Throw the sword down or I'll spike him like a lollipop.'

From his vantage point Matthias looked down. Far below him on the floor he could see Cluny holding the spike under Friar Hugo's chin.

Cluny gave the point a light jab. Hugo gurgled unhappily. 'You see? All it takes is a little harder push and he's dead. Now throw down your sword and get down here yourself, quick.'

Matthias peered over the rim of the Joseph Bell.

'All right, rat, you win. But how do I know you'll keep your word? First let the friar go, then I promise on my honour as a warrior that I'll come down.'

Cluny grinned wickedly. There it was again, that stupid thing called honour, the code of the warrior! But it was not his code: he had won!

'Get out of my sight, you snivelling little wretch,' he grated, thrusting Friar Hugo away from him. The frightened mouse dived back underneath the stairs. Cluny stood in the centre of the room, his one eye straining to catch sight of Matthias in the belfry. Blood dripped from the dozen wounds the mouse warrior had inflicted upon him during the course of their battle. But now he knew he had won; the voices had been right; he would soon see the last of the mouse warrior.

'Come on down, mouse, Cluny the Scourge is waiting for you,' he cried.

Matthias stood up on the wooden beam. With one mighty blow from the blade of the ancient, battle-scarred sword he severed the rope holding the Joseph Bell.

It appeared to hang in space for a second, then it dropped like a massive stone.

Cluny remained riveted to the spot, his eye staring

upwards. Before he had time to think it was too late . . . .

CLANG!!!

The Joseph Bell tolled its last, huge knell. The colossal weight of metal smashed Cluny the Scourge flat upon the stone floor of the bell tower.

Wearily Matthias the Warrior descended the spiral stairs, sword in hand. He led the sobbing little friar out of his hiding place. Together they stood and stared at the Joseph Bell where it lay, cracked clean through the centre. From beneath it there protruded a bloodied claw and a smashed tail.

Matthias spoke, 'I kept my promise to you, Cluny. I came down. Hush now, Friar Hugo. It's all over now. Wipe your eyes.'

Together the friends opened the door and walked out into the sunlight of a summer morning.

Redwall had won the final battle.

The bodies of both armies lay scattered thick upon the grass and stones where they had fallen. Many were sparrows, shrews, and woodland defenders, but they were far outnumbered by the slain rats, ferrets, weasels and stoats. Nowhere was there one of Cluny's infamous horde left alive.

Constance ambled up, her big flanks heaving, covered in wounds. She pointed to the bell tower and uttered a single word.

'Cluny?'

'Dead!' Matthias replied. 'Were all the horde slain? Did we take no prisoners at all?'

The badger shrugged wearily. 'A lot of them tried to escape. We didn't really stop them. They managed to unbar the main gate and ran out into the road. There were a big ginger cat and a white owl waiting for them. Hell's whiskers! I've never seen anything like it!'

Basil Stag Hare limped up and threw Matthias a wobbly salute. 'Squire Julian and Cap'n Snow. You can talk to them later on, young feller. Right now you're needed over in the cloisters. It's the Abbot. Better hurry.'

As fast as their tired limbs would allow them, Matthias, Constance and Hugo went together.

Abbot Mortimer lay in the cloister gardens surrounded by his mice and woodland friends. Everyone was there, from Queen Warbeak and Log-a-Log to Cornflower and Silent Sam, down to the humblest mouse. The poison barb on Cluny's tail had done its deadly work. The Father Abbot was dying.

Respectfully, the ranks opened to allow Matthias and his companions through. Constance knelt to cradle her old friend's head, Matthias gently clasped the wrinkled careworn paw. The Abbot smiled fondly at his young mouse.

'Matthias, my son, I see you have restored the sword of Martin to our Abbey. Is your mission completed then?'

Matthias rested his forehead against his Abbot's paw. 'Yes, Father, Cluny the Scourge is dead. I have done my task.'

The Abbot nodded slowly. 'So have I, my son, so have I.'

'Father Abbot, you must live,' said Constance in a gruff, choking voice.

The Abbot's old face broke into a weak smile. 'My old friend, I am not like the seasons. I cannot go on forever. It has to finish sometime.'

The tears rolled down Matthias's cheeks. He could not stop them. The Abbot patted his paw kindly.

'Ah, Matthias, Matthias, the brave one; wipe away your tears, my son. Death is only part of life. Tell me, can

411

you see the late rose?'

Matthias dried his eyes on the Abbot's wide sleeve. 'Yes, Father. It is in full bloom now.'

'And are all the little roses as red as blood?' said the Abbot.

'They are, Father,' Matthias answered.

The Abbot sighed. 'It is as it was meant to be. Is Brother Alf nearby?'

Brother Alf knelt before the Abbot.

'Ah, Brother Alf, my old and valued companion. When I am gone to my rest you will take my place as Abbot. You are a wise and compassionate mouse. I know you will look after my creatures for me.'

Abbot Mortimer closed his eyes for a moment before carrying on with his final instructions.

'What a great pity that it took so much bloodshed to unite us all. Henceforth the sparrows may come and go as they wish. They must share our food and use our Abbey, not only the roof but all of it. These good Guerrilla Shrews also – no longer will they be as gypsies roaming the woods: they will have a proper home here at Redwall. And now, Matthias my son, I must tell you my decision regarding you. It is my wish that you do not enter our order as a brother!'

A gasp of surprise arose from all those within hearing range. Matthias bowed his head. He was stunned by his Father Abbot's words.

The Abbot continued. 'No, my son. Your heart is far too brave. This Abbey needs you, but not as a Brother. Therefore, I name you Matthias, the Warrior Mouse of Redwall, champion of our order. From this day you will defend this Abbey and all of its creatures from evil and wrong. Your sword shall be known far and wide as "Ratdeath". Now, Cornflower. Where is little Cornflower?'

The young fieldmouse came. She stood by the Abbot waiting upon his word.

'There you are, dear Cornflower,' the Abbot smiled. 'A warrior needs a good wife. You are the beauty that will grace Redwall and rule the heart of our Matthias. The old gatehouse will be extended into a proper home. It belongs to you both. Guard our threshold wisely and well.'

There were no words to express the feelings of Matthias and Cornflower. They could feel the joy and pride singing from their hearts.

The Abbot looked up at Constance. 'And you, my oldest friend. Do me one last service. Lift my head a little and I will tell you what my failing eyes can see before I leave you.'

Obediently the badger raised the Abbot's head.

'Ah yes, I see the most beautiful summer morning of my life. The friends I know and love are all about me. Redwall, our home, is safe. The sun shines warmly upon us. Nature is ready to yield her bounty again in plenty this autumn. I have seen it all before, many times, and yet I never cease to wonder. Life is good, my friends. I leave it to you. Do not be sad, for mine is a peaceful rest.'

Thus did Mortimer, the Father Abbot of Redwall, die.

15

One year later.

The following is an extract from the annals of Redwall by John Churchmouse. It was he who took over as recorder from Methuselah. Here is part of his written record:

It is the Summer of the Talking Squirrel!

Only yesterday the young one known as Silent Sam was heard to speak. He was heard conversing with the son of Matthias and Cornflower. The young squirrel suddenly began to relate the saga of the late rose summer wars to the baby mouse. I fear that we will not be able to stop him talking, or his parents laughing with delight. The son of our warrior is a strong chubby little fellow. Everyone calls him Mattimeo because "Matthias Methuselah Mortimer" is too big a mouthful, but that was what his parents wished his name to be. Even now he tries long and often to lift the great sword Ratdeath. I think one day he is sure to succeed his father as Abbey Champion. Our Abbot, Mordalfus (no wonder he always preferred the name Alf, I mean, Mordalfus?) has declared that his first anniversary shall be marked by a huge feast. We are all invited. Constance has been pulling her cart around the woodland and meadows far and wide, bringing in guests.

The Guerrilla Shrews are out collecting honey from the bee folk; they have struck up a great friendship with the bees, even learning their language so that they can argue with them.

The Sparra Queen Warbeak has appointed herself deputy to Friar Hugo. She shows a great interest in the culinary arts, though I fear she will grow quite fat before too long. Lady Cornflower is out in the meadows with Mrs Churchmouse my wife and Dunwing the Sparra Queen Mother. They are gathering flowers for the tables. All about me the June sunshine is like liquid gold!

Basil Stag Hare has gone off on a journey to bring his friends Captain Snow and Squire Julian Gingivere back to the Abbey with him. Basil is ignoring the fact that it is the Abbot's anniversary. He constantly refers to it as 'A Regimental Reunion Dinner'. Winifred the otter, and the beaver, in company with the reprobate Ambrose Spike, are testing the quality of the October nutbrown ale. It must be particularly fine this year, judging from the sound of many rowdy ballads issuing from the wine cellars. Plumpen and his family of dormice are helping the Foremole and his crew dig a roasting pit. Early this morning our Father Abbot went out fishing with Matthias the Warrior. They consider it no less than their bounden duty to bring back a larger fish than last year. The Joseph Bell which was broken has been recast into two smaller bells. I can hear them now. They are named Matthias and Methuselah. My twin Churchmice, Tim and Tess, are grown quite sturdy over the past year. They are our Abbey bellringers, and a splendid job they make of it too!

The crops are growing well. The fruit trees and bushes in the orchard show much promise. The old gatehouse is now a beautiful rambling cottage. The grass is green, the sky is blue, *and the honey sweeter than ever before. I will finish my writing now and go to prepare myself for tonight's festivities, which will be held in their usual place, at Cavern Hole in Redwall Abbey. Please be sure to visit us if ever you are passing.*

     John Churchmouse (Recorder, formerly of St Ninian's)

Here ends the story.